THE FOUR LEGENDARY KINGDOMS

Also by Matthew Reilly

THE GREAT ZOO OF CHINA
TROLL MOUNTAIN
THE TOURNAMENT
SCARECROW AND THE ARMY OF THIEVES
THE FIVE GREATEST WARRIORS
THE SIX SACRED STONES
SEVEN ANCIENT WONDERS
HELL ISLAND
HOVER CAR RACER
SCARECROW
AREA 7
TEMPLE
ICE STATION
CONTEST

MATTHEW REILLY

THE FOUR LEGENDARY KINGDOMS

GALLERY BOOKS
New York London Toronto Sydney New Delhi

G

Gallery Books
An Imprint of Simon & Schuster, Inc.
1230 Avenue of the Americas
New York, NY 10020

Originally published in Australia in 2016 by Pan Macmillan Australia Pty Ltd.
Image on page 214 from the public domain.
All other internal illustrations by IRONGAV.

First Gallery Books hardcover edition May 2017

Manufactured in the United States of America

10 9 8 7 6 5 4 3 2 1

Library of Congress Cataloging-in-Publication Data is available.

ISBN 978-1-5011-6715-7
ISBN 978-1-5011-6716-4 (ebook)

This book is dedicated to
Gary "Smokey" Dawson
and
Wayne Dockrill.
Two true and loyal friends.

I CANNOT SEE IT.
THE OPTICKS OF MY TIME ARE NOT GOOD ENOUGH.
BUT THE MATHEMATICS ARE INESCAPABLE.
IT IS COMING.
IT WILL BE UP TO THE WISE AND NOBLE MEN OF FUTURE GENERATIONS WITH OPTICKS OF A MORE ADVANCED NATURE THAN MINE TO FIND IT IN THE NIGHT SKY AND INITIATE THE RETURN CALL.
OR ELSE ALL IS LOST.

SIR ISAAC NEWTON
THE CHRONOLOGY OF ANCIENT KINGDOMS

IT'S NOT THE SIZE OF THE DOG IN THE FIGHT, IT'S THE SIZE OF THE FIGHT IN THE DOG.

MARK TWAIN

FIRST CHALLENGE

THE ENTRY INTO HELL

And there along the shattered chasm's edge
We found the infamy of Crete stretched out—
The beast conceived inside the wooden cow.
And seeing us, the creature bit himself
As though tormented by an inward rage . . .

That is the way the Minotaur behaved.
My wary guide called out: "Run down towards
The crossing: best descend while he is mad."

DANTE'S *INFERNO*,
TRANSLATED BY SEAN O'BRIEN
(PICADOR, LONDON, 2006)

CHAMPION PROFILE

NAME: WEST, JONATHAN JAMES
AGE: 46
RANK TO WIN: ABOVE 10TH
REPRESENTING: LAND

PROFILE:

Captive participant.

A late inclusion to these Games, Jonathan (Jack) West Jr. is a wild card not to be dismissed lightly. He is, after all, the fifth greatest warrior of ancient prophecy. That said, that prophecy has no relevance here.

Ranked above 10th out of 16 to win the Games.

FROM HIS PATRON:

No supporting comment was issued by this champion's patron.

Jack West woke with a lurch, startled and gasping for air.

He was alone and in darkness.

He didn't know where he was, how he'd got here or how long he'd been here.

The air was cool and moist, like in a deep cave. The floor was dusty. The wall against his back was solid stone.

He was wearing jeans and a long-sleeved T-shirt, but no shoes.

His head was sore. He touched it . . . only to pull his hand away in shock.

His hair had been shaved off—

With a piercing shriek, the rusty iron door of his cell swung open and light flooded in.

A horrifying silhouette filled the doorway.

The outline of a bull-headed man.

A minotaur.

Or at least a man wearing a bull-shaped helmet.

He was well muscled, with knotty biceps and a stocky chest. While his upper body—save for the bull mask—was bare, on his lower half he wore modern black army-issue cargo pants and black combat boots.

I must be dreaming, Jack thought.

He didn't have time for a second thought because right then, with a roar, the "minotaur" charged at him.

A serrated hunting knife appeared in the masked man's right hand and it came slashing down at Jack.

Instinct kicked in.

Half rising, Jack grabbed the minotaur's knife-hand, twisted it and threw the man to the side, springing to his own feet as he did so.

The minotaur tackled him, and they rolled, struggling, wrestling, ending up on the ground with the masked man on top, straddling Jack and pressing down with the knife.

Clenching his teeth and using all his strength, Jack gripped the hilt of the knife, keeping its blade at bay, two inches from his own throat.

The blade edged closer to his Adam's apple, and in a faraway corner of his brain, Jack recalled that if you died in a dream, you woke up. He wondered if that would happen here.

Only what if it's not a dream, Jack . . . ?

His opponent pushed harder and from behind the black bull mask, Jack heard the man inside grunting with exertion.

It's just a man! his mind screamed. *It's just a man!*

And every man can be beaten.

Energized, Jack shifted his weight and reverse-rolled, sending the minotaur smashing headfirst into the stone wall.

It was a sickening blow. A dull crack echoed out—the sound of the minotaur's neck breaking—and the masked man slumped to the dusty floor and lay still.

Jack heaved for breath.

What a way to wake up.

Regaining his composure a little, he took in his cell for the first time.

The door was still open a little, letting in light. The cell looked exceedingly old: the walls were made of sandstone; the heavy rusted door sat on ancient iron hinges. As for what lay beyond the open doorway, God only knew.

On one wall of Jack's cell were two images carved deep into the stone:

The first one Jack knew: it was the ancient Egyptian hieroglyph *ankh*, meaning "life."

As for the second symbol, it looked like a swirling four-armed octopus. It was a variant of a rare and ancient symbol found in Hindu, Buddhist, and Neolithic cultures called a tetragammadion.

As he looked at it, Jack had the distinct feeling he had seen this symbol only recently, but he couldn't recall where.

He blinked, trying to remember. But it was no use. His mind was still too groggy.

Instead he tried to recall the last place he had been before he had lost consciousness and woken up here.

Pine Gap, he thought.

The top-secret base deep in the Australian desert.

He'd gone there to attend a meeting, a high-level meeting.

Something about the SKA Array . . .

He remembered arriving at the base outside the remote town of Alice Springs with Lily, Alby, and the dogs, and being allowed inside by the armed gate-guards.

And he recalled being met outside the observatory lab at Pine Gap by the tall, bespectacled figure of General Eric Abrahamson, the genial yet whip-smart man who had replaced Jack's longtime boss and friend, General Peter Cosgrove, after Cosgrove had been promoted to higher office.

They'd shaken hands and Abrahamson had introduced Jack to *his* soon-to-be replacement, a stern-faced general named Conor Beard. With his angular features and neatly trimmed red beard, Beard's operational call sign had been a slam dunk: since his early days in the military, he'd been known as *Redbeard*.

"Glad you dressed up for the occasion, Jack," Abrahamson had said wryly.

Jack had been dressed casually, wearing jeans, sneakers, and a blue shirt over an old white T-shirt. He wore a brown suede glove over his titanium left hand and a simple Casio G-Shock watch on his right wrist.

He'd smiled back at Abrahamson in the desert sun. "I don't work for you anymore, so I get to dress any way I like."

After exchanging greetings with Lily and Alby, Abrahamson bent down to pet the dogs. "Haven't seen these two since they were pups."

Jack said, "They own me now. Everyone owns me now. Zoe. Lily. The dogs. I was once the fifth greatest warrior, you know."

Abrahamson laughed. "What about Horus? What does she think of the dogs?"

Jack whistled sharply and a moment later, his loyal peregrine falcon, Horus, previously soaring overhead, had landed lightly on his shoulder. Looped around her neck was a leather collar from which hung a GoPro camera. She glared at Abrahamson and Beard, as if peering into their souls.

"She tolerates them," Jack said as Horus took to the air again.

"Come inside." Abrahamson guided them through the doors of the lab. "I have something important to show you."

And then nothing . . .

. . . nothing till he woke up here with a man dressed as a bull trying to kill him.

Still sitting on the dusty floor of his cell, Jack looked down at himself.

Somewhere in transit, his blue shirt and sneakers had gone missing. His long-sleeved T-shirt, a gift from Lily from a few years ago—back when she'd been a cute thirteen-year-old and not a worldly twenty-year-old—depicted Homer Simpson lying in an inflatable kiddie pool, passed out from drinking and surrounded by empty Duff beer cans, under the words:

WORLD'S GREATEST DAD

This is surreal, Jack thought.

He peered at the lifeless man in the bull mask on the floor beside him.

The mask, he now saw, was very modern, and was actually more of a helmet than a mask. It was made of high-tech lightweight resin and was painted matte black.

The visor of the bull helmet was a black mesh like that found on a fencing mask—it hid the identity of the wearer but allowed him full vision. Over the wearer's mouth was a gas-mask filter that looked like an animal's snout, thus making the whole thing look even more like a bull's head.

Jack yanked the mask off the fallen man . . .

. . . to reveal that it wasn't quite a man.

But it was something similar.

The "man" under the mask had a broad low-browed forehead, wide-set eyes, a flat nose, big mouth, crooked teeth, and thick matted black hair everywhere: on his jowls, in his ears, and forming a unibrow above his eyes.

The eyes, Jack thought, looking closer.

His eyes—frozen open in the moment of his death—were deep brown. They looked basically human yet somehow duller. If he didn't know better, Jack would have thought he was looking at some kind of half-evolved hominid, like a Neanderthal or Cro-Magnon man.

A tattoo on the half-man's hairy shoulder read N-016.

Jack gazed down at his dead attacker.

"What the hell are you and where the hell am I?" he asked aloud.

With a roar the hairy half-man sprang from the floor, snatching up the knife and lunging at Jack.

Jesus Christ!

But his attacker was weaker now, slower, fighting out of sheer fervor and frenzy. Jack parried the knife away and slipped round behind the half-man, wrapped his forearm around his throat and fully broke his neck.

The thing dropped dead for good this time.

"Fuck me," Jack gasped, sucking in air again.

Out of habit, he made to stroke back his hair and again he felt the rough stubble there. His head had indeed been shaved while he had been unconscious.

Lacking any other weapons, Jack patted down the dead minotaur. The only weapon the half-man had was the knife so Jack pocketed that. He removed the minotaur's combat boots and put them on. They were way too big for him but they were better than nothing.

With a shrug, he also took the armored bull helmet.

Then he walked out of the cell, stepping into the light.

In a cell just like Jack's—indeed, it was not far away from his—another man stood facing the steel door, waiting.

He was a tall man with unshaven ginger facial hair and battle-hardened eyes. Unlike Jack, he had come prepared.

He wore the combat gear of a British SAS operator: boots, cargo trousers, flak jacket, helmet. And he gripped in one hand a long serrated KA-BAR knife.

The cell's ancient door squealed open. Light rushed in and so did a minotaur.

It took three quick slashes from the SAS man's knife—two across the minotaur's hamstrings and a final killing blow across its throat—to kill the mask-wearing assassin.

Unlike Jack, the SAS fellow didn't bother to examine the corpse of his attacker.

No sooner was it dead than he just stepped over it and strode out of the cell, calmly wiping his knife blade on his trousers.

In a third cell, a United States Marine also waited tensely until, with a scream of rusty hinges, the door to his cell opened and a third minotaur thundered in.

Like the British SAS man, this Marine was prepared. That's to say he was dressed in desert fatigues and a helmet and he was armed with a telescoping nightstick. He wasn't entirely prepared though: while expecting an attack, he hadn't expected a crazed half-man dressed as a minotaur to come bursting in brandishing a knife.

Unlike Jack's ugly and awkward struggle, this fight was short, although not as ruthlessly quick as the SAS man's encounter.

The Marine's training kicked in and the clash ended with his knife buried in the sternum of the minotaur.

The Marine examined the body of his fallen attacker, touching the bull helmet, noting its modernness, and also assessing the odd semi-human creature beneath it.

Then he put on a pair of wraparound anti-flash glasses and walked out of the cell into the light.

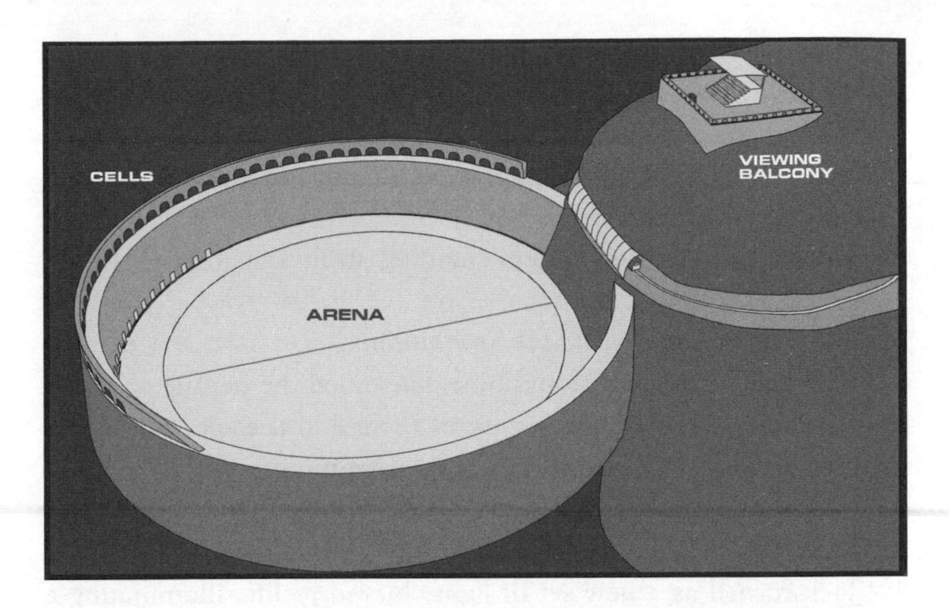

Jack emerged from his cell to find himself standing in what could only be described as a gladiatorial arena.

It was dark here, like night, but judging by the cool, still air, this arena was indoors, inside a sizable cavern of some kind.

The arena was wide and circular, built in the Roman style with a sawdust-covered sand floor, yet it was illuminated by modern floodlights. Like the minotaur he had just defeated, it was a curious mix of the very ancient and the very modern.

The door of his cell lay open behind him, embedded in the stone wall of the arena.

Fifteen similar doors were arrayed around the curved wall and standing in front of them, just like Jack, were fifteen other men.

Thirteen of them wore modern military attire: helmets and fatigues of various colors: desert, jungle, or night camo. Most were white, a few were black, and a couple were Asian. They variously held knives, short swords, or nightsticks but, Jack saw, no guns. The ones not wearing helmets all had shaven heads.

Outside two of the fifteen cells stood two minotaurs.

They stood rigidly to attention, short but erect, the knives gripped in their hairy hands dripping with blood.

And last of all, there was Jack, entirely unprepared, in his jeans, T-shirt, and newly acquired oversized boots. His titanium left wrist peeked out from the cuff of his sleeve, glinting in the artificial light. His face was filthy with sweat, dust, and blood, and he held his bull helmet and knife in his hands.

He eyed the two minotaurs standing stiffly outside two of the cells.

So not everyone defeated their minotaur . . .

Black-clad guards with machine guns lined the perimeter of the arena. There were perhaps twenty of them and it took Jack a moment to realize they were all helmet-wearing minotaurs.

"Greetings, champions!" a deep voice boomed from somewhere high above him.

Jack turned as a new set of lights blazed to life, illuminating a high stagelike balcony on the opposite side of the stadium.

A lone man stood on it, the man who had spoken.

That whole side of the arena was one giant rock face, the base of a grim black mountain that soared upward into shadowy darkness. The balcony on which the man stood jutted out from the mountainside eighty feet above the arena floor.

At the rear of the balcony was a set of bleachers, shaded by a large awning, and sitting on those bleachers—adding to the surreal weirdness of this place—was a crowd of about thirty men and women, all dressed in expensive suits and dresses. Even from where he stood, Jack could see the twinkle of sizable diamond necklaces on some of the women. They variously sipped champagne, smoked cigarettes, or gazed down at the line of "champions."

The man who had spoken was clearly their leader.

He was tall and powerfully built, perhaps in his mid-fifties. He was handsome, too, with a black beard and intense dark eyes. He wore a black modern designer suit with stylish crimson cuffs.

"I say again," he said, "greetings, champions. Welcome to the Great Games. I will be your host, your judge, your jury, and, if the need arises, your executioner.

"I have many ceremonial names. I am the Adversary of Light, the Accuser, the Fallen One, the Keeper of the Temple, the Prince of the Grigori, Iblis, Shaitan, Thanatos, Sataniel, Ruler of the Night-lands, Ba'al Zevuv, Beelzebub, King of the Fourth Kingdom, or simply, Hades, Lord of the Underworld. Welcome to my Games, champions. Welcome to the Underworld."

Jack couldn't believe what he was hearing.

Over the course of many adventures, he'd seen a lot of weird things.

He'd re-erected the capstone on the Great Pyramid of Giza during a dazzling solar event.

He'd seen Stonehenge come alive under the light of a Dark Sun.

Once, deep inside a Roman salt mine, he'd found the tomb of Jesus Christ . . . with Christ's body still in it.

And he had seen himself revealed as one of the five greatest "warriors" of history: an elite group of influential figures—warriors of battle and ideas—made up of himself, Moses, Genghis Khan, Napoleon, and Christ.

But the Underworld? Hell?

Now he knew he was dreaming.

The notion of an afterlife was common to societies all over the world. Every civilization had one, from the Egyptians to the Mayans to Japan and India and, of course, the three Abrahamic religions: Christianity, Judaism, and Islam.

In the Western tradition, the afterlife was divided into two places, Heaven and Hell, and the whole concept was infused with a moral element: good people went to Heaven and bad people went to Hell, a frightening realm located beneath the surface of the Earth, a place of fire, brimstone, and punishment for one's sins during life.

The afterlife of the Greeks, however, had no such moral element. They called their Hell "Tartarus" and in their myths, the Underworld could actually be accessed by the living, *if* one could find the entrance. Getting out again, though, was another matter. Only the major Greek heroes—Hercules, Theseus, and Odysseus—successfully visited and returned from the Underworld. It was a rite of passage if you were to become a legendary hero.

And it was the Greeks who had bestowed upon the king of this fiery kingdom the name "Hades."

Only Hell isn't an actual place, Jack's mind protested.

But then, as his eyes adjusted to the glare of the floodlights illuminating the arena, he began to see the area beyond it, in particular the dark mountain above and behind Hades's balcony.

It was astonishing.

It leaped skyward, a sharp dagger of black rock that rose high into the air. Various shadowy castles, fortresses, elevators, and staircases hung from its flanks, all at different levels and all looking decidedly menacing in the reflected glow of the floodlights.

One broad castle-like structure ringed the mountain at its waist, five hundred feet above the spot where Jack stood. The lights of many windows dotted it.

The whole mount was oddly similar in shape to the Eiffel Tower: wide at the base but tapering as it rose, at first slowly and then very sharply. Jack couldn't see what was at the summit—it was too dark up there—but he could make out some kind of netting spreading out from it, netting that blotted out the night sky.

Hades interrupted his thoughts, his voice booming in the enormous space. "You have all been brought here as representatives of the four eternal kingdoms to participate in history's greatest challenge, the Great Games of the Hydra."

Jack glanced at his fellow champions.

They all looked up at Hades as he spoke. The two minotaurs listened to him with particular attention, their chins raised proudly.

The man to Jack's left wore desert combat gear, a Marine Corps helmet and reflective anti-flash glasses.

He nodded at Jack's Homer Simpson T-shirt.

"Nice shirt, buddy."

"If I'd known I was coming to this party," Jack said, "I would've dressed differently."

"To prevail here," Hades boomed, "is to ensure that your name resounds throughout the ages. Songs will be sung about you, epics written, as they have of all past champions of these Games. In these hallowed arenas, tunnels and mazes, heroes have been born and legends have been made.

"And if I may say so, even before their vital purpose is realized, these Games are already historic. We have several notable champions participating: no less than *three* sons of kings are representing their fathers here. This is unprecedented."

The crowd behind Hades tittered and pointed. Jack saw three of his fellow competitors nod toward the spectators.

"And how could I forget?" Hades said. "We even have the fifth warrior himself competing."

His piercing gaze swung to face Jack.

Suddenly Jack felt every eye in the arena—competitors' and spectators'—land on him.

In his silly T-shirt, jeans, and oversized boots, he felt like he was in another dream: the one where you went to school without any clothes on.

Hades smiled at Jack. "My, my. The fifth greatest warrior himself. Never in the history of the Great Games has one of the five warriors participated. This is momentous."

Jack was really uncomfortable now. He could feel the accusing glares of his fellow competitors. He wished Hades would shut up about him.

Hades raised his arms.

"Forty days ago, the Star Chamber—the holiest shrine in my realm—opened for the first time in over three thousand years to welcome the return of the glorious Hydra. Which is why now, in accordance with the ancient laws, we gather to hold our Games. As the lord of this storied realm—one of a long line of lords—it falls to me to be the host and arbiter of these Games. It is a holy duty to preside over the Games and in the performance of that duty, I shall show neither fear nor favor."

He turned to the well-to-do audience on the bleachers behind him.

"I cannot be bribed.

"I will not accept entreaties for mercy.

"I will not grant special treatment. Not to the highest-born champion or to the lowliest minotaur.

"I can show neither leniency nor discretion. The rules of the Games are ancient and they are clear. It is my honor to enforce them . . . even if it should mean my own doom. My fellow kings, lords and ladies, distinguished guests and champions. Welcome to my kingdom. Welcome to the Great Games."

Jack's mind was racing, trying desperately to keep up.

It was bad enough to wake up, groggy and disoriented, in a strange place and have a man in a bull mask charging at you with a knife. Now he was hearing about Hell and Hades, Star Chambers that hadn't opened for three thousand years, and something called "the glorious Hydra" which was apparently returning from somewhere.

"Now then," Hades said, nodding at the pair of minotaurs standing outside two of the cells. "I see that two of our champions did not pass the First Challenge, so I must—"

"Wait!" someone shouted.

Everyone in the arena, including Hades, spun to face the champion standing immediately to Jack's right.

The crowd of spectators on the bleachers fell silent. They glanced at one another in horror. Some looked at Hades with trepidation.

Jack watched it all closely. So did the Marine to his left.

The man to his right, the one who had called out, was a tall Asian man with a shaved head and a ramrod-straight stance. He wore an olive-colored T-shirt, green combat trousers, and boots. It wasn't exactly a fighting outfit. More like something you wore in your barracks.

And it suddenly occurred to Jack that this man might have been brought here the same way he had—

"My name is Jason Chen," the man called in English, "and I am a captain in the Taiwanese Army, stationed in Taipei! I am here against my will! I was kidnapped! I wish to be released immediately!"

The crowd of spectators watched him with open mouths.

Most of the other champions, Jack saw, now stared forward or downward, trying to ignore the protester.

The entire arena was silent.

Hades's gaze fell on the Taiwanese man.

"I. Beg. Your. Pardon?" Hades said.

The Taiwanese captain stuck out his chest. "I said, my name is Jason—"

His head exploded.

It just popped, splattering outward in a hundred fleshy chunks like a pumpkin loaded with firecrackers.

Some blood and brain matter hit Jack's right cheek. The headless corpse collapsed to the dusty ground beside him, blood pouring from the arteries of the neck, forming a foul pool around Jack's oversized boots.

Jack snapped to look back up at Hades and saw that a second man had appeared at Hades's side, stepping out from behind him, an assistant of some sort.

The "assistant" lowered a small remote that he held in one gloved hand.

He was a most distinctive-looking man. He looked like some kind of high priest: he wore a long purple robe and was completely bald.

He also had the bulging eyes of someone with an overactive thyroid gland which, when combined with his bald head, made him look decidedly insect-like.

Horrified at the grisly explosion of his neighbor's head, Jack checked to see how the spectators on the bleachers were reacting to it.

He saw only casual indifference.

They just sipped their champagne flutes and shook their heads sadly.

Then it hit Jack and his hand flew to his own head, touching the back of his clean-shaven scalp . . .

. . . and he felt it.

A fresh scar, just above the nape of his neck.

That was why they'd shaved his head.

They had surgically implanted something *into his neck*: a small explosive. The same kind of explosive that had just blown off the Taiwanese captain's head.

This was how Hades guaranteed obedience.

Jack scanned the other champions and saw that all of them bore similar scars on their necks, plus one other thing: seared into the deformed skin of each man's surgical scar was a small yellow gemstone of some kind. But the amber-colored jewel was in no way modern; it was distinctly old. Touching his own scar, Jack could feel the hard edges of the gemstone embedded in it.

What have I been thrown into? Jack thought.

"Such a pity," Hades said. "And a pity for his support team, too."

Hades nodded to his assistant and, up near his balcony, just beneath it, some steel shutters opened, revealing four very peculiar train carriages standing on rails inside an open-faced tunnel sunken into the rock face.

The four carriages looked like the kind of train cars that were once used to transport circus animals: each was fronted by a waist-high fence of plate steel topped with sturdy iron bars. Their roofs were also barred. Jack counted four cells in each carriage, creating a total of sixteen.

Inside each cell he saw four or five people, all peering down at the arena anxiously.

Sixteen cells.

Sixteen champions.

"Kill Captain Chen's support team, please," Hades said simply.

His bug-eyed assistant raised his remote again and pressed another button on it.

In response, a torrent of a gray liquid came gushing out of the tunnel's ceiling above one of the train carriages and poured down powerfully into one of its cells.

It looked like cement, Jack thought, a kind of semiliquid conglomerate. And it was clearly hot, too. As it poured into the cell, it issued great clouds of steam.

And it was also *heavy* because when it came down it knocked the two men and two women inside the cell off their feet. They fell under the weight of the downward-pouring ooze, screaming as it forced them under.

Soon the screaming stopped and all that remained in the iron cell—judging by the gray ooze dripping over its waist-high front barrier—was a pool of the steaming liquid.

Jesus Christ, Jack thought. *They're hostage chambers.*

Hades sighed. "As I was saying before I was so rudely interrupted, two of our champions did not survive the First Challenge. As such, their support teams must also be liquidated."

He nodded to his assistant. "Monsieur Vacheron. Please kill the support teams of the two who failed the First Challenge."

At Hades's command, the assistant—Vacheron—pressed his remote again—

—and hot liquid cement was unleashed into two other cells of the train. More screams. More flailing.

When the occupants of the two cells were dead, Hades turned back to the arena.

"Of course," he said, "as has always been the case, the deaths of these two champions affords their conquerors the chance to take their places. In the cut and thrust of the Games, there are no social classes. Even the lowliest minotaur can compete against the highest-born champion and pursue the immortality of victory. Please, mark the minotaurs."

The two minotaurs standing in the line of champions—the two who had evidently killed the other champions in their cells—stepped forward.

Gold stripes were painted on their bull helmets, skin, and trousers, differentiating them from the regular black-clad minotaurs standing guard around the arena.

As he watched all this in horror and disbelief, a sudden thought struck Jack.

Sixteen champions and sixteen hostage chambers.

So who are my *hostages?*

"Oh, God . . ." Jack breathed, looking up.

His last memory was of visiting Pine Gap. He'd gone there with Lily, Alby, Sky Monster, Horus, and the dogs.

And then he saw them and his heart sank.

Peering out from behind the bars of one of the cells of the hostage train, high above the ancient stadium, were his twenty-year-old daughter, Lily, and her loyal friend, Alby Calvin.

Behind them was Jack's longtime pilot, Sky Monster, his bushy beard and wild hair framing his desperately worried eyes. In front of Lily and Alby, peeking over the waist-high wall of their iron cell, presumably standing on their hind legs, were Jack's dogs, Ash and Roxy.

"Oh, God, no," Jack said. "This can't be happening. This can't be happening."

Hades made eye contact with every one of the champions arrayed before him on the floor of the arena.

"I hope you are all now aware of what awaits your support teams if you fail in any of the challenges of these Games."

He smiled. "I will now hand you over to our Master of the Games, my loyal servant, Monsieur Vacheron."

The man with the bald head and bulging eyes stepped forward. He gazed at Jack and the other champions in what could only be described as a predatory way.

His shrill voice echoed loud and clear. "Lords and ladies! Esteemed guests! Allow me to present to you the arena for the Second Challenge! Open the pit!"

SECOND CHALLENGE

THE WATER PIT

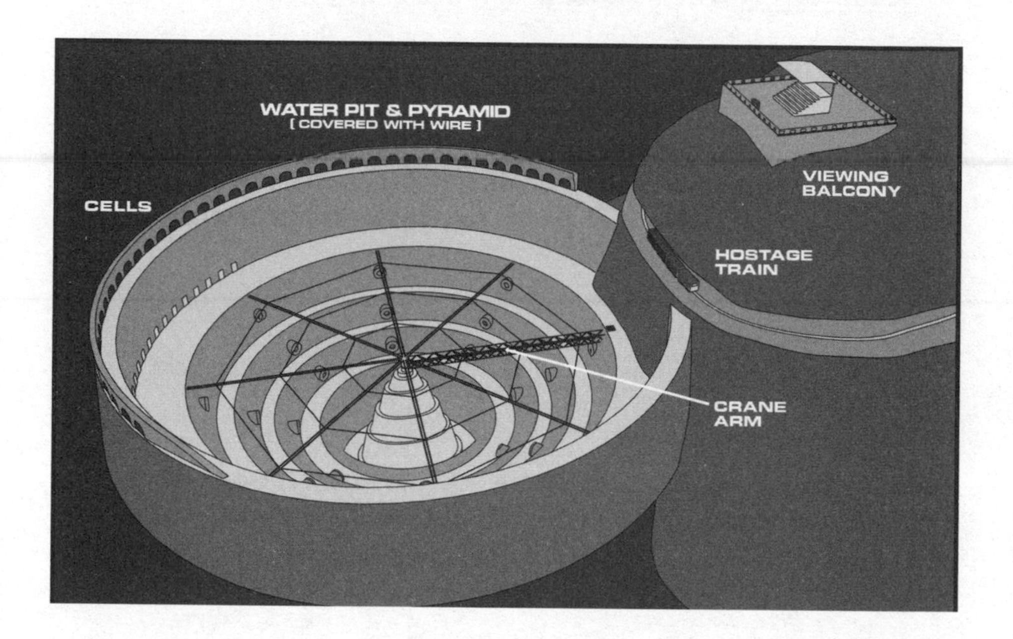

Long is the way and hard, that out of Hell leads up to light.

JOHN MILTON, *PARADISE LOST*

CHAMPION PROFILE

NAME: BRIGHAM, GREGORY JOHN
AGE: 32
RANK TO WIN: 1
REPRESENTING: LAND

PROFILE:

Major Brigham is an officer in the British SAS. Exceptionally skilled in hand-to-hand combat, he is also a man of impeccable breeding.

Educated at Eton. Fast-tracked through the Royal Military College. Distinguished service in Afghanistan and Iraq.

Son and heir to the Duke of Orkney. Betrothed to the daughter of the Duke of Avalon.

Ranked 1st out of 16 to win the Games.

FROM HIS PATRON:

"My house is very proud to have Major Brigham fighting on its behalf. When he wins these Games, his fame shall echo through the ages. He is my son in all but name. I look forward to giving my daughter to him."

Orlando, Duke of Avalon,
King of Land

At Vacheron's words, a colossal mechanism came to life in the arena around Jack.

With a deep rumbling, two huge flat doors set into the floor of the arena split in the middle and as sand cascaded off their edges, the two doors retracted into the walls.

An enormous circular pit opened before Jack.

"Oh, man," he breathed.

The pit dropped away in front of him, at least forty feet deep. It had four concentric levels that descended like giant steps, each fashioned in the shape of a trench. Protruding from the outer walls of the four trenches were large round pipes, each about the size of a man.

In the exact center of the pit, ringed by the four trenches, stood a circular steep-sided stone pyramid.

The pyramid's peak lay just below Jack, so that it was fully inside the pit. A narrow path wound up its curving flank, rising to its summit where there stood a beautiful altar.

On that altar was a most magnificent object.

A glowing crystal sphere.

It was about the size of a volleyball and it was absolutely gorgeous. It gave off an eerie golden glow.

At the sight of it, the spectators on the bleachers oohed and aahed.

Even Jack had to admit it was pretty stunning. It glimmered in the artificial glare of the floodlights, entrancing, mesmerizing.

Encasing the entire pit-and-pyramid was a taut wire-mesh ceiling.

It looked like a gigantic horizontal spiderweb. Radiating outward on eight steel arms, it was made of hundreds of fishing line–like wires.

Its function was clear: it allowed Hades and his guests to see down into the pit while at the same time the competitors could not escape from it. Small gates cut into the wire yawned open directly in front of Jack and the fifteen other champions.

There was one final feature of the pit that caught Jack's gaze: the exit.

Directly above the crystal sphere at the summit of the pyramid was a metal crane arm that hung from the wire-frame ceiling. If you crawled across the crane arm, over the width of the broad pit, you arrived at what appeared to be the pit's only exit.

When he spoke, Vacheron addressed the guests on the royal stage rather than the assembled champions.

"The Second Challenge for our heroes is a simple water maze. At its center is one of the nine Golden Spheres of the Ancients. The champion to exit the water maze with the Golden Sphere in his possession wins the challenge and gets the customary reward."

Straightforward enough, Jack thought. Except for the fact that he saw no water anywhere down there. And what was the "customary reward"?

"They will have to make haste, however," Vacheron added, "for the *last* champion to leave the pit will be rewarded with death."

That's not good, Jack thought.

"Of course," Vacheron said, "it would not be the Great Games if we did not have great hunters."

The assembled guests murmured keenly at this.

Two towering masked figures arrived beside Hades on his stage.

One wore black, the other white.

At first glance, in their ceremonial helmets, they looked similar to the minotaur Jack had killed in his cell, but as he looked more closely at them, Jack saw significant differences.

First, they were much taller than the minotaurs; hell, these guys were both probably six inches taller than Jack. They were not hairy half-men. They were men.

Then there were their helmets.

High-tech and fearsome, they were *not* bull helmets. Instead, they were fashioned in the shape of lion heads, male lion heads with great manes.

Lastly, unlike the shorter minotaurs, these two masked men did not have bare chests. They wore lightweight body armor: chest-plates, shoulder plates, combat trousers, and steel-toed boots. Only their well-muscled arms were uncovered.

Vacheron gestured toward them. "Meet Lord Hades's greatest hunters, Chaos and Fear. As the champions battle the maze, Chaos and Fear will hunt the champions. Beyond that, there are no rules save for the ancient Rule of the Arena: a champion may keep whatever he can carry from the battlefield, be it a weapon, a treasure, or even a gruesome trophy of conquest. Luck to all. Begin!"

At Vacheron's final command, a great noise erupted and to Jack's immense confusion, several things happened at once.

Surging torrents of water came bursting out from the pipes in the outer wall of the uppermost trench.

All fifteen of the champions beside Jack leaped off the mark like sprinters at the Olympics, jumping down through the gates in the wire ceiling into the first trench.

Jack paused.

What choice did he have? He glanced up at the barred hostage cell where Lily, Alby, and Sky Monster stood staring fearfully down at him. If he didn't compete in this, they would die.

Screw it, he thought and he slapped on his new bull helmet and jumped down into the maze.

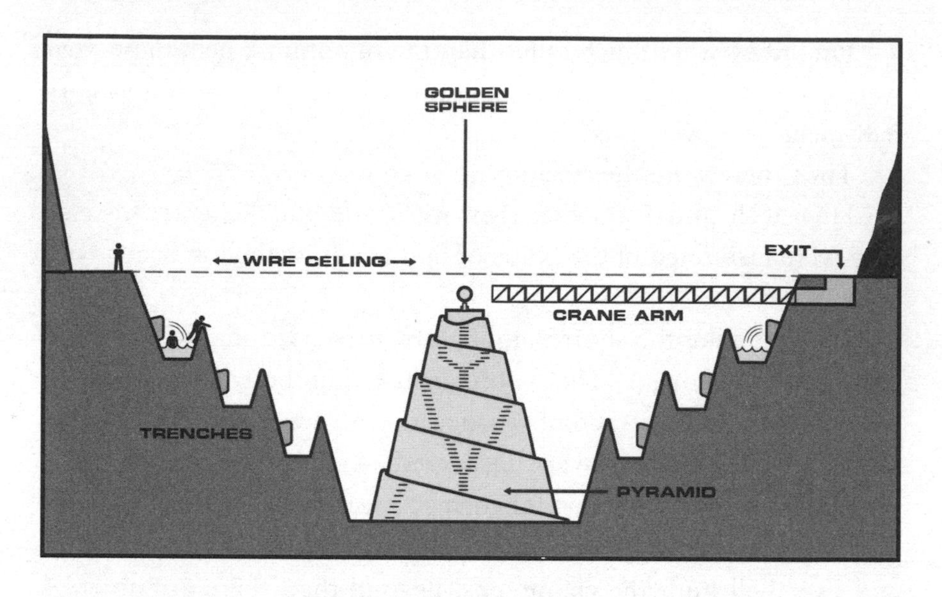

THE WATER PIT

THE FIRST TRENCH

Jack landed in a gray stone trench that was already knee-deep in sloshing water.

Noises came at him from every side.

Clang! Clang! Clang! The gates in the wire ceiling swung shut above his head.

The roar of the water surging out of the large pipes filled his ears. Thousands of gallons were gushing into the trench every second.

The trench wasn't wide—it could fit perhaps two people across—so it filled fast; but at seven feet deep, it was still high enough to crowd in over Jack.

He saw some of the other champions nearby.

They weren't wasting time.

They were all clambering up and over the inner wall of the curving trench in an attempt to get to the next, lower level before this one flooded.

And suddenly the whole concept of the pit became clear to Jack. When each concentric trench filled up with water, it would cascade over into the next, then the next.

Once the water hit the bottommost trench, however, it would start rising *up* again, *filling the entire pit*, consuming the pyramid before it eventually came level with the fish-wire ceiling.

If you didn't traverse your way down the trenches and then climb back up the pyramid to the exit crane arm in time, you'd drown when the water reached the wire ceiling and overcame you.

Once again Jack felt like the kid who had arrived at school unprepared for the exam. Everyone else seemed to know what was required but him.

The water was already up to his waist.

He thought for a second that he could wait for the water to rise some more and just ride it over the lip of the trench, but then he remembered the two lion-headed hunters who were coming to hunt them. He couldn't dawdle.

So Jack copied the others and started for the seven-foot-high inner wall of the trench—

—just as he saw *something* sweep into the trench, borne on the water, rushing into it from one of the pipes, something large with a speckled sickly green body.

Whatever it was, the animal disappeared beneath the sloshing waves.

"That can't be good," Jack said aloud.

He dived for the wall, his fingers scrabbling for purchase. Something large brushed against his leg just as he lifted it out of the water and fell over the wall into the next trench in a clumsy heap.

THE SECOND TRENCH

Jack landed hard on the dry stone floor of the second trench, the landing making his bull helmet fall askew. He threw it off and looked up—

—to see one of the two gold-painted minotaurs rushing at him with a knife!

Jack raised his own knife, the one he'd taken from the original minotaur attacker in his cell, and deflected the blow, falling backward at the force of the attack.

That must have been an unspoken rule of these Games, Jack thought: the combatants were free to kill any of their competitors at any time, as one less competitor gave you a better chance to win.

The golden minotaur swung again with his knife and Jack blocked the blow.

Then with a deafening roar, water came blasting out of the huge pipes on this level and it too began filling with water.

The gold minotaur kept advancing on Jack, swinging and slashing, and Jack backpedaled, desperately fending off the frenzied assault.

But then moving backward in this way, Jack stumbled into a column of water gushing from a pipe and slipped and fell.

The minotaur, knowing that it had him, lunged through the water at Jack—just as another large animal came rushing out of the pipe, carried on the water, and slammed into the minotaur, knocking him off his feet!

Jack propped himself onto his elbows to see some kind of fish—it was gigantic, easily eight feet long—mauling the hapless minotaur.

The minotaur's helmet came loose and the half-man screamed as the fish tore at him.

But then the minotaur started hacking at the fish with his knife and blood fanned out into the water.

Amid all the hacking and splashing, Jack got a good look at the animal.

It was a fish, all right, one of the ugliest fish in the world.

It also gave him a clue as to where he was.

It was a giant catfish, *Bagarius yarrelli*. Jack could tell by the flat head, the long greenish body with mottled spots, the vicious teeth, but most of all by its nasty-looking "barbels"—the long stringy filaments that extended out from its snout like cat's whiskers.

The giant catfish was a creature of southern Asia, ranging from the swamps of Vietnam to the deltas of Pakistan and the rivers of India.

Am I somewhere in southern Asia . . . ?

That didn't concern him now. As the now-helmetless golden minotaur got the better of the fish, the water from the first trench started overflowing into this one, and suddenly it began to fill even faster. The minotaur ignored Jack and leaped over into the next trench.

"Son of a bitch, this doesn't stop," Jack breathed as he dived for the next wall, looped an elbow onto it, hoisted himself over it, and tumbled downward again.

THE THIRD TRENCH

Jack landed with a splash inside the third trench.

Water was already flowing here. The helmetless golden minotaur scampered away to the left. No other champions could be seen. Jack figured his scuffle with the minotaur had allowed them to get well ahead.

He stood . . . just as he spied one of the lion-headed hunters—the black one, Chaos—striding around the bend from the right and raising a crossbow mounted on one of his forearm guards.

The crossbow fired . . . on a reflex, Jack dived clear . . . and the bolt whistled past him.

Jack landed in the water, lifting his head to take a breath, just as a giant catfish came lunging at him! He rolled again and the fish rushed by.

Jack was on his back now, half floating in the water, faceup, feet up.

The hunter dressed as a black lion continued to advance on him, raising the crossbow on his other forearm guard.

Jack had no defense.

The hunter fired.

Shwack!

The crossbow bolt slammed into the *heel* of Jack's left boot: the woefully oversized boot he had taken from the minotaur who had attacked him earlier. But the boot's sole was thick enough to absorb the bolt and Jack was, amazingly, unharmed.

Jack wasn't sure who was more surprised, him or Black Lion dude.

He wasn't going to stay and find out.

As water began to cascade over the upper wall of this trench—and now with a crossbow bolt sticking out of his left heel—he dived awkwardly over into the fourth and final trench.

THE FOURTH TRENCH

Once again, Jack landed in water, only this time it was *waist*-deep. The flooding was accelerating.

He saw the pyramid rising above him, the only way out.

The other champions were indeed well ahead of him. They were clambering up the pyramid, using either the ramp that spiraled up the outside of the almost-vertical structure or some hand- and footholds cut into its flanks.

A great cheer rose up as the leading champion reached the summit, grabbed the crystal sphere and held it aloft. He was a tall guy with a square jaw covered with rough ginger stubble. Kitted out in a flak jacket, lightweight hockey helmet, and combat boots, he looked to Jack a lot like a Navy SEAL or an SAS trooper.

The ginger-bearded trooper dived into the crane arm above the pyramid and crawled through it to the exit where he was met by more rousing cheers from the spectators.

Jack swore.

No cheers for me. I'll be happy just to get out of this pit alive.

He reached for the nearest handhold in the wall of the pyramid only to feel something clamp down on his right foot and yank him underwater.

★ ★ ★

A giant catfish had his right boot clenched tightly in its ugly jaws!

Jack lashed out with his left boot, kicking hard until—disgustingly—he stabbed the catfish *in the eye* with the crossbow bolt protruding from the heel of his boot.

The fish released him and Jack resurfaced, gasping.

Suddenly a colossal amount of water came tumbling over the trench wall above him, pouring over it in an unbroken stream: water from *all three* of the upper trenches was now cascading into this, the lowest level.

In an instant, Jack was neck-deep in sloshing water.

It was like the water itself was chasing him.

He reached for the handholds cut into the wall of the pyramid again and started climbing up its side as fast as he could.

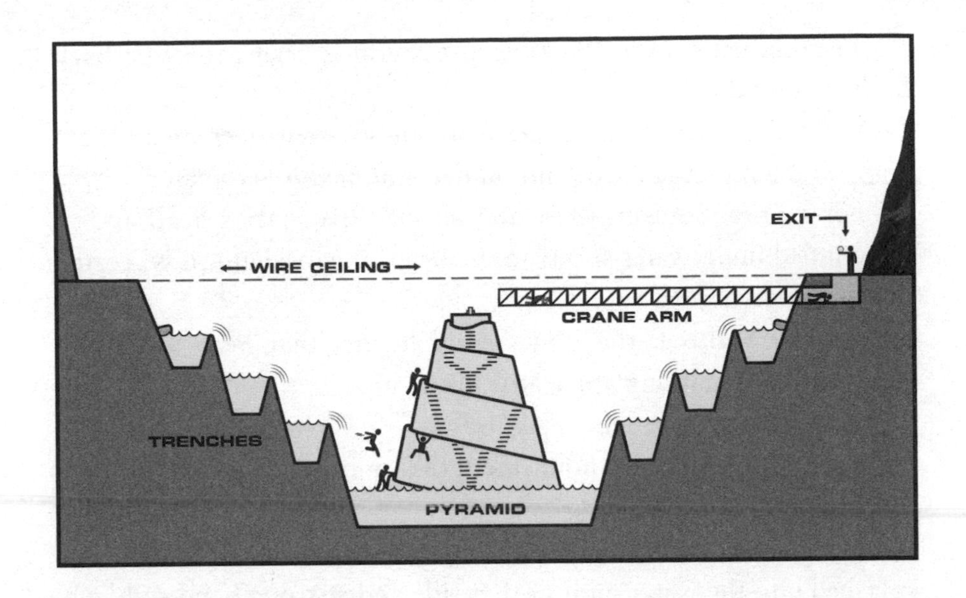

SCALING THE PYRAMID

Soaking wet, heaving for breath, his fingers shaking as they grabbed each handhold, Jack climbed the almost-vertical pyramid, pursued by the ever-rising water.

It was rising faster than he could climb. It rose up his body: over his knees, then his belt, then his ribs.

Jack looked up as he climbed, to see how far he had to go, when something flashed across his field of vision, something white, leaping across from the last trench wall onto the side of the pyramid.

It was the *white* lion-headed hunter.

Jack watched in horror as the white lion—Fear—landed on the side of the pyramid above him and grabbed the ankle of one of the other champions scaling the structure: one of the gold-painted minotaurs, the one who had lost his helmet while struggling with the catfish before.

Then, very deliberately, Fear leaped off the pyramid, taking the gold minotaur with him!

Both the white lion and gold minotaur fell down the face of the pyramid and splashed into the water right beside Jack.

The minotaur surfaced first, arms paddling, trying to swim back to the pyramid.

But then, as Jack watched from only a few feet away, Fear grabbed the minotaur, took him under, *and held him under*.

For a brief moment, the water sloshed over Jack's head and in the muffled underwater spectrum he heard the mechanical wheezing of a scuba-diving regulator.

And he realized: the lion-shaped helmet that Fear wore had some kind of breathing apparatus inside it.

This wasn't a fair fight.

Fear was going to hold the gold minotaur under until he drowned—

No sooner had the thought hit Jack than something large splashed into the water on his other side and a strong hand suddenly gripped his right boot.

It was the other hunter, the black lion named Chaos.

He yanked Jack down with tremendous force and Jack had time for one last deep breath before he went under.

Underwater.

It was grimly silent down here compared to the roaring world of gushing water above.

Jack saw Chaos beneath him, gripping his right boot, holding him under, using the helmet-mask to breathe.

He saw the gold minotaur beside him—still in the grasp of the white lion named Fear—struggling desperately, before the minotaur went limp and simply hovered in the void, dead.

Jack tried using the crossbow bolt sticking out from his left heel as he'd done earlier with the catfish. He unleashed a kick aimed at Chaos's throat, only to see the arrow bounce off the thick armored neckguard that Chaos wore.

Jesus . . .

Chaos kept gripping his other boot.

Jack wriggled and bucked and kicked with all his might, until—with a sudden jerk—his oversized right boot came off completely!

Jack planted his now naked foot on Chaos's lion helmet and pushed off it. He shot upward and resurfaced, gasping for air.

Thanks to the still-rising water, when he surfaced Jack found himself three-quarters of the way up the pyramid.

This was good and bad.

Good because he was closer to the summit.

Bad because at his current rate of climbing, the water would beat him there and he still had to crawl through the crane arm to the exit.

He gritted his teeth. Grim determination swept through him.

I'm not going to die here.

I can't stop now. I won't stop now.

I'm gonna get through this.

Jack snatched the nearest handhold cut into the stone and climbed. Climbed fast, as fast he could, racing the rising water.

It was going to beat him to the top.

But he kept going anyway.

Water swirled and sloshed around him. Giant catfish whooshed past him. They came so close their whiplike whiskers lashed his body.

He reached the peak of the pyramid long after the last champion had left the pit, at the exact moment that the rising water flooded the summit. Now the entire forty-foot pyramid, which had once stood proudly in the center of the pit, was completely submerged.

Jack saw the horizontal crane arm barely three feet away from him, stretching away for about seventy feet to the exit. The wire roof of the pit was right above it.

He dived for the crane arm as the relentlessly rising water swept up through its steel bars and consumed the whole crane arm and Jack as well.

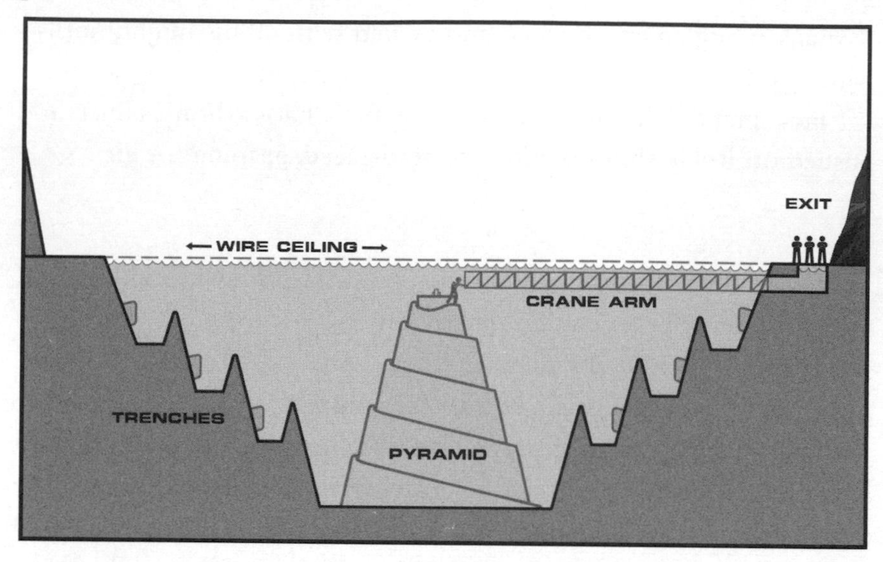

Seen from the viewing balcony, the entire circular pit was now completely filled with water.

It looked like a perfectly round pool, rippling with low waves. The shadows of several giant catfish could be seen prowling under the surface.

Hades's two huntsmen, the black and white figures of Chaos and Fear, were allowed to emerge from the entry gates.

The water went still.

There was no sign of Jack.

The crane arm led to a single hole cut into the floor of the arena and it, too, was now filled with water. It looked like a flooded manhole.

Hades watched it, curious.

The spectators watched it, hushed.

The other champions—soaking wet and breathing hard—watched it, waiting.

From their hostage carriage high above the arena, Lily, Alby, and Sky Monster watched it, holding their breath.

No movement.

No nothing.

No Jack.

And then there was a splash of water in the exit hole and Jack's head appeared.

He crawled out of it on his belly, panting, heaving, gasping for air, dripping from head to toe in his jeans, T-shirt, and single oversized boot.

He rolled onto his back, sucking in oxygen.

"Fifth warrior!" Hades called from his balcony. "You are the last to emerge."

Jack felt his blood run cold. Had he just survived all that only to have his head blown off now?

Hades smiled.

"Yet one other never left the pit, one of the promoted golden minotaurs," Hades said. "So while you are the last to emerge, you have not come last in this challenge. You have earned the right to continue in the Games."

He smiled at Jack, looking like he had very much enjoyed frightening the daylights out of him.

Hades turned to the tall man with the ginger stubble holding the crystal sphere.

"You. Champion. State your name and your house."

The champion removed his lightweight helmet to reveal a head of closely shaved orange hair. He spoke in a polished British accent. "I am Major Gregory Brigham, Your Majesty, from Her Majesty's Special Air Service, the SAS. I represent the mighty and glorious Deus Rex, the Kingdom of Land."

Hades said, "You have won the Second Challenge so you are entitled to the traditional reward: anything that is in my power to give, you may have. All you have to do is name it."

Major Brigham nodded. He seemed aware of this honor.

He jerked his chin at the champion next to him: a shaven-headed man wearing the combat fatigues of the American Army Rangers.

Brigham said, "I would like this gentleman to be killed, please."

Jack was gobsmacked.

Had he heard that right? Had the British guy just asked for the man beside him to be killed?

Hades shrugged. "So be it."

He nodded to Vacheron and Vacheron keyed his remote.

Blam!

The American's head exploded and his headless body crumpled to the ground.

Only Jack seemed horrified. Everyone else around him seemed to accept it without comment, as if they had expected it.

A moment later, a heavy gush of liquid stone thundered into one of the chambers in the hostage train—presumably that of the dead Ranger's hostages—drowning all its occupants.

When the cruel ceremony was over, Vacheron turned to the spectators. "The Second Challenge has been run and won. We shall let our champions adjourn for a short while to tend to their wounds and consult with their support teams, but not for long. The Third Challenge awaits."

The spectators cheered.

Jack sagged with relief.

Lily threw her arms around Jack in a deep relieved hug when he entered the hostage carriage a few minutes later.

The two dogs, their tails wagging furiously, bounced up to him as well. Roxy, the smaller of the two, a little black poodle, barked with unconcealed delight.

Jack returned Lily's embrace, holding her tight, closing his eyes. She was truly a young woman now, lean and beautiful, twenty years old, with long raven-black hair, olive skin, and a razor-sharp mind.

As he held her tightly, Jack glanced at Alby.

"This isn't a dream, is it?" Jack said.

"Definitely not a dream," Alby replied. "But we are through the looking glass, down the rabbit hole, and certainly not in Kansas anymore."

Alby was a different kid, too. Gone was the short, bespectacled, deaf, black nerd he'd been when he was eleven. Now he was twenty-one and while he still wore glasses—classy rimless ones—and a discreet hearing aid, he stood the same height as Jack.

Having been accelerated through his final two years of high school, he'd been fast-tracked to Caltech. It had been amazing for him. He'd blossomed there and he now spoke with a quiet and assured confidence that Jack liked.

Sky Monster clapped a hand on Jack's shoulder. The big bushy-bearded New Zealander shook his head. "Hades? The Underworld? Creepy dudes in animal helmets? What is this place, Jack? And how did we get here?"

A GIRL NAMED LILY

PART V

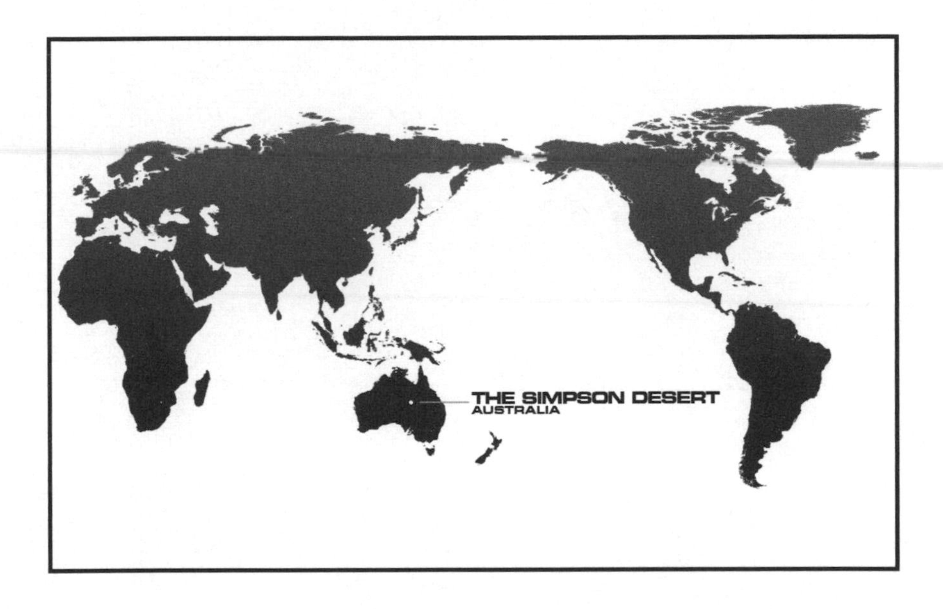

THE SIMPSON DESERT
AUSTRALIA

In the years after they saved the world in 2008, life was good for the members of the West household.

For Jack, after discovering that he was the fifth of the "Five Greatest Warriors" mentioned in an ancient prophecy and surviving a terrible showdown against his father in a giant underground shrine beneath Easter Island, the quiet life on his outback farm was just the ticket.

Long morning walks, reading books, going for drives in his Land Cruiser over the endless expanse of desert, and generally avoiding cataclysmic world-ending events; he loved it.

War veterans often said the same thing: once you have encountered the adrenalized exhilaration of combat, you either step away from the world entirely because you can't stand its more stupid elements or you re-up for more action.

For Jack's wife, Zoe, it was largely the same. She and Jack would sip their morning coffees on the deck, watching the sun rise above the dead-flat horizon. Although truth be told, she was perhaps still a little more restless for adventure than Jack—Zoe liked to fly off to see what their old friends were up to on archaeological digs at remote places or at special seminars given at the elite museums of the world.

For Lily, their adopted daughter, however, life was much different: she had grown up.

She had been eleven during the heady events of 2008. And after helping to save the world, what did an eleven-year-old girl want?

A puppy, of course.

A trip to the city of Adelaide had been arranged and Jack, Zoe, and Lily had visited a rescue shelter for dogs.

Lily had instantly fallen in love with a shy Labrador named Ash. A gentle dog, Ash had flunked out of guide dog school because she wasn't assertive enough, and her douchebag owners, when they suddenly moved overseas, had dumped her at the shelter on the way to the airport.

On that visit, Lily had cuddled her like a teddy bear. "This is the one," she said.

That would have been it had Jack not felt, as they were about to leave, a tiny tug on his pantleg.

He turned.

Sitting at his feet, pawing gently at his leg and looking up at him with beseeching black eyes, was a knee-high black poodle.

One of the women from the shelter came running up. "I'm so sorry. She's an escape artist, this one."

Jack looked down at the dog.

The dog just returned his gaze with steady eyes.

It was perhaps the least masculine dog in the world.

The woman tried to scoop it up, but the poodle ducked and dodged her, scurrying away. As Jack watched, he saw that it limped a little with each step.

Looking closer, he saw that there was something wrong with its front left leg: it was oddly crooked.

After a few tries, the woman finally caught it. "Let me put her back in her ca—"

"Wait," Jack said. "What happened to her leg?"

"Little Roxy here was living a very comfortable life in the sub-

urbs when, one afternoon, the two pit bulls from her neighbor's house dug a hole under the fence and attacked her.

"They mauled her horribly, almost tore her apart. Broke her leg, ripped open her throat. But Roxy fought back, held them off till someone came running.

"She arrived at our clinic soaked in blood. Looked like she'd been put through a meat grinder. We didn't think she'd make it through the night and her owners, when they saw her lying on the operating table, a bloody whimpering wreck, said they no longer wanted her. Their eight-year-old daughter, they said, wouldn't want a *broken* dog.

"Anyway, we patched her up as best we could and waited to see how she recovered. Within a week, she was standing gingerly. Within three weeks, she wanted me to throw her a ball and it was like it never happened."

Jack smiled. "'I never saw a wild thing sorry for itself,'" he quoted. "D. H. Lawrence. That's what I like about dogs. They don't feel sorry for themselves." He glanced from Roxy's crooked left fore-leg to his own artificial left arm.

Behind Jack's back, Lily had thrown a questioning look at Zoe.

Zoe shrugged as if to say: *I don't know where he's going with this*.

Then Jack smiled and said, "How about we take Roxy, too?"

And so life on the farm became life with two bounding dogs.

Lily loved Ash: played with her, fed her, let her sleep on her bed.

As for Roxy, she *adored* Jack. He was her world. Nothing else mattered. Whether he was riding in the Land Cruiser or reading in his office, she wouldn't leave his side. She followed him everywhere, often running several miles to find him somewhere on the farm. She was smart, too, and loved to be trained. Jack taught her to play dead, do a high five, and even fetch his slippers.

The dogs, it had to be said, were a bit of a shock to Jack's falcon, Horus.

The old bird tolerated them like a teenage girl tolerates a little brother. Horus would often sit on Jack's chairback studiously ignoring Roxy as the little black dog jumped up and down, begging her to play.

If Horus was particularly irritated by the poodle, she would fly down, pick up the dog's favorite pink tennis ball in her beak and place it on top of a bookshelf, way out of reach, while the dog barked in protest.

At these times, sitting at his desk, unseen by either animal, a small smile would creep across Jack's face.

As they had grown into their teens, Lily and Alby had remained friends, but Jack could see that in some ways they had grown apart.

For one thing, their university educations were very different. Alby was at the California Institute of Technology in Pasadena, just outside L.A., the preeminent astrophysics school in the world. Home to the Mars Rover project, the Hubble Telescope, and at least four Nobel Prize–winning physicists, it was the perfect place for him.

That said, to the shock of some of his fellow students, who were all mathematical whizzes with little interest in something as mundane as history, he took on a second degree at USC in Ancient History and Mythology. The closest his classmates got to mythology was playing *World of Warcraft* or reading *The Lord of the Rings*.

"I just like history," he'd tell them cryptically. "You never know when ancient history comes in handy in modern life."

Lily, on the other hand, while certainly gifted and clever, had not been accelerated through high school.

This was not entirely a bad thing, Jack thought.

She had learned how kids and regular people operated; how kind they could be and how petty. It grated on her when other girls were bitchy and many were the times when she complained to Jack: "We saved the world for people like *them*?"

Jack would just smile sadly. "Most people are good, kiddo. In the end—and this applies to every single person in the world—the only person anyone has to be true to is themselves. We all have to look at ourselves in the mirror and like what we see."

After graduating from high school, Lily had also gone to university in the US, to Stanford, where she studied Ancient History and a few ancient languages. While she didn't let anyone know that she was a member of a 5,000-year-old line of Egyptian oracles, gifted with the unique ability to read a superancient language, the Word of Thoth, it certainly helped with her studies.

Stanford was also just south of San Francisco, not far from Alby in L.A., and Jack was pleased to know they kept in contact.

But Stanford was not the same as Caltech.

An Ivy League–caliber school situated right on the edge of Silicon Valley, it was a university flush with talented and brilliant students. It also had a significant population of wealthy and privileged kids.

Lily had become friends with some students whose parents were gazillionaires, ultrarich types from some of the wealthiest families in the world.

She had become especially friendly with a handsome twenty-something lad from that crowd named Dion DeSaxe.

They'd been on a few dates and she was quite taken with him.

He was boyfriend material, she'd told Jack during one FaceTime call.

Jesus, Jack thought. It was scary enough to think of his little girl dating. But a boyfriend . . .

Dion, it turned out, was the scion of a very old-money French family. Jack met him when he swung through Stanford one time. He was handsome, clean-cut, with a square jaw, flowing jet-black hair, and the easy confidence of a young man who had grown up never wanting for anything.

Lily had nervously introduced them. "Dion, this is my dad, Jack West."

"Great to meet you, Jack," Dion had said familiarly as they shook hands. "Heard a heck of a lot about you."

Jack? Jack had thought.

He saw Lily shoot a worried look at him. She'd noticed it, too.

Jack wondered, *What ever happened to "Great to meet you, sir. It's a privilege to be dating your daughter"*?

He let it go.

Kids these days.

All things considered—dogs and boyfriends notwithstanding—life was pretty good.

And then came the day when General Eric Abrahamson called and invited him to Pine Gap.

"Jack. Eric Abrahamson," the familiar voice on the phone said. "We've found something we can't explain and thought maybe you could help us."

"Where?"

"Pine Gap."

"When?"

"Now would be good."

"What is it?"

"It's about the scar."

That got Jack's attention.

"I'll be there right away."

As it turned out, the call had come during university holidays, so both Lily and Alby were at the farm. They would come, too. Jack also contacted Pooh Bear and Stretch—his loyal companions from several past missions. They would meet him at Pine Gap.

Zoe, however, would not go. Two days earlier, she'd been called away to, of all places, the Mariana Trench off the coast of the Philippines by their good friends, Lachlan and Julius Adamson, the wonderfully geeky, freckle-faced identical twins who had also been part of their previous missions.

The Adamsons had been working with an American colleague of theirs, the renowned oceanographer and geophysicist Professor David Black, an expert on deep-sea ocean life and hydrothermal vents on the ocean floor. Working with Black in the Mariana Trench, the deepest point on the planet, they had found something.

The twins had sent Jack and Zoe a coded message: *There's something here that shouldn't be: a stone gate-like structure with text written on it in the Word of Thoth.*

Restless for some adventure, Zoe had volunteered to go and investigate while Jack had stayed at the farm with the kids, not expecting to get his own call shortly after.

And so, with Zoe away in the western Pacific Ocean, Jack had flown with Lily and Alby to Pine Gap on the *Sky Warrior*, his black Russian-made Concorde-like jet, piloted by Sky Monster.

After a short flight, the plane landed at the remote base outside Alice Springs in the barren heart of Australia.

Jack stepped out of the *Sky Warrior* onto the airstrip servicing the base, dressed in his way-too-casual clothes.

The black asphalt runway shimmered in the desert heat.

Lily, Alby, and the dogs hopped out of the plane after him. Sky Monster, as usual, said he would stay with the plane to tinker with a few things.

They were met by General Abrahamson and his soon-to-be replacement, General Beard, and guided inside the secret base.

Pine Gap is a very secret place, so secret that few know what really goes on there.

Some say it is a listening post. Others, a high-tech satellite-tracking facility. Others still claim that beneath the base, a giant iridium antenna bores down deep into the Earth and can track the slightest tremor: something which helps the United States (which owns the base) pinpoint any nuclear weapons test anywhere in the world.

As he stepped inside the base, into its clean and cool air-conditioned offices, Jack knew what was really there.

It was all of the above, plus one more thing.

Pine Gap was the data-collection and evaluation center for the SKA telescope array.

SKA stood for Square Kilometer Array, although people tended to tautologically call it the "SKA Array." It was a collection of radio telescopes in Africa and Australia that, when combined through complex computing algorithms, would give the highest-resolution images of stars and star clusters in the history of astronomy.

Indeed, the SKA processed so much information, it required specially built quantum computers that every *day* processed more information than passed through the entire Internet in a *year*.

It was a major project and a majorly secret one. The world's media had been told that the SKA would not be operational till 2020 but that, as Jack knew, was not true.

It was already operational.

After passing through the entry atrium of the base, General Abrahamson stopped in an air-conditioned waiting room.

"I'm afraid the kids and the dogs will have to wait out here. This is classified."

Lily and Alby understood and dropped onto the couches of the waiting room. Roxy was less enthusiastic about being parted from Jack. She barked softly as he headed through an inner door with Abrahamson and Beard.

They arrived in a subterranean room filled with large-screen monitors. It looked like Mission Control at NASA.

"So," Abrahamson said. "The SKA Array. The greatest telescope ever constructed. It cost four billion dollars to build and is capable of seeing farther into space than we've ever been able to do before. Isaac Newton would have killed for a telescope like this."

"And . . . ?" Jack prompted.

"And we turned it on a month ago," Abrahamson said. "And saw this."

He indicated the main viewing screen.

On it was a peculiar image:

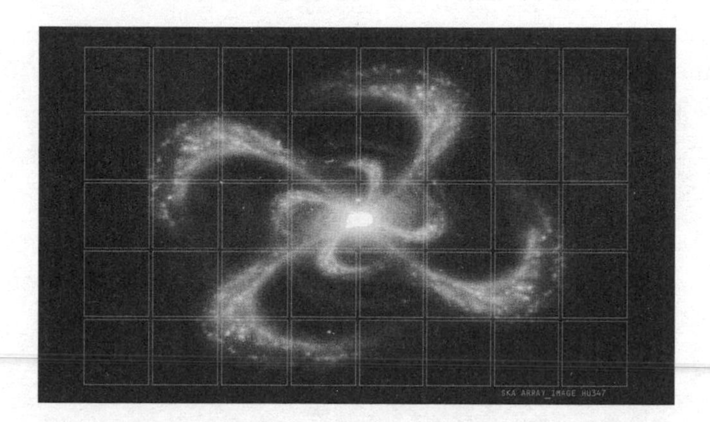

Jack found it oddly beautiful. It looked like a galaxy of some sort, with four large curling arms and four smaller inner arms that also curled slightly.

"What is it, a galaxy?" he asked.

"It's a galaxy, all right," Abrahamson said. "A runaway galaxy, hurtling through space at incredible speed, rocketing out from the center of the universe."

"How fast?"

"About 12 billion kilometers per hour."

"That's impossible. That's ten times the speed of light."

"We know, but it's what our readings say," Abrahamson said. "It seems to be riding on the crest of some kind of expanding gravitational wave, which moves like a ripple in a pond, expanding outward from the center of the known universe. This galaxy also possesses something called 'negative density' which allows it to travel faster than light without expanding catastrophically. I asked our physics geniuses and they said it's legit. Apparently, if gravity can keep light from escaping a black hole, it can also do the reverse and propel something faster than light."

Jack felt the back of his neck begin to tingle.

"How big is it?" he asked.

"It's approximately four hundred times the size of the Milky Way."

"And its course?"

Abrahamson said, "It's coming directly toward us, Jack."

The implications hit Jack immediately.

A galaxy that size, thundering across space at phenomenal speed, would wipe out everything in its path. When it came to our galaxy, the Milky Way, it would crash through it like a semitruck running over an anthill.

The Milky Way would be blasted apart. The sun and every planet in the solar system would either be vaporized in an instant or scattered into space.

And we'd never see it coming.

We would actually be long dead before the runaway galaxy smashed through the Earth. It was so immense, its gravitational effects so strong, it would rip the Earth asunder from many light-years away. Our deaths would be instantaneous—one second we would be here, the next we would not.

"How long have we got?" Jack asked.

Redbeard stepped in. "At its current velocity, we estimate that the runaway galaxy's destructive gravitational field will start to affect us in approximately two months. Earth has sixty days to live."

"Jack," Abrahamson said, "we're lucky we turned on the SKA Array when we did. We would never have seen this coming."

Jack stared at the galaxy depicted on the screen. "So what do you think I can do?"

Abrahamson said, "I don't know. But I do know that you've seen some crazy shit in your travels. I was hoping maybe one of your history books or ancient texts might mention this thing."

Jack looked again at the image on the screen. "It does resemble the tetragammadion . . ."

"The tetra what?" Redbeard asked.

"The tetragammadion. The symbol that today we call the 'swastika,' although this one is reversed," Jack said.

He grabbed a pen and paper and scribbled quickly. "It's usually drawn like this, with four curved or bent outer arms, four inner arms, and some dots nestled inside them."

"A swastika?" Abrahamson said distastefully.

Jack said, "Long before Hitler and the Nazis appropriated the swastika and made it a symbol of evil, it was actually a very *positive* religious symbol meant to bring good luck and ward off wickedness. In India, for example, it's sacred to both Buddhists and Hindus. There are also older examples. Swastika images have been found in the Ukraine that date back to 10,000 B.C. Oddly, no one has ever discovered what made the symbol so popular in those ancient cults. Maybe it was this galaxy."

Redbeard shook his head. "How could ancient civilizations know of a galaxy halfway across the universe? One that *we* couldn't see until now?"

Jack said, "It's happened before. The primitive Dogon tribe in West Africa knew that the star Sirius had two companion stars long before we confirmed it with modern telescopes."

"And how do you explain that?"

"I can't," Jack said. "No one can. Visitors from space? Time travelers giving them advanced knowledge? The world is full of things we don't understand. I've seen enough of them to keep an open mind."

Jack turned to Abrahamson.

"That's the best I can offer you, sir. Maybe I can look up the tetragammadion in some of my books and texts but, really—"

It was then that Jack smelled it.

An odd odor.

He frowned. He suddenly began to feel dizzy.

He spun . . .

. . . and saw the nearest air-conditioning vent.

A faint gas was issuing from it, causing the air to shimmer.

"There's something in the air ducts," he said just as, on a nearby security monitor, he saw masked men with assault rifles burst into the reception area of the base.

"We . . . have to . . . move . . ." His speech was slurring now.

Jack turned to face Abrahamson just as, to his horror, he saw Redbeard draw a pistol and fire it into the back of Abrahamson's head.

Then Redbeard calmly put on a gas mask.

Jack staggered away.

His mind was a blur and his legs felt like lead. Whatever the gas was, it was making him groggy, slow, dull.

Must get . . .

. . . to Lily and Alby . . .

He lurched pathetically away from Redbeard. Redbeard calmly followed him, gun held lazily.

"Don't worry, Jack," Redbeard said. "I'm not going to kill you. I need you. My royal house needs you."

His eyes watering, his throat tightening, his balance failing, Jack stumbled out the doors of the control room. He teetered a short way down a corridor and realized that he wasn't going to make it back to Lily and Alby.

He needed to do something.

He looked about himself and saw it: a kitchen. It looked like a regular office kitchen, with a microwave on the counter and a refrigerator by the door.

Jack fell into the kitchen and toppled the refrigerator so that it blocked the door, at least for a short while.

Thirty seconds later, General Conor Beard shoved aside the fridge and fully entered the kitchen, his pistol raised.

Redbeard smiled. “Don’t be afraid, Jack. You’ve been chosen for a very great honor. Who knows, maybe you *can* do something about this runaway galaxy.”

The last thing Jack saw, blurry and out of focus, was Redbeard’s gas mask–covered face.

Then he lost consciousness and everything went black.

He would wake up two days later in a dark stone cell in time to see a minotaur charging at him with a knife.

Two hours after the gas had been released throughout Pine Gap, two figures arrived at the secret base in a private jet bearing the markings of the United Arab Emirates.

They could not have been more different from each other.

One was tall and skinny; the other short and round. The tall one was clean-shaven; the short one had a heavy beard that was held in check by a jeweled brass ring. The tall one was handsome; the short one was not: he even wore a pirate-like eye patch over his left eye.

Their real names were Benjamin Cohen, former captain in the Israeli Mossad, and Major Zahir al Ansar al Abbas, second son of the Emir of the United Arab Emirates.

Despite their differences, they were the firmest of friends, brought together by a common cause and a mutual love of a little girl and her father.

They were known to their friends by the names Lily had bestowed on them many years ago: Stretch and Pooh Bear.

Bad weather over the Indian Ocean had delayed them and now they were two hours late for the meeting. They stood at the base of the airstairs of their private jet.

"Something's wrong," Pooh Bear said, his good eye scanning the base. "Where's the *Sky Warrior*?"

Jack's plane was nowhere to be seen.

"Where are the *guards*?" Stretch said. "This base is Level Nine Restricted. There should be a lot of men with automatic weapons out here and there's nobody."

They both drew their guns.

Then, very cautiously, they headed inside.

Inside the main building, they beheld the evidence of a fierce firefight.

The walls were shredded with bullet holes. Blood splatters were everywhere. Five dead guards lay piled behind the reception counter with bullet holes in their heads.

"Jack . . ." Pooh Bear started running, searching every room.

There was not a single person alive in the place.

They found the body of General Eric Abrahamson lying faceup, eyes open, inside a Mission Control–like room. They searched the rest of the building.

No Jack, Lily, Alby, or Sky Monster.

Pooh Bear and Stretch exchanged a look.

"Why kill everyone but take Jack and his crew?" Stretch asked.

Pooh Bear scanned the eerie rooms of the deserted, bloody base.

"Jack West Jr. doesn't emerge from his secret home very often," he said. "Maybe that was their goal: to take Jack. They got wind that he was coming here and they set a trap. Everyone else was just collateral damage."

Stretch sniffed the air . . . and frowned.

"Smells like chloroxipham."

"What's that?"

"A quick-acting nerve gas," Stretch said. "Nonlethal. They must've piped it into the air-con."

"Who uses it?" Pooh Bear asked.

"Western antiterror units mainly," Stretch said. "The British SAS are known to use it in siege situations. If terrorists take an embassy or a theater, they pump it into the air-conditioning ducts to knock out the bad guys but not kill any hostages."

Pooh Bear started striding down a corridor. "Hopefully Jack stayed conscious long enough to leave us a message."

He turned into the base's kitchen and went straight to the refrigerator tipped on its side.

It was a fallback protocol they had for use in emergencies.

If any of Jack's team were to encounter trouble at any place, they were to find the kitchen—since almost every venue had one—and there they were to leave a message in the one thing that most kitchens had: a milk bottle or carton.

Pooh Bear pulled a milk carton from the side-turned fridge and tipped its contents out.

Milk poured out of the carton . . .

. . . and so did something else.

A teaspoon.

It came tumbling out of the milk carton and clattered into the sink.

"Good work, Jack!" Pooh Bear said, snatching it up and examining it.

There was writing on the little spoon in black marker. It read:

"What is that symbol?" Pooh Bear asked.

"No idea," Stretch said. "And 'MM.' Do you think Jack means—?"

"Oh, man, yes."

Stretch looked from the spoon to Pooh Bear. "He must be in serious shit. MM. Mabel Merriweather. A most formidable woman once known as Mabel *West*. Jack wants us to go and find his mother."

Pooh Bear and Stretch dashed back to their plane.

They didn't want to be here when the authorities arrived. That would mean hours, possibly days, of explaining. If they were going to help Jack, they needed to get out of here right away.

Stretch pulled out his cell phone as he ran. "I'd better call Zoe," he said. "She's in the Pacific, checking out a find with the Twins."

The call went straight to voice mail.

"Damn it," Stretch said. "Phone's off or she's out of range."

"She could be 20,000 leagues under the sea right now," Pooh said. "We'll try again later."

Right then, as he raced across the tarmac, Pooh spotted something out on the desert floor: three wild dogs, or dingoes as Australians called them.

The dogs were moving cautiously, as a pack, surrounding something on the ground.

Pooh Bear paused, stepped closer, trying to see what they were hunting.

Then he saw it. A little puff of sand on the ground that they were slowly converging on.

It was an animal. A bird.

A downed bird.

One of its wings flapped limply, causing another puff of sand.

Pooh Bear went over to it . . . and when he recognized the bird, he hurried forward, yelling at the dogs to scat.

He fell to his knees beside the bird.

It was Horus, Jack's peregrine falcon.

The wounded bird lay on its side in a drying pool of blood, cooing weakly. Pooh Bear saw a bullet wound to her left wing.

"There, there," he said, cradling the brown falcon in his arms. "You're all right now."

He carried her back to the jet, climbing in and closing the door as Stretch hit the gas.

The private jet soared away into the sky, leaving behind the bloody crime scene that had once been the secret base of Pine Gap.

A SECRET HISTORY I

THE FOUR LEGENDARY KINGDOMS

There were other carvings, including one of four throned kings sitting shoulder-to-shoulder and flanked by five standing warriors . . .

FROM *THE SIX SACRED STONES*
(MACMILLAN, SYDNEY, 2007)

CHAMPION PROFILE

NAME: DEPON, TENZIN
AGE: 22
RANK TO WIN: 3
REPRESENTING: SKY

PROFILE:

A Tibetan prince from the Sky Kingdom, Tenzin Depon took his holy orders at the age of eight, forsaking his inheritance to become a warrior-monk.

He has been training full-time for these Games for the last fourteen years.

Ranked 3rd out of 16 to win the Games.

FROM HIS PATRON:

"This is Tenzin's time."

Kenzo Depon,
King of the Sky

On the balcony overlooking the flooded arena of the Second Challenge, the wealthy spectators chatted as they sipped champagne and ate hors d'oeuvres.

Snippets of their conversations could be heard:

"—I heard she wanted to marry him so she could weasel her way into the Rothschild bloodline—"

"—I love how newcomers to the White House think they have actual power—"

"—and then he said, 'Well, they *are* new money.' I almost laughed. *His* family's fortune only goes back to 1790. *He* is new money as far as I'm concerned!"

A few of the men commented on the champions:

"—The fifth warrior is out of his depth. He barely scraped through the first two challenges, and they are by far the easiest—"

"—My money's on the SAS fellow, Brigham. Iolanthe tells me he's been training for this for a year using replicas of previous mazes and arenas."

"—What about the US Marine? The one who took out Majestic-12?"

"—He did us all a favor, really. The Majestic-12 were out of control. Forgot who they were serving."

"—Keep an eye on the two warrior-monks from Tibet, especially the one named Tenzin. It says here in the official program that he's been preparing for this since he was eight years old."

★ ★ ★

In his team's hostage carriage above the arena, Jack sat with his back against the iron wall. After he'd calmed down a little, he had begun to recall more of the details of what had happened before his capture at Pine Gap. He told the others about the runaway galaxy in the shape of a curling tetragammadion that was hurtling toward Earth.

"So, where in the world are we?" Lily asked.

Jack said, "Judging from those catfish, somewhere in Asia, but I can't be sure." Roxy nuzzled up against his leg and he patted her.

Alby said, "Hades? The Underworld? What is all this and why are we here?"

"These," said a woman's voice, "are the Great Games of the Hydra, and you are here to represent my royal house."

Jack turned to face the speaker but he had already recognized her voice.

A beautiful woman with perfect porcelain skin, emerald-green eyes, and gorgeous auburn hair stepped into view outside his cell.

She stood with her hands behind her back and wore a sparkling figure-hugging silver gown that showed off her slender legs and narrow waist. She was a woman who over the course of several encounters with Jack had variously tried to kill, seduce, and even help him.

She was Iolanthe Compton-Jones, Keeper of the Royal Records for the ancient line of European kings known as the Deus Rex.

A man stood with her, a short bald guy wearing glasses and carrying a compact suitcase.

Iolanthe nodded to a nearby minotaur guard. "This is our house's personal doctor. Admit him."

The minotaur opened the barred door to Jack's cage, allowing the bespectacled man inside.

"Hullo," he said in a very British accent. "My name's Barnard. Dr. Harold Barnard. Now hold still, dear boy, and let me have a look at these scratches."

He opened his suitcase to reveal that it was full of medical equipment: bandages, pills, ampoules, syringes, even a pair of small portable defibrillator paddles.

Iolanthe remained outside the cell.

"Why, Jack," she said, "you didn't need to dress up for the occasion."

As Barnard tended to his wounds, Jack looked from his wet and dirty Homer Simpson T-shirt to Iolanthe's glamorous silver gown.

"Bite me, Iolanthe," he said.

Iolanthe turned to Lily. "And Lily, I'm so delighted to see you again. I am certain you will find this whole experience most stimulating."

"You're a real bitch, lady," Lily said.

Iolanthe smiled tightly. "How charming. Here, Jack, I brought you a gift."

Her hands emerged from behind her back holding a battered fireman's helmet. Its badge read FDNY PRECINCT 17.

She passed it through the bars of the cell. "It was on your plane. We can't have Jack West fighting without his famous helmet, can we?"

Jack took it. "Where are we and how did we get here, Iolanthe?"

"You know, Jack, you can't imagine how disappointed I was when I heard you'd married that pretty Irish girl, what's-her-name. Hearts broke around the world when it became known that the fifth greatest warrior was off the market."

"*Where are we and how did we get here?*"

"You are in India, Jack," Iolanthe said, suddenly serious. "Exactly where in India, well, I am not at liberty to say, but it is remote, in one of India's many desert regions. This," she waved her hand, "is the original ancient city of the Hydra: Old Hyderabad."

"And how did we get here?"

"Oh, I had you kidnapped," Iolanthe said simply. "From Pine Gap. You're a very hard man to find, Jack West. But I had someone at Pine Gap—General Beard—who informed me that you were emerging from your splendid isolation to go there for a meeting."

"Why am I here?"

"I would have thought you'd have figured that out by now. As I just said, you have been brought here to compete for my royal house in the Great Games of the Hydra."

She paused, looking at Jack closely.

"You've not heard of the Games?" she asked.

"No."

"Never?"

"Not ever."

"Oh, dear. Given your adventures, I'd thought you would know of them. I had better start from the beginning, then."

Iolanthe explained. "Do you recall in your travels around the ancient places of the world ever seeing a carving of four kings seated side by side on four thrones?"

Jack thought about that. After a moment, he saw it in his mind's eye: a carving on the wall of an ancient underground complex depicting five warriors standing behind four seated kings, a striking image that had stood out amid a larger adventure.

"Yes," he said, "in China. In a trap system under Witch Mountain devised by Laozi to protect the Philosopher's Stone. Four kings seated in front of five warriors."

"Right," Iolanthe said. "Those four kings represent the four eternal kingdoms, or the four legendary kingdoms as they are sometimes called. They are the four shadow families that rule the world: the Kingdoms of Land, Sea, Sky, and Underworld."

"The four shadow kingdoms that *rule the world*?" Alby said doubtfully.

"Yes," Iolanthe said. "Throughout recorded history, empires have risen and fallen, nations have been born and have died, wars have been fought, systems of government have collapsed. Through it all, ruling in the background the entire time, have been the four eternal kingdoms. By long-held convention, my royal family, which you know by the name of 'Deus Rex,' rules the kingdom known as Land."

This was news to Jack.

So far as he knew, based on his previous encounters with them, the Deus Rex were the so-called god-kings of Europe. They were a select group of royal families—including the British, Danish, Spanish, and Russian royals—who traced their lineage back to ancient times. Jack had the dubious distinction of having killed their leader, a Russian nicknamed Carnivore during a pivotal confrontation beneath Easter Island.

"Who's in charge of the Deus Rex now that Carnivore is dead?" he asked. "The Queen of England?"

"Her? Goodness no. The Duke of Avalon is now our king," Iolanthe said. "Queen Elizabeth is well down the line of succession, although one of her sons is here to watch the Games. The Kingdom of Land rules over the great landmasses of the world, those historically controlled by European powers: Europe, Britain, Russia, Africa, and Australia."

Jack said, "Hold on. You say these kingdoms rule the world together? When I was hunting down the Seven Wonders of the Ancient World, your family fought *against* America, against the Freemasons there."

"Saying that we rule *together* might be stretching the truth a tad," Iolanthe said. "There are always squabbles going on within the four kingdoms and between them, such as happened then. It has always been this way."

Iolanthe carelessly looped a strand of hair behind her ear.

"That incident was a spat between my royal house and the Kingdom of the Sea, now based in America and advised by the Freemasons. Houses will always seek to dominate and thus butt heads from time to time. My house—ably advised over the millennia by the historians of the Catholic Church and men of institutions like the Royal Society—has ruled for a *very* long time."

"The Kingdom of the Sea is America?" Jack asked.

"Technically, it is the kingdom of the Atlantic, Indian, and Pacific Oceans, which includes the Americas, but for now, yes, an American occupies that throne," Iolanthe said. "The Sky Kingdom is based in the mountains of Tibet and the famous Kingdom of the Underworld is here in India."

"Tibet contains an ancient kingdom?" Alby asked.

Iolanthe replied, "Why else do you think modern China has craved Tibet for so long? A thousand years ago, it was the other way around, and a royal household based in Tibet ruled over the backward Chinese. But over the centuries, things change and sometimes the ruled become the rulers."

Jack shook his head. "Okay, and on top of all that, you're saying places like Hell really exist?"

Iolanthe sighed. "For a man who has seen what you've seen, Jack, I would have thought this was rather easy to accept. And please don't say 'Hell.' It comes with all sorts of *immoral* connotations. Call it the Underworld. In the original myths, the Underworld was just a place you went to after you died—that's because this place began as burial catacombs. The dead were brought here. Only later, thanks to some troublesome priests, did it acquire the whole hellfire and damnation thing.

"No," she continued, "many of mankind's most enduring myths actually happened. The old gods, the old legends. While they may have been embellished and modified over the millennia, they happened. That is why they have stood the test of time.

"Take Zeus, the famed king of the gods, ruler of Olympus," Iolanthe said. "He was the Land King of his day and a most charismatic ruler. He dominated his three fellow kings who at that time were all from the same family. His brother, Hades, ruled the Underworld, this kingdom in India, while his other brother—"

". . . Poseidon . . ." Jack said.

"—ruled the seas. The failed rebellion of the Titans was a failed uprising *against the four kingdoms*. The Sea Kingdom's old capital and its famed destruction in ancient times has, of course, acquired its own mythic status as the story of Atlantis.

"Why, the names of the three previous winners of these very Games—Osiris, Gilgamesh, and Hercules—have resounded in history, even though the original cause of their fame has been lost. We view them today as fictitious gods or heroes when in truth they actually lived and did great things.

"So many things in our world derive from the four kingdoms: Star Chambers, debutante balls, the notion of *noblesse oblige*, even the Olympic Games began in Greece as an imitation of these Games."

"Wait," Jack said. "The Star Chamber. When he spoke earlier, Hades said something about a Star Chamber opening and that was why the Games are being held now. What was that about?"

Iolanthe smiled. "I always liked that about you, Jack. You pay attention. And you get right to the point. In the grand scheme of things, the Great Games are incredibly important. For they are, quite literally, man's chance to prove his worth and continue to exist."

"What does that mean?" Jack asked.

"During his opening address," Iolanthe said, "Lord Hades did indeed mention that the Star Chamber has opened. This kingdom, this mighty mountain-palace, is a most mysterious place. It was constructed by an ancient civilization, one that lived on this planet long before humans did, the same civilization that built the six-cornered Machine that you rebuilt, Jack.

"While it presents itself to us as a striking black mountain, it is much more than that. For this peak is curiously and inexplicably *alive*. Our scientists have analyzed it. It seethes with a peculiar kind of energy and it contains many unexplained mechanisms—like the one that opened the Star Chamber—that operate according to their own celestial calendars.

"The Star Chamber is an astronomical temple at the mountain's summit. Exactly forty days ago, *entirely of its own accord*, that temple opened. According to the ancient texts, this occurs when a galaxy known as the Hydra comes directly toward the Milky Way and Earth, an event that takes place approximately once every few thousand years.

"You yourself saw this galaxy, Jack. At Pine Gap. For the first time in history, thanks to the SKA Array, man has been able to see the Hydra."

Jack said, "The images captured by the SKA Array are top secret."

"*Are you listening to me?*" Iolanthe said. "The four kingdoms *own* every major government on Earth. Our people *designed* the SKA Array. We see the results before presidents see them. You should be honored to have even laid eyes on the Hydra Galaxy, Jack. Isaac Newton calculated its existence but never got to see it, much to his chagrin. As he once wrote, the optics of his time simply weren't good enough.

"But his mathematics were correct. It's out there and it's coming. And as it hurtles through space toward us, the Hydra is clearing the way for something far more important, a signal that will be sent from the very center of the universe, from the same civilization that built this place.

"They are searching for us, Jack, asking if we are still here and worthy of existing.

"In any case, these Games are a most ancient ceremony held in honor of the coming of the Hydra. In a series of challenges, the champions must acquire nine spheres of very rare gold quartz.

"Those Golden Spheres are then set in place in the two temples atop this mountain, in two separate ceremonies.

"The first ceremony involves laying five spheres in the Star Chamber, which we call the 'minor temple.' Only when they are laid will the second 'major temple' open. The final four spheres are then placed in the major temple in what is known as the Supreme Ceremony.

"This whole mountain, Jack, it's basically one giant ancient antenna. It starts deep underground and rises high into the sky. Once all nine spheres are set in place, they initiate the antenna, which sends a signal to the Hydra Galaxy, informing it that Earth is still populated by people advanced enough—worthy enough—to keep living. The Hydra will be diverted and life on Earth will continue.

"*Noblesse oblige*, Jack, the obligation of those who are highborn to look after the common people. This is why the royal houses exist, to preserve the ancient traditions of the Earth and thus keep everyone on it alive.

"As I said before, the Great Games have been held on three previous occasions, but this time is different. It has long been foretold that the Fourth Great Games will precede a great and terrible cataclysm. Much is at stake this time, more than just the fate of the Earth."

Iolanthe looked hard at him. "Right now, though, all you need to know is that Lord Hades's word is law. Make no mistake, he bears a heavy burden. With his crown came the sacred obligation to host the Games without fear or favor. If the champions do not acquire all the spheres, the major temple will *not* send out the return signal to the Hydra. And the Hydra Galaxy will crash through our galaxy and the Earth will be destroyed."

Jack was silent for a long moment. He eyed Iolanthe closely.

"That's not all there is to it," he said.

"I don't know what you mean," Iolanthe said.

"Why not just place the nine spheres and be done with it? Why host some elaborate Games?" Jack asked.

"Like I said, this mountain was built by a civilization far more advanced than ours. It was *designed* for this purpose, for hosting the Great Games. Just as the Star Chamber opened at a preordained time, so too do the Golden Spheres perform a preordained function. Each quartz sphere pulses with energy, as do the gemstones embedded in each champion's neck, since they are made of the same exotic mineral.

"As each sphere is won in each challenge—lifted from a pedestal by a champion branded with a gemstone—that sphere somehow *knows* that it was won in accordance with the ancient ritual. We cannot cheat at our task, Jack. We cannot fool the ancients."

"Okay, let me put it another way," Jack said. "*What's in it for you, Iolanthe?* For your kingdom? You didn't kidnap me to participate in this thing solely out of some ancient noble obligation to save the world. I know you. You don't work that way."

Iolanthe nodded slowly. "The Games are a test of humanity's worth, yes, but they do also serve another purpose. The king who *sponsors* the victorious champion wins for himself a most valuable and powerful reward."

"What's that?"

"Something that need not concern you right now," Iolanthe said. "Staying alive should be your primary concern."

Jack let it go. He had other questions which he wanted answered and only Iolanthe could answer them. "Those minotaur things. They're not quite human. What are they?"

"They are a form of subhuman," Iolanthe said, "an advanced primate that did not quite evolve to the level of *Homo sapiens*. Call them Neanderthals if you like. Anthropologists have long said that the Neanderthal people were never truly wiped out by *Homo sapiens*. They interbred with us and walk among us in our cities today. These, however, are purebred Neanderthals: dumb brutes fit only for menial labor and warrior fodder. Lord Hades has thousands of them. Under his direction, they maintain this glorious place."

"So they're his slaves?"

"A slave army, yes."

"Another question," Jack said. "Why me?"

"Oh, that was easy. Every champion here has trained hard for these Games. Some have trained their whole adult lives for them."

She nodded at the three cells to Jack's right. "The other champions representing the Kingdom of Land are the very capable Major Brigham from Her Majesty's SAS and two Brazilian special forces soldiers.

"Major Brigham has been preparing for this for years. The Brazilians, likewise. They were procured for us by our advisers in the Catholic Church. While Brazil is in South America and thus technically part of the Sea Kingdom, it still possesses the largest Catholic population on Earth, and with our deep Catholic connections, we were able to get them to fight for us. Our two Brazilians are *very* Catholic. Very bloodthirsty, too. My king thought it most humorous to do battle with the Sea King with men from his own territory. They have a private wager on the whole thing—"

"Again: why me?" Jack said flatly.

Iolanthe shrugged. "Our fourth champion was killed while training for the Games eight days ago and we needed a capable fighter to fill the fourth spot. Who better than you?"

"You decided that I be kidnapped and my family and friends held hostage while I compete in a series of death-challenges on your behalf?"

"Potato, pot*a*to."

"I agree with Lily," Jack said. "You're a bitch."

"Now, now," a deep voice said from somewhere nearby. "That's a little harsh."

A man stepped into view from behind Iolanthe.

Hades.

Hades stood before Jack's cell.

"So this is the fifth warrior." He looked Jack up and down. "Strange. I thought you would be more . . . imposing."

Jack evaluated Hades, too. "Funny, I was thinking the same about you, given you are the Lord of the Underworld and all."

It was a lie.

As Jack looked at Hades up close, the man was the living embodiment of imposing.

He was a big man, broad-shouldered, with a strong angular jaw and piercing maroon-tinged eyes. There was something in his gaze that was unnerving and it took Jack a moment to realize what it was. The man hardly ever blinked. He just stared at you with a steady unwavering gaze.

Hades's lips curled into a smile, but his eyes remained deadly.

He nodded at Jack's *Simpsons* T-shirt. "I must confess, I do enjoy modern cartoons. I especially liked the depiction of Satan in *South Park*. You seem rather unprepared, fifth warrior."

"I wasn't planning on all this when I left the house a few days ago."

"Then I do hope you are a quick learner."

"Do you enjoy this?" Jack asked suddenly. "Watching men scramble for their lives? Watching them die for your pleasure?"

Hades cocked his head at that. "You mistake me, fifth warrior. I do not find any pleasure in it at all. It is my duty to host these Games and it is that duty alone which motivates me.

"I have spent many years, the whole of my reign, preparing for this week. How many Lords of the Underworld have gotten to host the Great Games of the Hydra? Only three. Three. *In all of history*. My sole goal is to ensure the Games fulfill the requirements of the ancients.

"For my kingship is unique. I alone among the four kings cannot act in accordance with my own personal desires. When I accepted my crown, I swore to put my sacred duty above all else, including my allegiance to my home nation of France. I must also stand above the politics of the royal houses. I cannot play favorites, not even toward my own four representatives in the Games. If no champion proves worthy of the challenges, the world is not worthy, and thus it must end."

"What about that Taiwanese guy who said he'd been kidnapped?" Jack asked. "You killed him without even hesitating."

Hades shook his head sadly. "The world has changed so much over the centuries. Empires became republics, princes and princesses became celebrities, and as this thing called democracy has caught hold, ordinary people have begun to think that their opinions matter. They do not."

Hades's face became hard.

"Here, you will not find democracy. This is a true kingdom. It is *my* kingdom. My realm. I rule it with absolute power and iron discipline. No king could tolerate the insolence that man showed earlier, even if he really was wronged. To be the King of the Underworld is to be, if it is required, the man who condemns the entire population of this planet to death. That is my task. That is my duty.

"As such, I see only black and white. I do not see gray. That man refused to fight and so he had to die. My decisions, sir, are final. And I could well make the most final decision in all of human history."

He stared at Jack with his unblinking eyes.

Jack held his gaze and said nothing.

"But that was not why I came here," Hades said, suddenly smiling. "I came for her."

He nodded at Lily, huddled behind Jack.

Two guards opened the iron door to the cell, but Jack blocked them.

"You'll take my daughter over my dead body."

Hades's grin faded. "Mind your tone, fifth warrior. Remember what I said about insolence. And in point of fact, she is not your biological daughter. She is the daughter of the Oracle of Siwa. Her blood is pure. Indeed, it is of a purity that many would die to have and some would pay a fortune to marry."

Jack frowned. He didn't like the sound of that.

Hades held out his hand to Lily. "Come, child. Come with me to the royal balconies. Someone of your station, of your lineage, shouldn't be here with these . . . common folk."

Lily glared at Hades. "I think I'd rather stay here with my common dad and my common friends, you—"

"Lily," Jack said sharply. "No. Go."

"But Dad . . ."

Jack held her close and looked her in the eye. "If I die during the next challenge, everyone in this cell dies, too. If you go, it gives me one less person to worry about. It may also be like your grandmother always says."

Lily bowed her head and nodded, understanding the cryptic phrase.

It came from Jack's mother, a most unusual woman who, on those occasions when she'd spent time with Lily, had always encouraged her to try new things, go to unusual plays or movies, and most of all, to pay attention in school.

"*Who knows, you might just learn something*," she would always say.

Which was Jack's intent: go with Hades, because you might learn something about all this.

Lily turned to the Lord of the Underworld. "Okay. Fine. I'll go."

With a final kiss on the cheek to Jack, she left with Hades, Iolanthe, the British doctor, and Hades's guards.

A moment later, Monsieur Vacheron, the bald Master of the Games, appeared in front of Jack's cell and offered a leering smile.

"Hello, maggot," he spat. "For the Third Challenge, you may bring one weapon. You must also choose a companion and bind him to yourself."

Vacheron carelessly tossed something small through the bars at Jack. The object bounced off Jack's chest and landed on the floor with a clatter.

A pair of steel handcuffs.

Fifteen minutes later, Jack and Sky Monster stood in a tight iron-barred antechamber not much larger than a phone booth, facing a steel outer door, handcuffed to each other.

Stretching away from them on both sides were similar cages containing the other champions, all handcuffed to a companion of their own and all facing their own outer doors.

In the dark tight space, Jack felt like a racehorse in a starting stall, waiting with the other horses for the gates to spring open.

He and Sky Monster had been led here from their hostage carriage via a series of tunnels, before being pushed into the antechamber via a door in its rear.

Tense silence.

Jack now wore his fireman's helmet strapped tight around his chin along with his *Simpsons* T-shirt.

He still wore no shoes. The lone oversized boot he'd acquired in the water maze was no good and Alby had much smaller feet than Jack so his sneakers didn't fit; and Sky Monster was wearing his. Since Sky Monster had no weapon, Jack had given him the knife he'd taken from the minotaur at the very start of all this.

An odd trumpeting came from somewhere outside, beyond the door, followed by a muffled booming.

This must have been how Roman gladiators felt, Jack thought. *Waiting to fight, not knowing what lay on the other side of that door*.

His nerves jangled. His heart pumped loudly inside his head.

Beside him, he could see beads of sweat forming on Sky Monster's brow. The big Kiwi looked beyond petrified. He wasn't used to being on the ground and in the thick of things. He was normally up in the plane, circling, waiting to provide the getaway. He performed his heroics from a pilot's seat, which didn't require him to be lean or fit, and he was neither.

In the cage to their immediate right, Jack saw another pair of men cuffed together.

The older of the two was a short, wiry man with the dry caramel skin of a Nepalese. He wore a distinctive black bandana and—more importantly to Jack—he gripped in his hand a bent-bladed short sword.

Jack knew that kind of sword.

It was a *kukri* or *khukuri*, the traditional weapon of the Gurkhas, the legendary Nepalese warriors who had served with distinction for the Nepalese, British, and Indian armies over the centuries. Given their high-altitude Himalayan origins, Gurkhas were renowned for their endurance. They were also known for their ferocity in battle.

Jesus, there's a goddamn Gurkha here, Jack thought in despair.

Monsieur Vacheron paced behind the line of cages.

"Maggots!" he shouted. "This is the Third Challenge! A Golden Sphere sits atop the tower. The champion who acquires that sphere will be allowed to leave the arena via a special bridge that will then be retracted. Glory and honor await him. The rest of you shits will have to get out via the Coward's Route. Be quick about it. The last two champions left in the fighting space will have their heads blown off and their support teams liquidated."

Vacheron turned to walk away.

"Wait!" Jack called, stopping him. "What about our companions?" He indicated Sky Monster, cuffed to his left wrist.

Vacheron turned to face Jack, as if galled to be addressed by a champion. He glared at Jack and for a moment it seemed like he wouldn't answer.

But then he did.

"Your companions have even less value than you do, maggot. They are only here to weigh you down. It does not matter to me, Lord Hades, or to anyone else if they survive the test or not. Adieu."

Vacheron departed.

Beside Jack, Sky Monster began to hyperventilate.

"Hey. Monster." Jack put his face right up close to Sky Monster's. "It's okay. I'll be right there with you, right by your side. There's nothing outside those doors that we can't overcome together. Okay?"

Sky Monster nodded quickly. "Okay. Thanks, Jack. Thanks."

With a loud clang the outer door of their cage sprang open . . .

. . . and Jack beheld the enormous space beyond it.

"Holy shit . . ." he breathed.

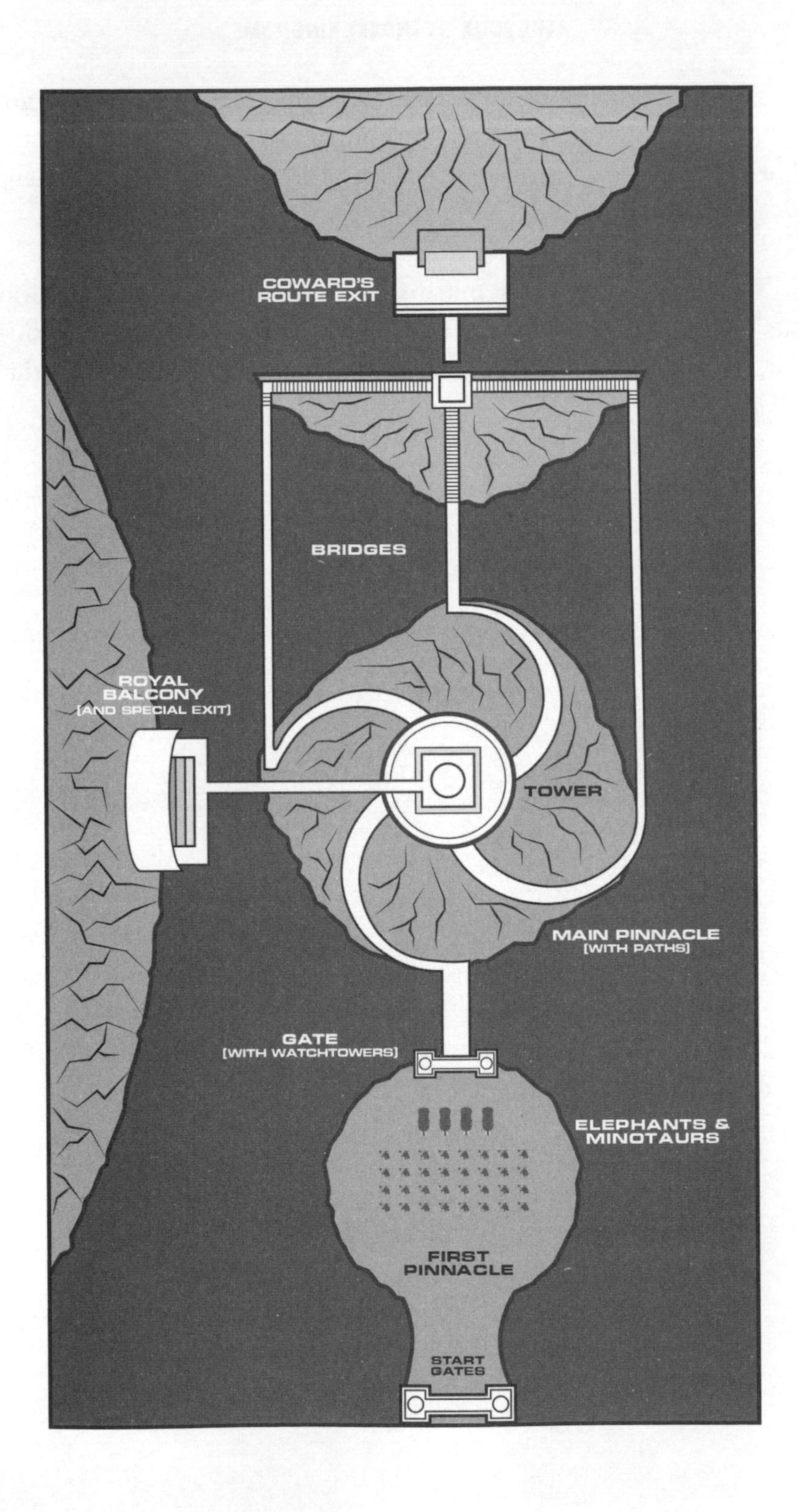
COWARD'S
ROUTE EXIT
BRIDGES
ROYAL
BALCONY
[AND SPECIAL EXIT]
TOWER
MAIN PINNACLE
[WITH PATHS]
GATE
[WITH WATCHTOWERS]
ELEPHANTS &
MINOTAURS
FIRST
PINNACLE
START
GATES

THIRD CHALLENGE

THE TOWER AND THE ABYSS

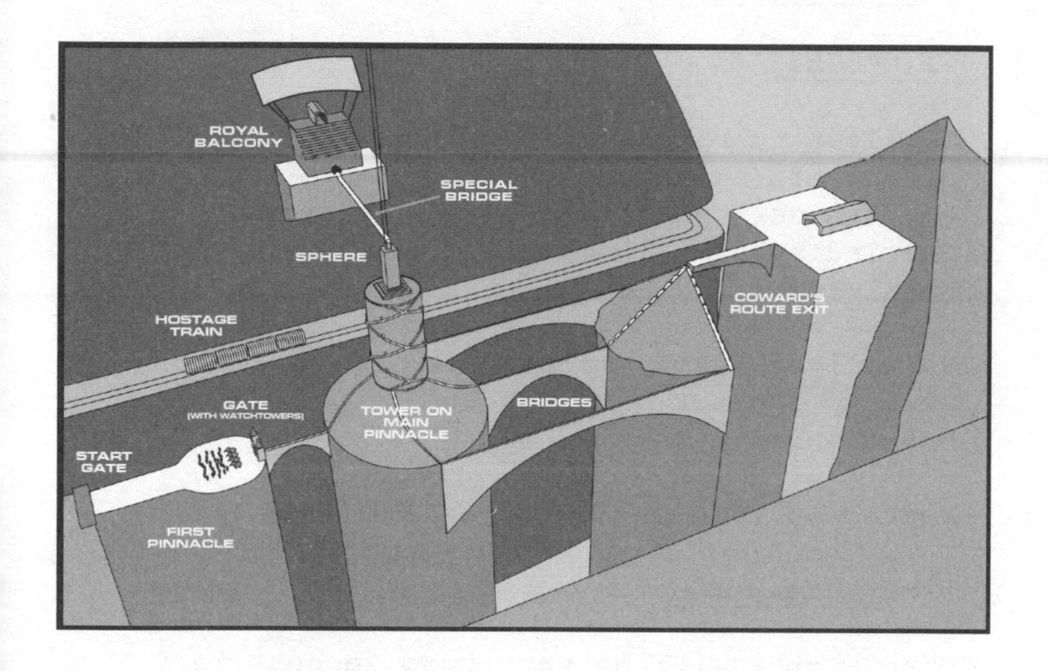

CHAMPION PROFILE

NAME: "THE GURKHA'
AGE: 31
RANK TO WIN: 6
REPRESENTING: SKY

PROFILE:

Nepalese by birth, the Gurkha is a member of one of India's most famed regiments, the 8th Gurkha Rifles. (While it is part of the Indian Army, members of the 8th are all Nepalese.)

He will be easily spotted, as he will be wearing a black bandanna and he will be brandishing a kukri.

Ranked 6th out of 16 to win the Games.

FROM HIS PATRON:

"The Gurkha will be very hard to beat."

Kenzo Depon,
King of the Sky

THE DASH ACROSS THE FIRST PINNACLE

A sight that was both spectacular and fearsome opened up before Jack and Sky Monster.

A huge abyss easily the size of three football fields stretched away from them.

Off to their left, flanking the abyss, was the side of the colossal mountain and on it—high, high up—was a viewing balcony for Hades and the other royal spectators. Beneath the royal balcony, arriving from the previous stadium on a set of rails, were the iron-barred hostage carriages.

Rising out of the abyss before them were two pinnacles of rock, connected by a narrow, railless bridge. The first pinnacle was small and flat-topped while the second one was simply gigantic. It rose far higher than the first and it also possessed something on it: a high cylindrical tower.

The tower was actually quite beautiful and it reminded Jack of ancient Babylonian architecture.

A series of pathways spiraled around the curved outer wall of the tower, crisscrossing one another at various intervals. The whole thing—the tower and the rocky pinnacle—rose at least ten stories above the spot where Jack now stood, so that its summit sat level with the royal viewing balcony.

Jack could just see a glowing Golden Sphere at the summit of the tower and near it, extending from the tower to the royal balcony, a tiny bridge suspended from cables.

That was the exit Vacheron had mentioned, the easy exit for the champion who grabbed the sphere, the one that would then be retracted. For now, Jack couldn't see the other exit—the Coward's Route—that would serve the remaining champions.

In all honesty, right then he didn't care for any exit. Of more immediate concern to him and Sky Monster was what lay between them and the lone bridge leading to the central tower/pinnacle:

A phalanx of about thirty minotaurs gripping swords and spears.

They stood in four rows on the first flat-topped pinnacle, in front of four elephants that wore armored plating and ceremonial red-and-black war paint. Each beast bore two minotaurs on its back and trumpeted loudly.

"Are those *elephants*?" Sky Monster said incredulously.

"Yep," Jack said.

The analytical part of his brain saw the small ears of the elephants. Asian elephants had smaller ears than African ones. Maybe Iolanthe had been telling the truth about their being in India.

He snapped out of it. The thought had made him pause.

The other champions hadn't paused.

They sprinted from their cages—running in tandem with their handcuffed partners—out across the flat-topped pinnacle toward the force of minotaurs and elephants.

The Gurkha who had been in the starting cage beside Jack's moved with particular speed and balance, in perfect sync with his short partner.

His partner.

It was then that Jack noticed—sadly—that nearly all the other champions had companions who were short, compact, lean, or small.

He glanced at Sky Monster beside him—tall and overweight—and wondered if, again, the other champions had had access to information that he hadn't. Speed and agility were clearly important factors in this challenge and unlike all the other companions Sky Monster was neither small nor agile.

A great roar banished those thoughts from Jack's mind.

The mini-army of minotaurs issued a war cry and, followed by the four thundering elephants, broke into a run and charged directly toward the champions.

The Third Challenge had begun.

The battle that followed was as vicious and chaotic as it was terrifying and loud.

There was movement everywhere: minotaurs running and slashing with swords, elephants rearing and landing with colossal booms, and champions dashing this way and that.

Amid all the chaos, Jack saw the Marine with the reflective glasses running low and fast through the melee, attached to a bulky female companion.

For a fleeting moment, Jack was pleased that someone else had a big partner, but then he frowned: he thought he *recognized* the big female Marine . . .

. . . but then his view was cut off by a rearing, roaring elephant and Jack ducked under the elephant's feet and, pulling Sky Monster with him, took off down the left-hand side of the pinnacle.

As he ran, Jack saw the British champion, the orange-haired SAS guy, Brigham.

Running with a short sword in one hand and his compact companion handcuffed to the other, Brigham hacked three minotaurs out of his way. He was heading for an arched gate that gave access to the bridge leading to the main pinnacle.

But then Brigham did something that was beyond anything Jack expected to see.

Momentarily free of attacking minotaurs, Brigham turned and without so much as a blink, hacked off *the hand* of his diminutive companion.

Jack blanched. "Jesus Christ . . ."

The companion screamed as his hand dropped off his wrist . . . along with the steel handcuff around it.

It was one of the cruelest things Jack had ever seen, but there was a ruthless logic to it.

Released from his connection to the smaller man, Brigham now bolted at much greater speed toward the gate, leaving his companion behind, bent over the bloody stump that was now his wrist.

Within seconds, the smaller man was set upon by two minotaurs and he wailed as they hacked him to pieces.

A few yards away from Brigham, Jack saw the Gurkha do the same thing: he slashed down with his vicious-looking kukri sword, severing the forearm of his partner.

His partner, however, didn't die as meekly as Brigham's. No, he hurled himself into the oncoming minotaurs—a sacrifice play to give the Gurkha time to sprint away.

"Good God," Jack said. "This is insane."

Sky Monster had seen both dismemberments. His eyes were as wide as saucers.

"Please don't do that to me, Jack."

"We get through this together or not at all, buddy," Jack said. "Come on."

As Jack and Sky Monster ran through the melee, all around them champions ducked and punched, ran and kicked, doing battle with the force of minotaurs.

Jack quickly noticed that, while outnumbered, the champions were more accomplished fighters than the smaller, half-human minotaurs.

The thirty minotaurs were intended to merely delay the champions on their way to the tower on the main pinnacle, to separate them.

Yet they were doing it with an enthusiasm and ferocity that was nothing short of shocking. They *hurled* themselves at the champions, leaping at them without a care for their own lives or safety.

With one exception.

Jack saw the remaining golden minotaur—one of the two who had been elevated to champion status—running unhindered with his companion through the ranks of regular minotaurs.

The minotaurs are favoring their own, Jack realized. *They may not be fully human, but they're not stupid.*

Just then an elephant—slashed across the belly by another champion in mid-charge—came crashing to the ground right beside Jack and Sky Monster.

The huge animal hit the ground with a great boom and started sliding toward them!

"Dive left!" Jack yanked Sky Monster and they dived full-length to the left as the elephant skidded past them and disappeared over the edge of the pinnacle, taking its minotaur riders with it.

Their dive had brought them close to the left-hand edge of the flat-topped pinnacle and as they got back to their feet, two minotaurs leaped at them.

"Monster! Clothesline!" Jack called and Sky Monster responded by raising his cuffed hand at the same instant Jack did and the first charging minotaur's throat hit the chain of their handcuffs and its feet flew up into the air while it dropped to the ground.

A split second later, Jack ducked and hip-tossed the second charging minotaur off the edge of the pinnacle.

"This is a madhouse!" Sky Monster called.

"Story of my life," Jack yelled. He pointed to the bridge leading to the large central pinnacle. "We can't stay here! We gotta get to that bridge!"

They ran through the melee.

Running fast and low, Jack swerved and dodged the inrushing minotaurs and rearing elephants, but the heavier Sky Monster was slower. He was huffing and puffing, breathless and red-faced.

He was slowing them down.

A three-story-high castle-like gate gave access to the bridge leading to the main pinnacle. It had two hornlike towers and a raised portcullis.

Looking past it at the much-larger main pinnacle, Jack saw that the golden minotaur and the British champion, Brigham, had already crossed the bridge and were now dashing up a curving ascending path cut into the pinnacle's lower reaches, closely followed by the Gurkha.

Jack and Sky Monster were still about twenty yards away from the gate. Only one other champion-pair was still on the first pinnacle and they were just now reaching the gate.

"We can't win this challenge!" Jack yelled above the din. "So let's just make sure we're not one of the last two champions in here!"

"Gotcha!"

It was then that the champion-pair that had just passed through the gate did something particularly nasty.

They found a lever and dropped the portcullis of the gate, sealing it.

"Bastards . . ." Jack gasped.

He and Sky Monster, already running last in this death race, were now stranded on the first pinnacle.

“This way!” Jack hauled Sky Monster toward the left-hand watchtower of the arched gate.

It was made of roughly hewn stone, which meant it was uneven, which meant handholds.

Sky Monster peered over the edge of the pinnacle and saw a mighty drop, many hundreds of feet deep, beneath them.

“Jack . . .”

“Don’t look down! Climb out onto the wall *now*!” Jack said, looking desperately behind them.

Up on the royal viewing balcony, Monsieur Vacheron commentated: “Ladies and gentlemen, if I may draw your attention this way: the fifth warrior and his companion are gamely attempting to climb *around* the bridge-gate.”

The crowd of royals all turned to look.

Standing among them, Lily had already seen what was happening and she watched anxiously.

Sky Monster reached for a handhold on the side wall of the watchtower and stepped out over the fathomless drop. Connected by the handcuff, Jack followed him.

They edged out along the outer wall of the watchtower, high above the deadly drop.

"Get further, further," Jack urged, "then go up—"

Sky Monster had gone about eight feet along the wall when, suddenly, a minotaur, heedless of its own safety, took a bounding leap clear off the edge of the pinnacle and flew right at Jack and clamped its hairy arms around both of his legs.

The result was instantaneous.

The extra weight caused Jack to lose his grip on the wall and he fell.

The assembled spectators up on the bleachers gasped as one.

Lily threw a hand to her mouth.

Jack dropped off the wall.

His left wrist, connected to Sky Monster's right, yanked Sky Monster's right hand from its handhold, and for a nanosecond Jack thought this was it: he and Sky Monster would fall to their deaths—

But then his fall stopped abruptly.

Sky Monster had somehow managed to hold on.

His teeth clenched, his big-bearded face going red with effort, Sky Monster was grimly gripping the wall with only his left hand, holding himself, Jack . . . *and* the minotaur up!

Jack felt a surge of inspired energy rush through him.

"You're the man, Monster!" he yelled and he kicked at the minotaur—once, twice, three times—until it fell off him and dropped away into the abyss at the very moment that Sky Monster's grip was about to fail—when Jack quickly regripped the wall and climbed up beside his partner, allowing Sky Monster to find a new handhold and catch his breath.

The two friends hovered there, perched a short way out from the pinnacle, where the crowd of angry minotaurs had gathered.

"Thanks, buddy," Jack said. "I'm sure glad I didn't bring a lightweight companion with me. He couldn't have done *that*. Come on, we gotta climb round this thing and get through this."

And so Jack and Sky Monster edged their way around the watchtower.

As they did so, far above and ahead of them, Major Gregory Brigham of the SAS, running free of any companion, powered up the series of narrow crisscrossing paths that circled the tower on the main pinnacle.

Close behind Brigham were the golden minotaur and the Gurkha. The Gurkha pounded up one of the paths, his mountain-born lungs aiding his climb.

On the royal balcony, Vacheron pointed them out.

"My lords and ladies, the leaders are approaching the summit of the tower. They should be wary, however, for the tower has its own defenses."

As he ascended the mighty tower, Greg Brigham heaved and panted. It was a brutal uphill run.

He heard grunting behind him, looked back and saw both the gold minotaur and the Gurkha clambering up the path a short distance below him.

Gaining.

The path Major Brigham was dashing up was not for the faint-hearted. It clung to the outer wall of the huge cylindrical tower and was wide enough only for one person.

On the inner side of the path, some shallow alcoves were cut into the wall at regular intervals, while a one-foot-high stone gutter rimmed the vertiginous outer edge of the path—

Suddenly Brigham heard great booms from somewhere above him.

He dove into the nearest alcove—a bare second before a huge spiked iron ball the size of a man came rolling around the corner, taking up the entire width of his path.

The ball was a vicious-looking thing: with many protruding red-hot iron spikes, blurring with motion. And it was built so that its rolling spikes fitted perfectly within the outer gutter of the path, stopping it from going over the edge. It rolled mercilessly down the pathway.

Brigham pressed himself into the shallow alcove, his back against the wall, and sucked in his stomach as the iron ball thundered past, its red-hot spikes so close they sizzled as they went by his nose.

The Gurkha leaped off the path, gripping its gutter with his fingertips, hanging from it to get out of the way.

The gold-painted minotaur and its companion, however, had no alcove into which they could dive and they saw the boulder too late to do what the Gurkha had done.

The iron boulder *plowed* into them.

Two of its cruel spikes stabbed the lead minotaur before the artificial boulder rolled over him and speared his companion as well and both the boulder and the screaming minotaurs toppled off the structure.

Jack looked up at the sudden screams.

Having climbed around the outer wall of the watchtower, he and Sky Monster were now hurrying across the bridge that gave access to the main pinnacle.

Behind them, the horde of minotaurs was massing around the gate. They were either trying to raise the portcullis or climb around the watchtower as Jack and Sky Monster had done.

Either way, the angry horde would be coming across the bridge soon.

At the sound of the screams, Jack snapped up and saw the two cuffed minotaurs and the iron boulder falling off the tower.

They fell a full two hundred feet before they hit the rocky slope of the pinnacle at the base of the tower, after which they tumbled down the slope and off the pinnacle, dropping into the abyss beneath it, falling who-knew-how-far.

Looking higher, Jack saw a couple of champions ascending the crisscrossing paths on the tower.

He could see the SAS guy, Brigham, leading the way, up near the summit, closely followed by the Gurkha, both of them dodging the iron boulders that tumbled down the tower's paths.

A few more champions were on the lower reaches of the tower, well behind. Others still, Jack saw, hadn't even bothered ascending the tower. Figuring that Brigham and the Gurkha were too far ahead, they were cutting their losses and already making for the Coward's Route exit.

A curving path led from Jack's bridge up the rocky slope to the tower. This curving path then became one of the paths on the tower itself, which meant that the iron boulders coming down the structure *continued* all the way down to where Jack was.

As they arrived at the start of this rising path, Jack and Sky Monster beheld an iron boulder that had stopped there at the end of its long downward roll.

Jack gazed at the deadly ball.

It was a savage thing: a six-foot-tall iron ball fitted with many red-hot spikes and several pairs of curving blades.

Now that it had stopped, Jack could also see that it was strikingly beautiful; the iron had been wrought into a vivid image: the heads of several ferocious snarling boars.

Indeed, the deadly spikes had been crafted to represent the tusks of each boar's head.

"Wow . . ." Jack breathed.

Sky Monster also stared at it in awe. "This is why I usually stay on the plane."

A roar made them both spin.

The minotaurs on the first pinnacle had got the portcullis open and were now running en masse through it, racing across the bridge after them.

"Move," Jack said. "We gotta get off this rock. We can't be one of the last two pairs left here."

They took off up the path.

While Jack and Sky Monster were beginning their ascent of the pinnacle, high above them, Major Gregory Brigham was reaching the summit of the tower atop it.

After dodging a few more iron boulders—and passing one of the four holes from which they had emerged—Brigham reached the summit of the tower only a few yards ahead of the Gurkha.

To the rapt approval of the watching royal spectators, Brigham clambered up some broad stone steps with wide vents in them, reaching the absolute peak of the enormous structure . . .

. . . where he found the Golden Sphere mounted on an altar.

Extending out from that altar-platform was a bridge suspended from cables which led to the royal balcony.

Brigham didn't waste a second. He grabbed the sphere and, gripping it like a football, raced across the bridge.

After a short vertigo-inspiring run, he stepped off the bridge with the sphere, panting and sweating, to the cheers of the royal spectators.

In stepping off the bridge, however, Brigham's boot landed on a trigger stone, and immediately the high bridge began to retract behind him, its extendable segments telescoping into each other, leaving the Gurkha stranded out on the tower.

Vacheron turned to the assembled royals. "My lords and ladies, we have a winner! But as I said, only he gets to escape the arena via this special bridge. All our other champions must be reminded how unworthy they are. They must escape via the Coward's Route."

At that moment, set off by the same trigger stone, a second terrible mechanism came to life on the tower.

Superheated liquid stone spewed out from the wide vents embedded in the steps supporting the altar on the summit. Thick, gray, and goopy, it glowed with red-hot embers and flowed like slow-moving lava.

The Gurkha turned and fled back down the nearest spiraling path.

The gray mixture oozed slowly out from the summit and, like lava pouring over the rim of a volcano, it began to creep down *all four* of the guttered paths that led down from the summit, toward all the champions still on the tower and the pinnacle.

THE COWARD'S ROUTE

Jack and Sky Monster were halfway up their curving path—with the small army of minotaurs charging up it behind them—when they saw the liquid stone come pouring over the rim of the tower's summit and start oozing down the curving paths on its flanks.

Jack saw all the champions on the tower reverse direction and start running desperately *downward*.

Having come halfway round the lower reaches of the main pinnacle, he now beheld the other exit from the vast cavern: three stupendous bridges spanning the abyss, all arriving at a mount where their three individual staircases converged at a single exit.

The Coward's Route.

The situation became clear to Jack.

What had until then been an upward race for the summit now became a downward sprint for the three bridges and the exit.

"Pick it up, Sky Monster!" he called. "We gotta get to that exit!"

And so they ran, ran as hard as they could, pounding up the steep curving pathway, pursued by the horde of angry minotaurs.

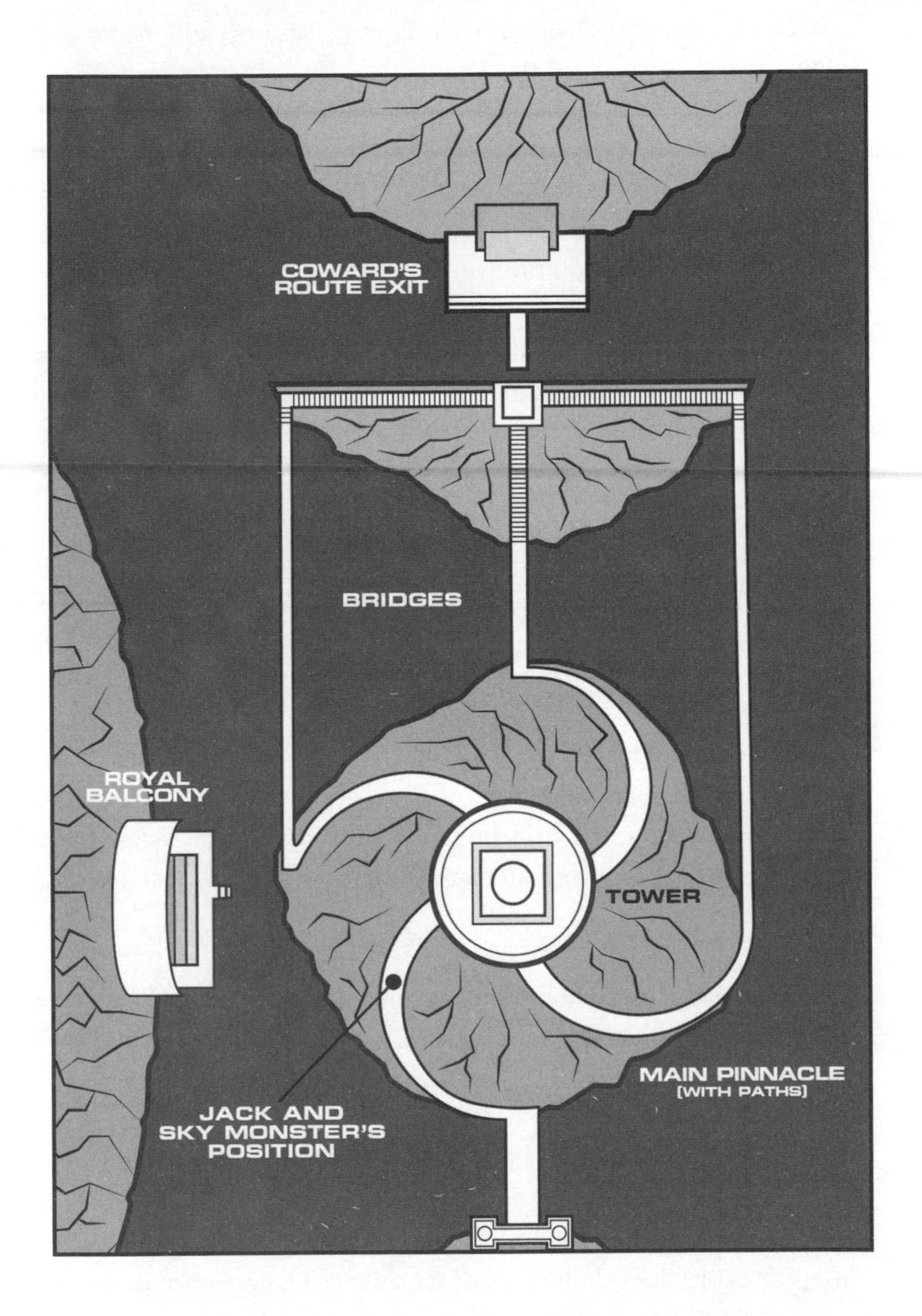
COWARD'S
ROUTE EXIT
BRIDGES
ROYAL
BALCONY
TOWER
MAIN PINNACLE
(WITH PATHS)
JACK AND
SKY MONSTER'S
POSITION

Sky Monster wasn't doing well. Panting and breathless, he was dragging Jack down.

They reached the spot where the rocky slope of the pinnacle met the base of the tower and as Jack looked up at an oncoming boulder, Sky Monster dropped to his knees.

"Keep running," Jack said, yanking him forward.

But Sky Monster didn't move.

"Sky Monster, buddy, we gotta—"

"Jack," Sky Monster said. "We both know it. I can't do this. I'm too fat, too slow. I'm weighing you down."

Jack glanced back at the ascending horde of minotaurs, then up at a descending iron boulder. Things were happening too fast. They didn't have time for this.

"Monster, please, we don't have time for—"

"No, but we do have time for *this*," Sky Monster said, suddenly shoving Jack roughly away from him, off the path, before he himself lay down and stretched his arm—his handcuffed arm—across the path.

Jack now dangled off the path, hanging from the handcuff, lying on the steeply sloping pinnacle.

A moment later, the iron boulder came rolling into view from the path above them and it thundered over Sky Monster's outstretched arm and—

Snap!

One of its blazing-hot spikes crunched down on the chain of their cuffs and snapped it in two. Another superheated spike lanced into Sky Monster's right forearm as it rolled past him and he roared in pain.

The deadly iron boulder tumbled away, rolling directly into the mass of minotaurs charging up the lower path. It took out the first five minotaurs before it stopped, wedged on top of one poor minotaur, pinning its foot under one of its spikes. The creature issued an agonized wail.

As for Jack, he stood up in surprise, suddenly untethered from Sky Monster.

"Go!" Sky Monster yelled at him. "You have to live, Jack! I don't! You were always special. I'm not. I'm just a pilot. Make my life worth something by getting out of this mess and kicking these assholes' assholes! Go!"

Jack didn't have time to argue so he just nodded to his friend and started running down the nearest path, heading for one of the three escape bridges.

Jack ran as fast as he could.

He flew down one of the sloping paths on the pinnacle and raced out onto one of the dizzyingly high bridges leading to the exit.

As he ran, he saw the other champions fleeing ahead of him.

They scampered up the three high stairways, reaching the point where the three stairways converged and then they leaped over a narrow chasm to safety.

Jack noted that this final leap was a downward one—a drop of about eight feet. Once you made the leap across, you couldn't jump back and reenter the arena. It was a mechanism, he guessed, to stop a champion going *back* into the arena, perhaps to save his partner.

He scanned the way before him. All the other champions were well ahead of him.

All but one.

The Gurkha.

He had gambled on reaching the summit of the tower first and winning the challenge. But that gamble had been a double-edged sword: after Brigham had gotten there first, the Gurkha had been left with the greatest distance to run to reach the Coward's Route exit.

Which meant the Gurkha was the only other champion left in the arena with Jack. Right now he was running along the middle bridge only a short distance ahead of Jack.

One champion is already dead, so I can't be the last one left here! Jack's mind screamed.

Jack sucked it up and increased his speed.

★ ★ ★

Up on the royal balcony, Lord Hades and his guests watched Jack's desperate sprint with keen interest.

"Why," Vacheron commentated, "look at the fifth warrior run. He knows the score. One champion has been killed, so now the last champion left in the arena will be the *second*-last one and that means death. He is literally running for his life."

The Gurkha was halfway up the middle set of stairs when Jack hit the base of his stairway.

Jack pounded up the stairs.

His rival—still gripping his short sword—was nearing the summit, running hard.

The Gurkha reached the summit first and leaped—

—just as Jack dived at him and grabbed his ankles with both arms, rugby-style, bringing him down with an ungainly thump.

Jack and the Gurkha untangled themselves and faced off on the small platform atop the triple staircase.

The Gurkha raised his short sword menacingly.

This was no longer a race to the exit.

It was now a fight to the death.

The Gurkha rushed at Jack, the blade of his sword flashing.

"Goddamn," Jack said.

Too exhausted to fight and too tired to care about doing it like a gentleman, he fought dirty.

One kick to the kneecap made a foul cracking noise and abruptly the Gurkha's left leg was folded back the wrong way and he screamed.

Jack's next kick to the unbalanced man's chest sent him toppling off the platform into the abyss. He screamed all the way down.

And suddenly Jack was alone on the platform.

The vast space around him was oddly silent.

The iron boulders had stopped tumbling down the tower's spiraling paths.

The horde of minotaurs—blocked by the iron boulder that had cracked Jack's handcuffs and facing the prospect of outrunning the

liquefied stone still oozing down the tower—had returned to the first pinnacle.

Hades, Vacheron, and the royal spectators all watched Jack in expectant silence, ready it seemed to break out into applause when he made the final leap.

The other surviving champions stood barely ten feet from him, across the narrow chasm, also watching. He had only to make the short jump to join them and exit the arena.

But then Jack did something that no one expected.

He didn't jump.

All the royal spectators watched, aghast, as to their complete and utter surprise, Jack West Jr. turned and jogged—jogged!—*back down* the high staircase, heading back toward the main pinnacle.

"What on Earth is he doing?" someone said.

Iolanthe watched Jack with narrowing eyes. "He's doing what he does."

Jack hastened back across the bridge, eyeing the oozing rivers of liquid stone still creeping down the crisscrossing paths of the tower.

They had almost reached the base of the tower.

He hurried up one of the curving sloping paths that led to the tower and arrived at the base of the tower just as the oncoming river of sludge crept into view ten yards away from him.

He found Sky Monster where he'd left him. The big Kiwi was just sitting there holding his bloody right forearm and staring at the ground.

He looked up in shock when Jack said, "Monster. Come on, it's time to go."

"Jack? You . . . came back? Don't you have to . . . get out?"

Jack smiled. "So long as we can outrun that ooze, we've got as much time as we need, my old friend. Leave no man behind, no matter how out of shape. Come on."

Jack led Sky Monster away toward the exit.

They had barely gone a few steps when Jack heard it.

A whimper.

A pained animal whimper.

Squinting, Jack peered down the sloping path that led back to the first pinnacle.

There, pinned underneath the iron boulder that had rumbled through here earlier, lying half-off the path—evidently as part of an attempt to dive clear of the boulder—was a minotaur.

One of its boots had been caught underneath the stationary boulder and now the half-man was hopelessly pinned underneath the heavy iron thing.

But it wasn't whimpering at Jack.

Rather, it was appealing for help from two other minotaurs standing further down the pathway. They shifted anxiously where they stood, unsure, uncertain. To attempt to rescue their comrade was to risk being caught by the oncoming sludge.

Then they made their decision . . . and bolted the other way.

The pinned minotaur yanked off his bull mask and wailed plaintively at their backs as they hurried away.

As Jack watched, the minotaur tugged desperately at his pinned foot, but it was no use. The boulder was too heavy for the half-man to move on his own.

Without his battle helmet on, the half-man looked far less fearsome: he had a mop of black hair, a low forehead, and a protruding jaw.

He looked more human.

And something inside Jack clicked.

This man, this thing, this half-man—whatever he was—was going to die horribly as he was slowly swallowed by the oncoming liquefied stone.

And so leaving Sky Monster at the base of the tower, Jack stepped down the path.

★ ★ ★

On the royal balcony, a handsome young prince came up beside Hades and whispered, "Is this legal, Father? Can he do this?"

Hades just kept watching Jack.

Then he said, "The champion is breaking no rules, as far as I can see."

The pinned minotaur still hadn't seen Jack.

Then Jack's bare feet crunched on the gravel of the path and the minotaur spun in surprise, eyes wide with fear.

Jack held up his hands.

"I don't want to hurt you. I want to help."

Without waiting for an answer—he didn't have much time; the river of liquid stone was almost at the base of the tower now—Jack just leaned forward and, to the pinned half-man's absolute amazement, grabbed one of the boulder's hot spikes with his titanium left hand and heaved on the boulder.

Up on the royal viewing balcony, the assembled guests now watched in open shock and disbelief.

"How ghastly," one of the women said.

"Preposterous," one of the men said.

Lily gazed down proudly at her father.

Near her, Hades just kept watching Jack with a cool gaze.

The heavy iron boulder rolled a short way down the sloping path, freeing the minotaur's left foot.

The half-man leaped to a standing position, hopping comically on his good leg, as if to defend himself.

Jack still held out his hands.

"Like I said, I want to help you."

He then quickly slipped himself under the half-man's left shoulder, took his weight and helped him up the path.

To the thunderstruck silence of the royal balcony, Jack and the minotaur rejoined Sky Monster at the top of the path and the three of them headed, together, down the opposite side of the pinnacle toward the bridges and the exit.

At the exit—the same spot where Jack had killed the Gurkha—Jack helped Sky Monster make the final leap across the chasm by tossing him across it.

Then, hefting the minotaur onto his shoulders in a fireman's carry—an image enhanced by the fireman's helmet he was wearing—Jack looked over at the royal balcony, at Hades and Vacheron.

"I can keep anything I can carry out of this arena, right?" he called.

Vacheron glanced questioningly toward Hades.

Hades nodded.

"You may," Vacheron said.

"Okay then," Jack said.

And with the injured minotaur draped across his shoulders, he leaped across the chasm to safety.

The royal balcony was abuzz.

Many famous things had happened at the Great Games over the millennia but never this: a champion saving a minotaur!

On the balcony at the end of the Coward's Route exit, the other champions stared at Jack in bewilderment.

Their baffled expressions said it all: Who *helped* a minotaur?

Hades held up his hand and the entire cavernous space fell silent. When he spoke, Jack could hear him even from this far away.

"Lords, ladies, champions! What a spectacle we are witnessing! Victorious champion. Step forward."

The SAS man, Major Brigham, stood before Hades. Reverently, he handed the Golden Sphere he had acquired during the challenge to the Dark Lord.

Hades said, "Champion. I am most impressed. You have won both of the last two challenges. Once again, for winning this challenge, your reward is yours to name. Anything that it is in my power to give. So speak."

Brigham nodded.

The royal audience waited in tense anticipation.

So did the champions on the other balcony.

After he had won the Second Challenge, Brigham had ordered the execution of his nearest rival. Would he do that again?

A few of the champions watched Brigham nervously, aware that the two lion-masked hunters, Chaos and Fear, had silently appeared behind them. Similarly, up on the royal balcony, Vacheron had appeared beside Hades with his deadly remote control unit.

Finally, Major Gregory Brigham spoke.

He bowed to Hades. “My Lord, I would like the Tibetan prince, Tenzin Depon, to be killed, please.”

The royal spectators murmured in approval.

The Tibetan prince was ranked third to win the Games. After his first win, Brigham had ordered the execution of the second-ranked champion. Now he was eliminating the next best challenger. This was a tried and tested strategy in the Games: win the early challenges and eliminate your key rivals.

Jack saw a muscly Tibetan warrior-monk standing near him. The young man closed his eyes, resigning himself to his fate a moment before his head blew apart and his body collapsed.

His companions in their hostage carriage were killed next: liquid stone gushed into their iron cage, drowning them.

Watching it all happen, Jack felt ill.

When it was over, Vacheron called formally: “My lords and ladies! That is all for today! All champions will retire to their hostage carriages! The Fourth Challenge shall commence tomorrow at dawn!” He bowed toward the royal guests. “I bid good evening to you all.”

A SECRET HISTORY II

THE TRUE HISTORY OF THE WORLD

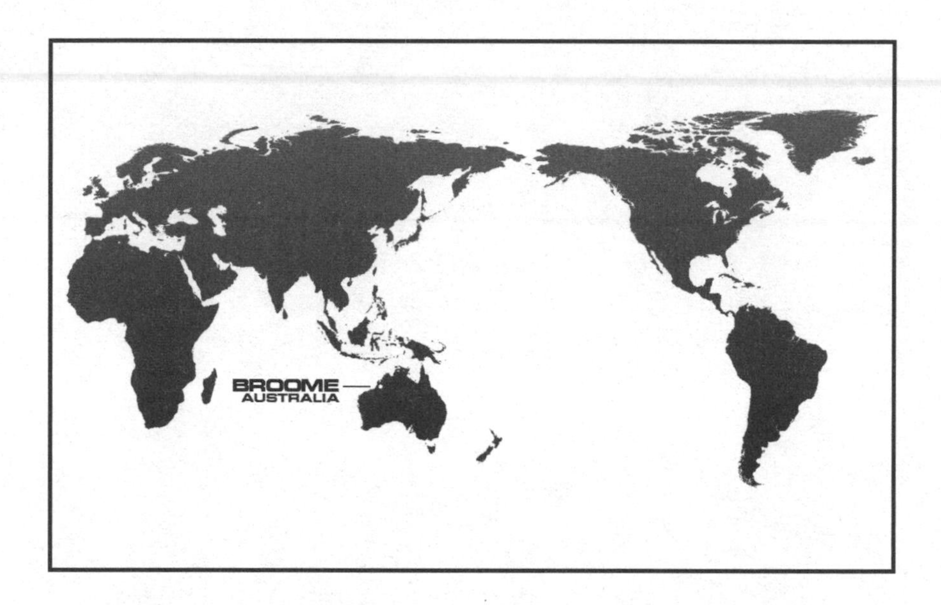

Newton was not the first of the age of reason. He was the last of the magicians, the last of the Babylonians and Sumerians, the last great mind that looked out on the visible and intellectual world with the same eyes as those who began to build our intellectual inheritance rather less than 10,000 years ago.

JOHN MAYNARD KEYNES

BROOME, AUSTRALIA

It was going on three in the afternoon when Pooh Bear and Stretch drove their rental car out of Broome regional airport in the remote northwestern corner of Australia.

It was blisteringly hot.

Perched on the coast at the edge of a mighty desert, in the winter months Broome was a popular holiday destination. But in summer it was just hot. For four months of the year, daily temperatures exceeded 44 degrees Celsius, or 110 Fahrenheit.

Pooh Bear and Stretch passed a cheerful sign that read:

WELCOME TO BROOME
POPULATION 14,052

"If you want to live at the ends of the Earth," Pooh Bear said, "this is it."

Stretch smiled wryly. "Mae certainly likes her solitude. And the world likes her to have it."

"What's her beef with you?" Pooh Bear asked.

"I'm too skinny. You?"

"My lack of a girlfriend," Pooh Bear said. "This is the woman who married Wolf and who raised Jack. She was always going to be formidable. What does she do up here?"

"She's a high school teacher. Teaches history."

"Jack's mother is a high school history teacher?"

Stretch turned to face Pooh Bear. "My friend, Dr. Mabel Merriweather is perhaps the most overqualified high school history teacher in the world."

Their car swung through the gates of Broome High School.

They'd timed their arrival well. School had just finished for the day and the students of Broome High were streaming out of the gates, heading home for the weekend.

Pooh Bear and Stretch waited in the reception area, having asked to see Ms. Merriweather.

After about five minutes, a short woman in her late sixties with a pixie face, bob haircut, and big glasses walked briskly into the reception area chased by a towering eighteen-year-old lad wearing a Broome High football jersey.

The boy pleaded, "But Ms. Merriweather, if I don't pass, I don't get to play in tomorrow's game!"

"Arthur—"

"Everybody calls me Bubba, ma'am."

She stopped walking.

Pooh Bear felt a chill descend on the room. The look she gave the boy could have frozen water.

"*Arthur*," she said. "Let me be very clear about this. I do not care for games. When you leave this school, it is not the number of football games you played that will garner you a job. My sole concern is your education. If you had studied for the test, you would have passed it. And if you had passed it, you would have been able to play your match. This is a good lesson for you: life comes first, games come second. You get to play when you earn it."

The giant boy bowed his head. Crestfallen, he turned and walked away.

Pooh Bear and Stretch—battle-hardened soldiers who had killed men in hand-to-hand combat—both just sat there, stunned.

"Now, then . . ." The little woman turned and her laser-like gaze landed on them.

"Benjamin Cohen," she said to Stretch. "Good Lord, lad, when are going to *eat* something? You're as skinny as a rake. And Zahir . . ."

Pooh Bear stood. Not many people used his real name these days.

"Found yourself a girl yet?"

"No, ma'am. Not yet."

"Any dates?"

"A couple, ma'am."

"Please, enough of this 'ma'am' business. Call me Mae." She gave them both a winning smile. "But if you ever call me Mae West, I'll cut your balls off with a butter knife."

"Yes, ma'am. I mean, yes, Mae," Pooh Bear stammered.

"Now," Mae said. "What's going on? Only one thing could bring the two of you all the way out here at no notice. What's happened to my son?"

They adjourned to Mae's office, a modest room overlooking a desert garden.

As he entered, Pooh Bear saw that all the bookshelves were filled with history books.

They ranged from the classic to the alternative: from Gibbon's *The History of the Decline and Fall of the Roman Empire* to *Chariots of the Gods* by Erich von Däniken and *The Secret Teachings of All Ages* by Manly P. Hall. All were arranged, Pooh Bear saw, in strict alphabetical order by author, their spines lined up with military precision.

"Jack's disappeared," Stretch said as he and Pooh Bear sat down in a pair of armchairs across from Mae's desk. "He was kidnapped."

"How do you know for sure?" Mae Merriweather may have had a cute pixie-like face, but her eyes—behind her big glasses—bored into Pooh Bear's. She looked to Pooh Bear like a killer librarian.

He pulled out his iPhone, played a video on it.

The video showed Pine Gap as seen from the air: a gliding, soaring view of the desert installation.

"This is footage from the GoPro camera that Horus was wearing around her neck when Jack disappeared early this morning."

On the screen, a gang of armed men—and one woman—walked into the base. They emerged soon after carrying the unconscious figures of Jack, Sky Monster, Lily, Alby, and the two dogs.

As they conveyed Jack across the sandy ground, the woman pointed up at the camera and one of the soldiers raised his pistol and fired and the camera view spiraled out of control before slamming into the ground and cutting to hash.

Pooh Bear grimaced. "They shot Horus and everyone at the base had been killed."

"Rewind it, please," Mae said firmly. "I want to see the woman's face."

Pooh Bear did so, freezing the image on the walking woman. As soon as he'd seen this footage, he'd recognized her. Like Jack, he knew the woman well.

"Her name is Iolanthe Compton-Jones," he said. "She's from a group we know as the Deus—"

"The Deus Rex," Mae said. "The god-kings."

Pooh was surprised that she would know this. "How do you know—?"

Mae said, "History teacher."

"Before he was taken, Jack managed to leave this for you."

He handed her the silver teaspoon from Pine Gap, with the message written on it in black marker:

"We can't decipher the symbol. Hopefully you can."

Mae turned the teaspoon over in her little hands, peering at it closely.

"A tetragammadion," she said absently.

Pooh Bear and Stretch said nothing, not wanting to interrupt her thoughts.

She looked up. "The base Jack was visiting, does it contain some kind of observatory? An astronomical observatory with a telescope?"

"Yes," Pooh Bear said quickly, hopefully. "The data site of a very powerful new telescope."

"Hmmm . . ." Mae frowned darkly and Pooh Bear suddenly felt like he'd done something wrong.

She stood abruptly and went to one of her bookshelves. She pulled from it a thick and very old leather-bound volume with no title on its spine.

She brought the book back to her desk and flipped through its pages.

When she found the page she was looking for, she read from the book aloud:

"*I cannot see it. The optics of my time are not good enough. But the mathematics are inescapable. It is coming. It will be up to the wise and noble men of future generations with optics of a more advanced nature than mine to find it in the night sky and initiate the return call. Or else all is lost.*"

Mae turned the book around for Pooh Bear and Stretch to see.

In the middle of the page, above the paragraph she had just read, was the symbol:

"Look familiar?" Mae asked them.

"Sure does," Pooh Bear said.

The text below the symbol, he saw, was handwritten in a very old style. The pages of the book were dry and brittle, brown with age.

"What is this book? And who wrote it?"

"This book," Mae said, "is nearly three hundred years old and it is one of only five existing copies. It is called *The Chronology of Ancient Kingdoms* and it was written by Sir Isaac Newton."

"This was why I asked if Jack was at an observatory when he was kidnapped," Mae said.

"There are many tetragammadions in the world—in Buddhism and Hinduism and also sadly in the Nazi swastika—but few refer to it in an astronomical sense. This picture, drawn by Newton himself, represents a distant galaxy known as the Hydra Galaxy."

"A galaxy he couldn't see?" Stretch said.

"Isaac Newton was a remarkable and brilliant man," Mae said, "perhaps *the* most brilliant man in all of human history. His work on the movement of planets was 250 years ahead of its time and the *Principia Mathematica* remains the most influential book ever written. Ever.

"Newton famously delved into some more *exotic* research that critics have dismissed as 'alchemy' or 'occult science.' His notes on these subjects—and Newton always kept very detailed notes—were notoriously obtuse, difficult to decipher. His work on the Hydra Galaxy is similar.

"Among other things, Newton was Lucasian Professor of Mathematics at Cambridge University, Master of the Royal Mint, and most importantly for our purposes, President of the Royal Society. This last post made him the head of a most powerful group, the Royal Society's inner elite: the Invisible College."

"The Invisible College?" Pooh Bear said.

"*Wisest of the wise, solemn advisers to the kings of old,*" Mae said. "That's their actual official motto."

"The members of the Invisible College were advisers to the British Crown?" Stretch asked.

Mae gave Stretch a look.

"No. I said they were *advisers to the kings of old*. To the kings of the four legendary kingdoms."

She saw the looks of incomprehension on Stretch and Pooh Bear's faces.

"Four legendary kingdoms?" Pooh Bear repeated.

Mae paused for a moment. She seemed unsure if she should go on.

"It was a topic I researched a long time ago, back when I had the energy and zeal of youth," she said. "My colleagues thought I was crazy. They said I was chasing legends, conspiracy theories, not real history. Only Jack's father encouraged me. I haven't thought about the four kingdoms in a very long time."

"Tell us about them," Stretch said.

"Gentlemen"—Mae's eyes were suddenly hard, focused—"if we are to proceed in this matter together, you are going to have to dispel some of your preconceived notions of kings and queens and nation-states, even of history itself. Can you do this?"

"Given what I've seen traveling around this world with your son, ma'am, I'm the most open-minded guy on the planet," Pooh Bear said. "I'm in."

"Mae," Stretch said. "Forgive me, but Jack West Sr.—Wolf—would never have married a plain old high school history teacher. What's your *real* area of expertise?"

Mae smiled. "While I genuinely love opening young minds, I like to think I am something more than your average high school teacher. All my life I have inquired into a single question. My search for the answer to that question has made me something of an expert in subjects as varied as mythical kingdoms, advanced astronomy, and famed individuals like Nikola Tesla and Isaac Newton."

"So what's the question?" Stretch asked.

"The question," Mae said, "is the greatest question of all: Who or what is God?"

"Who is God?" Stretch said doubtfully. "Are you talking about the Muslim god, Allah? Egyptian gods? Greek gods? Or the Christian God who supposedly sent his only son to Earth to be crucified and then rise from the dead? You do realize that Jack once found the tomb of Jesus Christ in a Roman salt mine *with the body still in it*."

Mae nodded. "I'm talking about all of them. And, yes, I am also very aware that Jesus the Nazarene was very much a man even if a sizable portion of mankind has made him into a god. Why do you think this has happened?"

Stretch shrugged. "He preached a popular philosophy. Peace, equality, be nice to others. He fed his followers with loaves and fishes. Healed the sick. And from what we learned back in 2008, he was also a member of a very ancient royal line—"

"That's right," Mae said quickly. "He healed the sick and he was a member of an ancient royal line. Imagine you're living in the Roman province of Judea and a guy comes out of nowhere with advanced medical knowledge and starts healing the sick? It'd cause a sensation. Christ's royal lineage made him an even greater sensation and his fame spread.

"It is my contention that a handful of royal lines have been privy to advanced *super*ancient learning handed down to them by a mysterious civilization from the distant past. This wisdom has given them a knowledge advantage over the general population and allowed them to appear, so to speak, god-like.

"Did you know that every single great ancient civilization mentions being visited by a white-skinned bearded man—it's always a man, he is always white, and he always has a beard—who bestows on them advanced wisdom and who often heals the sick?

"The Egyptians, the Maya, the Cambodians, all of them were visited by such an individual. The Egyptians called him Viratia. The Mayans called him Viracocha. The Cambodians: Viacaya. Sound consistent?

"I mean, if you're a simple society and someone comes to you and shows you how to build giant pyramids, predict solar eclipses, plant sustainable agriculture, and miraculously heals your ill, you'd think he was a god, wouldn't you?"

"Sure," Pooh Bear said.

"My postulation," Mae said, "is that our gods of old—from Zeus to Poseidon, to Anubis and Isis—were all royal beneficiaries of the superancient civilization that built the Machine. They were all members of a few high families who exist today as the four legendary kingdoms. The question of who or what is God is inextricably linked to the four kingdoms that rule our world from the shadows."

Again she saw the confused looks on Pooh and Stretch's faces.

"Okay, maybe I should backtrack a little," Mae said. "Think about everything you learned in history class at high school. All of that is wrong. History as you know it is not correct. What you need to know is the secret history of the world."

Mae took a breath. "The four legendary kingdoms have been amazingly successful at concealing their existence. Only a select few people know of their presence and power. If you look at a map of the world, you will see the borders of countries and nation-states; you will *not* see the invisible borders of the four ancient realms.

"But they are there. They most assuredly *do* exist. And these kingdoms have been affecting the course of human history since it began.

"They are the real rulers of the world. The kings of kings. The overlords of the world's monarchies."

"Like the Deus Rex?" Stretch asked.

"I could never prove it, but I always thought the Deus Rex were

one of the four kingdoms, yes. The one called the Kingdom of Land," Mae said.

"The four secret kingdoms are known as the Kingdoms of *Land*, *Sea*, *Sky*, and *Underworld*. Here, these are my old notes." Mae grabbed an old notebook from a shelf and leafed to a dog-eared page. "This will explain it better."

On the page were two maps of the world. The first was a regular map showing the usual national boundaries:

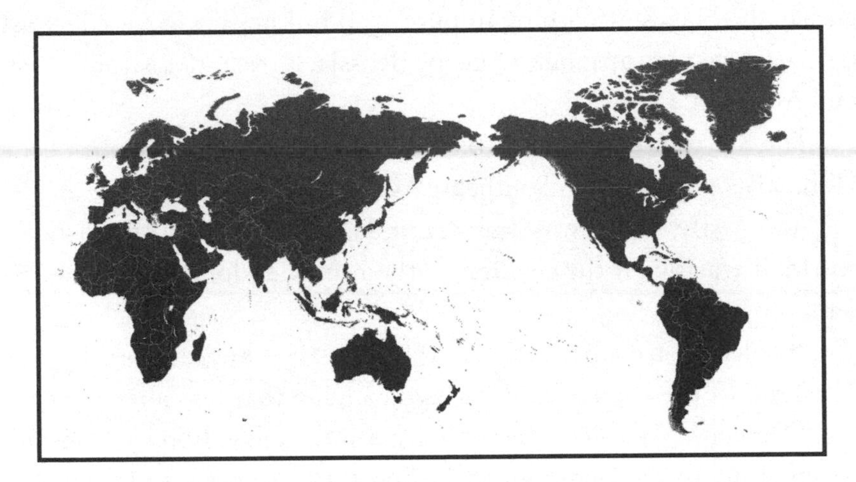

"This is your standard map of the world," Mae said. "You've seen it a million times. This is what people *think* is reality. Now look at this map."

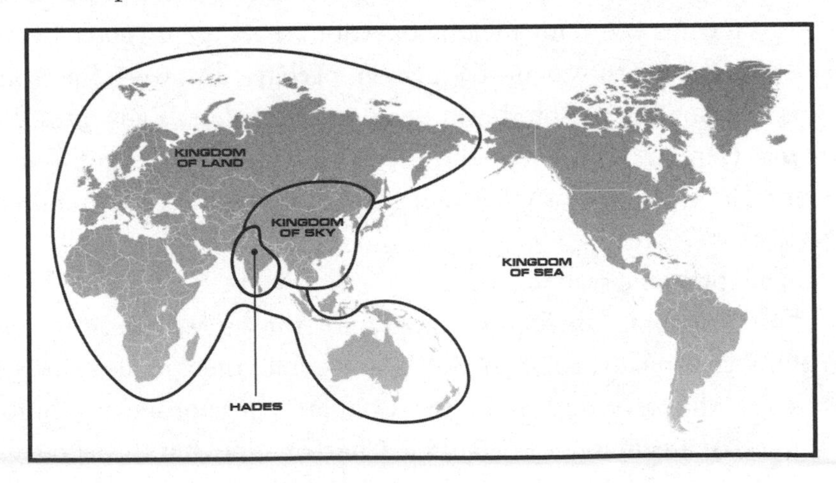

"*This* is reality," Mae said. "This is how the world is really governed."

Pooh Bear scanned the map closely. On it, the world was divided by hand-drawn lines into four regions.

The Kingdom of Sea was easily the largest of the four and it incorporated the Americas, Greenland, Japan, and all the world's oceans.

The Kingdom of Land was the next largest and, even at a glance, clearly the biggest according to pure land holdings: it covered a vast landmass that encapsulated Europe, Russia, Africa, the Middle East, and Australia.

The Kingdom of Sky was basically China and the nations of the Himalayas plus some of Southeast Asia.

And lastly, there was the realm labeled "Hades," the Underworld. It was by far the smallest of the four kingdoms and it was essentially India.

"Hades?" Stretch raised an eyebrow. "The ancient Greek god? The Lord of the Underworld? Are you saying that he's alive today?"

"The name *Hades* is merely a title that is passed on to each successive King of the Underworld. So yes, there is a man today, probably a very wealthy man living day-to-day by another name, who in royal circles is known as Lord Hades, King of the Underworld.

"Remember, Stretch, there are no gods, only people," Mae said. "This is the answer to my lifelong question: *there are no gods*. Every ancient god or hero was once a person, perhaps a powerful person, perhaps a famous person, but a person nonetheless. Zeus, Perseus, Athena, Hercules, they were all just people once. This is not a new theory. The Greek philosopher Euhemerus espoused it three hundred years before Christ."

She tapped the second map.

"*These* people, these four kings, are the secret rulers of the world. Occasionally, so great do they become, their names emerge from the shadows and enter the popular consciousness: Khufu, Rameses, Agamemnon, Constantine, Charlemagne. But this is rare.

"In their capacity as rulers, the four eternal kingdoms are stewards of advanced ancient knowledge, much of it astronomical, much of it written in the Word of Thoth in manuscripts that date back to the dawn of civilized man."

Mae held up a finger.

"The *source* of this advanced ancient knowledge is another part of the answer to my lifelong question: If there was a prior advanced civilization on this planet or if aliens visited the Earth, would *they* qualify as gods?"

Pooh looked at Stretch. Stretch looked at Pooh.

Mae went on: "The four kingdoms are the hidden hand that directs human history: every great war and famine, every revolution, migration, and depression, has been their doing.

"The four royal houses know that man must advance. They also know that wealth and glory inspire men to advance and so they allow men to acquire riches and power. To a point. For when some men rise too high—fly too close to the sun, if you will—the four kings ruthlessly cut them down.

"History takes on an entirely different character when viewed through this lens. Take, for instance, Louis XIV of France, the famous Sun King. Wealthy beyond imagining, he was one of these ancient kings, the King of Land. But his spoiled grandson, Louis XVI, was not half the man his grandfather was and he was passed over for the ancient crown. When Louis XVI dared to challenge this decision, the French Revolution was initiated and young Louis lost his head.

"The First World War: it was a squabble between some minor royal families. The Second World War was an alliance of all the royal households to quash a pair of troublesome nations, Germany and Japan.

"On three occasions, in 1929, 1987, and 2008, when the capitalist class rose too high too quickly and proclaimed themselves gods, the four kings promptly reminded them of their place.

"Presidents, prime ministers, nation-states, they are merely passing through. The royal houses use democracy as a tool to keep populations satisfied. Individuals rise, some even proclaim themselves 'kings' or 'sultans' but their wealth is nothing compared to that of the four kingdoms.

"Occasionally, to keep their bloodlines healthy and their minds fresh, the kingdoms will invite talented individuals into their secret aristocracy via strategic marriages.

"And over the last five thousand years, these royal households have been advised by the men—always men—of the Invisible College: advisers of surpassing wisdom, initiates in the wisdom of the 'Ancients,' the mysterious advanced civilization that built the Great Pyramid and the Machine that Jack reerected.

"Like the rulers they serve, sometimes the names of these advisers have entered the popular consciousness, too: men like Imhotep, Merlin, Richelieu, and Rasputin."

"And Newton," Pooh Bear said.

"And Newton," Mae agreed. "The Catholic Church, as a repository of much ancient knowledge throughout the Dark Ages and as the modern embodiment of the sun cult of Amon-Ra, has many such initiates within its ranks. And as you know, it advises the Deus Rex."

Pooh Bear held up his hands.

"Okay, okay, fine. There's a great big conspiracy of royal assholes ruling the world. How does all this help us find Jack?"

"Jack drew this tetragammadion symbol after visiting an advanced astronomical observatory," Mae said. "And then he was kidnapped by Iolanthe Compton-Jones, a member of one of the four legendary kingdoms. There are no coincidences when it comes to the kingdoms. They act in strict accordance with ancient laws and rituals.

"Something is going on, something to do with the Hydra Galaxy. Newton knew of that galaxy and he wrote his thoughts down in this book, *The Chronology of Ancient Kingdoms*. We need to find something in here or in his other work that can lead us to Jack."

"Now that's what I'm talking about," Pooh Bear said. "Ma'am, if you don't mind me saying so, you're pretty kick-ass."

"You have no idea." Mae Merriweather gave him an impish grin. "Oh, by the way, how is Horus doing? I like that bird."

"She won't be flying anywhere soon, but she's recovering," Stretch said.

"Good," Mae said. "Now, let's get to work."

THE UNDERWORLD
LOCATION UNKNOWN, SOMEWHERE IN INDIA

After the Third Challenge concluded, Iolanthe took Lily by the hand and led her off the royal viewing balcony.

"Come with me, darling," she said. "Tonight Lord Hades will be hosting the opening banquet and you simply *must* attend."

Iolanthe guided Lily to her own royal quarters.

Lily still had no idea where they were, or even if this "Underworld" was aboveground or below it.

But as she followed Iolanthe, she made a point of noting every detail. If she was going to help Jack, she needed to learn as much as she could about this place.

The royal balcony from which she had watched the Third Challenge seemed to be attached to a mountain of some sort.

From that balcony, Iolanthe had guided her back into the mountain, through a series of raw stone tunnels to a modern elevator hewn into the core of the peak. They went up.

The elevator opened onto another raw stone corridor, only this one was lined with plush carpet. Soft light issued from lamps on the gray walls. It looked like a stone-walled boutique hotel.

Iolanthe's quarters were sumptuously appointed—a broad room with a high bed, walk-in closet, and a marble bathroom.

A pretty young woman of perhaps twenty-five stood waiting for Iolanthe. She had brown hair and pale white skin.

"Ah, Chloe," Iolanthe said. "Be a dear and fetch my red ball gown. And my jewelry box, GHD, and makeup kit, too. We have some work to do on Eliza Doolittle here."

"At once, m'lady." The young woman named Chloe scurried away.

A single window offered a striking view: it looked out at a gigantic stone wall lit up by floodlights. The wall was about two hundred yards away and it was shot through with a mazelike pattern of horizontal ledges and vertical chutes.

At the top of the wall, stretching upward, there seemed to be some kind of camouflage netting. Beyond the netting was black darkness.

Lily wasn't sure but she got the feeling that whatever this mountain was, it was nestled in a crater of some kind.

Iolanthe looked her up and down, and shook her head disapprovingly. "You cannot attend a royal dinner wearing that."

Lily was still dressed in the casual clothes she'd worn to Pine Gap: hipster jeans, strappy sandals, and a pink Zanerobe hoodie. She frowned. She liked her jeans. They were very fashionable and had cost her a fortune.

Chloe reemerged from Iolanthe's dressing area with a red dress and a pair of high-heeled shoes.

Iolanthe was sizing Lily up, assessing her figure. "My, how you've grown. We're almost exactly the same size, you and me. Like sisters! Here, put this gown on."

Lily took the dress with a dark frown.

Her brain was trying to reconcile what she was hearing now with what she had seen: here was Iolanthe speaking ever-so-casually about banquets and ball gowns when men like her father had been fighting desperately for their lives.

"How can you think about stuff like this when people outside are dying?" she asked.

Iolanthe cocked her head to the side. "Darling. Child. This is the way things are. This is the way they've always been. For thousands of years. Trust me, you are not going to stop these Games. Now be a dear and put on that lovely dress."

Despite herself Lily did so.

Iolanthe smiled. "Now sit and let Chloe do your hair and makeup. She's an absolute magician."

Lily sat, facing the only mirror in the room, allowing Chloe to do her thing.

Looking at herself in the mirror, Lily thought that she had grown a lot over the past eight years. She was no longer a gangly little girl with big brown eyes and olive skin who added pink tips to her hair and who wore sparkly roller sneakers.

She was a woman now. Twenty years old, slim, and—she liked to think—attractive. She had grown into her features: her brown eyes and olive skin were radiant, a testament to her Egyptian ancestry. In cafes near Stanford, guys often came over and spontaneously asked her out. While she didn't get glammed up often, she knew she looked good in a skirt and heels.

"You have *great* shoulders," Iolanthe said, draping a diamond necklace over Lily's throat before nudging the ball gown's straps off her shoulders. "Never cover those shoulders up. They'll drive men wild. My God, you're gorgeous."

Lily stood and saw herself fully in the mirror.

The woman looking back at her surprised her.

The dress, so red and figure-hugging and so plunging at the neckline—the diamonds, so bright and sparkling—her hair, demure yet youthful. And the makeup, it was restrained and minimalist yet it artfully drew attention to her best feature: her big almond eyes. Lily had never seen herself looking so refined.

"Yes," Iolanthe said. "That will do nicely. This debut has been a long time coming. It is time, my dear, to present you to royalty."

Lily was ushered into a glorious dining hall.

Four colossal stone pillars—each carved in the shape of a vine-entangled tree—held up an intricately carved ceiling eighty feet above the floor. Dominating the main wall were four large shields, each of a slightly different shape, bearing unusual images and Latin mottos:

“The coats of arms of the four kingdoms,” Iolanthe said, seeing Lily’s gaze. “Land, Sea, Sky, and Underworld.”

Standing proudly in the center of the dining hall was a huge marble statue of a muscular Greek hero wrestling a minotaur. It was colossal; each figure must have been ten feet tall. The hero had a thick wooden club hanging from his belt.

“Hercules and the Cretan bull,” Lily whispered. “His Seventh Labor.”

“Well spotted,” Iolanthe said. “Most people think it is Theseus, not Hercules. How could you tell it was Hercules?”

“The club on his belt,” Lily said, pointing at the statue. “In the Greek myths, Hercules was famous for carrying a big club.”

The dining hall was filled with the royal spectators who had been watching the Games.

There were about thirty of them and they were all dressed in formal evening attire: tailored tuxedos for the gentlemen, ball gowns for the ladies, plus necklaces and earrings glittering with diamonds.

They sipped cocktails while a string quartet played chamber music.

A pint-sized jester in a red devil’s suit and a red-painted face bounced and capered among the crowd, performing magic tricks for them.

As Lily entered the hall in her stunning red ball gown, all conversation stopped. Even the jester froze in mid-leap to gawk at her.

Lily hunched her shoulders, feeling instantly self-conscious.

“Is it the dress?” she whispered to Iolanthe.

Iolanthe smiled knowingly. “It’s not the dress, darling. It’s you. In this world of ancient kings and pure lineages, you’re the most eligible young woman on the planet.”

Thankfully, the moment was broken and general conversation resumed and Lily took the opportunity to look at the four shields on the main wall.

Coats of arms, she knew, were designed to tell a story. Every little detail had meaning, be it the crest or the image on the escutcheon itself.

The first one, the coat of arms for Land, featured a crown atop it and had a picture of three pyramids.

Lily figured they represented the pyramids at Giza in Egypt, because the largest one, presumably the Great Pyramid, was being struck by a beam of light from above. Lily had seen this very image before: during the Tartarus Event that had required Jack, her, and their ragtag team to find the Seven Wonders of the Ancient World.

She read the motto: *Ad Majora Regis Gloriam.*

"'For the greater glory of the king,'" she translated aloud.

Iolanthe nodded. "Yes. My house, the Kingdom of Land, sometimes called the Deus Rex, maintains a special fondness for our king, as the King of Land has usually been the wealthiest and most powerful of the four kings."

Lily gazed at the second shield: Sea.

Surmounted by a trident, it depicted an ancient city on water; the city featured a pyramid, a domed building, two obelisks, and a lighthouse-like structure, all silhouetted by the blazing sun.

Its motto, *A Magnitudine, Vires* translated as "From size, strength."

"Nice trident," Lily said.

"A great Sea King of old wielded it in battle many centuries ago, giving rise to the myth of King Neptune and his trident."

Lily looked at the third coat of arms: Sky.

It depicted a mountain landscape: three mountains, the largest and darkest of which was topped by a bright star that was itself ringed by the sun.

This shield, Lily saw, was the only one to have no sharp edges. All of its corners and points were rounded off into gentle curves.

"Why doesn't that one have any sharp corners?" Lily asked.

"The Sky Kingdom is the most spiritual of the four legendary kingdoms. A keeper of ancient knowledge and rituals, it prides itself on not being hostile. The gentle corners of its royal shield are designed as an expression of its peaceful nature."

"*Potestatem ex Alto*," Lily read. "That means 'Power from above.' That's not exactly peaceful. Nor are these Games."

"Not all power is physical," Iolanthe replied. "And even those who preach peace must sometimes stand and fight."

Lily turned her gaze to the final shield, the coat of arms of Hades's kingdom, the Underworld.

Alone among the shields, it did not depict the sun. It was decidedly dark and grim.

Also, instead of a stylized crest sitting above the shield, it bore two horns, like those of a bull. The image on the shield was of a forbidding mountain with ramparts and towers on it. Looming behind the grim mount, instead of the sun, were the curving tentacle-like arms of what she guessed was the Hydra Galaxy.

Iolanthe said, "We are standing inside that mountain right now."

"It looks like the Eiffel Tower," Lily said.

"Or perhaps the Eiffel Tower looks like it," Iolanthe said.

Lily read the motto—*Ad Majora Natus*—and frowned.

"That's odd," she said. "It's the only one that's not about glory or power. *Ad Majora Natus* means—"

"'Born for greater things,'" a voice said from behind her.

Lily turned, and found herself staring into the eyes of Lord Hades himself.

"The new Oracle," Hades said. "It is an honor and a pleasure to meet you under more formal circumstances, not in amongst those crude carriages. I fear we were not properly introduced."

Hades was much more striking when seen up close, Lily thought.

His dark eyes were piercing and his dark beard perfectly groomed. His crimson-edged suit was intricately woven with symbols sewn into the weave. From head to toe, he was truly an ancient lord.

Standing dutifully one step behind him was his chief aide, Vacheron, the Master of the Games.

Standing on his other side like a bodyguard was a gigantic man in a glistening silver dog helmet. This man's armor was amazingly modern: all bi-Kevlar mesh and carbon-fiber plating. The two Glock pistols in holsters on his thighs were very modern indeed.

"Okay, sure. Hey there," Lily said to Hades, deliberately not using any kind of formal address. "I'm Lily West."

Hades saw what she was doing and smiled indulgently. "Greetings, Miss Lily. My name is Anthony Michael Dominic DeSaxe, the fourth of that name to be appointed Marshal of France and also the fourth of that name to be appointed Lord of the Underworld."

"DeSaxe . . ." Lily said softly.

No, she thought, *it couldn't be*. She shook the thought away.

"I like your motto," she said. "I was just saying to Iolanthe, it's not like the other three. They're all about strength, power, and glory, but yours is not. How do you interpret it?"

Hades nodded, impressed. "Mine is an ancient duty, a duty greater than all others, so my house's motto speaks to that. I mean no disrespect to the other kings. They are all remarkable men from remarkable houses. I, however, was born to be a steward of this historic kingdom and to host these most important Games: I was quite literally born for greater things."

"Like putting on a death show?" Lily asked. "And acting like some kind of Roman emperor?"

"If killing men is part of my greater duty, then I must do it even if I do not like to. Many rituals in this world have lost their original meanings and so have become empty ceremonies, but the ritual behind these Games has not been lost. These Games are not held for *my* pleasure. They are held for a reason. They are a signal that the inhabitants of this planet are still worthy of the existence we were given."

"A signal to whom?"

Hades looked at Lily closely. "There are many things in this world that cannot be explained, young one. Some of them you yourself have experienced: ancient buildings like the pyramids and Stonehenge; underground temple-shrines like those of the Machine that your father reerected. Who do you think built those wondrous things? Men?

"Or perhaps individuals far more ancient? Ask yourself, how did life itself arise on this remote planet? I am sure you are aware of the Cambrian Explosion, the sudden burst of complex life that occurred on Earth 500 million years ago. What caused it? How did life begin here?

"Humanity has been watched from afar for a long, long time and every now and again—through rituals like the Tartarus Rotation and the Dark Star of Nepthys and the Great Games of the Hydra—we must prove that we have attained a level of sophistication that warrants the continuation of our existence."

Lily mentally noted the words "Tartarus Rotation" and "Dark Star of Nepthys." She and Jack had been pivotal players in the episodes of the Tartarus Sunspot and the Dark Star.

Hades said, "In the case of Tartarus and Nepthys, important ancient knowledge was lost and had to be refound. Some of the other kingdoms partook in those quests, Iolanthe's among them."

He nodded at Iolanthe, who bowed graciously.

"I myself did not participate," Hades said. "If the world is to end through the careless loss of sacred knowledge, then so be it.

"But here, now, there is no loss of ancient knowledge. These Games were never lost. And the role they fulfill is an important one. When we lay those nine Golden Spheres—first five, then four—we tell the Ancients that we as a people are worthy of living. If men die in the process, then they die for a noble cause."

He bowed, ever the gracious host. "Forgive me, Miss Lily, I have other guests to attend to. Enjoy the evening. You cannot imagine what a joy it is to have you here."

He swept away, followed by his dog-helmeted bodyguard, leaving Vacheron standing there, staring at them with his bulging eyes.

"Holy Oracle, it is truly an honor," he said to Lily, bowing low.

When he turned to Iolanthe, his expression transformed into one of pure joy. He smiled, revealing foul yellow teeth.

"And Princess Iolanthe, it is as always an exquisite pleasure to see you. If you need anything during your stay here, anything at all, please call me. I am your humble servant."

The Master of the Games bowed again, kissing Iolanthe's hand, and departed.

Lily looked at Iolanthe. "I think someone's got the hots for you."

Iolanthe grimaced. "Monsieur Vacheron has long been Hades's loyal servant and emissary to the other kingdoms. He is one of those types who delights in associating with the highborn. More than anything in the world he desires to marry into royalty, to officially enter the social stratosphere he so admires. I am of royal blood and unmarried, so he flatters me constantly."

"Do you like him?"

"The man is a pig," Iolanthe said. "A loathsome, ambitious pig. Do not confuse being royal with being all-powerful, Lily. I may be royal. I may have almost limitless resources at my disposal, but I am not free to do *everything* I please. For one thing, it is not for me to choose whom I marry. It is my king who will do that. And he will make that choice based on all manner of reasons, many of them political and strategic. I detest Vacheron but if it is decided that it is advantageous that I marry him, then I will and I will have no choice in the matter."

Lily glanced from Iolanthe to the departing figure of Vacheron.

She thought about Iolanthe. Over the years, Iolanthe had been both a deadly rival and a convenient ally to her family. She was the most ruthlessly amoral person Lily had ever met, but right now Lily couldn't help but feel sorry for her.

After Vacheron took his leave, Iolanthe guided Lily through the crowd of royals.

Lily saw a few people she recognized from newspapers and magazines—members of the British and Danish royal families mostly—but the rest she did not know. They were the shadow-royals of the world.

She also saw a wide-screen TV with a list on it:

THE CHAMPIONS

KINGDOM OF LAND	1	Maj. Gregory Brigham	UK
	2	Sgt. Victor Vargas	Brazil
	3	Sgt. Mauricio Corazon	Brazil
	4	Capt. Jack West Jr	US/Aus
KINGDOM OF SEA	1	Maj. Jeffrey Edwards [Delta]	US
	~~2~~	~~Lt. Barrett Johnson [Army]~~	~~US~~
	3	W.O. DeShawn Monroe [Navy]	US
	4	Capt. Shane Schofield [USMC]	US
KINGDOM OF SKY	~~1~~	~~Tenzin Depon~~	~~Tibet~~
	2	Renzin Depon	Tibet
	~~3~~	~~The Gorkha~~	~~Nepal~~
	~~4~~	~~Capt. Jason Chen~~	~~Taiwan~~
KINGDOM OF THE UNDERWORLD	1	Zaitan DeSaxe	France
	2	Capt. Sachin Singh [MARCOS]	India
	~~3~~	~~Lt. Wasim Nasiruzzin [MARCOS]~~	~~India MINO~~
	~~4~~	~~Lt. Ravi Mano [LRRP]~~	~~Sri Lanka MINO~~

The champions. Their names being crossed off as they were killed. She saw her father's name in the box containing the four representatives of the Kingdom of Land: Capt. Jack West Jr US/Aus.

Suddenly a man dressed in the red robes of a Catholic cardinal stepped in front of her, blocking her view of the television. He had a thin pencil moustache, darting eyes, and he was smiling with unbridled joy.

Lily did a double take. She could have sworn she'd met him somewhere before.

"Young madam, it is an honor of honors to meet the Oracle of Siwa!" he exclaimed, taking Lily's hand and bowing low.

Of course he was honored, Lily thought. She had known for some time that the Catholic Church was the modern incarnation of an ancient Egyptian sun cult, the Cult of Amon-Ra. From their priestly garments featuring blazing suns to the many obelisks decorating Rome and the Vatican, everything about the Church was devoted to the worship of the sun. For a cardinal to meet someone directly descended from ancient Egyptian royalty would indeed be an honor.

Iolanthe said, "Lily, this is Cardinal Ricardo Mendoza. Cardinal, this is Lily West, true daughter of the last Oracle."

The cardinal looked Lily up and down in a way that Lily didn't like at all. He did it like a horse buyer assessing a filly.

"How old are you, Lily?" he asked.

"I'm twenty."

"And are you still a virgin?"

The question caught Lily off guard. Who asked *that*? "With all due respect, Cardinal, that's none of your fucking business."

Cardinal Mendoza was now looking unashamedly at her breasts and stomach. He didn't even seem to hear her. "It is no matter. You are magnificent as you are. Just *magnificent* . . ."

Creepy as this encounter was, Lily couldn't shake the feeling that she had met this man before.

Then it hit her.

She had not met him but she had *seen* him: at Pine Gap, during a security briefing way back during the mission to find the Six Ramesean Stones.

She had seen this man's photo and biographical data on a computer screen.

After the murderous Father Francisco del Piero had died during the Seven Ancient Wonders mission, Cardinal Ricardo Mendoza had been appointed leader of the Church's most powerful Curial department, the Congregation for the Doctrine of the Faith, a department that had once been known by a different name, the Inquisition.

Mendoza was the Church's expert on all things ancient and their adviser to the Deus Rex, the god-kings, the Kingdom of Land.

Mendoza smiled vilely at Lily. "You will make a wonderful wife to a lucky man someday, my gorgeous Oracle. Do enjoy the Games."

He departed, leaving Lily standing there feeling dirty.

"That was creepy," she said.

Iolanthe shrugged. "The Church has its uses. That it went down a men-only path is a shame. It has not been good for them. It colors their thinking, dulls their minds. Here, there is someone I'd like you to meet."

Iolanthe guided Lily to a pair of younger royals closer to her own age.

They were both men. One was pudgy, Persian, red-faced, and sweaty; he gripped a wineglass and drank from it in huge gulps. The second younger man was facing the other way; he was well built and black-haired.

He turned around and smiled.

Lily froze at the sight of him and felt a deep uneasiness in the pit of her stomach.

It was Dion. Dion DeSaxe from Stanford.

"Hello, Lily," he said with his perfect confident smile.

Lily's mind whirled.

Like many women her age, in her darker moments she'd wondered why this charming guy from Stanford had asked her out when there were so many other girls to choose from.

She'd hoped it was because he'd been attracted to something special about her: whether that was brains, looks, or even just her smile.

The last thing Lily had thought was that anyone at Stanford might know of her mysterious history or that they would date her because of that.

But that now seemed to be precisely the case.

Dion knew.

Had known all along.

Lily felt betrayed, cheated, swindled. Worse than that. She felt like a fool.

Iolanthe made the introductions.

Indicating the fat prince: "Lily West, may I present to you Prince George Khalil, cousin of the House of Hades." She gestured to the handsome one: "And Prince Dionysius DeSaxe, first son of our host, Lord Hades, Crown Prince and heir to the Kingdom of the Underworld."

Dion kissed Lily's hand formally. "We already know each other.

I was not expecting her to be here at the Games, but I am delighted that she is."

He held Lily's gaze with his deep brown eyes. The cocky look on his face said: *Yes, I knew who you were all along.*

Lily noticed two pretty princesses dressed in expensive pink gowns watching their exchange closely, eyeing the handsome son of Hades.

Then the fat one named George broke the moment by blurting: "So, how are you enjoying the Games so far, Lily?"

Lily stiffened. "I'm learning a lot."

Prince George babbled drunkenly, "Well, *I* think they are simply *brilliant*. Champions, minotaurs, slashing swords, exploding heads, death by combat. *Brilliant*! Did you see the fifth warrior take on the Gurkha at the end of the last challenge? It was a pure do-or-die moment. God, it's all simply marvelous entertainment!"

Lily looked at him askance. "Entertainment? You consider all this to be *entertaining*?"

George said, "Of course! I mean, sure, some of them die. It's not as if they have royal blood or anything. They should be honored to die in front of us."

Lily just stared at the fat drunk prince.

He lowered his voice, whispering conspiratorially. "And it's going to get better. I have it on good authority that the maze for the Fourth Challenge is simply astonishing; Vacheron tells me we may see the Hydra warrior for the first time, too. And the Fifth Challenge, my goodness, apparently it is of a scale never seen in the Games before. Oh, it's just so delightful to be here. Just *delightful*!"

Thankfully, at that moment, a bell chimed, calling all the guests to the dining tables.

Dion leaned close to Lily. "Please, forgive him, and forgive me, too. I honestly did not know you would be here. If I can arrange it with my father, I would be delighted if you would sit with me at a later meal so I can explain myself. For now, let me escort you to your table."

He held out his elbow . . .

. . . Lily didn't take it. The two pretty girls nearby gasped in horror.

"Iolanthe can take me," she said curtly as she walked off toward the dining tables.

Lily ate dinner next to Iolanthe, at a table occupied by six other members of her royal household.

There were five large dining tables in the gigantic stone-walled hall. Four for the royal households and one—set higher than the others—for Hades and the three other kings.

Flanking their table like enormous statues were the two lion-headed warriors from the Second Challenge in the water pit. They were both big men, Lily saw, but not as big as Hades's dog-helmeted bodyguard who, as always, loomed behind his master.

Lily watched the four kings curiously.

All were stately-looking men of about sixty. They all seemed sharp-eyed and obviously healthy; they looked after themselves. In fact, as Lily looked at them more closely, she felt they resembled modern chief executives more than ancient royal lords.

Taking pride of place in the middle of the five tables was an altar on which sat the two Golden Spheres that had been the focus of the Second and Third Challenges.

Seeing them up close for the first time, Lily was dazzled.

They were exquisite.

Each was the size of a volleyball and they glowed with an ethereal luster that came from somewhere deep within them.

Then Lily noticed their outer surfaces and she gasped.

Each Golden Sphere depicted the surface of the Earth and the outlines of the continents. The shorelines of the continents were not quite right, as if they depicted the world from another, earlier age.

These were not just gold *spheres*, they were gold *globes*.

"What exactly are these things?" Lily asked Iolanthe.

"They are very ancient," Iolanthe said. "They have always been kept in a sacred vault here in the Underworld, a vault that only opens when the Star Chamber opens."

"What are they made of?"

"In previous eras, they were simply believed to be possessed of the power of the gods," Iolanthe said. "But as man has advanced in knowledge and wisdom, he has found less need for divine explanations.

"The current Lord Hades is a wise and curious man. When the vault opened a little over a month ago, he conducted some experiments on the spheres. He found that they are made of a variety of quartz not found on Earth.

"Quartz is a very peculiar substance. It has conductive properties: it can *store* vibrations and resonances, kind of like a natural hard drive. Lord Hades told me that each of those golden globes pulses with an inner energy on wavelengths unseen anywhere in nature or in modern electromagnetic science."

"An inner energy?"

"Whatever it is, the fate of humankind depends on it," Iolanthe said. "For it is the placement of these spheres that will divert the incoming Hydra Galaxy."

There was one other extra guest at Lily's table, the winner of the Third Challenge: the SAS commando, Major Gregory Brigham.

As the winner of the most recent challenge, he ate at the banquet as his king's esteemed guest.

And as she sat there surrounded by these bejeweled women and powerful men, these shadow-rulers of the world, Lily just shook her head.

She would have preferred to eat a hamburger with Jack any day of the week.

Just then, some music played and Hades's pint-sized jester bounded out onto a stage accompanied by a minotaur. Dressed in his red devil's suit, he mugged and danced jauntily.

The crowd of royals laughed.

"Ah, Mephisto," someone near Lily sighed.

Lily now got a better look at the jester and what she saw frightened her.

The skin on his face was red, but this had not been achieved through makeup. It was *tattooed* red. And a pair of triangular bones had been surgically implanted beneath the skin of his forehead, to create very realistic-looking horns. Most frightening of all, though, were the little man's teeth: they had all been filed to sharpened points.

This was not a children's clown. Everything about Mephisto was cruel, nasty, perhaps even demonic.

The red jester began to poke and prod the minotaur with his little red trident.

He would playfully stab the minotaur and then somersault quickly through its legs as it turned and then stab it again.

The whole act was like a comical version of a bullfight. At one point, the minotaur lunged at the jester, only for the jester to step lightly out of the way, sweeping aside an imaginary bullfighter's cape.

The audience of royals laughed and clapped.

And then the jester pulled a curious weapon from his belt: it had a wooden handle from which hung a pair of weighted brass balls on two short lengths of chain.

"It is a flail," Iolanthe whispered to Lily. "An ancient weapon and a most difficult one to master."

With a deft swirl of his wrist, Mephisto twirled the flail, causing the two heavy balls to spin so rapidly they blurred with motion.

Then with a flick of his arm, the flail lashed out and the two brass balls were suddenly wrapped around the minotaur's head and they came crashing together at the poor beast's temples, crushing his helmet horrifically inward.

The half-man in the bull mask froze instantly. Blood dribbled out from under his cracked mask yet he remained standing.

Lily was thunderstruck.

Beside her, Iolanthe continued to eat her appetizer. She picked a stray piece of lettuce from between her teeth.

The audience gasped, then clapped in admiration.

As she watched, Lily's eyes met those of the little red jester and she saw delighted malevolence in them.

As the jester eyed Lily, he kicked the still-standing minotaur behind him.

The minotaur fell to the stage with a dull thud. It lay motionless, dead, as the jester broke eye contact with Lily and bowed theatrically for the crowd.

They cheered enthusiastically.

"I am truly in Hell," Lily whispered to herself.

While Lily was dining in luxury and splendor, Jack, Alby, and Sky Monster sat together on the cold steel floor of their hostage carriage eating out of tin bowls.

While the bowls weren't exactly of the finest quality, the food was actually pretty good: pasta, rice, chicken. Energy food for men who needed lots of energy.

Nestled beside Jack were his two dogs, the big Labrador Ash and the small poodle Roxy.

In front of all of them—its bull helmet removed and its injured foot now bandaged—was the minotaur Jack had saved at the end of the Third Challenge.

Looking at the hairy half-man with his broad forehead, flat nose, and unibrow, Jack thought about what Iolanthe had said earlier about the minotaurs being purebred Neanderthals.

Archaeologists and anthropologists had once believed that *Homo sapiens*—modern man—had killed off the smaller-statured Neanderthals.

More recent theories, however, postulated that the world's Neanderthal population, rather than being exterminated, had just been thinned and, in some regions, had interbred with *Homo sapiens*. It was entirely possible that the slightly hairier, shorter, hunched-over person in your office had some Neanderthal blood in them. That a society of purebred Neanderthals might have survived in a remote and contained ancient citadel was not out of the question at all.

With his hunched stance and protruding lower jaw, Neanderthal man had also gotten a bit of a raw deal when it came to estimations of his intelligence. Neanderthals, it was thought, could build weapons and structures, count and speak.

Jack's dogs had their own responses to the hairy half-man.

Ash, imperturbable as usual, just ignored him. Roxy, also as usual, adopted a guard-dog role: she stared daggers at the minotaur, growling suspiciously at him.

"Here." Jack handed his bowl of pasta to the half-man. "Eat something."

The hairy half-man took the bowl tentatively.

"Can you speak?" Jack asked.

The half-man nodded. "Little."

"What's your name?"

The half-man pointed to a tattoo on his left shoulder that read *E-147*. Jack recalled that the minotaur that had attacked him in his cell at the very start of all this had had a similar tattoo on its shoulder.

"I . . . Minotaur E-147," the Neanderthal said.

"Okay. I'm Jack."

"Jack?" the half-man said, trying to wrap his mouth around the word. "Jack."

Roxy barked at the half-man, making him jump.

Jack patted the little poodle. "Never mind her. She's kinda protective."

The hairy man said, "Jack help E-147 when other minotaurs run. Why?"

"I don't like watching anyone get left to die," Jack said.

E-147 looked directly into Jack's eyes. "E-147 surely die without Jack's help. E-147 thank Jack. E-147 consider Jack friend."

"You're welcome," Jack said. "This is Sky Monster and this is Alby—"

"Why Jack keep dogs?" E-147 interrupted. "For eat later?"

"*What?* Oh, no." Jack shook his head. "We don't eat dogs. The dogs are my friends. Good friends."

"Oh." E-147 looked a little saddened by that.

"Tell me," Jack said. "How many minotaurs are there?"

"There many minotaurs," E-147 said. "N minotaurs, S minotaurs, E minotaurs, and W minotaurs."

Jack saw the pattern: north, south, east, and west. Wherever these minotaurs lived, they were divided into geographic areas.

"Where do all you minotaurs live?" he asked.

"In minotaur city. Known as Dis. Is great underground city. It protect only land entrance to Underworld."

Alby said, "An underground city?"

Jack said to him, "Iolanthe said Hades has thousands of these guys. E-147, how many E minotaurs are there?"

E-147 said, "Most high number is E-900."

Jack said, "Four groups of minotaurs, with almost a thousand to each group. We're talking several thousand minotaurs all up."

"Jesus," Sky Monster said.

Jack turned back to E-147. "If you don't mind, I just have to ask, *what* are you?"

E-147 cocked his head to the side, frowning. "I . . . E-147. I . . . me."

Jack smiled to himself. "I'm sorry. I shouldn't have asked that. That's right. You're you."

At that moment, another voice spoke—a man's voice, a young man's voice.

"Jack? Jack West Jr.? It *is* you . . ."

Jack turned.

Through the bars of the hostage carriage, two cells away, he saw a young male US Marine dressed in combat trousers and an olive T-shirt.

It was a Marine he knew well but had not seen in a long time.

It was Lieutenant Sean Miller, call sign *Astro*.

Jack and Astro's relationship went way back, back to the mission involving the Six Ramesean Stones.

It had not started out well: when the mission began, Astro had been inserted into Jack's international team as a representative of the United States. What neither Astro nor Jack knew at the time was that Astro's shadowy superior back home had been Jack's father—a villainous colonel known as Wolf—whose plans were not as noble as Astro had thought they were.

During a vicious battle at a gigantic underground temple-shrine in Japan, Astro had betrayed Jack and, thinking he was doing the right thing, sided with Wolf. But a short time later, Astro was shot and the duplicitous Wolf left him for dead.

The person who'd saved Astro was Jack. They had been friends ever since.

"Astro?" Jack said. "How'd you get roped into all this?"

"Same as you, I'm thinking," the young Marine replied. "They found my file, saw that I'd had some history with all this ancient stuff, and called me in. But I feel terrible—because of me, these guys got pulled into it, too."

Jack noticed that Astro was sharing his cell with three other United States Marines, two men and one woman. At that moment, the woman stood up to look at Jack.

She was a very distinctive female Marine. She was absolutely gigantic, at least six foot two, with a shaven head and a grim dark-humored smile.

It was the big burly woman Jack had seen during the Third Challenge, the one accompanying the other US Marine, the one with the reflective glasses. The hostage chamber between theirs was now empty, half-filled with liquid stone, its occupants sacrificed after the Third Challenge. Until now, Jack hadn't realized that he and the Marines were quartered so close to each other.

He recognized her, but he hadn't seen her in a very long time, not since some very secret joint US–Australian special forces operations in the 1990s.

"Do my eyes deceive me or is that Jack West Jr.?" the big woman said. "The famous Huntsman, the biggest pussy in the crack Australian SAS?"

"What's a nice girl like you doing in a place like this, Gena?" Jack said.

The woman grinned back at him. After all these years, she hadn't changed a bit.

She was Gena Newman of the United States Marine Corps, call sign *Motherfucker*, or just Mother for short.

"What happened to you, Jack?" Mother said. "Back in the 90s, you were hot shit. Ranked in the top ten in the world. Geez, your escape from Iraq in Desert Storm in Saddam Hussein's own fucking plane went down in military legend, man. And then you just vanished. Disappeared. Where the hell did you go?"

"A mission that turned into my life," Jack said. "In '96, I was assigned to protect a little girl and that mission didn't end till 2008. I adopted her. Got married. Found out I was part of an ancient prophecy."

"Prophecy?" Mother said.

"You kinda get used to the epic historical side of it all," Jack said.

Mother snorted. "Yeah, well I haven't seen something this freaky since I saw Cirque du Soleil in Vegas. Creepy French circus shit. Got any ideas on how to get out of this clusterfuck?"

"Not yet. I'm still playing catch-up myself," Jack said.

"Hey, you still got that plane you stole from Saddam?"

"The *Halicarnassus*? Sadly, no. I destroyed it when I had to smash my way into a big underground shrine. Real shame. Got a new plane, now. Stole it from one of these royal assholes after I killed him. It's a Russian knockoff of the Concorde. Fast."

Jack jerked his chin at their grim surroundings. "So how'd you get involved in all this? This ain't your regular Marine Corps op."

"As I said, it's my fault," Astro said. "I was on tour in Afghanistan, based at Leatherneck in Kandahar, when I got called into a tent and found the Commandant of the Marine Corps sitting there waiting for me. He was surrounded by some powerful dudes in suits. They knew a lot: asked me about our mission back in '08, the Six Sacred Stones, the Vertexes, the prophecy of the Five Greatest Warriors and all that. Then they asked me about Mother and our CO, the captain here. Asked if I knew anything about them and a group called 'Majestic-12.' I didn't. I just said they were two of the best Marines I'd ever seen. Put Tomahawk with 'em and you've got one hell of a team."

He turned to the two other male Marines sitting below the waist-high wall of their cell, out of Jack's sight. "Excuse me, sir, but I got someone here I think you should meet."

The most senior Marine stood and Jack got a good look at him for the first time. He was lean and fit, his muscles hard and wiry. He had dark hair that had been shaved short to accommodate the explosive chip and gemstone in his neck and a weathered handsome face. He wasn't wearing his reflective antiflash glasses now, so Jack could see his eyes.

They seized his attention.

Two hideous scars—one for each eye—slashed vertically down across them.

Astro said, "Captain Jack West Jr., formerly of the Australian SAS, call sign *Huntsman*, meet Captain Shane Schofield of the United States Marine Corps, call sign *Scarecrow*."

The Marine with the slashed eyes stared at Jack for a long moment, before nodding.

"Captain," he said cautiously. "What's with the arm?"

Jack glanced down at his titanium left arm. One of the reasons he wore a glove on that hand and a long-sleeved T-shirt was to cover it up, to *not* draw attention to it. But this Scarecrow guy had spotted it instantly.

Jack could have said it was a state-of-the-art, fully articulated, motor-controlled arm built for him by his late mentor, Wizard, after his real arm had been seared off by a curtain of falling lava in a volcano in Uganda, but instead he just said, "Lost the old one in a tight spot. This one's better."

"So what do you know about this place and these Games?" the Marine named Scarecrow said.

"Not much more than you," Jack said. "I was drugged and kidnapped. Woke up in a cell to find a minotaur charging at me with a knife. How about you?"

Scarecrow said, "We were brought here under false pretenses. Along with Astro, Mother, and Tomahawk"—he nodded at the fourth and last Marine in the cell, a younger blond-haired man—"I was informed that we would be performing a joint op with four Delta operators in southern Afghanistan. Boarded a plane with the D-boys, short flight, maybe an hour, but when we landed, it was at a remote desert airstrip near a coast. Afghanistan has no coast. It's landlocked. We weren't in Afghanistan anymore.

"The airstrip we'd arrived at was little more than a runway of hard-packed sand. No buildings, no civilization in sight. Only a single man, that guy Vacheron, and a pickup truck with a cage on the bed. Our Delta companions seemed entirely unsurprised. They just got in the cage."

He nodded at the four men in the next barred hostage chamber.

"That's Major Jeff Edwards, call sign *Ricochet*, and his three douchebag buddies from Delta Force. Typical Delta assholes. They're better than you and they know it. I suspect they've been training for this. But we had no idea.

"Anyway, we got in the pickup's cage and black bags were put over our heads. When my bag was removed, I found myself alone in a cell and a few minutes later, one of those minotaurs came charging at me, just like you."

"Do you know any of the other champions?" Jack asked.

Again, Scarecrow paused, eyeing Jack warily, assessing him. He struck Jack as a careful man who didn't like surprises.

At last, Scarecrow said, "That big African American dude over there with the tattoos on his arms is Warrant Officer DeShawn Monroe. Navy SEAL. Trained killer, tough son of a bitch. Known as *The Finisher*, 'cause that's what he does, finishes things. He's the only other one I know."

Jack nodded. "Well, if Astro vouches for you, you're good with me. I'd trust him with my life and with my little girl's, too."

"Forgive me if I withhold judgment on you for a while," Scarecrow said. "Right here, right now, I don't trust anyone."

"I get that," Jack said. "In the meantime, a question: What did the coast look like? The coast near the airstrip you landed at?"

Scarecrow shrugged. "Just a barren desert coast. No trees, no life. Tropical blue water, but with a tinge of reddish-orange at the edges. Given the short flight time from Kandahar, I figured we were somewhere on the edge of the Arabian Sea, but honestly we could be anywhere in the region: Yemen, Oman, Iran, Pakistan, even India."

"We're in India," Jack said. "So I'm told."

"India," Mother spat. "I hate fuckin' India."

"Why is that?" Jack asked.

"Because India gave the world yoga, and now when I go to Starbucks to get my morning coffee, I have to deal with all these fucking yoga-loving yuppies dressed in tight pants who think they're living on some higher celestial plane when they're really just asshole followers-of-fashion."

Jack allowed himself a smile.

Scarecrow looked at Jack seriously. "Captain West—"

"Please, call me Jack."

"Captain West. I've seen some strange shit in my time. For instance, Astro, Mother, and I once survived a very unusual mission together at a secret base called Hell Island. But I've never found myself in a place calling itself the Underworld, ruled by a guy calling himself Hades, fighting for my life against guys in bull and lion helmets. My question for you is: What are we going to do to get out of here alive?"

Jack looked at Scarecrow for a long moment.

"I don't know," he said. "I really don't know."

Shortly after, in the eerie darkness that surrounded the hostage carriages, all the champions drifted off to sleep.

After the exertions of the first three challenges—the minotaurs in the cells, the water pit, and the tower—they all slept soundly.

All except Jack.

He couldn't sleep.

Leaning against the bars of his cell, he peered out at the darkened Underworld, at the tower and the abyss of the Third Challenge.

This whole place baffled him. The Underworld. Was it a cave? It looked like a cavern, but it didn't feel like one. The air was too fresh. But he couldn't see the sky either; above him there was nothing but inky black. No stars, no moonlight.

Jack was awake when, late in the night, Major Brigham returned from the banquet and reentered his cell. He was greeted by his companions but soon they were all sleeping.

Jack remained awake, sitting up against the waist-high fence of his cell, head resting against the bars, thinking. Then fatigue overcame him and his eyes began to droop and he nodded off—

A shuffling sound woke him.

A figure in a hooded robe crept past Jack's cell, moving quickly and lightly.

Jack didn't move. He didn't know how long he'd been asleep for, or what time it was, but it was still dark, the dead of night.

He followed the robed figure with only his eyes, feigning sleep.

The figure stopped at a cell a few doors down from Jack's and whispered something to one of its occupants before fleeing as quickly as it had arrived.

Jack watched the robed figure leave.

What was this?

He shook his head, not sure if he was asleep or awake. His weary brain tried to make sense of it but he was unable to ponder the matter any further, for right then all the fatigue and stress of the previous day finally overcame him and he fell into a deep dreamless sleep.

Jack was awoken by a sharp jolt and the clang of metal on metal.

His carriage was moving. The train of hostage chambers shunted slowly along its track.

Sunlight rushed into Jack's cell and as the train moved away from the pinnacles of the Third Challenge, he saw the landscape around him for the first time in the cold light of day.

Alby, Sky Monster, and E-147 awoke with the movement and joined Jack at the bars.

On the far side of the pinnacles, they saw a colossal stone wall, perfectly vertical and gently curved.

Alby said, "Looks like we're inside a meteor crater . . ."

Jack couldn't yet see the whole mountain-like formation that housed their movable cell, but he could now see why he had been confused as to whether or not this Underworld was situated in a large cavern.

Looking upward through the bars of his cell, he saw camouflage netting extending out from somewhere high above him over to the rim of the curved stone wall opposite him.

The camouflage netting caused the landscape inside the crater to be shrouded in dense shadow. Only the odd shaft of sunlight pierced it. At night the netting had made it too difficult to even see stars in the sky.

But it also allowed fresh air to get in, hence the half-cave, half-not effect.

The carriages came around a bend and suddenly Jack saw something else on the vertical wall of the crater opposite him.

A vast and complex vertical maze protruded from the face of the sheer cliff. In front of it was a broad lake of steaming yellow-tinged liquid.

"What is *that*?" Alby gasped.

"That, I'm guessing," Jack said, "is the arena for the next challenge."

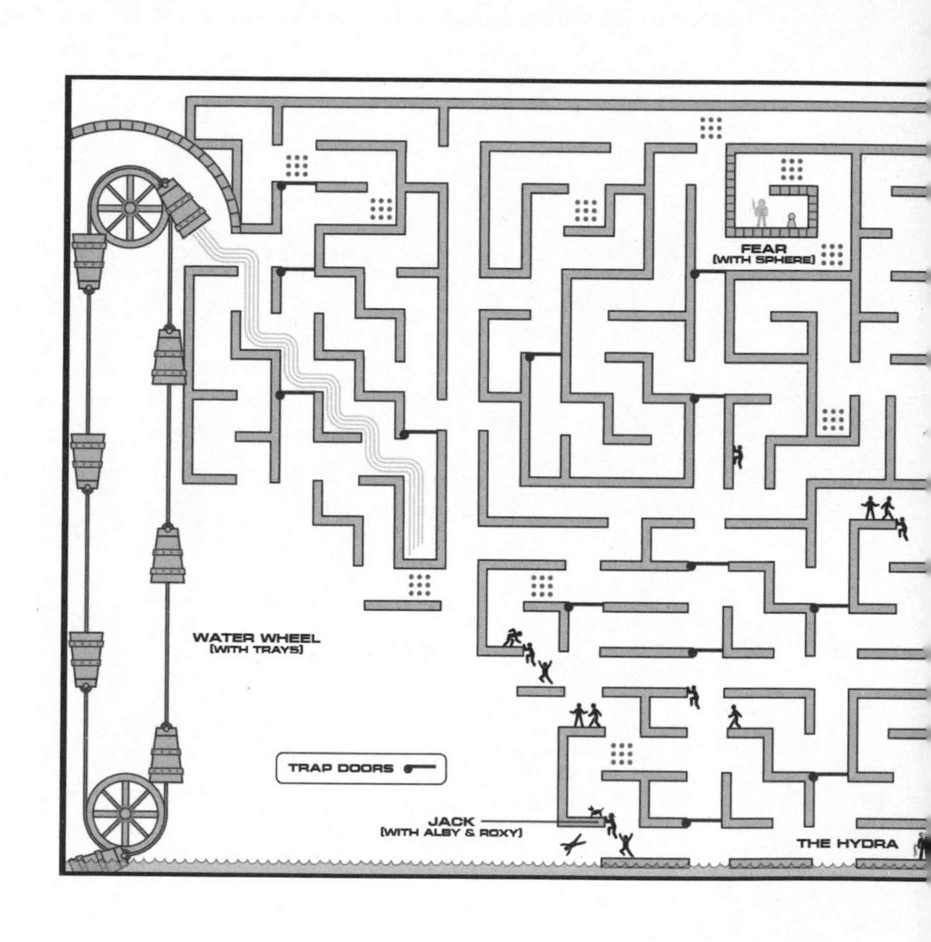

FEAR
(WITH SPHERE)
WATER WHEEL
(WITH TRAYS)
TRAP DOORS
JACK
(WITH ALBY & ROXY)
THE HYDRA

FOURTH CHALLENGE

THE VERTICAL MAZE

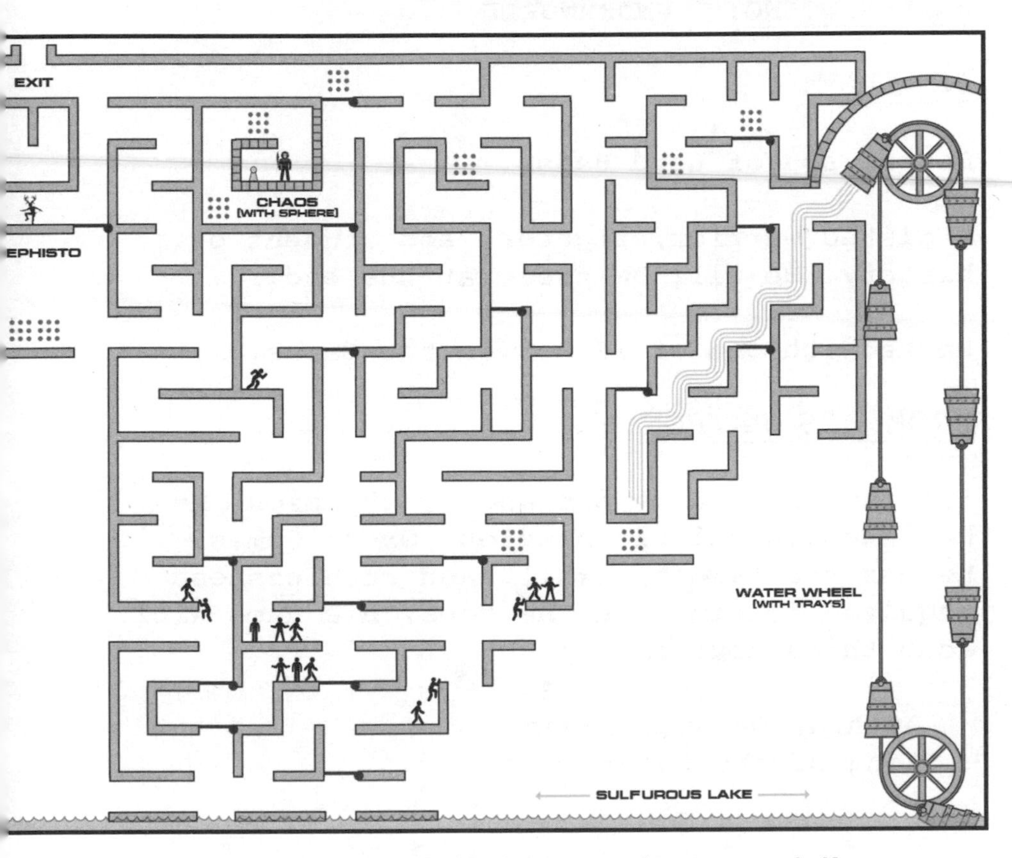

Why do we loathe Hades more than any god, if not because he is so adamantine and unyielding?

KING AGAMEMNON
THE ILIAD, BOOK IX,
BY HOMER

CHAMPION PROFILE

NAME: ZAITAN DESAXE
AGE: 22
RANK TO WIN: 4
REPRESENTING: UNDERWORLD

PROFILE:

Second son of Lord Hades.

A gifted warrior, fighter, and student of history. He will be there at the end.

Ranked 4th out of 16 to win the Games.

FROM HIS PATRON:

"Zaitan is both my son and my champion. He has studied all the previous Great Games. He has the talent, skill, and ruthlessness required to win. When he does, his name will echo throughout the ages."

Anthony DeSaxe, Hades,
King of the Underworld

Jack stood on a low stone bridge in front of the dizzying vertical maze.

He was still not wearing any shoes.

Sky Monster wore a size thirteen: way too big for Jack. And E's boots were similarly too large.

His bare feet stood only inches above a broad lake.

By the smell of it and the steam rising from it, the lake was fed by some kind of sulfurous thermal spring.

It lapped against his stone bridge, leaving a yellow residue near his feet. It looked hot and unpleasant and the odor it gave off smelled toxic, almost cancerous.

Don't fall in, Jack thought.

Even though he was standing in front of the elaborate wall-maze, Jack had his back to it. He was looking in the opposite direction.

Having stepped a short way out onto the sulfurous lake via the bridge, he could now, in the full light of day, see Hades's mountain-palace in all its glory.

It stood in the center of what was indeed a vast circular meteor crater, and in addition to the various castles and fortresses Jack had seen before, he now saw an observatory-like structure high up on this side.

Looking lower, he saw the hostage carriages. The rails on which they stood ran in a flat circle that swept all the way around the bottom reaches of the mount, below a few royal viewing balconies.

In the better light, he could also see the summit of the peak now.

An elaborate cupola-like structure occupied the summit and from it, like an immense spiderweb, spread the vast camouflage netting that shaded the entire crater.

"The Kingdom of Hades," Jack said softly.

His thoughts were cut off by Monsieur Vacheron, speaking into his microphone.

"My lords and ladies, welcome to the Fourth Challenge! The famous vertical labyrinth. Ten champions shall enter the maze, but there is only one exit from it. Once that exit is used by *seven* champions, it will be closed and sealed.

"As you can see, two Golden Spheres sit inside the maze. To the champions who emerge from the maze with the spheres, the usual rewards shall go."

Jack looked up at the maze.

It was cut into a sheer flat-faced slab of stone that jutted out from the curved wall of the crater. Roughly twenty stories tall, it was a confusing tangle of horizontal walkways and vertical chutes, all cut at right angles to each other.

As he gazed up at the monstrously complex labyrinth, Jack saw the two Golden Spheres sitting in separate dead-end sections on either side of the central axis.

Jack tried to take in all the different levels of the maze.

As he did so, he noticed that not every horizontal section of walkway was made of thick stone.

Some sections were thinner and they seemed to be attached to hinges.

Trap doors, he thought.

Jesus . . .

Two gigantic water wheels turned at either end of the massive maze, lifting foul yellow water out of the lake in large steel dump trays.

Each tray probably held three hundred gallons, Jack guessed, and every few minutes, they dumped their contents into the maze. Gravity and a mechanism that caused the trap doors to open did the rest: the occasional trayloads of water plunged down through the maze as powerful waterfalls, ready to knock the unwary to injury or death.

Vacheron wasn't done.

He grinned malevolently. "It is not just the maze that defends the spheres."

At that moment, Hades's two lion-headed warriors, the black-clad Chaos and white-clad Fear, entered the maze via the exit at the top and quickly climbed down to the two dead ends containing the spheres, one for each sphere.

"To get the spheres, our champions will not only have to negotiate the maze, they will also have to best Chaos or Fear."

Vacheron grinned. "Although, keep your eyes open, for we may also see the arrival of another of Lord Hades's finest warriors," he said teasingly.

The royal audience murmured their awe and approval.

Up on the royal balcony, standing beside Iolanthe, Lily watched all this fearfully. She had spent the night in a very comfortable spare bedroom in Iolanthe's quarters, even though she would much rather have stayed with Jack and the others in their cell.

Vacheron held up a finger.

"As we all know, the goddess Artemis has always favored brave hunters, so there is one other way for a champion to escape the maze, *even after the exit is closed*. If a champion can catch the goddess's prize stag and bring it to the exit, he shall be allowed out. Of course he must do this while he himself is being hunted. Now, I hear you ask, what will be the Sacred Stag?"

At that moment, a small figure dressed in red appeared at the top of the maze.

Lily gasped.

It was the jester from the previous night's dinner, Mephisto. The cunning little fellow who had casually murdered the minotaur to entertain the royal guests.

The little jester wore a gaudy crown of antlers on his head. He waved his deadly flail and bowed gaily for the royal crowd.

From his position on the lake, Jack could only just see the little man in red with the antlers. He didn't know what to make of him.

Vacheron said, "Finally, each champion has chosen two companions to accompany him on this challenge. They will not be shackled to him this time. They may help him. They may hinder him. But their survival is not necessary. Only the champion's is. Luck to all."

Jack had been informed of this requirement when Vacheron had come to the hostage carriages earlier, and so now he stood on his stone platform with his two chosen companions:

Alby and Roxy, his little black poodle.

THE BRIDGE TO THE MAZE

To be fair, once he had laid eyes on the vertical maze and seen what it would require to traverse it, Jack really didn't have much choice in the matter of his partners.

Sky Monster's right forearm had been badly hurt during the Third Challenge: he wasn't going to be able to climb, let alone leap across voids or hang from edges. And Lily was away with the royals.

Which left Alby and the two dogs.

He could count on Alby. The kid, now twenty-one, was reliable and smart. When it came to a maze, Jack would've picked Alby anyway.

Since Roxy was smaller and lighter than Ash, he could carry her, like he was doing now. It helped that she was a dog with a serious protective streak. Who knew, maybe she could sniff out danger ahead of them.

Vacheron called, "Let the Fourth Challenge commence!"

And the madness began.

The other champions bolted off the mark, racing over the low stone bridge that led across the stinking lake to the base of the maze.

Alby made to move but Jack held him back with his hand.

"Wait. Not yet."

"Why?" Alby said.

And then it happened.

Two of the champions—a handsome young man wearing the crimson uniform of Hades's team and one of the Brazilian special forces men that Iolanthe had pointed out earlier—ran ahead of the others and leaped up to the lowest level of the maze . . .

. . . leaving their companions, two each, to take up defensive positions behind them, blocking the way of the other champions.

Those four defensive men then began fighting the other champions as they tried to get to the maze.

Punches were thrown. Men flew every which way. One fell into the steaming lake and screamed on contact with the hot yellow water.

"Jesus . . ." Alby breathed.

"It's a time-winning gambit," Jack said. "I figured someone might do it. Those four defensive guys aren't going to hold off all the other champions for long. It's literally a sacrifice play."

He was right.

The four defensive men were soon overwhelmed by the oncoming champions and tossed into the deadly pool, but not before they had taken out three men—all companions. In the meantime, their two champions, Hades's man and the Brazilian, had already reached the second level of the maze.

A great head start.

Jack turned to Alby. "Okay. Focus now. I want you to look at this maze, figure out a path through it and memorize it."

Alby blanched. "Memorize a way through *that*? It's like looking at a plate of spaghetti."

"Once we're in it, we won't be able to see anything, so we'll be guessing," Jack said. "Do the best you can. Pick one side, left or right. That cuts it in half. Count the levels next, so we always know how far we are from the top. Then try to memorize the exit."

"Okay, I'm on it—" Alby replied, before he cut himself off.

Something over Jack's shoulder had caught his eye.

Jack spun.

An absolute giant of a man was striding down the bridge behind them, having emerged from a doorway set into the base of Hades's mountain.

Like the two lion-helmeted warriors up in the maze, this man wore an elaborate helmet, only his was forged into the shape of a snarling snake. He wore modern body armor, with forearm and shin guards, all painted deep gray.

Most distinctively, however, he carried two vicious-looking whips, one in each massive hand.

Jack recognized them from his history books.

They were a particularly nasty variety of whip called a *scourge*. Used by the Romans, the scourge was a short whip, with perhaps five strands of rope or leather stretching out from a wooden handle. At the end of each rope were sharp blades designed to slash the skin of the victim.

The blades at the ends of this fellow's whips glistened in the light.

On the royal stage, Vacheron held up his hands in delight.

"My lords and ladies, welcome the Hydra!" he called. "There is no backing out of this challenge now!"

The royal spectators started clapping.

Lily just stared down in horror at Jack and Alby as they took off for the maze, fleeing from the advancing snake-headed warrior.

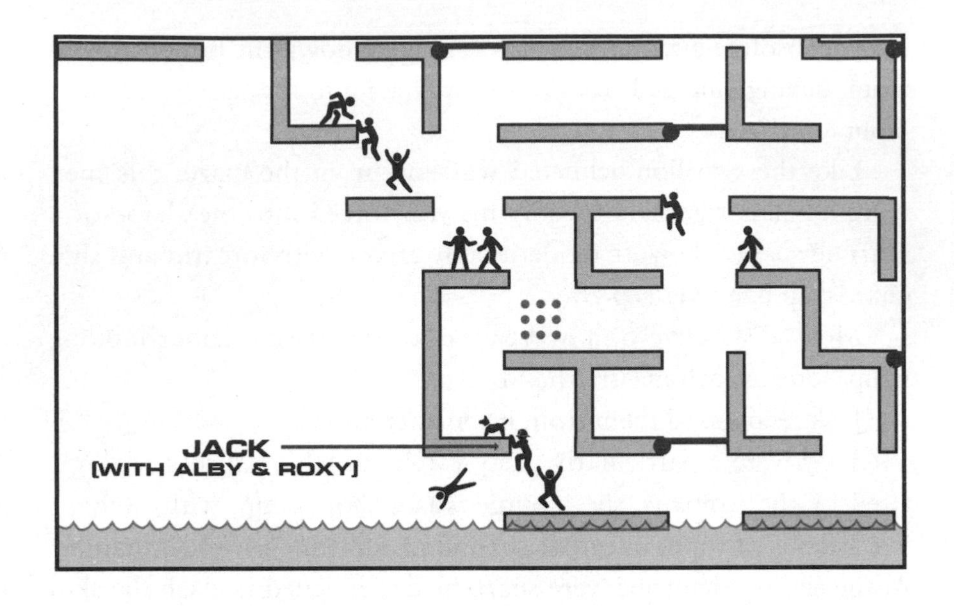

THE LOWER REACHES OF THE MAZE

"Go left!" Alby yelled to Jack and they made for that side of the maze.

The vertical labyrinth soared up into the air above them, eighteen levels high, as tall as an office building.

Its railless ledges were shallow and they were positioned at intervals of about six feet.

There were several ways to advance up the maze.

First, you could scale the vertical chutes using ladderlike handholds cut into the sheer walls of each chute.

Second, you could leap across a short void to another level. This was harder: it would take a healthy upward leap to wrap your elbows over the edge of the next level and then you had to haul yourself up onto it.

And third, well, the maze did face outward: you could—if you dared—climb up and around the *forward* edge of a ledge, dangling precariously above the sulfurous lake below.

Jack tucked Roxy inside his T-shirt as he leaped up from the ground level to the first level, poking his head above the ledge just in time to see a bulky Navy SEAL—a companion of the American champion named Monroe, left behind by his boss—come lunging at him with a knife!

Before Jack could even react, Roxy exploded from his T-shirt, barking and snapping, and she clamped her jaws around the SEAL's knife hand and clung to it like a terrier.

Startled, the SEAL recoiled, giving Jack the chance to reach up, grab him by the arm, and hurl him down into the lake, yanking his poodle from him as he did so.

The Navy SEAL splashed into the stinking lake and shouted in pain before going under.

Jack placed Roxy down on the ledge.

"Good dog," he said as he clambered up, then reached back down for Alby.

Alby joined them on the first level.

"Christ, a maze is hard enough," Jack breathed. "But getting through one with all these assholes also in it, that's just messed up. Come on."

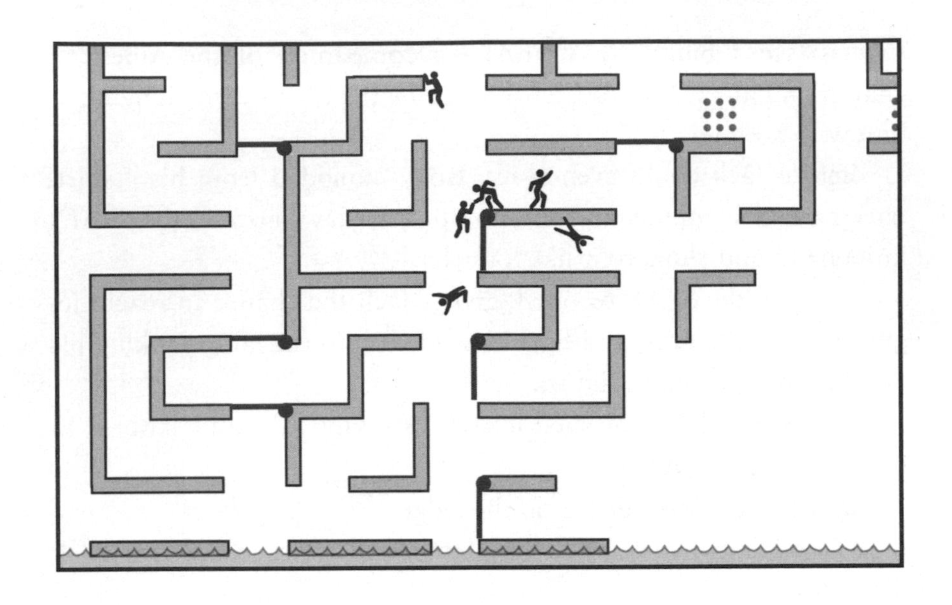

SCARECROW VS. THE INDIAN MARCOS

The US Marine named Scarecrow had chosen the right-hand side of the maze.

He ran with Astro and the other male Marine, a nuggety lieutenant with sandy blond hair named Tim Bowles, call sign *Tomahawk*. Seeing the maze from his hostage carriage—and the nimbleness it would require to scale it—Scarecrow had decided to let Mother sit this one out.

After ascending five levels, his crew had come face-to-face with the team of another champion: an Indian soldier who wore the black headband of the elite Indian Marine Commando force, abbreviated as MARCOS.

A scuffle ensued as the Indian commando fled, leaving his men to fight—and delay—Scarecrow's crew.

Scarecrow tossed one of the Indian's companions off the ledge and he plummeted to the foul lake thirty feet below.

Tomahawk grappled with the other companion and they fell to

the ledge together. They rolled for a few moments until the floor beneath them just spontaneously dropped away!

Trapdoor.

As the two men fell through the trap door, Astro dove forward and grasped Tomahawk's wrist, stopping his fall.

The Indian man wasn't so lucky. He fell all the way down the chute, splashing into the scalding water.

Jack and Alby also encountered more hostile foes.

When they were four levels up, they were confronted by the other swarthy companion of the Navy SEAL, DeShawn Monroe, who had also been left behind by his champion.

The SEAL lunged at Jack with a knife, but Jack ducked, grabbed the man's wrist, and threw him judo-style, slamming him down onto the ledge—

—only to discover it wasn't a solid section of ledge but a trap door.

The moment the SEAL hit it, the small section of floor beneath him flipped downward on a hinge and, to Jack's surprise, the man instantly dropped from view.

Watching from the royal balcony, Lily saw the SEAL drop through the trap door and fall.

Thanks to a fiendish mechanism of the maze system, *all the trap doors* positioned directly beneath the one he had fallen through opened at the same time: causing the SEAL to fall *all the way* to the bottom of the maze, where he plunged into the stinking lake with a pained shout, never to surface again.

Lily gasped. "Oh my God."

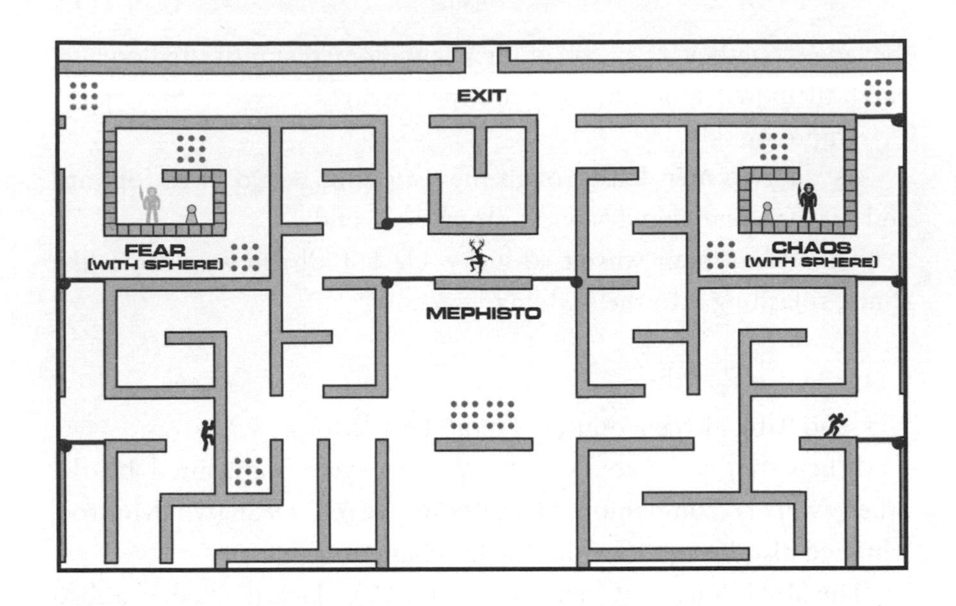

THE GOLDEN SPHERES

When viewed from the royal balcony, the maze was alive with movement.

With ten champions in there and each—at least initially—accompanied by two partners, there were close on thirty people zigging and zagging, climbing and leaping, searching and prowling through the vertical labyrinth.

To Lily it looked like an ants' nest: a convoluted series of ledges and shafts filled with moving people.

And then she saw the two leading champions—the pair who had left their partners on the bridge to delay all the others—as they came to the two dead ends containing the Golden Spheres, up in the higher reaches of the maze.

The first champion was one of Iolanthe's two Brazilian men.

His name was Sergeant Mauricio Corazon and he had once been a member of the Brazilian Army's crack special forces unit known as the *Comando de Operações Especiais*. After being found guilty with five other troopers of the gang rape of a pretty young secretary on their base, he had been dishonorably discharged and sentenced to twenty years in prison.

After Corazon spent a year in a filthy São Paulo prison, his local bishop appeared one day and offered him and his five comrades their freedom in exchange for participating in a holy mission: the Great Games.

Having scaled the right-hand side of the maze, Corazon arrived at the fifteenth level, at the dead end containing one of the Golden Spheres.

Standing in front of the glimmering sphere was the black lion-helmeted figure of Chaos. He gripped a sinister-looking scimitar in one hand.

Corazon's eyes narrowed. He knew how to fight. Like all special forces operators from his country, he was an expert in capoeira, the deadly Brazilian martial art. He could take this guy in his stupid helmet.

Corazon drew his knife.

Up on the royal balcony, standing beside Lily, Iolanthe watched the confrontation intently.

Beside her, Cardinal Ricardo Mendoza did the same.

Iolanthe said, "Now we find out if your Brazilian psychopaths are worthy."

Mendoza nodded. "They are more than worthy."

Corazon attacked Chaos with a flurry of flashing knife moves.

Chaos parried his every blow—easily—before ducking and slashing Corazon's throat with his sword, almost decapitating him.

The black lion-headed warrior then hurled the dead Brazilian off the ledge and the limp body sailed fifteen levels down the face of the maze before it landed with a splash in the lake far below.

★ ★ ★

Iolanthe turned to Cardinal Mendoza and raised her eyebrows.

Mendoza swallowed. "Oh."

In the left-hand dead end containing the other Golden Sphere, a different kind of confrontation took place.

The young man wearing the crimson colors of Lord Hades arrived there to find the white lion, Fear, guarding the Golden Sphere with his own curving sword, waiting for him.

Again, the royal spectators watched keenly.

Lily heard a few of them whisper, "It's Zaitan. Hades's second son . . ."

Lily saw Hades himself watching the encounter closely.

She also saw Dion—Hades's first son and heir—watching with extreme interest.

Zaitan drew his own short sword and stared levelly at Fear.

They engaged.

This fight was far more evenly matched.

While Fear was taller, Zaitan moved faster, and rather than try to match the lion-helmed warrior for strength, he moved quickly, parrying blows and then diving away, making Fear chase him.

Lily frowned as she watched the fight.

There was something wrong about it. Something odd. She had the distinct impression that Fear wasn't fighting as hard as he should; definitely not as hard as Chaos had fought the Brazilian commando.

And then, as Fear lunged at him with a lusty swing, Zaitan slipped under the swipe, scooped up the sphere and slid *out and over* the front edge of the ledge, quickly dropping to the level below, with the sphere.

The royals gasped, then cheered.

Bearing the precious Golden Sphere, Zaitan now moved with greater speed and confidence. He raced away from the dead end, lest Fear come after him, and slithered up the last three levels before popping out through the exit at the top of the maze.

Safely out of the deadly labyrinth, he looked over at the royal balcony and with a broad grin on his face, thrust the sphere above his head triumphantly.

The royal spectators roared with delight.

Hades clapped approvingly.

Dion clapped vigorously, cheering loudly at his brother's achievement.

Further down on the left-hand side of the maze, Jack and Alby both spun at the roar from the royal balcony.

Alby turned to Jack. "Someone's got a sphere already."

"Keep going," Jack said. "We can't stop moving."

There was one other dangerous element lurking in the maze.

Mephisto the jester, wearing his gaudy antlers.

He danced jauntily around the middle levels of the labyrinth, Charlie Chaplin–style, twirling his deadly double-balled flail as if he didn't have a care in the world.

And then he stopped, hearing something, and with frightening speed, he suddenly descended two levels, moving with incredible lightness and nimbleness out over the forward edges of the ledges before he landed without a sound right behind a lone champion.

It was the Indian MARCOS commando: the one who had thrown his partners at Scarecrow and fled.

After leaving his men to fight Scarecrow, the MARCOS commando was now hopelessly lost.

He had stumbled across the center of the maze and into a dead end and had had to backtrack out of it. Alone, afraid and desperate, he had completely lost his bearings and now all he wanted to do was find a way upward.

He held in his hand a long serrated knife with a steel knuckle-duster grip.

Mephisto crept up behind him, gripping his wicked flail.

The Indian commando didn't know he was there.

The royal spectators saw it all, but Mephisto turned to them and put a finger to his grinning lips: *Shhhh!*

Then, still stalking the hapless Indian commando, he began theatrically raising and lowering his feet, as if walking on tiptoes.

Lily watched the scene in total horror. These Games were a foul awful thing, but she found the jester's jokey treatment of the violence he was about to inflict somehow even more frightening.

The little red jester crept closer to the oblivious Indian.

The crowd held their breath.

Then Mephisto tapped the Indian on the shoulder.

The Indian spun around, raising his knife.

But as the Indian turned, quick as a whip, Mephisto ducked around him, so that the little man again stood behind the commando's back.

Mephisto shrugged comically toward the royal balcony.

The royal spectators laughed.

The Indian commando whirled again and this time, Mephisto raised his double-balled flail until it was spinning like helicopter rotors and he flung it . . . and the two heavy brass balls, joined by their connecting chain, wrapped around the poor Indian commando's head.

The result was fast and devastating.

As the chain hit the Indian in the forehead, the two brass balls whipped around his head *and came back*: they slammed into his eyes with phenomenal force, crashing into the sockets with twin explosions of blood before driving into the poor man's brain.

The Indian stood for a few seconds, but he was already dead.

Mephisto stepped forward and unwrapped his flail from the dead man's face—revealing the hideously smashed-in eye sockets—before he let the body collapse in a heap to the ledge.

The Indian commando, a member of the MARCOS, one of the finest commando units in the world, had been defeated in seconds by the jester.

Mephisto bowed for the royal crowd.

The crowd applauded appreciatively.

Then Mephisto placed his boot on the Indian's body like a victorious hunter and flexed his arms in a muscleman's pose.

The royals laughed.

Lily didn't. She just swallowed in fear.

Then suddenly Mephisto's head jerked up—he had sensed someone else nearby—and looking down below the jester, Lily saw another champion and his partners unwittingly approaching Mephisto's position from below.

Jack, Alby, and Roxy.

Mephisto scurried away.

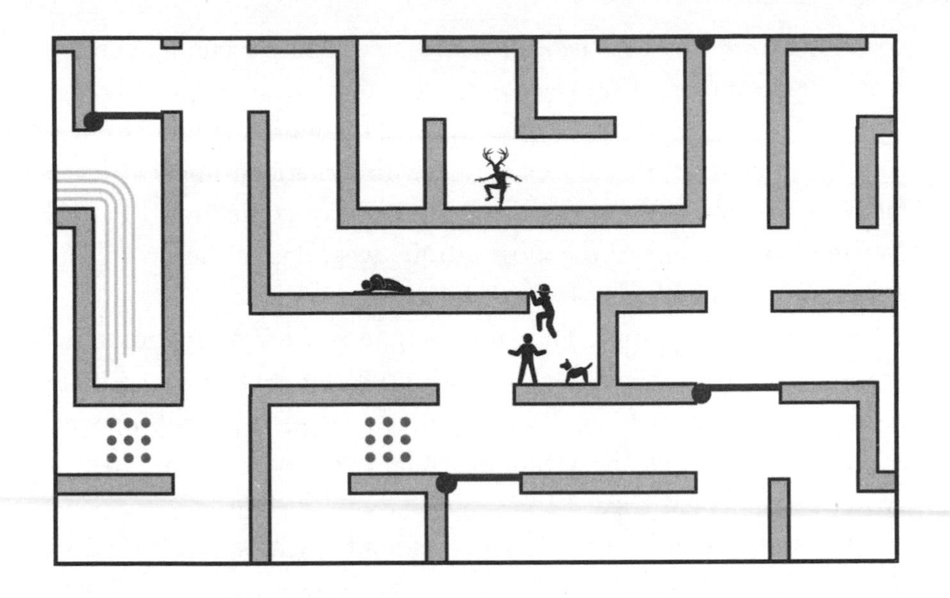

JACK VS. MEPHISTO

Jack hauled himself up onto a new level and immediately saw a body lying on the flat stone ledge in front of him.

It was the corpse of the Indian commando.

He froze, instantly cautious.

The killer might still be nearby.

Jack turned to Alby, waiting on the level below, holding Roxy. "Alby, hang back a second. Don't come up yet."

Jack drew his knife as he slowly approached the slumped body. It was lying facedown.

Reaching forward with his bare right foot, Jack rolled it over.

The face of the dead MARCOS commando stared back at him with its crushed eye sockets.

"Christ," Jack said, wincing.

He bent over the corpse, examining it.

The Indian commando had died so suddenly, he was still clutching his knuckle-duster-gripped knife.

Jack checked the body for more weapons.

"Now *that*'s useful," he said aloud, unclipping a gun-like device from the dead man's belt.

Like many special forces units around the world, the Indian Marine Commandos often do exercises with American units to learn from them. One weapon that the Indians have copied from the US Marine Corps is one of the most unique weapons of the world: the Armalite MH-12 Maghook.

A variety of grapple gun, the Maghook fires a gas-propelled grappling hook that, thanks to a high-powered magnet, can adhere to sheer metallic surfaces. Because of its complex propulsion and cable-reeling systems, the Maghook has proven to be difficult to replicate, but India has tried.

The Indian copy of the Maghook is made by its special weapons division, the ARDE, so they call it the ARDE-7 grapple gun. It is a crude copy, to be sure, but it's compact and it works.

And this poor asshole won't be needing his anymore, Jack thought as he took the dead man's ARDE-7.

Bent over the commando's body, Jack never saw the small red-clad figure slowly and silently lowering himself out and around the ledge above him.

Mephisto moved like a calculating monkey, dangling from one arm high above the lake, his double-balled weapon held in his spare hand.

On the royal balcony, all the royal spectators held their collective breaths as they watched Mephisto lower himself behind the unsuspecting Jack.

Lily leaned forward, opening her mouth to shout a warning—

"Ah-ah-ah," Hades said from beside her. "Don't say a word. We must not give our champions any assistance."

Lily bit her lip, feeling totally powerless, as over on the maze, Mephisto's feet landed silently on the ledge immediately behind Jack.

Beside her on the balcony, other royals—including an old lady in pearls—sipped champagne from crystal glasses as they keenly watched the scene.

Lily glanced from the old lady to Jack to Hades before she ever so casually bumped the old lady's arm, knocking the champagne glass from her hand, sending it sailing over the balcony's railing.

"Oh dear, I'm terribly sorry," Lily apologized.

A second later, the crystal glass smashed against the mountainside twenty feet below the balcony, exploding into a thousand pieces, the noise ringing out like a gunshot.

Jack had just clipped the dead Indian's grapple gun to his own belt and was rising to stand when, from across the lake, he heard the champagne glass smash and he spun at the sound—only to see the bizarre figure of Mephisto, short, red and deadly, standing there *right behind him.*

"What the hell—?" he gasped as Mephisto swung his flail, cracking it like a whip.

Jack ducked and the two brass balls clanged loudly as they slammed together at the exact spot where his head had been.

Then Mephisto was leaping at Jack and it was all Jack could do to fend off the demonic little jester's blows.

Mephisto swung his flail, Jack rolled and the heavy brass balls made deep dents in the stone ledge.

Mephisto lashed out with his clawlike fingernails and one fingernail drew a slashing line of blood across Jack's left cheek.

Jack raised his knife, only to see Mephisto crack his flail again. One of the heavy balls hit Jack's knife hand and the knife went flying from his grasp, tumbling into the lake below.

Jack actually managed to land a good punch on Mephisto then, knocking the jester toward a nearby chute . . . only for the little man to jam some kind of handheld pneumatic mountain-climbing device into the stone wall and use it as a handhold to stop his fall.

Then Mephisto was back in Jack's face and he swung his flail again and this time one of the brass balls hit Jack a glancing blow on the side of the head and he saw stars and dropped to his knees.

Jack's vision clouded. He was about to lose consciousness. He wanted to roll off the ledge and swing down to the one below, but his muscles wouldn't obey.

Out of the corner of his eye, he saw the demonic little red man standing over him, raising his flail to finish him off.

Whack.

Alby hit Mephisto in the back of the head with the dead Indian's knife, leading with its knuckle-duster grip.

Mephisto dropped instantly, out cold.

Alby slid to Jack's side, started slapping his face. "Come on, Jack! Stay awake! Stay awake!"

Jack shook his head, regaining some clarity, and raised himself up on one elbow.

He looked from Alby—with Roxy snuggled inside his zipped jacket—to the unconscious jester and back to Alby again.

"Thanks."

Jack stared at Mephisto, at his red tattooed face, his subdermal horns, his sharpened teeth. "What is *that*?"

Suddenly, Mephisto groaned.

Alby said, "I don't know, but I sure don't want to be here when he wakes up. Let's get moving up this maze."

They hurdled the slumped body of the jester and sprinted away into the maze.

On the royal balcony, after glancing down at the smashed champagne glass, Hades gave Lily a meaningful look.

Lily simply returned his gaze and shrugged. "Alcohol makes people so clumsy. Your guests really should be mindful of their drinking."

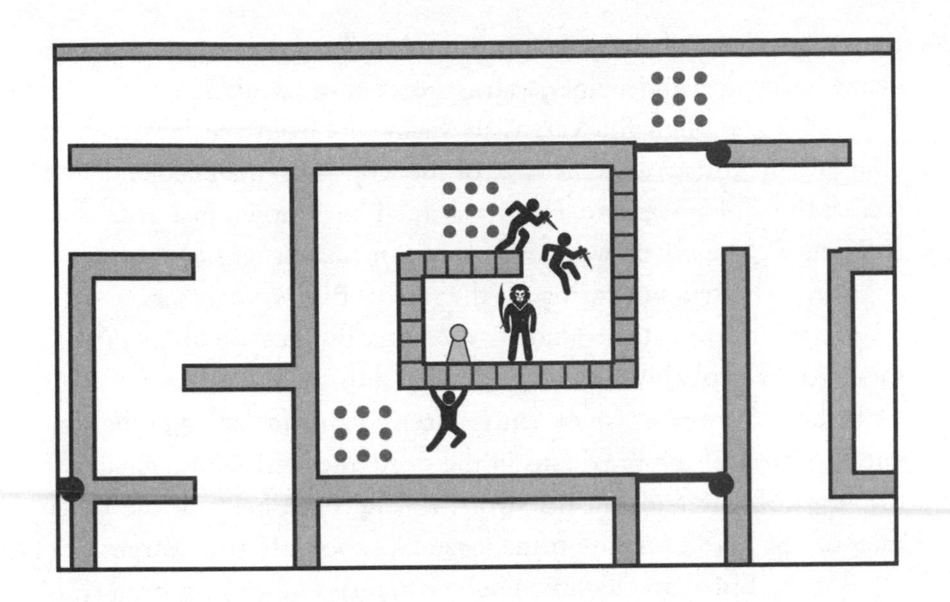

THE SECOND GOLDEN SPHERE—VARGAS VS. CHAOS

While Jack was doing battle with Mephisto on the left-hand side of the maze, high up on the right-hand side, another champion was making a run at the second Golden Sphere, the one defended by the black lion, Chaos.

It was the second Brazilian champion. His name was Sergeant Victor Vargas and he hailed from the same disgraced special forces unit as Sergeant Mauricio Corazon.

Unlike Corazon, Vargas had not raced headlong up the maze alone. Rather, he had done it with his two partners and now they closed in on the dead end containing Chaos and the second sphere.

Having seen Corazon's body go sailing down the face of the maze, Vargas had conceived a different plan to get the sphere.

He sent his two partners into the dead end ahead of him while he remained on the level below.

His two partners stormed the dead end, attacking Chaos with knives.

Chaos responded with terrible blows from his massive sword,

but the two Brazilians were quick and agile and they managed to evade his swings and swipes, at least for a short while . . .

. . . long enough for Vargas to sneak up from the level below, climbing up and around the edge of the ledge into the dead end, and snatch the Golden Sphere. He then leaped back down just as Chaos, still fighting the other two, saw him out of the corner of his eye.

Vargas bolted, not caring for the fate of his two partners.

He hadn't told them that it was actually part of his plan that they would probably die, and die they did: seeing Vargas race off with the sphere sent Chaos into a frenzy and in his rage, he dispatched both of the Brazilians in the dead end with him. He cut off the head of one and ran his sword through the belly of the other then tossed both of them off the maze and took off after Vargas.

But the Brazilian champion had gotten too much of a head start and he nimbly ascended the last couple of levels of the maze, and just as Chaos rose onto the topmost level behind him, Vargas slithered through the exit with the all-important Golden Sphere in his possession.

The spectators on the royal balcony cheered.

Chief among them was Cardinal Mendoza. He gave Iolanthe a smug knowing smile as he clapped heartily.

On the left-hand side of the maze, Jack once again heard cheers coming from the royal balcony.

"Damn it," he said. "Someone must have gotten the second sphere. Now we gotta be one of the seven to get out through the exit. Can you remember the way up?"

Alby gulped. "I don't know but I can try."

"Alby, there's no other person in the world I'd rather follow through a maze," Jack said. "Lead the way."

Jack wasn't the only champion to hear the cheers from the royal balcony. All the other champions had heard them and they also knew what they meant.

The other champions had begun to converge on the uppermost level of the maze—some with their companions, some without—and one after the other, they climbed out through the exit hatch.

Two levels below the escape level were Scarecrow and his team.

"Pick it up, Marines," he said to Astro and Tomahawk. "Let's get out of this death trap."

The three of them came to a void leading to the second-to-top level of the maze. Astro led the way, followed by Tomahawk, with Scarecrow bringing up the rear.

"This level is clear," Astro said, peering forward, as Tomahawk reached back down to lift Scarecrow—

—just as a huge fist seized Scarecrow's left ankle and yanked him back down to the level below.

Scarecrow landed on his back, hitting the ground hard, and looked up to see the flashing blades of one of the Hydra's scourges rushing at his face.

Scarecrow rolled. The blades slashed the stone beside his head, creating sparks. The other scourge came down. He rolled again and it missed again.

From his position on the ground, Scarecrow unleashed a powerful upward kick at the Hydra's groin.

Whack!

But the Hydra just stood there staring at him, unharmed. The codpiece on his armor was too strong.

"Right . . ." Scarecrow said.

But then he glimpsed a weak point in the big warrior's armor: beneath the jawline of the man's snake helmet, there was a sliver of bare skin. It was the only section of bare skin visible on his entire body.

Scarecrow sprang up from the floor, leading with a superfast fist. The blow connected with the Hydra's exposed throat and the Hydra doubled over, gagging.

Scarecrow didn't hang around to finish him off. He just leaped like a hurdler *onto* the bent-over Hydra's back and used him as a human platform to jump up into Tomahawk's waiting hands.

The three Marines then took off, found an aperture that took them up to the topmost level, and moments later, to their great relief, they slithered up and out through the exit hatch.

On the royal balcony, Vacheron kept the spectators updated.

"Ten champions entered the maze! Two have been killed—one of the Land Kingdom's champions from Brazil, killed by Chaos during an attempt to grab a sphere, and one Indian commando representing our illustrious host, the Lord of the Underworld, who met his fate at the hands of that little rascal Mephisto."

Vacheron grinned. "Of the eight still alive, six others have now left the labyrinth. Two remain: the fifth warrior representing the Land Kingdom and Warrant Officer Monroe from the Sea Kingdom. But when the next champion leaves the labyrinth, the exit will be sealed. The other champion left in the maze will be hunted by Chaos, Fear, and the Hydra until he is dead or . . . if he dares . . . until that champion catches Mephisto in his capacity as the Sacred Stag and brings him to the exit. Some would say it is better to die at the hands of Hades's warriors than to attempt such a task."

★ ★ ★

Jack and Alby hurried through the maze, carrying Roxy between them.

Up they scrambled, guided by Alby, racing across the horizontal ledges, hurdling voids and trap doors, and scaling the vertical shafts.

Because of the route Alby had taken, they had gone almost all the way to the left-hand edge of the maze, over near the giant water wheel there. The great wheel turned, dumping hundreds of gallons of superheated sulfurous water into the maze every so often; cascades of the sickly yellow fluid would tumble down several chutes before falling to the lake in spectacular waterfalls.

At length, they reached the topmost level and saw the exit: it was in the exact center of the eighteenth level, an illuminated square hatch cut into the stone ceiling perhaps twenty yards away.

"Nice work, Alby," Jack said.

Standing on the top level of the maze was like standing on the roof of an eighteen-story building. The maze dropped away beneath them. The steaming lake at the bottom was a long way down.

"No lingering," Jack said. "We don't know how many other champions have already left the maze—"

Just then, another champion popped up out of a vertical shaft a short way in front of them—halfway *between* them and the exit—bloodied and alone and scrambling on his hands and knees . . .

. . . because right behind him was the white lion, Fear.

The champion scrambled away from Jack, Alby, and Roxy, heading for the exit. Fear followed him, his back to Jack.

Jack recognized the champion.

It was the black Navy SEAL with the tats on his arms: DeShawn Monroe, The Finisher, the guy who had left his companions behind earlier to fight.

And right now, he wasn't doing well.

He had blood all over his face and neck, and as he half ran, half crawled down the length of the ledge, he favored his left leg.

Fear, on the other hand, was moving freely, unhurt. He was casually stalking the wounded SEAL. Fear kicked Monroe from behind, sending the wounded man sprawling forward.

Then Fear calmly wiped the bloody blade of his sword on his pantleg, preparing to finish off The Finisher.

Jack clenched his teeth.

Whether it arose out of loyalty to a fellow soldier or from an overdeveloped sense of justice at seeing a wounded man about to be callously killed, either way, what Jack saw just plain pissed him off and despite himself, he charged forward.

Since he'd lost his knife in the fight with Mephisto, he just took ten quick strides forward and launched himself at Fear from behind, slamming into his back, crash-tackling the giant warrior.

Fear grunted as he dropped to his knees and Jack went sprawling on top of him.

The Navy SEAL, Monroe, turned in surprise. He'd clearly thought he was done for and now this had happened.

Fear kicked Jack off him, almost tossing him off the ledge and down the face of the maze. But Jack landed on his feet and he unleashed a big sidekick to the kneeling lion-helmeted warrior's mask.

The kick sent Fear's head flailing backward and it hit the rear wall of the ledge hard.

The blow against the wall cracked the visor of Fear's helmet and in a fleeting instant, as the warrior turned back to face Jack, Jack saw his eyes.

Angry brown eyes.

Jack called, "Finisher! Help me! We can beat him together!"

The Finisher was still lying dumbly on the ground on the other side of Fear, clearly stunned at this turn of events.

Fear began to stand.

"I can't beat him by myself," Jack urged. "Help me!"

Inhaling deeply, gathering his strength, The Finisher rose to his feet . . . and bolted away down the ledge, loping toward the exit.

Jack's mouth fell open. "Son of a bitch . . ."

Fear reached his full height.

And now stood between Jack and the exit to the maze.

Jack watched as DeShawn Monroe climbed up through the exit. No sooner was he out than a hatch slammed shut and the illuminated exit hole went dark.

"Oh, no," Alby gasped. "He must have been the seventh champion to get out. The maze is closed. We're stuck in here unless we . . ."

Jack backed away from the advancing figure of Fear. "Unless we find that jester dressed as a stag and bring him to the exit. Quickly! Go back down, now!"

Alby leaped back down the nearest chute, with Roxy tucked into his jacket. Jack followed as Fear broke into a run down the topmost ledge after them.

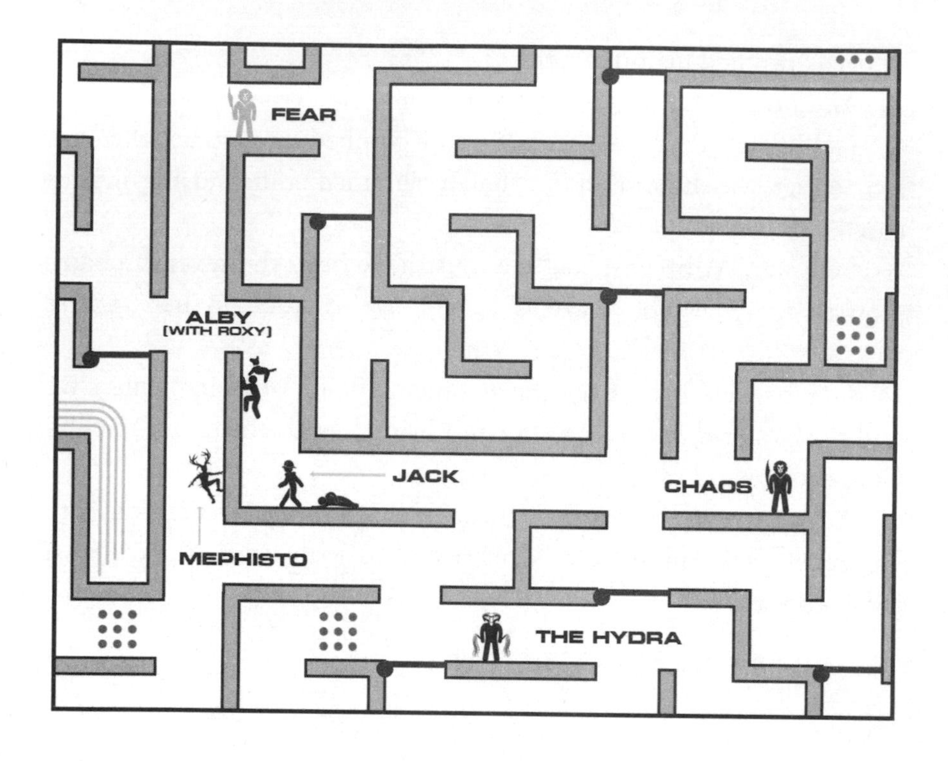

THE HUNT FOR THE SACRED STAG

The Fourth Challenge entered a new phase.

The maze was quiet now. The sounds of men running and shouting and of swords clashing had ceased.

The creaking of the two water wheels on either side of the maze and the sloshing of their buckets collecting water from the lake were the only sounds.

It was now a three-sided hunt: while Jack and Alby hunted the antler-clad Mephisto, Chaos, Fear, and the Hydra hunted them.

The spectators on the royal balcony watched with rapt attention as Jack, Alby, and Roxy descended through the left-hand side of the maze, heading for the spot where they had left the unconscious Mephisto.

While Jack couldn't see it, the royals could: Hades's three warriors were closing in on him from three sides. White Fear from above, black Chaos from the right, and the gray-suited Hydra from below.

With Alby and Roxy behind him, Jack came to the ledge where he had last seen Mephisto.

Stepping down onto it from a vertical shaft, he saw the body of the dead Indian MARCOS trooper lying exactly where he had last seen it.

Jack whispered to Alby: "That creepy little red guy should be just on the other side of that corpse—"

He stepped down fully onto the ledge.

The jester's body was gone.

Mephisto was no longer lying unconscious beside the corpse of the Indian commando.

Jack spun. "Shit, he woke up—"

A shrill cackle echoed out from somewhere nearby.

"Looking for *meeeeee*?" a high-pitched voice sang out.

The royal spectators were enthralled.

Mephisto *was barely four feet from* Jack, on the other side of the vertical stone wall that separated them.

"Such good theater . . ." the prince named George said.

Gripping the balcony's handrail with white knuckles, Lily scowled at him.

Jack hadn't heard Mephisto speak before, but now that he had, he wished he hadn't. The jester's twee voice sounded like fingernails on a chalkboard.

"Because I *seeeeeee* you!" he called.

Jack whirled and glimpsed the little man above and behind him—a moment before Mephisto yanked his head from view.

He's playing with me.

"Be careful when you hunt the Sacred Stag!" Mephisto's voice called. "We wouldn't want the hunter to become the hunted."

A sudden thump made Jack turn again and now he saw the towering black figure of Chaos standing on his level, not twenty yards away and approaching fast.

Jack turned to Alby. "Go! Follow that jester!"

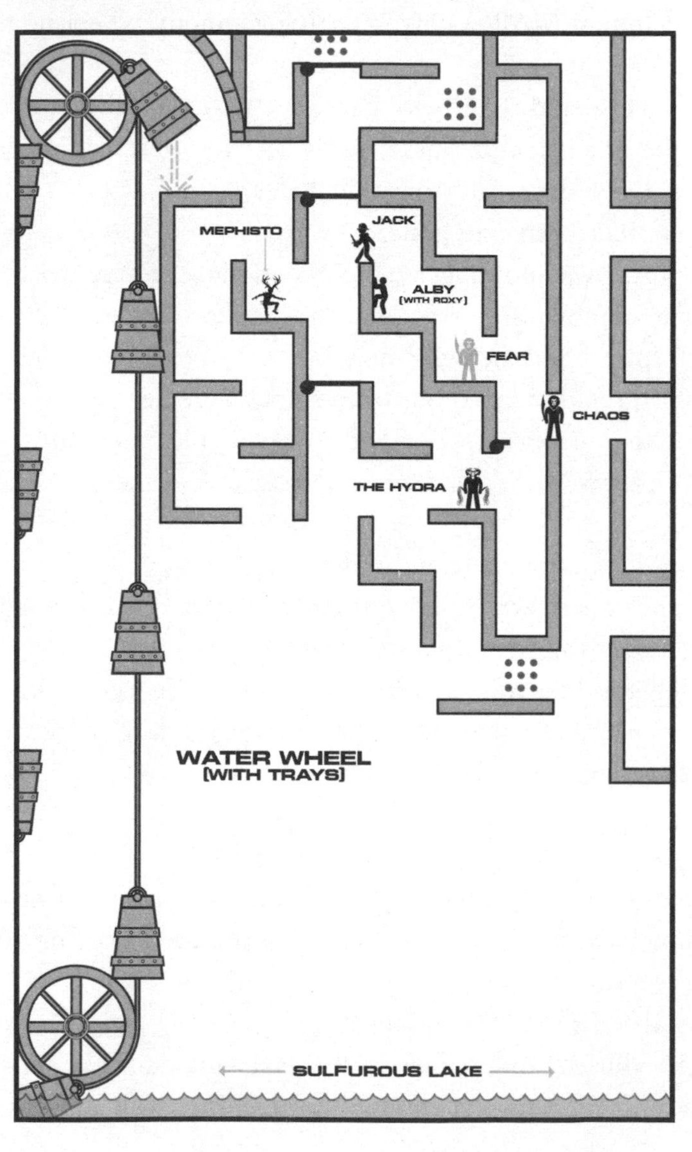

Mephisto danced away into the far left-hand reaches of the maze, heading toward the slow-turning water wheel there.

Jack and Alby gave chase, crossing a vertical chute before moving up a steplike section of ledges and shafts.

As they moved, Jack would periodically turn to look behind them.

Their pursuers were close now: Fear, the Hydra, and Chaos.

Jack pressed on. He couldn't see it but he guessed his three pursuers would fan out and seal off all the available escape routes from this section of the maze.

Lily watched the deadly endgame taking place in front of her.

"They're fanning out," the prince named George explained to the woman beside him. "Fear, Chaos, and the Hydra are sealing off all the escape routes. The fifth warrior is a rat in a trap. This won't take long."

"Got any ideas?" Alby asked breathlessly as he scaled a vertical wall behind Jack. Roxy's furry black head poked out of his jacket's front zipper.

"I remember this section of the maze," Jack said. "There's only one vertical outlet and two horizontal ones. I imagine that little red creep is blocking the upper exit. He lured us in here and now those other bastards are blocking the horizontal outlets behind us."

"He lured us here?" Alby asked, looking at the ledges around them.

"I imagine these assholes have practiced in this maze many times before the Games," Jack said. "Probably practiced by hunting some poor minotaurs. To finish someone off, you lure them into a containable section of the maze, a section with few exits, and then you slowly close the noose."

"So, do you have a plan for getting out of this noose?" Alby asked anxiously.

Fear was only a couple of diagonal ledges below them now and closing in. A sudden gush of stinking yellow water from the water wheel whooshed through the ledges near them.

Jack looked out and around their ledge. His gaze fell on the slow-turning water wheel at the edge of the maze, its iron dump trays going up and down. The dump trays looked like heavy-duty mine cars.

"Maybe . . ." he said absently.

He turned back to Alby. "If we're gonna live, I have to catch this slippery little red guy and he's not gonna give up without a fight. I can't win this in a straight-up fight. I'm gonna have to 'win ugly.' "

At that moment, Jack reached the top of their ascending-diagonally path and peered over it . . .

. . . to behold Mephisto standing on a ledge on the other side of a narrow void, lazily twirling his flail, smiling nastily at him, waiting for him.

Jack turned to Alby and whispered, "Okay, listen. When the fighting starts, you'll have a chance to get out through the top outlet. Go through it and get to the top level of the maze. I'll meet you up there . . . if I live."

"If you live," Alby said softly.

"Alby Calvin," Jack said, taking the Indian's knuckle-duster knife from Alby and looking him in the eye. "If I don't survive this, you won't either. They'll hunt you down and kill you. So let me say this: I love you, kid. You've been a loyal friend to Lily and to me. You've grown into a fine young man and I love you like a son. If this is it, give 'em hell."

He held out his hand and they clasped firmly.

"No matter what happens, we'll see each other again," Jack said, and with those words, knife in hand, he leaped across the little void to do battle with the jester.

Jack landed in front of Mephisto.

It was a small ledge. It had a wall on one side. On the other there was nothing but a short drop down a chute to a trap door. Below that trap door, Jack knew, was nothing but a long drop to the deadly lake below.

"Greetings, fifth warrior," the jester said in his eerie voice. "Are you ready to die?"

"Let's dance," Jack said flatly.

The jester bared his sharpened teeth. "Let's."

With shocking speed, he rushed at Jack, hurling his blurring flail.

Only for Jack to do a most unexpected thing.

He held his knife out in front of him, pointing the blade vertically.

The deadly flail wrapped around the blade, its speeding brass balls clanging together loudly and harmlessly two feet in front of Jack's face.

Mephisto frowned, perplexed. This was the only way to defuse the power of a flail: give it something other than your own head to wrap itself around.

As the jester paused, Jack took his chance and did something that he figured Mephisto had never experienced in his practice sessions in the maze.

He grabbed the jester by the lapels and leaped off the ledge with him, dropping back-first down the nearby chute toward the trap door one level below.

Jack slammed into the trap door and, as it was designed to do, at the impact, it swung open . . .

. . . and suddenly Jack and Mephisto were clear of the maze, falling together through open air toward the lake.

The royal spectators gasped as one as they saw the two tiny figures of Jack and Mephisto drop from the left-hand end of the maze.

As he fell, Mephisto squealed in terror. He definitely hadn't anticipated this.

But Jack had.

As he fell, he drew from his belt the grapple gun he'd taken from the dead Indian commando earlier and fired it up and to the left.

With a gaseous *whump*, the gun's grappling hook flew upward, its cable extending out behind it, and it grabbed purchase on one of the ledges near the extreme left-hand edge of the maze.

With a sudden snap, the cable went taut and abruptly Jack—still gripping Mephisto roughly—swung to the left, toward the slow-turning water wheel.

Their swing curved upward and Jack landed perfectly on one of the large iron dump trays that lifted water from the lake, his feet standing on its four-inch-thick rust-covered edge.

The moment they were on the dump tray, Jack ruthlessly slammed the little jester's head against the iron edge. The jester's head bounced hard off it and he went limp, knocked out for the second time in an hour.

Jack then reeled in his grappling hook and, to the astonishment of the royal audience, rode the water wheel upward.

★ ★ ★

When he leaped off the water wheel up near the top of the maze, Alby was there waiting.

Holding the limp antler-headed body of Mephisto over his shoulder, Jack landed beside him.

"Nice plan," Alby said.

"Like I said, win ugly. Let's move," Jack said.

Chaos, Fury, and the Hydra were still rising up through the levels below them.

Jack and Alby bolted for the exit.

They arrived at the closed exit hatch just as their three pursuers appeared on the topmost level, running hard.

Jack pounded on the hatch, yelling, "We have the stag! We have the stag!"

The hatch was opened from above.

Jack pushed Alby up through the exit hole, handed Mephisto up to him and then leaped up and out of the deadly maze a bare few seconds before Chaos arrived behind him.

Jack and Alby lay on their backs on the roof of the giant maze, panting and breathless, nineteen stories above the lake.

"I don't know . . . how much more of this . . . I can take," Jack gasped between heaving breaths.

"Me neither," Alby agreed.

Roxy crawled out from Alby's jacket front and began licking Jack on the nose.

Beside them, Mephisto groaned. Slowly, painfully, he opened his eyes.

Still lying on his back, Jack looked over at the deadly jester.

"Got you, motherfucker," he said.

A SECRET HISTORY III

THE OMEGA EVENT

THE EGYPTIAN SYMBOL ANKH

Knowledge must continually be renewed by ceaseless effort, if it is not to be lost.

ALBERT EINSTEIN

MAE MERRIWEATHER'S HOME
BROOME, AUSTRALIA

"Okay, so what have we got?" Mae said.

She, Stretch, and Pooh Bear sat in her living room, surrounded by a mess of books, scrolls, three laptop computers, two iPads, and even some statues.

They had worked through the night looking into any and every reference to the Hydra Galaxy and the tetragammadion that had been used over the millennia to represent it.

"This Hydra image appeared all over the ancient world," Stretch said. "There are records of it being carved into temples and shrines in places as diverse as India, Pakistan, Ireland, England, Belize, Guatemala, Australia, Cambodia, even Easter Island."

He glanced at Pooh Bear. "We never got there ourselves, but Easter Island was where Jack—"

He caught himself before he said it, throwing an awkward glance at Mae.

"It's okay, Benjamin," she said. "Easter Island was where my son confronted and killed his father, my ex-husband. It's all right. Jack told me everything about that incident. For the record, his father was a jackass who got what was coming to him. More importantly, where was the symbol found on Easter Island?"

Stretch checked his notes. "On a small rocky islet just off the southern shore of Easter Island called Motu Nui."

"Motu Nui . . ." Mae said, thinking. "Ever heard of Motu Nui, Benjamin?"

Stretch shook his head. "Should I have?"

"Easter Island is famous for its long-faced stone statues called *moai*. But few know about Motu Nui. As a geographical feature, it's not that special, just a small rocky mount half a mile off the southern tip of the island. But it played a key role in Easter Island's most important ritual. Motu Nui was the islet that the Easter Islanders used for their famous ritual contest, the Birdman Race."

"What was that?" Pooh Bear asked.

Stretch said, "Jack mentioned it once, back when we were finding the Six Ramesean Stones. It was a race between warriors. They had to swim across the shark-infested strait between Easter Island and the little islet, grab a bird's egg from up near its summit, and then return with the egg. Whoever won the race became the chief of Easter Island for the next year. Something like that."

"Close," Mae said, "but not quite. It was indeed a race between warriors, but it wasn't the *warrior* who got to be the chief of Easter Island. It was his *sponsor*. That man became *chief of chiefs*, first among the various chiefs of Easter Island, a king of kings, so to speak . . ."

Her voice trailed off.

"What is it?" Pooh Bear asked.

Mae frowned, thinking. "The king of kings," she said absently.

She looked up sharply.

"Four kings rule the four legendary kingdoms, but who is the *first* among them, the king of kings? In royal matters, someone is always preeminent. How do they choose him?"

She opened her laptop and scrolled through many photographs until she found a certain image: one of a striking Greek urn.

Mae said, "This is an ancient Greek urn that Jack discovered at the lost library of Alexandria. As you can see, painted on the urn is a

beautiful artistic rendition of the Twelve Labors of Hercules. See those words written around the rim in Greek? They translate as:

THIS URN COMMEMORATES THE COMING TOGETHER OF THE FOUR KINGS TO CELEBRATE THE GREAT GAMES. EACH BROUGHT CHAMPIONS TO REPRESENT HIM TO DECIDE WHO WOULD BE THE KING OF KINGS.

"The king of kings . . ." Pooh Bear said.

"They brought champions to represent them," Mae said, "just like the Easter Islanders did. Like the *moai*, the Birdman Race is a unique peculiarity of Easter Island. There is no record of anything like it being performed anywhere else in the world.

"Where did the race come from? Why did the Easter Islanders perform such a ritual? And for our purposes, knowing the connection Easter Island has to the advanced civilization that built the Machine, was the Birdman Race derived from that civilization?"

"So what are these Great Games?" Stretch asked, nodding at the urn.

Mae said, "As far as we know, they're a myth. The concept of 'games' in the ancient world could mean many things: gladiatorial battles, chariot races, or even the series of athletic events like those put on by the ancient Greeks which became the Olympic Games.

"I've only encountered one reference to any kind of *Great* Games in all of my research, and that was a mention by Plato. He said the Great Games were a mythical series of deadly challenges held in the Underworld and reputedly hosted by Hades himself. Of course, I took that with a grain of salt since Plato is also the source of the Atlantis legend."

"Interesting," Pooh Bear said. "After you showed us that page from Isaac Newton's book mentioning the Hydra Galaxy, I had a hunch: if Newton, as a member of the Invisible College, was an adviser to one or all of the four legendary kingdoms and knew all about their astronomical wisdom like the Hydra Galaxy, I thought that maybe the present-day members of those kingdoms might be in the business of acquiring Newton's writings. So I looked up recent auctions of Newtonian works."

"And?" Mae said.

"There's a French family, a very wealthy family by the name of DeSaxe, that over the last decade has bought several original works by Isaac Newton. One of them was the only drawing done by Newton in his most famous book, the *Principia*. This drawing."

Pooh Bear turned around his laptop so the others could see its screen:

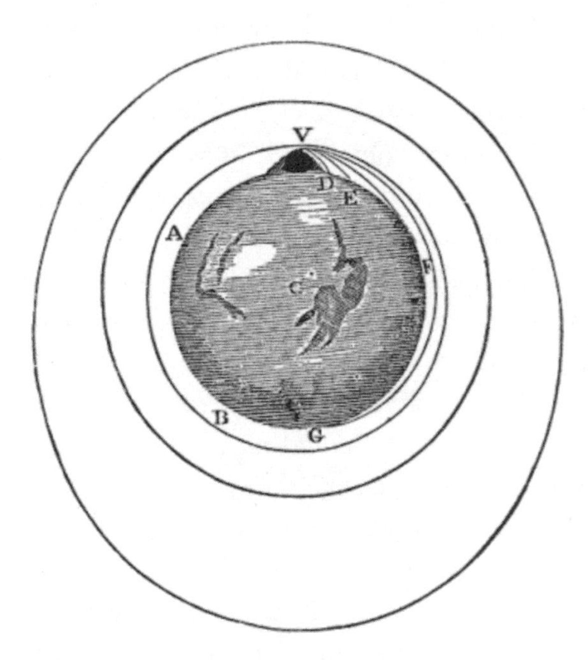

On it was a picture of a planet, presumably the Earth, with a mountain sticking up from the northern pole. A series of arcs, circles, and ellipses ringed the planet.

"It's called Newton's Mountain," Pooh Bear said. "It's a thought experiment about gravity and orbits. If you fire a cannonball from the top of the mountain at different speeds, it will do different things because of the Earth's gravitational pull. Fire it softly and it'll drop to the Earth. Fire it faster and it will fly in an orbit around the world. Fire it faster still and it will escape Earth's gravitational pull completely and fly off into space.

"Last year, the head of the DeSaxe family, Monsieur Anthony DeSaxe, bought Newton's original drawing at a private auction for a cool $22 million."

"Twenty-two million bucks?" Stretch whistled. "Must be a hell of a drawing."

Pooh Bear turned to Mae . . .

. . . and he paused.

She was looking at him with her mouth open and her eyes wide.

"What?" Pooh said. "What did I say?"

"The DeSaxe family," Mae said slowly. "I haven't heard that name in years. I encountered them several times in my early research. It is a very old family, *very* highly regarded in French society, and very mysterious.

"Their lineage goes way back. Several of the DeSaxe men were Marshals of France. The patriarch of the family, Anthony 'Tony' DeSaxe, attended several royal weddings in Europe back in the 90s, which made me wonder if he was a member of the Deus Rex, the Land Kingdom. I still don't know if that's the case, but at the time I thought he must at least know them. I didn't know about the purchase of the Newton drawing, though."

"It wasn't reported in the media," Pooh Bear said. "I found it through French tax records. Mr. DeSaxe kept the purchase very quiet."

"He's a secretive man," Mae said.

"He is indeed, so I looked him up," Pooh Bear said. "Anthony Michael Dominic DeSaxe IV. Fifty-six years old. Estimated net worth: twelve billion dollars. Inherited two billion from his father, but turned that into twelve billion through two primary businesses: mining and shipping.

"His private family company owns over forty mines around the world, ranging from coal to gold to rare-earth minerals. There are a couple of mines in Brazil and a few in South Africa, but most of his mines are in India, in and around the Thar Desert.

"As for shipping, the DeSaxe Shipping Corporation both constructs and deconstructs container ships and oil tankers. They build them at a shipyard in Toulouse and rip them apart on a thirty-mile-long stretch of private beach in the remote northwest of India, in Gujarat Province, where the Thar Desert meets the Arabian Sea."

"I saw that ship graveyard on the news once," Stretch said. "It's amazing: a whole line of massive rusting ships beached on the shoreline, all slowly being broken up. The story was about an environmental controversy, some kind of spill."

"That's right," Pooh Bear said. "DeSaxe Shipping employs poor Indian workers to strip decommissioned vessels on that stretch of the Indian coast. Often when they're stripped, the ships leak oil, arsenic, and all manner of other toxins into the ocean. There was a leak last December. Greenpeace protested and tried to drum up media support, but the DeSaxes don't like publicity and the matter was resolved very quickly with a call to the Indian prime minister."

Mae pulled up an image on her laptop.

"Mr. DeSaxe also has a connection with our Hydra symbol. Ten years ago he purchased a 3,000-year-old Assyrian lion statue. The statue is generally unremarkable—the Assyrians carved a lot of lion statues—but one of my search algorithms found the Hydra symbol carved into its base. This is what the symbol looked like."

Stretch and Pooh Bear peered at the image.

"It looks sort of like a coat of arms," Stretch said.

"What's that weird mountain covering the Hydra symbol?" Pooh Bear said.

"No one knows," Mae said.

Pooh Bear turned to her. "Tell me, what was the purpose of the lion statue? Ancient statues always had a purpose, a meaning. What was this statue's purpose?"

"You're absolutely right, Zahir," Mae said. "The statue was one of a pair of lions, but its twin has long been lost. Its podium proclaimed in ancient Urdu: "I AM CHAOS, ONE OF THE TWIN GUARDIANS OF THE UNDERWORLD." According to Assyrian legends, two lions guarded the gates to Hell. The other lion's name was Fear."

Pooh Bear pulled out his cell phone. "I want some more information on the mysterious Mr. DeSaxe. I'm going to call in some favors. See if my father's intelligence agency has anything on him: government mentions, suspect donations, phone intercepts, anything."

After Pooh Bear had left the room to make his call, Stretch said, "Since we've been looking into the Hydra Galaxy, I looked up places dedicated to the Hydra. Two stand out: two cities in central Asia that are both named *Hyderabad*—one is in India and the other is in Pakistan. Carvings of the symbol for our Hydra Galaxy have been found at both."

"Interesting," Mae said.

At length, Pooh Bear returned from the other room. "I just spoke with UAE Intelligence. I asked them to patch into America's ECHELON system—it monitors every phone conversation around the world—and do a cross-check of several words: DeSaxe, games, Hydra, kingdom, Underworld, Iolanthe Compton-Jones. We got two hits straight away."

He read from his notes: "The first call to mention some of the search terms was intercepted two months ago. In it, a male voice speaking with an Indian accent and identified as Mr. Sunil Malik

said, 'It's a wonderful specimen, Mr. DeSaxe, one of the best I've ever seen. The tablet dates from the 14th century B.C. and is completely intact, which makes it exceedingly rare. It's a collector's dream.' "

Mae's eyes narrowed. "Sunny Malik . . ."

"You know him?" Stretch said.

"Oh, yes. You could say that Sunny and I work in the same field—the world of ancient history—only he operates in a very murky corner of it," Mae said. "Sunny Malik is one of the world's premier dealers in blood antiquities. He is also a very dangerous individual, a gang lord and a gunrunner. Works out of Karachi, Pakistan."

"Blood antiquities?" Pooh Bear asked.

"Ever heard of conflict diamonds or blood diamonds?"

"Sure."

"Same thing. When they attack an ancient city, militant groups like the Taliban and ISIS raid all the museums and wealthy homes and grab any artifacts or antiquities they can find. Then they sell those artifacts—'blood antiquities'—to people like Sunny Malik who onsell them to collectors on the black market. This is worth following up. And the second call, Zahir?"

Pooh Bear said, "The second call was intercepted only eight days ago. In it, an adult male voice said, 'Iolanthe, it's Anthony DeSaxe. Of course, you may substitute a new champion for the Games. It will be lovely to see you again next week.' "

They were all silent for a moment.

Mae said, "That was eight days ago, you say? Iolanthe Compton-Jones and Anthony DeSaxe spoke about arranging a substitute for the Great Games? That would mean the Games are being held *now* . . ."

Stretch said, "You think the Great Games of the Hydra are being held right now . . . in the Kingdom of the Underworld . . . and that Iolanthe grabbed Jack to compete in them?"

"That's exactly what I think," Mae said. "Zahir, Benjamin. We may have just stumbled upon the greatest gathering of the four royal kingdoms in the last three thousand years and my son has been thrust into it. We need to find out where it's happening."

"How do we do that?" Stretch asked.

Mae stood. "We go to Karachi and pay Sunny Malik a visit. And we find out exactly what it was he sold to Mr. DeSaxe."

THE UNDERWORLD
SOMEWHERE IN INDIA

After surviving the vertical maze, Jack, Alby, and Roxy were escorted back to their hostage carriage by some armed minotaur guards. For some reason that no one deigned to tell Jack, the two winners of the wall-maze challenge—Zaitan and the Brazilian, Vargas—would not be given their rewards straight away. That would happen later.

Scarecrow and his two Marines—Astro and Tomahawk—were likewise taken back to the hostage train.

"I just gotta say it," Scarecrow said to Jack as they walked together. "You're one bloody-minded son of a bitch. Going after that jester was ballsy."

Jack nodded. "You do what you've got to do."

Astro laughed grimly. "Scarecrow knows all about that. Over the course of some crazy-ass missions, his heart has stopped twice and he's still alive and kicking."

Scarecrow said, "I just wanted to say it now, because I've got a feeling things are going to get nastier. If they put the two of us in a pit and tell us to fight to the death, well . . ."

"Let's hope it doesn't come to that," Jack said.

They arrived at Scarecrow's carriage, where Mother was waiting.

"You both survived!" she said. "Woo-hoo! Hashtag: my boys survived another ancient death-challenge."

Jack said his good-byes and kept walking.

Scarecrow and Mother watched him go.

When Jack was out of earshot, Scarecrow said, "This can't end well. This whole thing is one giant elimination. The sixteen champions are slowly being whittled down to one. It's got to get to a point where he and I will have to fight it out. What do I do?"

They both watched Jack walking away, heavy with fatigue.

Mother said, "You know what I think of you, boss. As far as I'm concerned, you're the fucking man. You won't stop fighting till your last breath. That guy"—she jerked her chin at Jack—"is just like you. He may not be the soldier you are now, but once upon a time, he was one of the best. And he's determined. He can dig deep. My official opinion? If you two have to fight it out hand-to-hand, you can take him . . . but he's gonna take some killing."

Scarecrow eyed Jack closely from behind.

The remaining champions all arrived back at their hostage carriages, where they were once again locked inside.

No sooner were they in their chambers than two downpours of liquid stone came blasting out of the roof of the train tunnel and drowned the hostages of the two champions who had died during the challenge: the Brazilian, Corazon, and the Indian MARCOS commando.

When the foul deed was done, the carriages shunted forward on their tracks and moved once again around the base of the mountain.

Jack turned away from the sight of the recently flooded hostage chambers. He didn't want to think about that. To take his mind off it, he gazed out through the bars of his moving cell.

Alby came alongside him. "Jack, I don't know if you're noticing it, but I'm starting to see a pattern in all these challenges."

"They're rituals," Jack said softly, still looking outward.

"Yes," Alby said. "Elaborate rituals. A minotaur charging into your cell. Special assassins wearing lion, dog, and snake helmets. That jester dressing as a deer. There's more to this than we know right now. It might all be *one big ritual*. If we can figure out what that ritual is, we might just improve our chances of surviving."

At that moment, the hostage train rounded a corner and began clanking to a halt.

Jack leaned forward as a new arena came into view below them.

"Oh my Lord . . ." he breathed.

It was colossal, easily the largest arena they had seen so far.

Alby gasped. "It looks like the Circus Maximus."

It did indeed, Jack thought.

An enormous racetrack opened up below them. High stone walls flanked its dirt floor.

The track, however, did not run in a circle or oval. Rather it had three straights that switched back and forth in an *S* shape until the final straight shot into a great yawning tunnel bored into the wall of the crater.

Jack swapped a glance with Scarecrow over in his cell.

"What do you think?" Scarecrow said.

"I think," Jack said, "that the next challenge is going to be big."

Moments later, the train thunked to a gaseous, wheezing halt.

Vacheron appeared in front of it and addressed the eight remaining champions in their cages.

"Hello, maggots! Rejoice, for today, you are all the recipients of a great and rare honor. Before the Fifth Challenge begins this afternoon, you have all been invited to a lunch hosted by Lord Hades himself. Here the rewards for the last challenge will be dispensed.

But we can't have you dining with royalty covered in blood and sweat and smelling like animals. Clean yourselves."

Buckets of water and sponges were brought to each carriage.

Vacheron himself brought a bucket to Jack's hostage carriage.

He sneered down his nose at Jack. "For some reason, *you* have earned a special preluncheon audience."

"With who?" Jack said.

"A king has asked to meet you in person," Vacheron said. "To see you for himself."

"Which king?"

"His." Vacheron jerked his nose at E-147. "He asked for you and the minotaur to meet with him."

"A minotaur king?" Jack said, thinking. Then he looked up sharply. "I want to bring one of my people with me," he said, glancing at Alby.

"For this audience, bring whomever you like. I care not." Vacheron waved a hand dismissively. "But for your lunch with Hades, you come alone."

They came for Jack ten minutes later: eight minotaur guards wearing crimson-and-gold sashes over their shoulders.

Having quickly washed himself with the water and sponge, Jack still wore his Homer Simpson T-shirt and jeans. He still had no shoes, so he went barefoot.

Alby and E-147 walked with him.

Jack had wanted to bring Alby for two reasons: one, because two heads were better than one and if he was going to see more weirdness, he wanted Alby to see it, too; and two, because he wanted to talk to Alby and he saw this as an opportunity to do it alone and out of range of inquiring ears.

They were led a short distance from their carriage and down a superlong and superhigh staircase that ran down the lower reaches of the western flank of Hades's mountain.

As they walked down the immense staircase together, Jack said, "Alby, I need you to help me with something."

"Sure."

"This explosive charge in my neck," Jack said. "So long as I have it inside me, I'm their prisoner. I can't leave. That asshole, Vacheron, used a remote earlier to detonate the explosives in those other guys' necks. Which means the explosive charge uses a radio signal. I need you to figure out a way to jam that signal."

Alby glanced at the ugly scar on the back of Jack's neck and the sparkling yellow gemstone embedded in it. "Hmmm. If we had a jamming device, we could disrupt the signal either near the charge itself or near the source."

"The source?" Jack asked.

Alby looked up behind them as they walked down the staircase, back at the colossal mountain-palace.

His searching eyes landed on one of the fortresses hanging off the Eiffel Tower–shaped mount, the second-highest fortress.

"There," he said, pointing.

Jack followed his gaze . . .

. . . and saw the fortress Alby was looking at.

A cluster of modern antennas—radio, satellite, and cell phone—sprang upward from one of its towers.

"I'm guessing that antenna array is your source," Alby said. "I can't see any others. The way I see it, you've got three options: (a) jam or remove the device in your neck; (b) jam or destroy those antennas; or (c) . . ."

"Yes?"

Alby shrugged. "Steal Vacheron's remote. He probably has another one somewhere, but it could buy you time, at least for a while."

Jack turned to him and smiled. "I've always liked the way you think, kid."

They came to the base of the giant staircase. A broad flat plain stretched away from them for about two hundred yards, ending at a most imposing and intimidating structure: a grim castle embedded in the western wall of the crater.

The castle looked incredibly strong: two superhigh crenellated ramparts bookended a colossal gate. The gate's huge iron portcullis was currently open, and beyond it, stretching away into darkness, was a paved roadway.

A lone figure stood in the mouth of the mammoth gate, looking like an ant underneath the enormous ancient structure.

It was a minotaur, but a big one, with broad shoulders and a thick neck.

Even from this distance, Jack could see that the horned bull helmet he wore was more elaborate than those of the regular minotaurs. He was also dressed in flowing purple robes that glinted with gold edging.

E-147 hesitated, turned to Jack. "This is great moment for Jack and for E-147. That is Minotaur King."

Jack's audience with the Minotaur King took place in the yawning maw of the gate of the grim castle.

Jack stopped in front of the Minotaur King.

Up close, he saw that the Minotaur King's helmet was incredibly ornate. It was embedded with rubies and sapphires.

The king removed the helmet, and Jack saw his Neanderthal face, hairy and broad.

But his eyes were like lasers. They glistened with intelligence.

"Greetings, champion," the king said. "My name is Minotus. I am Minotaur King."

"I'm Jack West. This is my friend, Alby Calvin. And this is—"

"E-147," King Minotus said. "I know. He is reason I wish to meet Jack West."

Jack glanced at E, who bowed his head.

Minotus said, "Jack West save life of E-147 during challenge. This most unusual. Why Jack West do this?"

Jack cocked his head in surprise. He had wondered why the head of Hades's minotaur army would want to meet him, but he had not anticipated this.

"I didn't want him to die," he said simply.

Now it was Minotus who cocked *his* head.

"Why Jack West care for minotaur? Minotaur lowly scum. Minotaur dirty slave. Minotaur's life not worth dirt on Jack West's boot."

Jack frowned at those words.

"E-147 didn't want to die. I felt sorry for him. And he's not lowly scum. Nobody is lowly scum, not even a minotaur."

Minotus's eyes went wide, as if Jack had uttered something sacrilegious.

He looked away for a moment, then he spun back to face Jack.

"For twelve thousand years, minotaurs live in service of King of Underworld. For twelve thousand years, minotaurs serve many different Kings of Underworld. Some kings good and fair rulers. Others mean and cruel.

"Being Minotaur King is difficult job. Must balance Lord Hades's wishes with needs of minotaurs. Much depend on nature of King of Underworld.

"This King, this Hades, he decent man. Hard but fair. Good to minotaurs. Treat minotaurs as loyal servants not slaves. He has even say to me that after these Games, he let minotaurs live free here in Underworld.

"But his sons not fair. Sons cruel. His first son and heir, Prince Dionysius, is very vicious man. Kill minotaurs for sport. Kill minotaurs when drunk. Dionysius sometimes hunt minotaurs with Vacheron and his younger brother, Zaitan. When Hades die and Dionysius become King of Underworld, it will be dark time for minotaurs."

The Minotaur King bowed his head and looked down at the ground, contemplating this dark future.

Jack watched him closely.

"Why did you really bring me here?" he asked. "Why did you want to meet me?"

The Minotaur King's head came up and he looked hard into Jack's eyes.

"In twelve thousand years, over the course of three Great Games, no champion ever save the life of a minotaur in a challenge. Ever."

Minotus stood a little taller and suddenly Jack saw something in him—in this Neanderthal, this half-man, whatever he was—something that even the lowliest person had.

He saw pride.

"Yet Jack West do exactly that," the king said. "As king of

Minotaurs, I wanted to meet this man, this Jack West, and, on behalf of all minotaurs, give him thanks for saving E-147."

He extended a hairy hand.

Jack took it.

"I wish Jack West good fortune in remaining challenges," Minotus said. "Please forgive my minotaurs for their acts in next challenge. They must do job for which they are trained. But know that the other slaves of the Underworld cheer for you."

Their audience over, Jack, Alby, and E-147 were escorted back to the mountain-palace by their minotaur guards.

Jack ascended the giant staircase, deep in thought.

"What are you thinking?" Alby asked.

Jack squinted up at the mountain-palace above them.

"I'm thinking that this whole affair—these Games, this mountain—is based on big-picture issues. Ancient rituals, royal houses, distant galaxies." He turned to face Alby. "Wouldn't it be strange if it all turned on one small act of kindness to a lowly minotaur?"

A few minutes later, they came to the spot where the long staircase went over the tracks of the hostage train.

There Jack parted ways with Alby and E-147. They were directed back to their carriage, while he kept on going up the stairs to attend his lunch with Lord Hades.

Flanked by minotaur guards and still wearing his dirty T-shirt and no shoes, Jack was led into the royal dining room of the Lord of the Underworld.

Jack gazed at the glorious hall with its high ceiling and marble floors. His eyes took in the many paintings and statues and, of course, the crests of the four legendary kingdoms:

His eyes scanned the four coats of arms. He saw the pyramids in the one for Land; a watery city in the one for Sea; mountains for the Kingdom of Sky; and for Hades, the Hydra symbol and the mountain-palace in which he now found himself.

The giant statue in the center of the hall of Hercules wrestling the Cretan Bull caught his attention.

It was a common statue, one that appeared in public parks all over the world, from the Tuileries in Paris to Hyde Park in Sydney. Jack had seen different versions of it many times. Now, however, he looked at it differently. After his own recent encounters with bull-headed half-men, he kind of felt a kinship with Hercules.

A bust of an ancient king stood beside the entryway. The stern-faced man depicted in the stone wore the same crown that Hades wore now.

A previous King of the Underworld, Jack thought.

Cut into the base of the bust were the words:

EVRYSTHEVS
DIS PATER

"I bet you were an asshole, too," Jack whispered to the bust.

"I guarantee he was," Scarecrow said, appearing at Jack's side, escorted by two minotaur guards. "What does 'Dis Pater' mean?"

"Dis is another name for Hell or the Underworld. So it means Father of the Underworld. Lord of Hell."

Standing in the doorway to the dining room, they were soon joined by Gregory Brigham and the other champions.

Brigham had dressed up for the occasion, in full dress uniform. So had the Brazilian trooper Sergeant Vargas who, along with Zaitan, had won the Fourth Challenge.

Jack hadn't.

Even if he'd had fresh clothes, he wouldn't have worn them. They'd kidnapped him to come here and fight. He wasn't going to dress up for anyone. He quite liked that he wasn't wearing any shoes.

He noticed that Scarecrow had done the same. He just wore his dirty battle fatigues.

The royal spectators were already seated at their tables and they stood and applauded as the champions entered the dining room.

Hades sat at a high table. He also stood and clapped as the

champions entered. Standing guard behind Hades, ever watchful, was his giant dog-helmeted bodyguard.

Scarecrow said, "One of the other champions told me that dog is the best of Hades's warriors. Name's Cerberus, just like Hades's dog in all the Greek myths."

Jack looked sideways at Scarecrow. "A Marine officer who knows Greek myths? You're not the average Marine, are you?"

"You have no idea."

Jack also saw Mephisto standing close to Hades.

The little red jester glared at Jack, his eyes burning with hatred. He had not liked being outwitted and captured in the vertical maze.

I've made an enemy, Jack thought. *The worst kind. One with substantial killing skills and who holds a grudge.*

The champions were guided into the hall.

As he moved through the room, Jack saw a wide-screen television with a list on it:

THE CHAMPIONS

KINGDOM OF LAND	1	Maj. Gregory Brigham	UK
	2	Sgt. Victor Vargas	Brazil
	~~3~~	~~Sgt. Mauricio Corazon~~	~~Brazil~~
	4	Capt. Jack West Jr	US/Aus
KINGDOM OF SEA	1	Maj. Jeffrey Edwards [Delta]	US
	~~2~~	~~Lt. Barrett Johnson [Army]~~	~~US~~
	3	W.O. DeShawn Monroe [Navy]	US
	4	Capt. Shane Schofield [USMC]	US
KINGDOM OF SKY	~~1~~	~~Tenzin Depon~~	~~Tibet~~
	2	Renzin Depon	Tibet
	~~3~~	~~The Gorkha~~	~~Nepal~~
	~~4~~	~~Capt. Jason Chen~~	~~Taiwan~~
KINGDOM OF THE UNDERWORLD	1	Zaitan DeSaxe	France
	~~2~~	~~Capt. Sachin Singh [MARCOS]~~	~~India~~
	~~3~~	~~Lt. Wasim Nasiruzzin [MARCOS]~~	~~India MIA~~
	~~4~~	~~Lt. Ravi Mano [LRRP]~~	~~Sri Lanka MIA~~

For the first time, Jack saw the names of all sixteen champions.

He noticed that eight of the names had been crossed out.

The dead ones, he thought.

Two names at the bottom had "MINO" written beside them. Jack guessed that these were the two champions who had been killed and replaced by the gold minotaurs after the First Challenge. Now that the two gold minotaurs were also dead, those additions had lines through them, too.

Walking beside Jack, Scarecrow said, "They're eliminating us, one by one."

"For their amusement and entertainment," Jack agreed.

"Stay sharp, Huntsman. We're not dead yet," Scarecrow said as he was guided away from Jack to be seated beside his patron, a distinguished-looking gray-haired man in a tailored suit.

Jack, Major Brigham, and the Brazilian named Vargas were escorted to a table where Iolanthe and the Catholic cardinal, Mendoza, sat with another man: a handsome blond-haired man in his late forties who looked a lot like Iolanthe.

Jack ignored them as the last person at the table dashed from her seat and leaped into his arms.

"Dad!" Lily exclaimed.

She was wearing a beautiful floral day dress, demure high heels, and was all made up—the exact opposite of Jack in his grimy T-shirt and bare feet. She looked glamorous, yes, but also sexualized, as though she were being displayed for these royals.

As they embraced, their lips came close to each other's ears and they whispered softly.

"You okay, kiddo?"

"For now. Look who's sitting with Hades."

Jack's eyes found Hades's table . . . where he saw Dion DeSaxe sitting beside Hades and Zaitan.

Jack recalled the Minotaur King describing the cruel first son and heir of Hades as Prince Dionysius.

"Dionysius . . . Dion . . ." Jack's face darkened. "The preppy kid from Stanford? The one who took you out?"

"Yes," Lily said bitterly. "He is Hades's son. He knew who I was all along."

They separated and sat.

Iolanthe made the introductions.

"Major Gregory Brigham, Captain Jack West Jr., and Sergeant Victor Vargas, meet your patron"—she indicated the blond-haired man—"my brother, Orlando, Duke of Avalon, Patriarch of the Deus Rex, and King of the Noble and Ancient Realm of Land."

The Brazilian, Vargas, bowed and shook Orlando's hand reverently.

After patting Brigham familiarly on the shoulder, the Land King extended his hand toward Jack. "The famous Captain West. The fifth greatest warrior. It is indeed a pleasure."

Jack didn't take his hand, just left it hanging there. "I met your predecessor, a Russian named Vladimir Karnov, a descendent of the Romanovs and then-head of your family. Knew him as Carnivore. I pumped a hundred rounds of heavy-bore antiaircraft ammunition into him. Turned him into pulp. Nice to meet you, too."

Jack sat at the table, leaving Orlando standing there with his hand held out.

Jack grabbed a bread roll and wolfed it down.

"Right . . ." Orlando said, throwing Iolanthe a meaningful glance.

She just shrugged. "We *did* kidnap him, brother dear."

As he ate, Jack noticed that the Brazilian, Sergeant Vargas, was deep in whispered conversation with Cardinal Mendoza.

A glass tinkled, garnering everyone's attention.

Up on the main table, Hades stood.

"My fellow kings, lords, ladies, and champions, welcome. Sixteen brave champions began these Games, now only eight remain.

The Fifth Challenge awaits and historically it is the longest and most difficult challenge of the Great Games. Today it will be no different. Our Fifth Challenge is, without doubt, the most deadly and grueling challenge our dauntless heroes will face, so it befits us to celebrate them now and give them a meal to fill their bellies. It is also time for the winners of the Fourth Challenge to claim their rewards."

Jack felt his blood run cold.

He had forgotten about this part.

This was the moment when one of the other champions could demand his death and there was nothing he could do about it.

The two winners of the challenge in the vertical maze stood: Vargas and Zaitan, Hades's second son.

Hades said to them, "You both secured a Golden Sphere in the Fourth Challenge. As such, anything that is in my power to give, you may have. All you have to do is name it."

He looked at Zaitan.

Zaitan bowed low. "My Lord, I would like exemption from the next challenge, please."

The crowd of royal spectators nodded. A wise option.

Hades said, "So be it. You are exempted from the Fifth Challenge." He turned to Vargas. "And you, champion? What is your reward to be?"

Sergeant Vargas stood. For a long moment, he stared down at Jack, looking deep into his eyes and Jack knew that he was done for.

He was no longer flying under the radar—his actions in the last two challenges had shown him to be a threat—and the Brazilian now saw him as exactly that, a rival who had to be eliminated.

He guessed that this had probably been the subject of Vargas's intense conversation with Cardinal Mendoza.

Still eyeing Jack, the Brazilian spoke.

"Lord Hades," he said, "I, too, would like exemption from the Fifth Challenge."

Jack released the breath he'd been holding.

But he quickly found himself contemplating a new thought.

What did this Fifth Challenge involve that would make these two well-informed champions use their precious rewards to avoid it?

"Very wise choices," Hades said, nodding to Zaitan and Vargas. "They show a keen and classical understanding of the history of the Games. The battle race that is the Fifth Challenge is fraught with perils. Two champions in the past used this very reward to skip it and focus their energy for the critical later challenges. I myself have always said that only a classically educated champion can prevail in the Games."

He shifted his stance. "At the conclusion of the Fifth Challenge, we will lay the first set of Golden Spheres in the minor temple atop this mountain. After that ceremony, the Games will enter a second phase, one featuring different kinds of challenges.

"Eight champions sit among us now. The next challenge will determine how many proceed to the second phase." He locked eyes with each of the champions. "Please do not hate me for testing you so searchingly. I am not trying to crush the world's greatest heroes. I am trying to find them. Enjoy this lunch, especially if it is to be your last."

Hades sat and lunch began.

Jack surveyed the scene in a kind of stunned awe, observing conversations and chatter that seemed entirely unaffected by the bloodshed that had been occurring and which, by all accounts, would continue.

The Catholic cardinal sitting beside Iolanthe turned to Jack. "Captain West, forgive me, but it feels so strange to be sitting here with you."

"Why is that?"

"Because although we have never met, I feel that I know you. I have followed your career for a long time. I have read so many con-

fidential files on you, from the time you emerged from seclusion with the daughter of the Oracle of Siwa to the time you found the Seven Ancient Wonders and killed my colleague, Francisco del Piero."

"He was a gigantic asshole, who—" Jack said.

"—you threw into a jet engine."

"—who got what he deserved."

"Father del Piero was committed," Mendoza said. "He was a believer. Like I am."

"Committed to what?" Jack asked. "To this? Rich assholes ruling the world?"

"The ruling elites do not rule because they *want* to," Mendoza said. "They rule out of a sense of obligation."

Jack gestured to the assembled diners around them. "They don't seem to be suffering too much from that obligation."

He rounded on the cardinal. "I've seen files on you, too, Cardinal Mendoza. I know who you are. The files say you're a member of the Catholic Church's 'Omega Group' and an expert on the 'Trismagi.' Tell me, what are they?"

Mendoza nodded slowly. "As you have already discovered, the Catholic Church is merely the current name for a cult of priests that has survived for over five thousand years since Egyptian times. It is a cult devoted to the worship of the sun and the stars and the wisdom of an ancient civilization that once flourished on this Earth. It is the civilization that built the Sphinx and the pyramids, the stone circles of England and the three secret cities of Thule, Atlas, and Ra. The civilization that gave us the two sacred trees and the Life Stone itself.

"The Omega Group is a small elite within the Church that for over five thousand years, during wars and famines and the Dark Ages, has kept secure the most critical ancient knowledge of that incredible civilization."

"And what exactly is the most critical knowledge of that civilization?" Jack asked.

"Knowledge about the Omega Event. The end of all things."

"You mean the end of the world?"

"I mean the end of *all* things," Mendoza said firmly. "Our world is but an outpost in a much larger cosmos, Captain. An important outpost, to be sure, but still part of a greater whole. The Omega Group are custodians of the Ancients' knowledge pertaining to the end of the entire universe."

Jack sat back in his chair. "The end of the universe."

He threw Iolanthe a look.

She said, "We are living in a momentous time, Jack. The time when mankind proves its worth. The Tartarus Rotation, the Dark Star, they were but initial tests, preliminary tasks to let whoever is out there know that intelligent life is still here on Earth."

"They didn't feel like mere preliminary tasks to me," Jack said.

"They weren't *supposed* to be hard, Jack," Iolanthe said. "They were only hard because the ancient knowledge regarding the Golden Capstone and the Machine had been lost and had to be found again. The knowledge behind the Great Games was never lost, which is why this time it's different."

Cardinal Mendoza said, "Even the three previous passes of the Hydra Galaxy were merely exploratory visits to test our worth. The three Games held in honor of those passes were thus minor tests for mankind. They occurred in 10,000 B.C., 2700 B.C. and 1250 B.C., and were won by Osiris, Gilgamesh, and Hercules, respectively. This time it is different, for this time the coming of the Hydra Galaxy heralds the Omega Event."

"Which the Omega Group knows about?" Jack said.

"Yes." Cardinal Mendoza leaned forward. "Captain, listen to me closely. We all know the universe is expanding. Newton knew it. Einstein knew it. Modern telescopes have proven it. What few know is that when the universe expands to its limit, *it then begins to contract*. This contraction ends in the ultimate singularity—the colossal implosion of all matter in the universe into a single black hole—which scientists have crudely labeled 'The Big Crunch.'

"Throughout the ages, the universe has progressed through a constant cycle of Big Bang–expansion–contraction–Big Crunch. Each Big Crunch is like the core of a nuclear weapon imploding: in a single instant it extinguishes the universe and in the next instant *it causes the next Big Bang* and so the cycle continues.

"Whatever you call it—ultimate singularity, universal implosion, Big Crunch—*that* is the Omega Event. The great ancient civilization knew about this cataclysmic event and how to prevent it, too."

"And the 'Trismagi'?" Jack asked. "What does that mean? Three magicians?"

Mendoza said, "That is the literal translation, yes: *three magicians*. But in older times, anyone with advanced knowledge was considered a magician. Think of them as the three most senior initiates of the Ancients, three individuals who are privy to that civilization's most prized wisdom."

"Are they here at these Games?" Jack asked, glancing around the hall.

"No," Mendoza said. "They are the keepers of the three secret cities, the guardians of those extraordinary places. Occasionally, the three of them come together to pass on their knowledge. The three wise men who arrived at Christ's birth by the light of a star were the Trismagi of that age. After these Games are done, the Trismagi of our time will—hopefully—guide us through the dreaded Omega Event."

At that moment, Iolanthe's brother, Orlando the Land King, spoke. "Cardinal, you are, as ever, far too dour."

He slammed his glass down on the table, causing some of the wine in it to slosh out. He was clearly drunk.

"Do not cast a cloud over these Games. This is a time for celebration, not foreboding. The Games will be won, the golden apples will be set in place in the two temples atop this mountain, the Mysteries will be given to the winning king, and the world will be saved. As for the death and maiming part, well, I know of no greater pleasure than watching capable men get cut to pieces."

He drained the remainder of his wine in one messy gulp and stood abruptly.

Iolanthe, the cardinal, Major Brigham, and Vargas all immediately stood respectfully. Jack and Lily didn't.

Orlando said, "But right now, I need to take a fucking piss."

Jack stood as well. "If you could point me in the right direction, I need to go, too."

"I'll take you via the scenic route," Orlando said as he and Jack stepped away from the table.

Wobbling slightly, Orlando led Jack onto the balcony outside the dining room. The balcony ringed the mountain and one could, it seemed to Jack, walk all the way around it.

Orlando lit a cigarette while Jack beheld the vast crater of the Underworld.

Looking up, he saw the immense camouflage netting encasing the entire crater. It swooped from the summit of the mountain down to the crater's rim. Dappled sunlight filtered through it. The sun, Jack noted, was still high in the sky.

Below him, Jack beheld the broad circular crater.

He saw the wall-maze far below, off to the right, and the Circus Maximus–like structure directly in front of him. To his left, also down at the base of the crater, nestled against the wall, was the grim castle of the minotaurs.

"What's that castle?" Jack asked Orlando, feigning ignorance.

"It's where all the minotaurs live," Orlando said. "Dirty fucking things. Live in squalor. There's a whole city back there behind that gate. But they're good workers, I'll give them that."

In his drunkenness, Orlando had become very chatty. If Jack could keep him talking, he might be able to get some useful information out of him.

"They built this mountain?" Jack asked, looking up at the towering palace around them.

"Oh, goodness, no," Orlando said. "They're not smart enough to do that. They're ignorant brutes. Neanderthals. This place was built a *long* time ago by a civilization far more advanced than us. The minotaurs are Hades's slaves, his subhuman army, and the source of every myth about Satan's infernal servants."

Orlando took a long drag on his cigarette. "They do all the grunt work here and are happy to do it. Vacheron designed all the arenas and mazes for the challenges and the minotaurs built them under his direction."

"That's an enormous logistical operation," Jack said. "Where do they source all the material?"

"They bring in all the food, vehicles, and construction materials from the west dock."

Jack kept his eyes on the view of the crater, trying to look casual, trying not to let his concentration show.

A western dock . . .

He recalled something E-147 had said earlier: that the only land entrance to this place was inside the minotaur city somewhere. He must've meant this dock that Orlando mentioned.

"How do all you royals get here?" he asked lightly. "Do you fly in?"

Having walked partway around the balcony, Orlando opened a door leading back inside.

"How else would we get to this godforsaken shithole? We fly in on helicopters from one of Hades's mines. There's a chopper platform and hangar up on one of the fortresses near the top of the mountain.

"The four kings are all board members of Hades's mining company, so a trip to India like this is passed off as a 'board inspection tour' of the mines. Hiding in plain sight, as they say. Hoping to figure a way out, eh? Don't get your hopes up, Captain. The odds of you leaving this place alive are infinitesimal. My advice to you: fight a good fight and die a good death."

He led Jack inside and down a short corridor to the men's room.

★ ★ ★

Back in the dining room, Shane "Scarecrow" Schofield sat with his patron, the King of the Sea, a man by the name of Garrett Caldwell.

In his sixties, with sweeping silver hair and the tan of a man who played a lot of tennis, Caldwell was a gracious and refined host.

Two other American champions sat at the table with Scarecrow: the Navy SEAL named DeShawn Monroe and the Delta operator, Jeff Edwards.

As the lunch wound down, their patron stood to take his leave and, one by one, shook hands with each of them.

Scarecrow didn't take much notice of the ritual until Caldwell shook his hand and surreptitiously left something in it:

A small syringe, with a curious red liquid inside it. The label on the syringe read "HYPOX-G4–62."

Scarecrow knew what that was. Every elite soldier did. It was a hyperoxygenated blood additive, designed to give you extra stamina in the battlefield by upping the oxygen levels in your blood. It was the military equivalent of anabolic steroids.

Scarecrow had never used it, but he knew guys who had. Exhaustion was the biggest enemy in the field, and "Hypox," as the men called it, kept you energized and alert for many hours.

Caldwell smiled at Scarecrow. "A little pick-me-up, should you need it. Could be the difference between life and death. Best of luck."

In a cubicle in the men's room, Jack folded down the lid of the toilet seat and sat down on top of it, thankful for a moment's solitude during which he could gather his thoughts.

A thousand things ran through his mind.

Hades. The Great Games. The mountain in the crater, all of it covered by camouflage netting. The minotaurs and their gated city. The lion-helmeted killers, Chaos and Fear. The deadly jester, Mephisto.

Snippets of recent conversations:

Mendoza speaking about the end of the universe.

Orlando talking of arriving here by helicopter from a mine in India.

And one odd statement: Hades saying that only a *classically educated champion* could prevail in the Games.

The sound of a door opening made him look up.

Two men had entered the men's room, chatting.

The first one was saying "—that last challenge was simply *brilliant*! Your brother, Zaitan, was *on fire*. And Mephisto was fucking livid that the fifth warrior caught him. That jester is cunning and it's not often that he gets outwitted by anyone. He'll be gunning for West during the second phase."

"*If* West survives the Fifth Challenge, George," the other one said and Jack recognized his voice as that of Dion DeSaxe, Hades's son and the prick who had gotten close to Lily at Stanford. They were standing at the urinals.

The one named George said, "You don't know the half of it, Dion. Seriously, the next challenge is massive. I saw Vacheron do a trial run a month ago. The circus, the course, the chase pack. It'll be fucking mayhem. Fucking *brilliant*."

Dion said, "Vacheron has done well with his challenges. I heard someone say that if the Games are a success, as a thank-you gift, Orlando will give his sister, Iolanthe, to Vacheron as his wife."

"Vacheron has long wanted to become royal," George said. "It's his greatest desire. He has a lot riding on these Games."

There was a pause as they urinated.

"Tough shit for the hostages, eh," George said.

Jack frowned as he heard this.

Dion said, "What are you gonna do? After the Fifth Challenge, there's no further need for them. The champions fight alone in the second phase, so slaughtering all the hostages is perfectly reasonable."

"I know, but—"

"Honestly, George, don't think of the hostages as people. In the grand scheme of things, their lives don't mean shit. They should be honored to die doing something important."

The two men zipped up and left the men's room.

Jack remained in the stall for several more minutes, to give them a head start.

When he emerged, his eyes were set in a determined stare.

This was no longer just about surviving challenges to protect his friends.

He now had to figure out what he was going to do after the next challenge, because at the end of it, no matter how well he performed, Alby and Sky Monster—not to mention Scarecrow's hostages, Astro, Mother, and Tomahawk—would all be killed.

Jack whispered softly to himself. "What the hell am I going to do?"

★ ★ ★

A few minutes later, he returned to the dining hall.

As he was about to step through the main doorway, a figure blocked his way.

Major Gregory Brigham.

"You're dangerous," Brigham said, his eyes hard.

"Is that so?" Jack said.

"When all this started, you didn't know shit from Shinola. Looked like a deer in the fucking headlights. But you learn fast. Which means now you're dangerous. No offense, but when I win this next challenge, I'm going to use my reward to blow your fucking head off."

Brigham shoved past Jack, bumping his shoulder on the way.

"No offense taken," Jack said after him.

Jack returned to his table and sat beside Lily.

He gazed forward, deep in thought, as if in a trance.

"Dad?" Lily asked, concerned. "You okay?"

He looked up quickly.

Then he leaned in close to her and whispered, "They're gonna kill all the hostages after the next challenge. Can you do something for me *during* the challenge?"

Lily turned to face him and for the first time in two days, she dared to hope. This was the Jack West Jr. she knew.

"Of course. If I can."

"Good. It's time to bust our people outta here." He told her what he needed her to do and she nodded gamely.

"It'll be tough, but I can try," she said.

Moments later, the guards returned and took Jack away to compete in the Fifth Challenge.

After the champions departed, the dining hall emptied quickly, the various royal households decamping to the viewing balcony for the Fifth Challenge.

Iolanthe was about to guide Lily that way when three young men arrived in front of them.

Dion, his friend George, and Dion's brother, the champion from the Underworld named Zaitan.

"Princess Iolanthe," Dion said. "If you don't mind, before the next challenge begins, we'd like to show Miss Lily one of the more remarkable places in the palace."

Iolanthe looked warily at the three princes. Lily could see that she wasn't happy about this, but Dion, as Hades's heir, clearly outranked her.

"But of course, Dion," she said.

Leaving the dining hall, Dion guided Lily to an internal elevator that descended through the core of the mountain.

"Lily, this is my younger brother, Zaitan," Dion said. Zaitan was a shorter, more muscular version of Dion: square-jawed, handsome, and, like Dion, he knew it.

Zaitan looked Lily up and down lasciviously. "She is just as you described her, brother. *Ripe*."

"Indeed," Dion said.

The elevator stopped and the three princes led Lily through some winding rough-hewn tunnels.

"Where are we going?" Lily asked.

"My father and his guests are so *old*," Dion said. "In age and in attitude. We're going to where the young people are."

They stepped out onto the railway tracks behind the hostage train. Lily tried to catch a glimpse of her people in their hostage carriage but she couldn't see into it from this angle. Looking out from the open-faced tunnel, however, she could see the odd-looking racetrack for the upcoming Fifth Challenge.

Dion guided her away from the hostage train before cutting into a tight stone-walled passageway that delved into the tunnel's inner wall.

After walking a short way down this passageway, Lily emerged inside a large chamber and stopped dead in her tracks.

She was in a dungeon, an enormous ancient dungeon.

Arched alcoves lined the walls, some of them veiled by ragged curtains, others sealed with iron bars. Torture devices were everywhere: in the alcoves, on the walls, hanging from the ceiling.

And there were many kinds. Racks, cages over hot coals, firebrands, spiked sarcophagi. The whole place was lit by fire pits, giving it a truly hellish aspect.

Dion grinned. "There's a reason why the Underworld got a reputation for punishment and damnation. Welcome to the fabled dungeon of Hades."

Some of the royal princesses from the luncheon were here, casually drinking wine as they sat on some racks.

It was then that Lily saw the minotaurs.

Three whimpering minotaurs were chained to a long wall, their arms stretched high above their heads. Red-hot brands hung from ropes an inch in front of their petrified faces. If they moved even slightly, their noses would be scorched.

Dion stood in front of them but didn't even notice them.

"I've been thinking, Lily," he said. "About the future. About our future together."

"You have got to be joking," Lily said.

Dion smiled wanly.

He casually pushed a hanging brand into the face of the minotaur nearest to him.

The minotaur wailed in utter agony as the red-hot brand seared the skin of his face.

Dion let the brand swing away. The minotaur hyperventilated.

Dion looked closely at Lily. "You don't know it, but you are a catch. There is no finer prize in my world than the beautiful Oracle of Siwa."

Lily was appalled but not cowed. "And there is no greater coward than a man who tortures a defenseless creature bound to a wall. You're psychotic."

Dion grabbed a rusty sword lying nearby, tested its weight in his hand . . .

. . . then he nonchalantly thrust it into the belly of the defenseless minotaur, killing it.

Lily clenched her jaw tightly, now more angry than appalled.

Dion withdrew the sword from the now-limp minotaur and gazed thoughtfully at the blood on its blade.

"I have asked my father for your hand in marriage and I think he will give you to me."

"*Give* me to you? Are you insane?"

Dion snuffed a laugh. "It is customary at the halfway point of the Great Games for Lord Hades to bestow gifts on nobles: titles, land, brides. I know it is customary for a young man to ask the permission of a girl's father for her hand, but let's be honest, it wouldn't be proper for someone of my station to ask anything of your father."

Lily shook her head. "What makes you think I would marry you?"

"Oh, I think this might," Dion said, pulling aside a curtain . . .

. . . to reveal an arched alcove set into the wall.

Chained to the wall of the alcove in the same manner as the minotaurs, flanked by the princes Zaitan and George, was Alby.

★ ★ ★

Lily lunged forward but Dion seized her arm and held her back.

Alby quivered as he hung from the wall, trying desperately not to move, lest he touch the red-hot brand hanging inches in front of his nose.

Dion said, "Great times are upon us, Lily. Over the next few years, monumental things will happen and the four kings will be central to them. *I will be one of those kings* and far sooner than nature intends."

Lily looked incredulously from Dion to Zaitan. "You plan to *kill* your father, Hades? The two of you?"

"My brother and I are of like mind on this matter," Dion said. "My father—unyielding as he may be—is far too beholden to notions of duty and fairness. For thousands of years, the Lord of the Underworld has been feared, but today he is merely *respected* for his adherence to the rites of old.

"No. Hades should be feared. The mere mention of his name should inspire cold dread. When I take that title, with my brother by my side, I will be feared by all, by kings, by commoners, by my minotaur slaves, and most especially by the wife who will bear me many children. When the time is right, at the end of these Games, my dear father will have a most unfortunate accident. I will claim his throne and then I will rule this kingdom with an iron fist."

Dion moved in front of the sweating, quivering figure of Alby. He hovered one hand beside the hot brand hanging so close to Alby's nose.

"Lily. Darling. You will be my wife. You will be my wife and you will keep my secret because you know that I can pluck your friends and loved ones from any place in the world, bring them here and torture them just like this."

With a sudden—unexpected—move, Dion unclasped Alby's chains, letting him drop to the stone floor, gasping and free.

While Lily watched, Dion crouched in front of Alby. "As for you,

Albert, my secret is safe with you, too, since no matter what happens, you will be liquidated at the end of the next challenge."

Dion nodded to George. "Take him back to his carriage." He held out his arm for Lily. "Shall we adjourn to the viewing balcony?"

This time, despite how furious it made her feel, and with a final desperate look at Alby, Lily reluctantly looped her arm in Dion's.

FIFTH CHALLENGE

THE BATTLE RACE

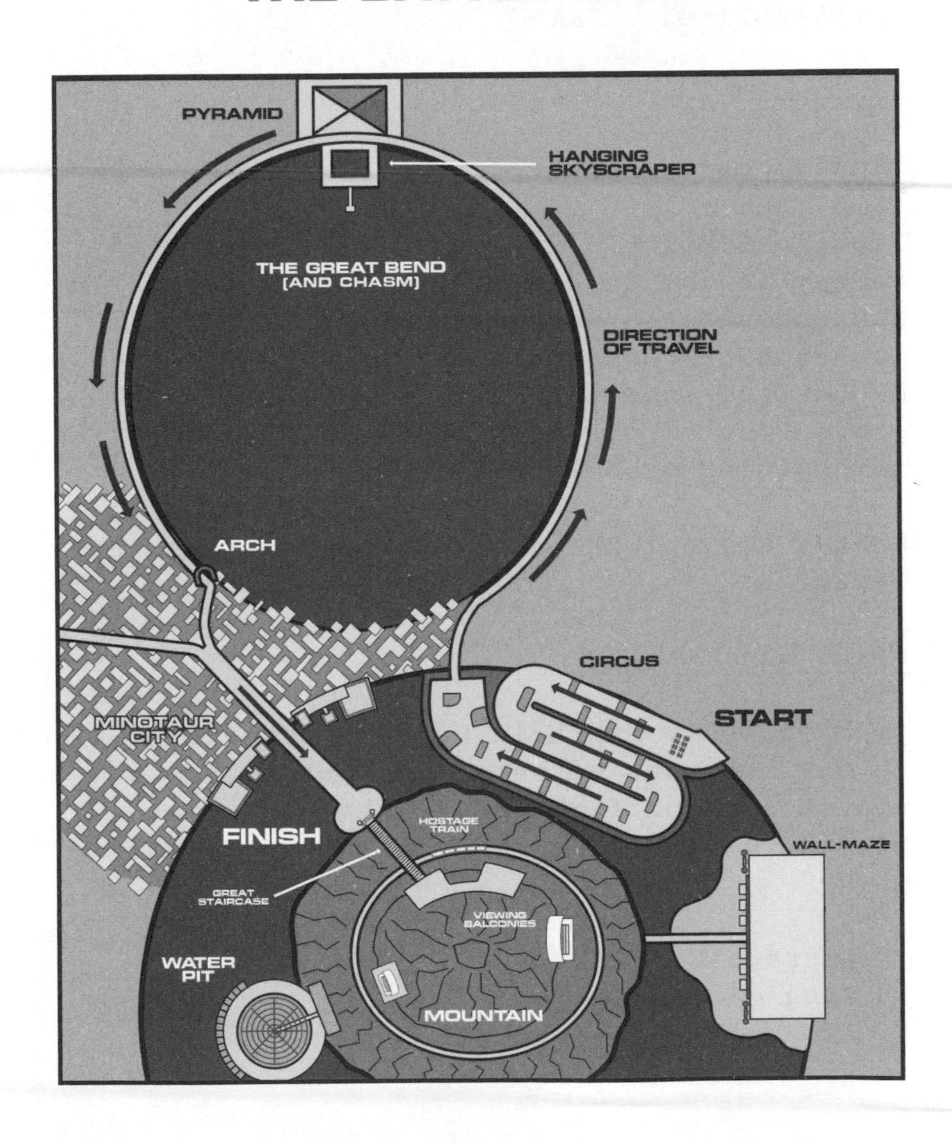

CHAMPION PROFILE

NAME: SCHOFIELD, SHANE MICHAEL
AGE: 42
RANK TO WIN: ABOVE 10TH
REPRESENTING: SEA

PROFILE:

Captive participant.

Captain Schofield has had a distinguished career in the United States Marine Corps. He has encountered our world on one previous occasion, although he does not know it: he battled (and defeated) the Majestic-12 group, one of our agencies tasked with maintaining global order.

Ranked above 10th out of 16 to win the Games.

FROM HIS PATRON:

"I have every faith in Captain Schofield. He may not want to serve me, but he has a reputation for fighting to the very last breath. I like that kind of man representing me."

Garrett Caldwell,
King of the Sea

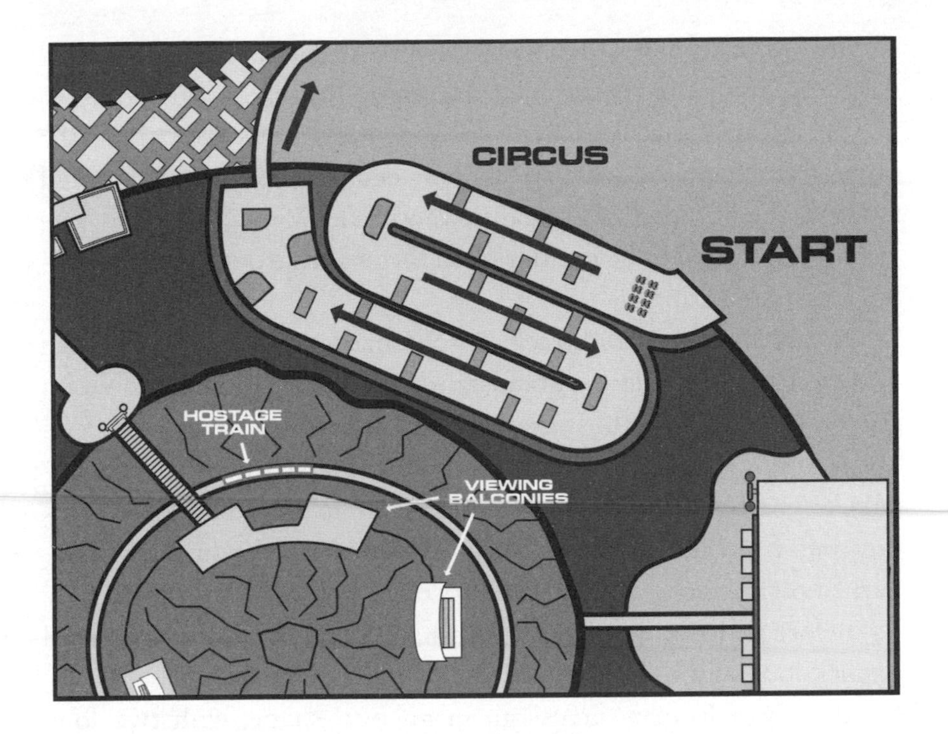

THE CIRCUS

Thirty minutes after he'd left the dining hall, Jack found himself sitting in a stripped-down motor car, wearing his trademark fireman's helmet.

The car was a Light Strike Vehicle, or LSV, a small dune buggy used by various armies in desert environments. As a car, there wasn't much to it: it was little more than a black frame on four wheels, with two front bucket seats and a single rear seat, a steering wheel, and a rear-mounted engine. No windows, no doors, no extra weight: everything about it was light and fast.

Sitting with Jack in the car were Sky Monster and E-147 since he was allowed two companions for this challenge. Jack had planned to bring Alby with him for this one, but when he'd returned to their cell, for some reason Alby wasn't there. Jack had seen him return moments after he and the others had left.

Sky Monster now sat in the driver's seat—his right arm bandaged tightly—while E occupied the seat in the rear.

Their car—as well as five other identical LSVs containing the other five champions—stood at one end of a long dirt-covered straight, the first part of a gigantic racetrack. With Zaitan and Vargas having elected to be exempt from the challenge, only six champions were competing.

It was an ancient racetrack, an old chariot-racing arena known as a circus. Massive stone grandstands flanked it, looking down on the track. Right now, those grandstands were eerily empty.

Looming above the grandstands was Hades's dark mountain-palace. The royal spectators watched from an elevated balcony jutting out from it. Far below their balcony was the hostage train, parked on its tracks, allowing the hostages a clear view of the circus.

Before he had been deposited in his LSV, Jack had been granted a quick look at the circus.

Usually, a Roman circus ran in an oval shape, with two long straights and two bends, but this one had been modified.

It had three straights that ran in a flat *S* shape before the track curved into the tunnel hewn into the outer wall of the crater. Each straight, however, was fitted with a peculiar set of obstacles: broad square pits, all filled with water.

"Champions!" Vacheron called from a podium above the track. "Welcome to the Fifth Challenge, the famed Birdman Race! In years gone by, this race was staged with chariots. Today, we use a modern kind of chariot, but the race itself remains true to its heritage.

"The course consists of three parts: the circus, the Great Bend, and a final dash through the minotaur city of Dis.

"A single Golden Sphere lies in a cavern at the far end of the course, in a monument devoted to the birds beloved by the war god, Ares. To the champion who returns that sphere to the royal balcony will go the final reward. There is no punishment for coming last in this challenge: all who complete it will progress to the next phase of challenges.

"At the conclusion of this challenge, the first sphere-laying ceremony will be held. After that, the second phase will begin. Luck to all. Start your engines!"

Jack froze.

Not at Vacheron's final words, but at something he had just said.

In a monument devoted to the birds beloved by the war god, Ares.

"The birds beloved by Ares," he said aloud. "The Stymphalian Birds."

Sky Monster frowned at him. "What are you talking about?"

Jack didn't answer.

Things were suddenly becoming clear to him.

The First Challenge: a man charging at him, dressed as a *bull*.

The Second Challenge: being pursued through the water maze by men dressed as *lions*.

The Third Challenge: the deadly iron boulders, with their protruding blades fashioned to look like the tusks of *boars*.

The Fourth Challenge: in which the jester had been dressed as a *deer*.

And all of it done in honor of a *hydra*.

Jack recalled the giant statue of Hercules wrestling the Cretan Bull in the dining room.

"It's been staring me in the face the whole time," he said.

He even remembered the bust in the dining room of a stern-faced King of the Underworld labeled: EVRYSTHEVS.

"Eurystheus . . ." Jack said. "Son of a bitch."

Sky Monster said, "Would you mind explaining your realization for those of us in the cheap seats?"

Jack turned to face him. "Sky Monster, these Great Games are not just any old Games. They are a series of challenges, trials, *labors*. They are the greatest and most famous labors ever recorded in history. These Games are the Twelve Labors of Hercules."

Jack counted them off on his fingers.

"The First Labor of Hercules was to defeat the Nemean Lion, a beast with skin that could not be penetrated by arrows or swords. Here we have Hades's thugs, Chaos and Fear, with their lion helmets and modern armor.

"The Second Labor of Hercules was to defeat the Lernaean Hydra. This has all been about defeating the Hydra Galaxy.

"The Third Labor of Hercules was to catch the Ceryneian Deer, which I did in the last challenge in the wall-maze, while the Fourth required Hercules to catch the Erymanthian Boar—remember those iron balls in the Third Challenge?

"The Seventh Labor was fighting the Cretan Bull, like I had to do in the First Challenge.

"And the Eleventh Labor was to find the Golden Apples of the Hesperides. What have we been searching for during all these challenges? Golden Spheres. Orlando even called them 'apples' one time.

"And who was the guy who gave Hercules all his Labors? A famous king named Eurystheus, who is represented in a bust up in Hades's dining hall, a bust labeled *Dis Pater*, Lord of the Underworld.

"Classical historians have often wondered how a petty and cowardly king named Eurystheus could have bossed around a warrior as tough as Hercules. Here's the answer: Eurystheus was the Lord of the Underworld and the ancient figure we know as Hercules was a champion in these Games.

"The Twelve Labors of Hercules have long been considered metaphors. Because they were. They were ritual challenges that used animal motifs like boars, lions, bulls, and birds."

Sky Monster stared at Jack. "That's all well and good, Jack, but how is that going to help us?"

"Hades said it himself," Jack said. "Only the classically educated champion will succeed in these Games. I think a few of my fellow champions knew about this when they came here, while I didn't. But, Sky Monster, I just caught up."

Just then, with a great clanking, a series of large garage doors set into the wall behind the six small Light Strike Vehicles rumbled open.

Jack turned and saw eight very large vehicles emerge from the garages.

Six of the eight vehicles were giant black trucks. Jack recognized them: they were brand-new six-wheeled Typhoon assault trucks.

Built in Russia by the Kamaz corporation, they were brutish things, designed to withstand mines and missiles and pretty much anything else that exploded. Standing on six massive tires, they could carry sixteen men in their boxlike rear compartments.

These Typhoons, Jack saw, had rear compartments that were open on both sides, allowing him to see clearly into them.

He didn't like what he saw.

Each huge black truck held twelve sword-wielding minotaurs.

"I'm starting to see what this challenge involves," Sky Monster said. "While we race, they chase."

"Uh-huh," Jack said, swallowing. "Hey, E. Any chance those minotaurs might show you some preferential treatment?"

E-147 shook his head. "These minotaurs from different region of minotaur kingdom to E-147; from south region. They train long time for this challenge. It great honor for them to kill or eliminate champion. Make no difference to them that E-147 be here with Jack."

The other two chase vehicles were smaller than the Typhoons, but still larger than the Light Strike Vehicles.

They were Spartan armored personnel carriers: steel-plated four-wheel drives popular with SWAT teams.

Jack saw one other thing about these Spartans. Whereas the Typhoons were driven by minotaurs, the two Spartans were driven by men: by Fear and the Hydra.

He looked at the thin frame of his Light Strike Vehicle. While it had speed and nimbleness on its side, it looked positively puny compared to the chase vehicles.

Jesus.

In the LSV beside Jack's, Scarecrow, Mother, and Astro were also looking at the enemy vehicles looming behind them.

"Can't help feeling the odds have been stacked against us," Scarecrow said.

"Fuckin' A," Mother added. "I haven't been this bummed since Zayn left One Direction."

Jack was looking at one of the Spartan APCs when the little red figure of Mephisto jumped onto its running board, whispered to its driver, the white lion-helmeted Fear, and then pointed directly at Jack.

"I think we're in for special treatment," Jack warned Sky Monster. "Man, I hate that little red guy."

A horn trumpeted from somewhere and Mephisto scrambled off the track, joining Vacheron up on the podium that overlooked the starting line.

Vacheron called, "Champions! Prepare for the race of your lives! Begin!"

He thrust his arms high and the six Light Strike Vehicles blasted off the mark and the Fifth Challenge began.

What followed was mayhem: total vehicular mayhem.

The six LSVs of the champions whipped down the first straightaway at phenomenal speed, kicking up dust clouds behind them as they skidded and weaved to avoid the wide square pits in the ground.

Behind them, the pack of black Typhoon trucks thundered down the track, engines roaring, minotaurs leaping from their open troop-holds and landing on the fleeing LSVs and wrestling with the champions.

The minotaurs on the two Spartans had even better firepower: they fired shoulder-launched rocket-propelled grenades at the champions' cars.

In short, the racetrack became a moving battlefield of speeding cars, trucks, explosions of dirt, and crisscrossing RPGs.

Sky Monster drove hard while Jack pivoted in his seat, searching for enemy vehicles coming up behind—

"Monster! Brake left!" he called as one of the other Light Strike Vehicles swung in toward them and tried to ram them into one of the deep water-filled pits.

It was Gregory Brigham's car, driven by Brigham himself. Brigham gave Jack a tart salute as he shot off ahead of them.

And then their little car jolted violently, struck from behind by Fear's Spartan four-wheel drive. It rumbled along right behind them.

A crossbow bolt whistled past Jack's ear—fired by Fear, extending his arm out his window.

"Get us out of here, Monster!" Jack urged.

Sky Monster gunned it and their LSV whipped around the next pit before swerving to avoid another one, forcing the Spartan to swing in behind it.

Lily watched it all from the royal balcony.

From her elevated position, she could see that the pits on the track were arranged in such a way that one could not drive in a straight line for long. As such, the six little cars of the champions swerved constantly while they were pursued by the six minotaur-filled Typhoons and the two Spartans of Fear and the Hydra.

She watched in ever-increasing anger as the big Spartan APC harried Jack's tiny LSV.

Jack and Sky Monster's car skidded at speed around the first turn of the circus, kicking up a spray of sand.

Dust swirled all around them. Engines roared. The walls of the circus sped by in a blur.

They were mid-field, traveling in the center of the pack of Light Strike Vehicles, tucked in behind Scarecrow's car. Up ahead, leading the way, were the cars of the Navy SEAL, DeShawn Monroe; the Delta operator, Jeff Edwards; and the Brit, Gregory Brigham.

But then as they came to the end of the second straight, Brigham suddenly cut across the nose of Edwards's car, forcing it toward one of the water-filled pits at the end of the straight.

Edwards's car careered toward the pit, but Edwards was a skilled driver and he managed to skid to a halt and avoid the pit . . .

. . . only to stop right in front of Jack and Sky Monster's car.

Sky Monster yanked his steering wheel left and did a full 360-degree lateral skid. It was an amazing evasive maneuver, but it cost them precious speed and suddenly, as they sped in a wide arc onto the third and last straight of the circus, they had two enemy ve-

hicles pressing close on either side of them: Fear's APC on the right and a massive minotaur-filled Typhoon on the left.

Minotaurs began leaping from the Typhoon onto the struts of their LSV en masse.

One, then two, then three . . .

As Sky Monster drove, Jack and E punched and kicked them off.

It quickly became clear to Jack that this was hopeless: no sooner would they dispatch two minotaurs than two more would take their places.

He looked over at Fear in his white helmet—and an idea hit him. A way to get out of this. This *whole* thing . . .

"Sky Monster!" he called above the wind. "Whatever happens, keep driving! Keep going!"

"What are you doing?" Sky Monster shouted.

"Using my classical education to get us out of this!"

With those words, Jack leaped off their LSV onto the running board of Fear's Spartan and in one quick movement, grabbed the crossbow attached to Fear's forearm guard and fired it *across the hood* of the LSV . . . and hit the driver of the minotaur-filled Typhoon on the other side, right in his eye-visor!

Its driver dead, the Typhoon peeled left before its wheels clipped the outer wall of the circus and the whole massive truck suddenly rolled, tumbling down the straightaway, hurling minotaurs this way and that, before it slammed to a crunching halt on its side. It lay still, shrouded by a cloud of dust and dirt.

Freed from the bad-guy sandwich, Sky Monster powered ahead in his LSV.

Jack remained standing on the running board of the Spartan, holding on to the side mirror with one hand while with the other he grappled with Fear.

Two things struck Jack about his opponent: one, the big warrior in the lion helmet was fucking strong and, two, he had all the leverage. Jack wasn't going to win this fight.

Better do something then, his mind screamed.

He looked ahead and saw that the straightaway bent to the right, heading toward the tunnel set into the crater wall. A final pit, filled almost to the brim with water, yawned before him.

Jack leaned close to Fear. "You wanna dance, asshole? Let's dance."

He then released his grip on Fear, reached inside the cab and yanked on the steering wheel.

The big black APC swung left and with Jack on it, it plowed straight into the oncoming pit with a monumental splash.

The crowd of royal spectators gasped as one as the Spartan went plunging into the pit with Jack hanging on to its side.

"Fucking *brilliant*!" the prince named George exclaimed.

Beside him, Lily watched in horror as the big armored truck sank into the inky black water, taking the fighting figures of Jack and Fear with it as it slowly disappeared from view.

Inside the sinking Spartan, Jack and Fear grappled ferociously.

Fear was trying to bring around his other forearm, with a second crossbow mounted on it, while Jack—standing awkwardly, half-in, half-out of the driver's window—tried to hold his arm at bay.

Water flooded over the top of Jack, gushing in through the window in a constant stream—but he couldn't let go of Fear's arm. To do so would mean death.

Then, with frightening speed, the Spartan went vertical and with a *whoosh*, went entirely underwater.

On the track above the pit, all the other cars and trucks raced out of the circus and disappeared into the tunnel leading to the next section of the course.

The royal spectators, however, were all glued to the water pit, waiting to see who would emerge from its sloshing waters, Fear or Jack.

A minute passed.

The water went still.

Neither combatant emerged.

Lily watched the pit with desperate eyes. "Come on, Dad . . ."

Another minute passed.

The water in the pit was now perfectly still.

Lily despaired. No one could hold their breath for that long, not even Jack.

"Look there!" Prince George called. "Over in the far corner! Someone's surfacing!"

Hope surged through Lily as she peered to see who it was. She saw a man break the surface on the far side and step up out of the pit.

She didn't need to see his face.

His white lion helmet said it all . . . so did the battered fireman's helmet gripped in his right hand.

Tears began to well in her eyes.

Prince George pumped his fist. "Fuck yeah! The fifth greatest warrior is toast."

The royal spectators all began cheering and applauding as, on the empty racetrack far below them, the familiar figure of Fear—in his lion helmet, white body armor, and combat boots—turned to face them.

Then he removed his helmet.

And they all instantly fell silent.

Only Lily smiled, through tear-streaked eyes.

It was not Fear.

It was Jack.

The fight between Jack and Fear inside the cabin of the Spartan had been as brutal as it had been desperate.

As they struggled over the crossbow, Fear had hit a button on the side of his helmet.

Jack knew what he was doing.

He recalled the Second Challenge in the water maze, when he'd noted that Fear's helmet had scuba capabilities: Fear had used it to hold the golden minotaur underwater and drown him.

Fear was switching on his helmet's scuba breather.

But in doing this, Jack saw, he had revealed his weakness, his classical weakness: *a bare section of skin between his helmet and his throat*.

In his mind, Jack recalled how, according to the legend, Hercules had killed the Nemean Lion. After his arrows had bounced harmlessly off its impenetrable hide, Hercules had shot it with an arrow through its only weak point: its mouth.

That was Fear's weak point.

Jack figured that the Nemean Lion in the legend had actually been a warrior like Fear dressed in similar armor.

Buoyed by this knowledge, Jack lunged forward and twisted Fear's forearm guard with the crossbow on it so that it pointed upward. Then Jack fired it up into the gap between Fear's helmet and his throat, at the exposed skin there, right up into his mouth.

The arrow lodged deep in Fear's brain and he went instantly still, dead.

Then as the water filled the sinking truck around them, Jack grabbed the dead man's helmet and put it on, biting down on its internal scuba mouthpiece just as the incoming water consumed him fully.

Now, he would wait—wait for all his enemies above to think him dead and leave the circus. In that time he grabbed Fear's body armor and boots and put them on.

That was another thing his classical education told him to do.

After slaying the Nemean Lion, Hercules had used its own claws to cut off its pelt and head. He'd then used the impenetrable pelt *as his own armor* in the other Labors.

Jack was starting to see the symbolism of the Games. He not only had to achieve what Hercules had achieved, he needed to do it in the same *ways* Hercules had done it.

After a few minutes had passed, he decided it was safe to surface and he swam upward.

Jack stood on the deserted racetrack, now wearing Fear's white battle gear over his jeans and T-shirt.

On one forearm, he wore Fear's crossbow and in his other hand, he gripped a rocket launcher and a couple of RPG rounds.

He tossed Fear's white lion helmet to the ground and put his own fireman's helmet back on.

He glared up at the royal balcony and called, "Hades! I know! About the Labors! So now I know what I have to do!"

The assembled royal spectators whispered to each other in shock. Champions did not dare address Hades in such a fashion. They all recalled what had happened to the Taiwanese soldier who had defied him at the start of the Games.

Vacheron, who had returned to the balcony by this time, turned to Hades and held up his remote. "Shall I punish this insolence, my Lord?"

Hades shook his head. "Heavens, no. This is not insolence. This is courage."

He called back to Jack. "I am glad to hear you know what you must do, champion! Honor us and do it!"

Down on the track, Jack whirled on the spot, looking for a car or truck he could appropriate.

All the other vehicles were gone, all except one.

The crashed Typhoon, the one that had rolled earlier, hurling clear all of its minotaur crew.

Dented and dusty, it stood on the track about fifty yards from Jack.

He hurried over to it, jumped into the driver's seat and keyed the ignition.

Nothing happened.

He tried again and only got a weak wheezing noise from the engine.

Even from this distance, he could hear the royal spectators laughing at him.

And then an LSV came blasting back out from the tunnel in the crater wall and Jack raised his weapons, tensing for the fight.

Only then did he recognize the driver of the Light Strike Vehicle.

Sky Monster.

The big New Zealander swung the little car to a skidding halt beside Jack. E smiled a goofy Neanderthal grin from the backseat.

"Need a ride?" Sky Monster said. "We got a short way into that tunnel but then I figured it didn't matter if we finished this race. It only matters that *you* do."

Jack leaped into the LSV.

"Thanks, buddy. Let's do some fucking damage."

The LSV's rear tires kicked up dirt as the little car roared off the mark and raced out of the stadium, into the tunnel that led to the next section of the course.

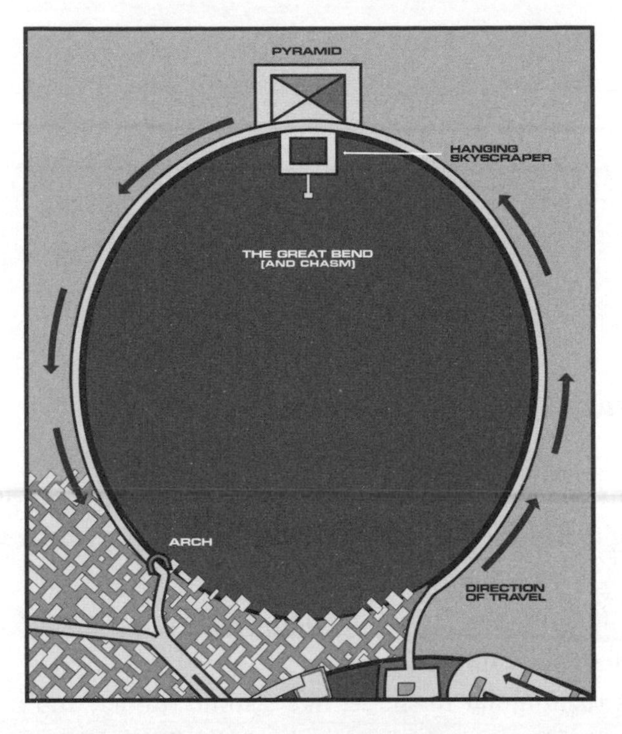

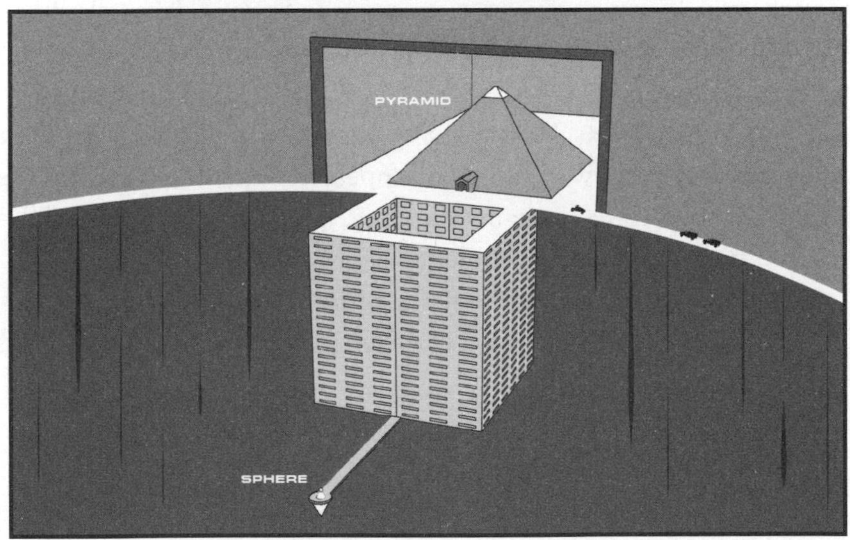

THE GREAT BEND

THE GREAT BEND

In his introduction to this challenge, Vacheron had mentioned something called the Great Bend. Now Jack knew why it was called "Great."

Upon leaving the circus, he and Sky Monster shot through a short stone-walled tunnel.

It was rectangular in shape, like a mine tunnel, and it was wide enough only for two vehicles to travel side-by-side. Its walls, floor, and ceiling were cut from solid stone. There were no crevices or recesses in them.

Then, abruptly, as Jack and Sky Monster sped along the dark tunnel, the left-hand wall simply disappeared and all of a sudden the tunnel only had three sides: floor, ceiling, and the right-hand wall.

An utterly immense chasm fell away to their left.

There was no guardrail or fence protecting that side; the roadway simply ended at a sharply cut edge. The chasm below it seemed to drop away forever.

Floodlights illuminated the enormous underground space.

And what a space it was.

Jack saw that this ledge-like road ran in a long sweeping curve around the circumference of the gigantic chasm. It was essentially a superlong bend: a Great Bend.

He saw the five cars of the other champions, the five Typhoons, and the one remaining Spartan racing around the track, doing battle with one another, tiny against the colossal landscape.

If the big circular bend were a clock face, Jack had entered it at five o'clock. He saw a distant exit on the opposite side of the chasm at seven o'clock. The other champions were at one o'clock. To get to the exit, Jack would have to drive counterclockwise all the way around the chasm, passing through the centerpiece of the cavern at twelve o'clock.

And that centerpiece was, quite simply, stupendous.

An enormous pyramid, easily two hundred feet high, stood inside a box-shaped shelf cut into the wall of the cavern.

In front of it, overhanging the dizzying chasm, was a building-sized stone structure.

It looked like a New York skyscraper that had been attached to the wall of the chasm, only instead of rising upward, it plunged downward perhaps twenty or thirty stories.

Scores of horizontal recesses could be seen on the hanging building's flanks, each one the size of a large coffin. A square shaft seemed to run down the building's core and its walls were also dotted with recesses.

Jutting out from the lowest point of the upside-down skyscraper, infinitesimal in the distance, was a half-bridge that extended out over the abyss. The half-bridge had a podium at its tip on which stood a single Golden Sphere.

"Floor it, Monster!" Jack called.

Up ahead of Jack and Sky Monster, Scarecrow was driving hard, trying to stay ahead of a Typhoon truck filled with minotaurs while not tipping off the edge of the roadway.

Without warning, a minotaur charged onto the hood of the Typhoon directly behind him, took three bounding steps forward and dived like a maniac onto the back of Scarecrow's Light Strike Vehicle.

Mother grabbed the little bastard by the horns of his helmet and tossed him off the speeding LSV into the chasm. The little figure fell away into darkness, falling forever, squealing all the way down.

Further ahead, the Navy SEAL DeShawn Monroe was leading the pack and his LSV blasted out of the three-sided roadway onto the enormous shelf that housed the pyramid and the hanging skyscraper.

He swung his Light Strike Vehicle onto the roof of the hanging skyscraper and quickly leaped out of it, leaving his SEAL companion to take the wheel.

Monroe himself began climbing down some ladderlike handholds cut into the face of the skyscraper. The handholds ran in a vertical line in between the many coffin-sized recesses carved into the structure, leading to the sphere's platform.

Monroe was so intent on his task, he didn't look into the shelflike horizontal recesses.

He just ran out onto the elongated half-bridge, snatched the sphere and began his return climb.

He reached the top of the skyscraper and ran back to his partner in their LSV—

—just as a crossbow bolt slammed into Monroe's forehead, a bolt fired by Gregory Brigham in his incoming LSV, using a crossbow he'd taken from a minotaur.

Monroe collapsed to the ground, dead, the sphere still gripped dumbly in his hand.

His partner spun, searching for the source of the bolt, but his only reward was a bolt to his own face, shot by one of Brigham's partners. The Navy SEAL snapped back in his seat under the weight of the shot, his face exploding with blood.

Brigham's LSV swept to a halt beside Monroe's corpse. Brigham leaned down and scooped up the sphere.

His car then sped off, away from the pyramid and the upside-

down skyscraper, beginning the return journey down the other side of the Great Bend.

Jack saw it all from his own speeding car, far behind.

He recalled Brigham's words at the luncheon and how, if he won the challenge, he would use the reward to have Jack killed.

"Monster," he said. "We gotta catch that asshole. It's time to clear the road."

Racing at outrageous speed along the first half of the Great Bend, Jack's LSV closed in on the last Typhoon truck.

As Sky Monster brought them closer, Jack stood in his seat, hefted his stolen RPG launcher onto his shoulder and fired it.

The RPG lanced forward, issuing a dead-straight smoke trail before it slammed into the rear axle of the Typhoon and detonated.

The rear end of the Typhoon was lifted off the roadway before it began to fishtail and wobble . . . until one of its outer tires tipped off the edge of the roadway and the whole truck fell into the abyss. It dropped away into the void, taking its crew of minotaurs with it.

On the royal balcony, the assembled spectators were now watching the challenge on large plasma-screen monitors.

They were all glued to the screens, watching them with rapt attention.

No one noticed Lily step up beside Vacheron as he stared at the big screens.

Likewise, no one noticed when she slipped her hand into one of the pockets of his robes and removed his remote control from it.

THE RETURN BEND

There were now two races going on.

Out in front was one pack. It was led by Gregory Brigham, streaking away with the sphere, hurtling down the roadway on the far side of the chasm.

He was closely followed by the Delta man, Jeff Edwards, and Scarecrow. Immediately behind them were the Hydra in his Spartan and two minotaur-filled Typhoon assault trucks.

The second pack of vehicles was only just going past the pyramid and the suspended skyscraper.

In this pack was one other champion—a Tibetan prince named Renzin Depon, brother of the dead champion named Tenzin—plus two more Typhoons, and last of all, Jack, Sky Monster, and E-147.

As they sped out onto the wide shelf containing the pyramid, Jack eyed the rearmost Typhoon.

A couple of the minotaurs standing in its open-sided hold were firing long-barreled sniper rifles at the fleeing Light Strike Vehicles ahead of it.

"That's what I need," Jack said as he reloaded his RPG launcher, hoisted it onto his shoulder and fired it at the Typhoon.

The shot hit the truck's right rear tire, sending it careering up the sloping flank of the pyramid before it rolled onto its side—throwing the minotaurs clear—and tumbled to the base of the pyramid, smoking and broken.

Sky Monster brought their LSV to a halt beside the crashed truck. Jack and E-147 leaped out and scooped up two sniper rifles that had been tossed clear of the wreck. A couple of dazed minotaurs charged at them, but Jack dispatched them with quick hits from the butt of his newly acquired rifle.

As he and E-147 jumped back into the LSV and Sky Monster gunned it off the mark, Jack looked backward, taking in the magnificent suspended skyscraper.

He saw the many shelflike recesses cut into its outer flanks and also the ones cut into its hollow core.

He squinted.

There were objects *inside* each of the recesses.

Nestled inside each rectangular alcove there was a coffin-like sarcophagus. Each sarcophagus appeared to be cut from brilliant silver and depicted on their surfaces were eerie carvings of men with the heads of long-beaked birds. The bird-heads had the distinctive hooked beaks of ibises.

A half-man/half-ibis, Jack thought. *A birdman. And also the common depiction of the ancient Egyptian god of wisdom, Thoth.*

And he knew all about Thoth.

The Word of Thoth was the ancient language that only Oracles of Siwa like Lily could read. It was the language that had been at the center of his adventures over the past twenty years: from the Golden Capstone that had sat atop the Great Pyramid at Giza to the locations of the Six Sacred Stones and the prophecy of the Five Greatest Warriors.

Perhaps most important of all was the fact that the ancient Egyptians had claimed that Thoth himself was a mysterious visitor who had brought them advanced knowledge and wisdom.

This is all coming full circle, Jack thought.

He gazed down at the many coffins, sitting in their rectangular alcoves.

There must have been hundreds of them.

But what was inside them?

Jack didn't have time to dwell on that. He had to catch Brigham before he won the challenge and condemned Jack to death. If he survived these Games, Jack figured he could always come back later.

Jack looked across the wide chasm and saw Brigham's LSV whipping away along the return bend, well ahead of all the other vehicles. The British major was about to reach an archway that marked the end of the return bend: the exit.

"E!" he called. "Where does that tunnel go?"

"To minotaur city," E-147 replied. "Minotaur city is last segment of course."

"Sky Monster!" Jack yelled. "If that British asshole wins this challenge, we're all dead. We have to slow him down. Pull over."

Sky Monster stopped the car at the beginning of the return bend.

Jack leveled his sniper rifle, balancing its barrel on one of the struts of the Light Strike Vehicle.

Through the crosshairs of its telescopic sight, he saw Brigham's fleeing LSV, speeding away.

In a few seconds, Brigham would reach the archway and disappear into it.

Jack squinted as he looked through the crosshairs and gently squeezed the trigger.

Blam!

A spark kicked off the ground behind Brigham's speeding LSV. He'd missed.

Jack chambered another round. Took aim again. And just as Brigham's car whipped into the archway at the far end of the bend, he fired.

Brigham's LSV zoomed into the archway . . . just as its left rear tire was punctured by the sniper round . . . and suddenly the Light Strike Vehicle fishtailed wildly, bouncing off the arch before it skidded through it and came to a screeching 180-degree halt.

Jack hit Sky Monster on the back. "That'll hold him up for a little while. Go! Go! Go!"

Sky Monster gunned the LSV around the long sweeping return bend. The stone-walled roadway was still tight and the drop on the left-hand side was close.

There was now only one Typhoon immediately ahead of them plus the car of Renzin Depon. Scarecrow, Edwards, the Hydra, and the other two Typhoons were further ahead, about to rush through the archway.

"Get in behind that truck," Jack said.

Sky Monster did so, bringing their speeding car right up close to the rear bumper of the Typhoon.

The three minotaurs in the Typhoon's hold were so preoccupied with the chase going on ahead of them that none of them saw Jack creep out onto the hood of his Light Strike Vehicle and leap forward onto the tailgate of their Typhoon.

From there, he shimmied along its left side, hanging high above the fathomless chasm below.

Lifting himself up, he surprised two minotaurs in the rear hold and hurled them from it into the abyss.

A third shocked minotaur was holding an RPG launcher. Before he could react, Jack grabbed his launcher by the barrel and used it to hurl that minotaur out of the hold, too. He then climbed fully into the hold and crept forward into the driver's cab of the Typhoon, and fired the RPG *out through the windshield*.

After shattering the windshield, the RPG shoomed low over

Renzin's LSV and hit the Typhoon ahead of it, blasting its rear half to pieces.

The Typhoon swerved left and nose-dived off the edge, sailing into nothingness.

Jack was left in the cab of his Typhoon with its very shocked minotaur driver. One kick and he was out the door and falling to his death and suddenly Jack was at the helm of a Typhoon assault truck.

He stopped the truck, allowing Sky Monster and E to climb aboard.

"Now, this is more like it," Sky Monster said, sliding behind the wheel and hitting the gas.

The big truck shot off after the rest of the fleeing vehicles.

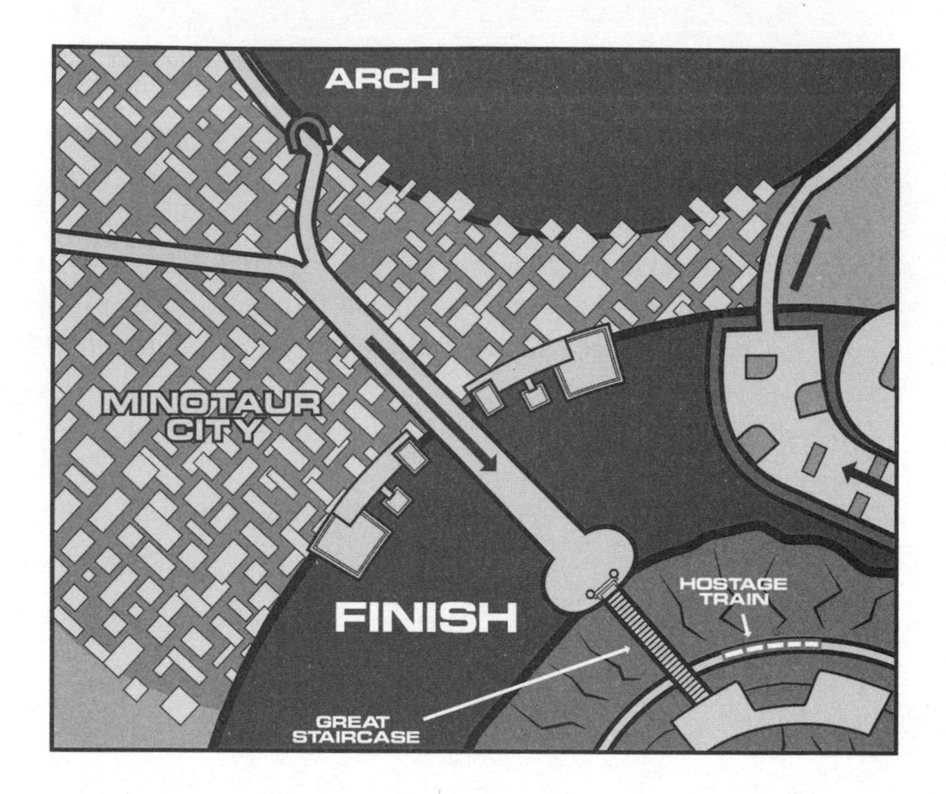

Up ahead, Scarecrow was in the middle of his own drama.

Jack's long-range shot at Brigham's Light Strike Vehicle had done more than just slow down Brigham.

It set off a chain reaction that affected almost every vehicle in the convoy.

When Brigham's rear tire was hit, his car had skidded through the archway and swung to a lurching backward-facing halt.

The car immediately behind Brigham's—that of the Delta man, Edwards—swerved to avoid the suddenly stationary car. But it clipped Brigham's wheels and went bouncing off to the right, rolling onto its side before sliding to a halt on its roof.

Scarecrow's car came next.

He also swung right as he burst through the archway, narrowly avoiding both Brigham's and Edwards's cars, as he sped out into a larger space.

He looked back to see Brigham dive out of his car with the Golden Sphere gripped in one hand, leaving his two partners in the stationary car—a split second before the Hydra's Spartan four-wheel drive came rampaging *right over* the stationary LSV, crushing both the car and the men still in it!

A second later, a Typhoon truck crunched right *into* the remains of Brigham's LSV and the two vehicles became one and they skidded sideways as a single unit past the shocked figure of Gregory Brigham before crashing into a wall.

As the other vehicles overshot the crash site, Scarecrow took in this new space around him.

A ramshackle city in a high-ceilinged cave spread out before him. It looked like a colossal slum, a vast tangle of ungainly shacks and sheds, all of different shapes and sizes, all made of rusted metal or corrugated sheet iron.

The minotaur city, Scarecrow realized.

It reminded him of the townships of Johannesburg or the refugee slums of Kenya. A metropolis for those deemed by their superiors as unworthy of the niceties of life, a slum city for the wretched workers of Hell.

Thousands of minotaurs sat on rooftops and balconies—or any elevated vantage point—eagerly waiting to see the racers emerge from the Great Bend.

They were not wearing their helmets, Scarecrow saw, so their hairy Neanderthal features were visible. He'd forgotten that they were actually people—of a sort—with faces, friends, and even moments of joy. This race, it seemed, was clearly a highlight of their otherwise hard lives.

The road on which Scarecrow and the others had been traveling continued *over* the city as a freeway-like concrete bridge that bent and curved between the taller structures of the underground metropolis.

At the far end of the elevated roadway stood a giant thick-walled castle with a massive medieval gate in its center. Beyond that gate, Scarecrow could see the base of Hades's mountain-palace.

More cars came bursting out of the archway: the LSV of the Tibetan, Renzin Depon, and . . . one final black Typhoon truck.

Brigham still stood out on the roadway, looking this way and that, trying to figure out his next move while not getting killed.

The Typhoon swept past him, rushing by perilously close to him, and Scarecrow's eyes widened in surprise as he saw a figure lean out from the passenger side of the Typhoon and deftly snatch the Golden Sphere from Brigham's hands.

It was West!

"Told you he was a determined son of a bitch," Mother said.

But then, to Scarecrow's even greater surprise, Jack's Typhoon suddenly pulled up right beside his car.

"Scarecrow!" Jack called. "Catch."

He threw the Golden Sphere to Scarecrow, who caught it like a football. He looked up at Jack in shock.

"What are you doing?" Scarecrow asked.

"We don't have much time, so I'm gonna make this quick. Hades is gonna have *all* the hostages executed after this challenge. But there's an exit from this place through the minotaur city: a supply tunnel of some kind to a western dock. The way I see it, this is our only chance to get our friends and hostages out of here. If you want your people to survive this thing, send 'em over to my truck now. As for you, I need you to go and win this challenge and these Games while I break out our other hostages."

"They'll kill you," Scarecrow objected. "As soon as they see you running, they'll blow the charge in your neck."

"I'm hoping I've got that eventuality covered, at least for the time being," Jack said. "Right now, I just want to free our hostages."

Scarecrow turned to Mother and Astro. He bit his lip in thought.

"Go," he said to them. "Go with him."

Mother began to object. "Now, wait a sec—"

"No," Scarecrow said. "He's right. If I have to go it alone from here, I'm not going to watch you guys get executed. I'd rather you had a fighting chance to live. Go and help him."

With a scowl Mother jumped out of the LSV and with Astro beside her, boarded Jack's Typhoon truck.

"You better be right, Huntsman," she said to Jack. "Okay. Where to?"

Jack's gaze became fixed and his jaw clenched. "Back to Hades's mountain. We shepherd your man home and then we bust our people out."

Two cars shot along the elevated roadway that ran above the rambling minotaur city: Scarecrow's Light Strike Vehicle and Jack's stolen Typhoon truck.

Racing a short distance behind them were the chase cars and the LSV of the very confused Renzin Depon. With their cars smashed and overturned, both Brigham and Edwards were out of this race.

The road was raised about thirty feet off the ground, so that it was roughly level with the rooftops of the shacks of the city. The Neanderthal population assembled on those rooftops cheered as the vehicles shot past them.

Among them was the Minotaur King, watching the proceedings with thoughtful eyes.

From the passenger seat of his Typhoon, Jack peered forward.

In the very heart of the city, the elevated road arrived at a fork: one road bent to the left, heading back toward the main crater and Hades's mountain-palace; the other branched to the right, heading westward.

As they shot through the junction, taking the road that led back to the palace, Jack stared down the westward one. It disappeared into a modern-looking tunnel cut into the wall of the cavern.

"E, does that road lead to the west dock?"

"Yes," E-147 said. "To supply dock."

Jack turned to Mother in the rear compartment of the truck's cab: "After we get the hostages, that's where we're going."

They turned left at the fork, onto the homeward stretch of the roadway, and Jack beheld a magnificent sight: this final piece of road stretched away from him in a dead-straight line that ended at Hades's mighty mountain-palace.

Of course, he knew that the road had been built this way so that Hades and his royal guests could watch the final mile of road *from* the mountain-palace, but he let that thought slide.

The road lanced ahead of him, cutting through the minotaur city before entering the main crater through the castle gate and arriving at the enormous staircase that climbed the lower reaches of the mountain to a royal balcony where Hades and the royals waited.

"Faster, Monster!" Jack yelled.

The two cars sped down that final stretch of roadway, streaking away from their pursuers.

They whipped through the gate and roared out into the open space of the main crater, arriving at a broad vehicle turnaround at the base of the colossal staircase leading up the mountain.

"Go!" Jack yelled to Scarecrow as the two cars skidded to simultaneous halts at the bottom of the staircase.

With a nod, Scarecrow took off up the stairs, gripping the Golden Sphere in the crook of his arm.

Watching from the royal balcony at the top of the enormous staircase, Hades frowned.

He saw Scarecrow bounding up the Great Staircase with the sphere. That was to be expected.

But the fifth warrior, West, was not clambering up the stairs. He was dallying in the cab of his truck, which was odd.

"Monsieur Vacheron," Hades said. "What is the fifth warrior doing?"

Vacheron looked down at Jack and he also frowned.

★ ★ ★

From his position in his hostage carriage, Alby watched Jack, too.

"What are you doing, Jack?" he whispered softly.

At the base of the massive staircase, Jack was waiting for Scarecrow to get to a certain spot up the staircase.

"Come on, Scarecrow, hurry up . . ." he said to no one.

For the staircase stretched up and over the railway track on which the hostage carriages stood and he couldn't do what he had to do until Scarecrow got past them.

Vehicles began to appear all around him: the car of the last remaining champion, then the dented and damaged chase trucks of the Hydra and the minotaurs.

Then Scarecrow, pounding up the Great Staircase, ran over the top of the hostage carriages and Jack made his move.

He leaped out of the cab of his Typhoon with the rocket-propelled grenade launcher already on his shoulder and aimed up at the mountain-palace . . .

. . . and he fired.

Up on the royal balcony, Hades's eyes went wide.

Beside him, Vacheron's mouth opened in horror.

He snatched for his deadly remote control, only to find his pocket empty.

"What the—?" he gasped.

The RPG shot out of Jack's launcher and streaked upward, its smoke trail stretching out behind it.

It wasn't aimed at the royal balcony as Hades and Vacheron feared, but rather at the railway tracks immediately underneath the first hostage carriage.

The RPG hit its target and exploded.

Rocks and debris showered out from the side of the mountain . . .

. . . and the tracks beneath the first hostage carriage were suddenly no longer there. Now there was just a void.

And the little train began to roll forward into it.

As his hostage carriage began to roll slowly forward, Alby saw the future and it was not good.

"Oh, God," he said.

He scooped up the two dogs with one arm and gripped the bars of the slowly moving carriage with the other.

They were about to go for a very bumpy ride.

★ ★ ★

As the hostage train rolled forward into the newly created hole in front of it, it only had one way to go: down.

The first carriage tipped into the hole and dropped off the tracks . . . taking the rest of the hostage train with it!

The entire four-car train rolled off the tracks and began to bounce down the rocky slope of the mountain at a diagonal angle.

It crashed through crags and bounced off boulders, making a terrible noise as it thundered down the slope: a mix of groaning iron and smashing rock.

Inside the train, Alby and the dogs were thrown around like rag dolls.

The heavy iron-barred train careered down the slope at this oblique angle for a full hundred yards before it *slammed* into the side of the staircase that Scarecrow had run up.

The train took a chunk out of the massive staircase as it bounced off it. The deflection set it on a more vertical path down the lower reaches of the mountain, so that it was now rushing *straight down the slope*.

It roared down the last section of the mountain, blasting through some rocky outcrops—turning them instantly to dust—before it shot out onto the turnaround at the base of the stairs. It ground into the flat concrete of the turnaround, hitting it so hard that it gouged a trench in the concrete before, with a squeal of rending metal, it came to a lurching halt in a billowing cloud of dust.

The whole scene looked like something from a disaster movie: the crashed train, half-turned on its side, enveloped in the immense dust cloud.

"Fuck me," Mother gasped. She turned to Jack. "I think you and me are gonna get along fine."

"Get your guy," Jack said, already racing toward Alby's carriage. "I'll get mine."

"What about the hostages of the other champions?" Mother said.

Jack grimaced. "We can't save everyone. Besides, those hostages knew what they were getting into when they came here. Ours didn't. Hurry now, we gotta get out of here!"

Alby was curled awkwardly on his back inside the side-turned carriage, still gripping the two dogs protectively. All three of them were covered in rock dust. Roxy whimpered, licking Alby's face.

The iron-barred door of their cage had been thrown open by the crash of the train. Beyond it, Alby could see nothing.

The dust cloud had created a gray fog-like effect around the whole crashed train.

Suddenly a figure burst out of the fog, stood over him and lifted him to his feet.

It was Jack.

"Come on, kid. Time to get out of Dodge."

Others were reacting in different ways:

From the royal balcony, all that could be seen at the base of the staircase was an enormous billowing dust cloud. It had enveloped the entire lower half of the stairs plus all the vehicles down there.

No one could see a thing.

Lily watched from a corner of the balcony. While everyone was looking at the devastating scene, she surreptitiously stripped the battery from Vacheron's remote and tossed the remote off the balcony.

The royal spectators murmured in hushed whispers, some excited, some alarmed. Many glanced fearfully over at Hades.

For his part, Hades just stared impassively down at the dust cloud.

"Monsieur Vacheron, I presume you have a response for this," he said.

Vacheron was speaking quickly but firmly into a radio. He nodded to his master. "Yes, my Lord. Of course, my Lord. I do apologize. This is most unfortunate. I can't imagine what he's doing."

Hades never took his eyes off the dust cloud.

"I know what he's doing. He's trying to rescue his friends."

Jack threw Alby and the two dogs into the back of the Typhoon just as Mother and Astro returned with the fourth Marine, Tomahawk.

Jack climbed into the Typhoon's cab. "Sky Monster, go! Get us out of here!"

Sky Monster floored it and the Typhoon blasted off the mark, now heading away from the mountain-palace, *back toward* the minotaur city.

Disoriented by the dust cloud and with Vacheron's voice yelling in his helmet's earpiece, the Hydra gave chase in his Spartan, but Jack had a hundred-yard head start on him.

Watched by the shocked Neanderthals on their rooftops, Jack's Typhoon shot back down the elevated road of the minotaur city, heading the wrong way. When the truck came to the junction, it swept left, heading west.

It shot into the tunnel at the end of that elevated road and suddenly it was blasting through darkness, the only light the beams of its headlights.

This tunnel was nothing like the ornate, ceremonial roadways of the Fifth Challenge.

It was simple, utilitarian, all concrete and rough-cut stone walls. A supply tunnel.

A few hundred yards behind Jack's fleeing truck were the headlights of eight vehicles: the Hydra's Spartan led the way, followed by seven new Light Strike Vehicles driven by armed minotaurs that had been scrambled in response to this emergency.

A chase pack.

After racing through the darkened tunnel for about four miles, Jack's Typhoon burst out into a larger space.

Jack saw ten container trucks parked at loading docks, with their rears pointing toward four massive industrial-sized garage doors cut into the far rock wall.

Sunlight lanced through gaps in the garage doors. Low, fading sunlight. Late-afternoon sunlight.

Western sunlight.

"The west dock," Jack breathed. "We made it."

A crew of minotaurs standing near the trucks looked up at the sudden arrival of the Typhoon.

Armed with AK-47 assault rifles, they'd been forewarned by radio of Jack's approach and now they covered the industrial-sized garage doors. But they looked uncomfortable holding the guns, gripping them in an unfamiliar way.

These aren't fighting minotaurs, Jack realized. *They're workers. Just a loading-and-receiving team.*

Jack leaned out the passenger door of the Typhoon and raised his rocket launcher to his shoulder.

"Don't slow down," he said to Sky Monster.

The minotaurs opened fire . . .

. . . just as Jack fired the rocket launcher.

It shot through their midst before it slammed into the left-most garage door and exploded.

When the smoke cleared, a great ragged hole yawned open in the garage door and a thick beam of orange sunlight illuminated the big receiving cavern.

Sky Monster aimed the speeding truck right at the hole and the little gang of minotaurs dived clear as the Typhoon thundered past them, smashed through the hole in the door and raced outside into the light.

The speeding Typhoon burst out into sunlight and from his seat in the cab, Jack beheld a spectacular view.

A wide, flat sandy beach spread out before him. It sloped gently down to the water's edge, where it met the dead-calm waters of the Arabian Sea.

The setting sun sat low on the horizon, reflecting off the ripples in the water. Jack guessed there were perhaps thirty minutes of daylight left.

On the landward side of the beach was a high cliff of hard-packed sand. At least a hundred feet high, it prevented access to the beach from the desert. They had emerged from a squat concrete structure built into the face of that cliff.

It was deathly silent. No birdsong. No insect noise. No hum of city life.

Located somewhere on the remote west coast of India, Hades's kingdom was clearly a long way from anywhere.

Jack's eyes took in the wide beach.

It would have been gorgeous had it not been for one singular feature: the many rotting hulks of gigantic cargo and container ships that lay strewn along its length, beached on the shore.

They were hideous ghostlike things. Rusted and cannibalized, they looked like the emaciated skeletons of once-great oceangoing behemoths.

Jack had read about beaches like this. It was a ship graveyard.

Decommissioned cargo ships were brought here to be stripped—by hand, by impoverished laborers—for reusable parts.

It was notoriously dangerous work: fumes from leftover fuel often overcame workers; fires were common; arsenic used to strip away paint and rust poisoned workers; and sometimes whole sections of the boats simply collapsed on top of them, killing them.

The derelict boats stretched away from Jack to the north and the south.

He counted twenty of the giant things, but there were many more than that. The nearest skeletal ship towered above his Typhoon truck, twenty stories high, but as the beach extended into the distance in a broad curve, the ships shrank in size, vanishing into the haze.

"Which way do we go?" Mother asked.

"North," Jack said. "If this really is India, then going south doesn't help us. There's only ocean that way. Going north gives us options. Not good ones, but options: Pakistan, Afghanistan, borders."

To Jack's right, a paved asphalt supply road ran up the side of the cliff, leading to the desert.

Sky Monster said, "Do I take the road?"

Jack bit his lip in thought. "No. If they have reinforcements, they'll come from that direction. Go north along the beach itself."

"Gotcha." Sky Monster peeled the truck onto the beach, kicking up a geyser of sand as he swung northward—

—a split second before the chase pack, led by the Hydra's Spartan, blasted out of the wrecked door of the supply dock and opened fire with every gun they had.

The wave of bullets strafed the hull of a derelict container ship as Jack's Typhoon swung in close to it, whipping underneath the giant steel support struts that held the massive ship upright on the beach.

They were racing down the side of the colossal ship, heading toward the sea.

Grabbing whatever weapons they could find in the Typhoon, Mother, Astro, Tomahawk, and Alby all returned fire at the pursuit vehicles behind them.

"There's too many of them!" Mother called to Jack.

"I'm on it!" Jack shouted, hefting his RPG launcher onto his shoulder and firing it—not at the chase cars but at the struts holding up the beached ship.

The shot hit its target and a gout of sand sprayed upward, taking three of the support struts with it and with a great moan of straining metal . . .

. . . the container ship began to fall sideways!

The immense shadow of the slow-falling ship enveloped the cab of Jack's Typhoon.

"Go faster, Monster!"

"My foot is on the floor!" Sky Monster shouted.

"Then put it through the floor!"

Groaning loudly, the massive ship toppled sideways, coming down on top of them and the chasing pack. The Hydra saw what was coming and he pulled his Spartan out and away from the falling ship. Most of his fellow chasers did the same, except for three of the minotaur-driven LSVs. They just hammered forward, trying to outrun the falling ship and catch Jack's fleeing truck.

Jack's Typhoon skidded around the stern of the toppling ship just as it came down.

The sound it made when it hit the sand was colossal. A tremendous deafening *boom*.

The three LSVs speeding along behind Jack's truck failed to outrun it by mere yards and the ship pulverized them, crushing them to nothing when it landed on top of them.

Guided by Jack, Sky Monster drove like a demon, charging northward up the ship-strewn beach.

They skidded around a second beached ship and then whipped right through a tunnel-like hole in a third.

The chase pack was close behind them, firing, harrying, gaining.

And then a black-painted assault chopper roared over the cliff guarding the landward side of the beach and unleashed a withering barrage of 30mm rounds at Jack's Typhoon.

As Sky Monster peeled away from the fusillade, Jack snapped to look up at the chopper.

It was a Kamov Ka-52 Alligator gunship. Possibly the sleekest attack chopper ever built by the Russians, it was incredibly maneuverable, thanks to its two coaxial contrarotating main rotors.

It was a state-of-the-art gunship built to carry one thing: firepower. It had two side-mounted 30mm cannons, twelve Vikhr-M antitank missiles, and a pair of deadly rocket pods. With its side-by-side pilot configuration, it even had ejection seats: rare for a chopper.

In a distant corner of his mind, Jack noted that the Ka-52 Alligator was brand-new. Only the Russian military used it. He wondered if Iolanthe's royal Russian relatives were in the military-helicopter business and had donated a few models for Hades's use.

The Alligator thundered by overhead. Two missiles lanced out from its pods.

"That way!" Jack yelled to Sky Monster. "Go into that ship!"

Sky Monster obeyed and swung them hard over, and their Typhoon bounced straight *into* the next beached container ship.

The big truck took air as it plowed into the ship's rusted, gutted hull. It was now hurtling lengthways down a vast empty hold designed to house hundreds of shipping containers. Beams of sunlight coming through gaps in the walls illuminated the bones of the great ship: a complex network of girders and catwalks.

The two missiles roared in behind the speeding truck and, overwhelmed by the forest of targets now in front of them, they detonated against a pair of girders well behind the Typhoon.

"Huntsman!" Mother called. "That chopper is packing too much heat!"

"I know, I know!" Jack yelled.

She was right. Their Typhoon truck was a seriously tough piece of hardware, but compared to the Alligator, it was a lightweight. It would only be a matter of time until it nailed them.

He had to do something about that chopper.

At that moment, the Hydra's Spartan four-wheel drive swung into the ship behind them and charged down the length of the cargo hold.

"Sky Monster, stay inside this ship, inside this hold! Do loops until you see my signal to get out."

"Your signal?"

"You'll know it when you see it. Alby, get up here!"

Alby appeared in the doorway connecting the cab to the rear hold of the Typhoon.

Jack said, "Okay, listen up. No matter what happens to me, you've all got to get away from here. Alby, you know more about the ancient world and our enemies than anyone here. I'm putting you in charge. Find a radio or a phone. Call Zoe, Stretch, Pooh Bear. But not anybody in government—we don't know who is compromised. Call someone we trust and bring back the cavalry for Lily."

"What about you?" Alby said.

"No matter what happens now, I'm a dead man," Jack said. "As soon as they figure out a way to do it, they're going to blow my head off with the explosive in my neck. The best I can do now is get you guys out of here. You got that?"

"Yes, sir." Alby nodded sadly.

"Mother?" Jack said. "You good with that?"

"I've picked boogers out of my nose that were bigger than this kid, but if you say he's got a brain, that's good enough for me," Mother said.

Jack began to stand but then Alby grabbed him by the arm.

"Jack. Thanks. Thanks for everything."

Jack smiled grimly. "No problem. Now, I gotta go and break some shit. Sky Monster, slow down a little. Let that Hydra asshole get closer behind us."

"Closer?"

"Yes." Jack got out of his seat and hustled back into the hold of the Typhoon.

He then threw open the rear door and saw the Hydra's Spartan right behind them.

Without missing a step, Jack leaped out of the Typhoon and onto the hood of the speeding Spartan, took two steps along it and, to the Hydra's great shock, jumped onto the Spartan's roof.

There he yanked open a hatch and jumped inside. As he landed inside the cab of the Spartan, he kicked the steering wheel, causing its airbag to explosively inflate *right in the Hydra's face*!

With the Hydra stunned by the impact of the airbag, Jack kicked him out of the speeding vehicle and suddenly he owned the Spartan.

And as Sky Monster's Typhoon began doing laps in the shelter of the derelict ship's massive cargo hold, Jack swung the Spartan onto a spiraling access ramp that led upward.

At the same time this was happening, the two pilots of the Alligator chopper were flying it alongside the container ship, searching for the Typhoon inside.

When they saw it through some gaps in the hull, whipping along inside the cargo hold, they swung the chopper into a hover beside the beached ship and waited till they could draw a bead on it.

The pilot gripped his control stick, trigger finger at the ready, waiting for the Typhoon to reappear—

It reappeared.

He jammed his finger down on the trigger.

A tongue of muzzle-fire blazed out from the Alligator's side-mounted cannons.

But only for an instant.

For at that exact moment, a Spartan four-wheel drive armored personnel carrier came sailing out of the sky from the foredeck of the container ship—and landed smack-bang on top of the twin rotors of the Alligator.

The same Spartan Jack had taken from the Hydra and driven up onto the foredeck of the ship.

Only Jack wasn't in it now. He'd gunned it toward the edge of the foredeck and leaped out at the last second, sending the Spartan flying off the edge of the deck, aimed straight at the gunship.

Eight tons of armored personnel carrier came crashing down on top of the helicopter.

It crushed the chopper's twin rotors in an instant and the whole tangled thing came crashing down beside the container ship, landing in the sand in a huge flaming explosion.

Inside the Typhoon, Mother saw the blazing wreck hit the ground.

"Fuck me, that crazy bastard knocked out the chopper."

"I think that was his signal," Sky Monster said.

"Damn straight," Mother said. "This is the best chance we'll have to get out of here. Gun it!"

With a sad look back at the wreckage of the Spartan—and with no way of knowing if Jack was in it or not—Sky Monster did as he was told.

By sacrificing himself and taking out the two biggest threats of the chase pack—the gunship and the Spartan—Jack had given them a chance to get away and they had to take it.

Alby patted Sky Monster on the shoulder. "Go north," he said. "Go north as fast as you can."

Now free of the Spartan and the Alligator, Sky Monster's Typhoon sped north along the ship graveyard, shooting past the rotting, rusting hulks, speeding under their towering bows and sterns.

The four remaining minotaur-driven Light Strike Vehicles maintained their pursuit for a short while, but then they must have received radio instructions to abandon the chase, for they all suddenly turned as one and headed back down the beach toward the concrete supply dock that serviced Hades's kingdom.

Standing in the rear door of the Typhoon, Mother watched them go.

"What are you thinking?" Astro said from beside her.

"I don't think they're gonna just let us go, but if they want to give us a head start, we should get as far away as we can," Mother said.

The Typhoon shot away up the beach, heading north in the dying light of the sun.

As for Jack, without a car or a truck to call on, he just sat on the foredeck of the derelict ship, watching the sun dip below the horizon, waiting for them to come for him.

It didn't take long.

Within twenty minutes, the minotaurs on the four remaining LSVs returned and with the Hydra leading them—his armor scratched and dented from his fall from the Spartan—they surrounded Jack on the foredeck.

He offered no resistance when they cuffed him and shoved him into one of the LSVs.

Then they drove him back in the direction of the western supply dock, back toward the Underworld, where, no doubt, Jack thought, retribution awaited him.

The four LSVs pulled to a halt at the base of Hades's mountain-palace.

Whereas before the palace had been sleek, tall, and imposing, now it was horribly scarred, its symmetrical lines mutilated by the damage caused by Jack West Jr.

The train tracks that had housed the hostage carriages lay askew, blasted apart by Jack's RPG attack. Rubble and debris had cascaded down the lower reaches of the mountain, creating a layer of ugly scree.

And that was the thing: what had once been ancient and elegant was now defaced and deformed.

The assembled royal guests stood in appalled silence as Jack was shoved by the Hydra out of his LSV at the bottom of the Great Staircase.

Of course the Great Staircase was now a lot less great.

It had a gaping dent halfway up its length, the result of the runaway hostage train slamming into it.

Hades, Vacheron, and Lily stood at the top of the staircase, above the broken tracks on which the hostage train had previously stood.

Hades looked imperiously down at Jack.

Vacheron glared at him in apoplectic rage, the veins on his forehead bulging.

The remaining champions stood off to the side, watching warily.

The Hydra guided Jack up the stairs. They stopped at the edge of

the dent halfway up the staircase, a hundred feet below Hades, Vacheron, and Lily.

Hades nodded to his Master of the Games.

Vacheron spoke. "My lords and ladies, may I offer my most sincere apologies. Never have these Games seen such an outrageous act, such an abomination. Champions do not flee the Games. Champions do not try to free hostages. This champion foolishly attempted to do both and in doing so, has brought shame on himself and embarrassed his sponsoring king."

Vacheron pulled something from behind his back and Jack's heart sank.

It was another remote. A second remote control unit that detonated the explosive charge in his neck.

"You thought I would not have a spare?" Vacheron waved the remote at him. "You are lucky I retrieved it only *after* you were apprehended. But, then, now everyone gets to enjoy your death."

Vacheron held up the remote.

"There can be only one punishment for this outrage and that is death. Immediate death."

He aimed the remote at Jack and Jack squeezed his eyes shut, waiting for the end—

"Wait!" a voice called. "Not yet!"

A figure stepped out from the group of champions, gazing up at Hades and Vacheron.

Jack opened his eyes again and looked at the figure in shock.

It was Scarecrow.

Scarecrow held up the Golden Sphere from the challenge as he said, "I won the Fifth Challenge and I haven't claimed my reward. I wish to claim it now. I want Captain West spared."

Vacheron was speechless.

The royal spectators were aghast.

Lily's eyes lit up.

But Hades's face was a mask. He gave nothing away. He stared at Scarecrow long and hard.

Scarecrow just returned his gaze, eyes level and unblinking. "My reward is anything that is in your power to give, is it not? And you can spare his life with a single command."

Every eye in the space was now turned to the Lord of the Underworld.

Hades kept staring at Scarecrow.

Jack was thunderstruck. Not even he had expected this. But Scarecrow was clever: he'd backed Hades into a corner by making this a test of his power, of his authority in his own kingdom.

At last, Hades spoke.

"Champion," he said. "Never in the history of the Great Games has one champion asked for another to be spared. Are you sure this is your wish? This man could kill you in a later challenge."

Scarecrow said, "It is my wish, yes."

Hades shrugged. "The rewards for winning challenges are ancient. They are not mine to choose nor are they mine to deny if they are within my power to give. Your reward is granted, champion. The fifth warrior's life is spared and he may thus continue in the Games."

Audible gasps were heard from the royal balcony. Whispers and murmurs abounded.

Lily grinned with relief.

Jack exhaled.

He threw Scarecrow a nod of thanks and Scarecrow returned it.

Vacheron scowled, his face blazing with fury.

Hades turned. "Monsieur Vacheron, if you will, please prepare the minor temple for the First Ceremony. Once the ceremony is completed, we shall commence the second and final phase of the Games."

KARACHI, PAKISTAN

While Jack had been whipping through the early straightaways of the Fifth Challenge, an old rental van had been whipping through the streets of Karachi at unusual speed.

It was unusual because Karachi—Pakistan's largest city and a sprawling grimy metropolis of twenty-four million people—was not known for fast driving. Normally it was a traffic nightmare, but today was not normal. For today a big cricket match was being held at the National Stadium—a Twenty20 exhibition match between Pakistan's beloved national team and a specially selected World XI team—and it seemed as if the whole city was watching it. The streets were delightfully empty, so Mae and Pooh Bear made good time.

Mae drove, while Pooh gazed out at the vast city with his good eye. Stretch wasn't with them.

"Karachi," Pooh Bear said. "What a dump."

"Highest murder rate in the world," Mae observed. "Warlords, slumlords, crimelords, ganglords. It's a viper pit of terrorists from Afghanistan and all kinds of ethnic criminal gangs who hate each other. Karachi is the birthplace of 'target killing': masked assassins on motorbikes who pull up beside your car and gun you down."

"Who is this guy we're seeing again?"

"Sunny Malik, illegal antiquities broker. According to your phone trace, he sold some kind of artifact to Anthony DeSaxe two months ago. I want to know what it was."

"He has the expertise to know about it?" Pooh Bear asked.

"Not every authority on a subject resides in a university, Zahir," Mae said as she drove. "Sunny won his expertise in the toughest environment of them all: the black market. A dealer in blood antiquities knows history better than a tenured professor at Yale."

"Can we trust him?"

"Not for a second," Mae said. "In addition to his international trade in historical artifacts, Sunny Malik is a local Karachi gangster who'd shoot us as soon as look at us. Once we get the information we need, we should be ready to run."

The van pulled to a stop in front of a walled mansion just off Ghosia Road, about a mile from the National Stadium. The polished mansion was an island of cleanliness in a sea of dust and grime. The roars of the crowd at the stadium could be heard, even from this far away.

Pooh Bear and Mae got out.

After a short discussion with the two armed gate guards—during which a call was made and both Mae and Pooh were patted down for weapons—they were ushered inside.

Mae and Pooh Bear entered a wide marble-floored room where four Pakistani men sat gathered around a gigantic television.

On the television, of course, was the cricket match, and watching it with three goons was Sunny Malik.

Sunny sat in a huge leather La-Z-Boy recliner. He swiveled it around to face his visitors.

He was an enormously fat man of sixty, with a bulging belly, a bushy gray moustache, and multiple chins. He wore a loud Hawaiian shirt, open at the neck, and he practically glittered with gold: three chunky chains around his neck, four bracelets on his wrists, and a pair of garish 70s-era Elvis sunglasses over his eyes.

Sunny lazily blew cigarette smoke into the air above him as he spoke.

"Mrs. Mabel West. Mother of Jack West Jr., ex-wife of the late Jack West Sr., a.k.a. Wolf. It is an honor to finally meet you. I was a fan of your articles in the historical journals before you went into hiding after your divorce. I must say I was glad to see your work reappear after Wolf's untimely death. It's always a pleasure to meet someone as interested in the ancient world as I am." He grinned slyly. "What brings you to my humble abode this fine day?"

"Information," Mae said. She held up a wad of hundred-dollar bills that Pooh had provided. "And I'm willing to pay for it."

Five minutes later, Mae and Pooh Bear stood with Sunny in an office adjoining the television room, looking at Sunny's computer screen. On it was a photo of a beautiful ancient tablet covered in cuneiform.

"This is what I sold DeSaxe," Sunny said. "A clay tablet found in Mosul a year ago. 14th century B.C. It's the ninth tablet of the Epic of Gilgamesh."

"The ninth tablet, you say?" Mae said. She glanced at Pooh Bear. "The Epic of Gilgamesh is one of the earliest and greatest poems in history. Gilgamesh was a hero not unlike Hercules: a great king and warrior who went on arduous quests. The Epic of Gilgamesh consists of twelve tablets. The ninth tablet describes Gilgamesh's journey to an 'Underworld' at the ends of the Earth."

Her eyes began scanning the cuneiform text.

"And the buyer was Anthony DeSaxe?" Pooh Bear asked.

"No, it was his son, Dion. Said it was a gift for his father, for a special occasion. I like Anthony DeSaxe. He has bought several quality items from me over the years. Discreetly, of course. I'm less fond of Dion. He's a cocky fucking brat."

Mae looked up from the tablet. "It's the ninth tablet, all right. Although it has some extra lines I've never seen before. It seems to be giving directions." She translated: "'Gilgamesh began his journey

at the northern city of the Hydra and proceeded toward its southern twin until three-fourteenths of the way, he came across a tunnel guarded by two hairy men giving entrance to the realm of the Lord of the Underworld . . .' "

Mae cut herself off. "Three-fourteenths of the way . . ."

She blinked as she looked up at Sunny, trying to hide her excitement. "This tablet was found in Mosul, you say? Islamic State?"

"They are the best looters since the Nazis," Sunny said, smiling.

Then he removed his gaudy sunglasses to reveal hard bloodshot eyes that stared directly at her. He'd seen her excitement.

"Mrs. West, nothing in this world pains me more than selling something for less than market value. Dion DeSaxe paid me US$600,000 for this tablet yet now I get the feeling I should have charged him more. Much more."

"No, no . . ." Mae stammered. "It's nothing that makes it any more valuable to you—"

"But it's something that makes it very valuable to *you*," Sunny said. "People think I deal in artifacts, guns, and drugs, but I don't. I deal in *value*. I deal in anything that people want."

"We should go—" Mae said.

"Only after you tell me what this is all about," Sunny said. "Or perhaps I should call Anthony DeSaxe and ask him why Mabel West just turned ashen white when she read the tablet I just sold to his son. Boys—"

The three thugs watching the cricket stood up, drawing pistols. They entered the office . . .

. . . just as Pooh Bear yanked off the jeweled brass ring holding his long beard in check and threw it at their feet.

The small wad of C-2 plastic explosive that he always kept hidden inside the ring went off like a flash-bang grenade, hurling Sunny and his henchmen off their feet.

Pooh Bear grabbed Mae by the hand and they rushed out the door.

They burst out into sunlight, dived into their van and peeled out just as Sunny's henchmen ran out onto the street after them, guns drawn.

Sunny appeared behind his men. "Kill the Arab! Bring the woman back to me!"

The thugs mounted some nearby motorcycles and sped off after the van.

Pooh Bear swung the van at speed onto Ghosia Road, chased by the three bikes. Thanks to the cricket match, traffic on the wide straight road was still moving pretty well and Pooh Bear banked and weaved through the various vehicles on it.

He glanced in his side mirror and glimpsed one of the riders behind him raising an AK-47. The gun flashed and his side mirror exploded.

"Target killers!" Mae shouted above the din.

The first motorcycle-riding assassin sped up, slicing through the traffic on his sleek bike, and swept up alongside their crappy little van, aiming his rifle a split second before he was blasted clear off the bike by a shot that no one heard. It was as if he'd been yanked backward by an invisible rope. One second he was there, the next he wasn't. His riderless motorcycle kept going for twenty yards before it clattered to the roadway.

"Leave it to the last second next time," Pooh Bear said.

"*Sorry, there was a truck in my sight line*," Stretch's voice said in Pooh Bear's ear.

Stretch sat perched on a rooftop at the far end of Ghosia Road, beside an enormous Pepsi billboard, in a perfect sniper's position that looked all the way down the dead-straight road. Through the crosshairs of his Barrett sniper rifle he saw Pooh and Mae's van coming toward him, chased by the killers and weaving through all the slower-moving vehicles on the dusty road.

★ ★ ★

At that moment, the remaining two killer-bikers zoomed up on *both* sides of Pooh's van and opened fire on it.

"*I got the one on your right!*" Stretch called. "*You take the one on the left!*"

Pooh Bear heaved left on his steering wheel and rammed the armed biker on that side up against a truck in the next lane. The biker was crushed for a moment before he dropped out of sight, tumbling with his motorcycle beneath the wheels of the truck.

At the same instant, the killer on the right-hand side of their van was hit by a sniper round right in the heart and he was hurled backward.

Now free of their pursuers, Pooh Bear swung his van left, off the main road and into a maze of back alleys.

Sunny Malik would find the van two hours later, abandoned in a lane at the base of a building with an enormous Pepsi billboard on its roof.

He saw the dirty tire marks of two trail bikes on the floor of the van's rear compartment: Mae and the Arab had come prepared. If they were on bikes now, speeding away through the labyrinth that was Karachi, Sunny's people would never catch them.

Sunny gazed at the empty van with narrowed eyes and began to think.

Inside Pooh Bear's jet parked at a private airport west of Karachi, Mae, Stretch, and Pooh sat down in front of a laptop computer.

"Benjamin, could you pull up India and Pakistan on Google Earth, please," Mae said.

Stretch did so.

"Now, pinpoint the two cities named Hyderabad in India and Pakistan, and plot a line between them."

After a few clicks of Stretch's mouse, the map looked like this:

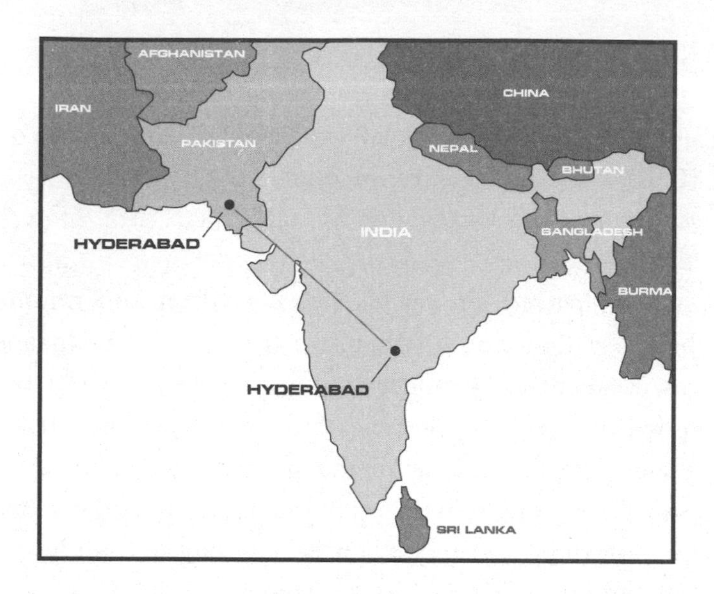

"Okay. Starting at the northern one, plot a point three-fourteenths of the way *between* the two Hyderabads," Mae said. She looked at Pooh Bear. "If it worked for Gilgamesh, maybe it'll work for us."

After a few more mouse clicks, a point appeared on the line.

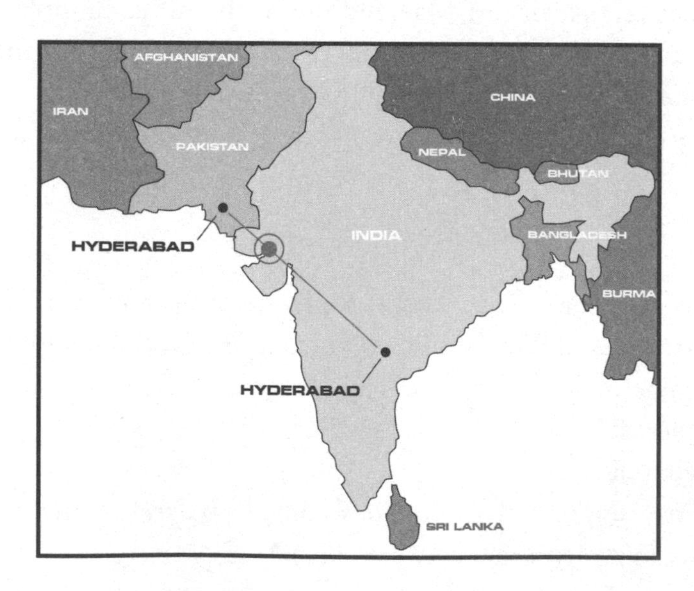

The point between the two Hyderabads was situated in north-western India, where the Thar Desert met the Arabian Sea.

"If this is right, the Underworld is in Gujarat Province, India," Mae said, "near the coast of the Arabian Sea. That's seriously remote, a long way from anywhere . . ."

". . . yet suspiciously close to where our wealthy friend Mr. Anthony DeSaxe has several mines and a thirty-mile stretch of private beach with a ship graveyard," Stretch said. "A modern mine would be a great cover for an ancient underground kingdom."

Pooh said, "You think *DeSaxe* might be the modern Lord Hades?"

Mae said, "He has the wealth, the royal connections, and the bloodline. His blood is as blue as it gets. He'd be an excellent candidate."

She tapped her finger on the computer screen. "Zahir. Benjamin. In the absence of any other viable alternatives, this is where we need to go next."

A SECRET HISTORY IV

THE FIRST CEREMONY

**THE SUMMIT TEMPLES
(BEFORE CEREMONY)**

Jack West shot skyward in eerie silence.

He was standing inside a modern gantry elevator that rose up the side of Hades's gigantic mountain-palace. With its steel-girdered skeletal shaft bolted to the outer flank of the mountain's upper reaches, the elevator made a soft *whir* as it glided upward.

Jack stood with the other remaining champions, covered by armed minotaur guards and the black lion, Chaos.

He saw Chaos eyeing his own new armor: the white armor he had taken from Chaos's brother-in-arms, Fear. The outfit already looked odd over his jeans and T-shirt, but it looked even odder when combined with his fireman's helmet.

There were only seven champions left now: Jack, Scarecrow, Major Brigham, Sergeant Vargas, the Delta guy Edwards, the Tibetan monk Renzin Depon and, of course, Hades's own son, Zaitan.

They variously looked dirty and weary, beaten, and bruised—except for Vargas and Zaitan, who had wisely exempted themselves from the Fifth Challenge. They looked fresh and rested.

As he'd entered the elevator, Jack had overheard someone saying that all the other remaining hostages had just been executed.

The elevator rose. Jack noticed Zaitan staring smugly at him.

"Can I help you?" Jack said.

Zaitan smirked. "No."

"Then maybe you can help me," Jack said. "What's this ceremony we're going to? What's it all about?"

"It's about informing the universe that someone is still here on Earth," Zaitan said.

Jack said, "You don't seem bothered that your hostages just got killed."

Zaitan shrugged. "They served their purpose."

A moment later, the elevator stopped and the doors slid open and the champions were guided out of it.

Jack stepped out onto a narrow steel catwalk suspended high above the world. They were right up near the summit of Hades's mountain.

Far beneath him, he could make out the various stadiums of the challenges he had survived thus far: the round water maze of the Second Challenge, the chasm and the bridges of the Third Challenge, the wall-maze of the Fourth, and the circus of the Fifth. He was so high up, they looked tiny.

The camouflage netting that encased Hades's crater fanned out from dozens of sturdy-looking brackets mounted just above his head.

To the side of the elevator was a set of metal spiral stairs that jutted out over the drop and led upward . . . above the camouflage netting.

The champions were shoved toward those stairs and they climbed them, one after the other.

When he reached the top of the stairs, Jack stepped up onto a platform above the camouflage netting and at the sight that met him, his breath caught in his throat.

Night had fallen and Jack found himself standing in open air, on a superhigh platform underneath the star-filled sky.

Hades, Vacheron, and all the royal spectators were already there. Iolanthe and Lily stood together. Jack nodded to Lily and she waved back at him tentatively.

A vast desert plain stretched away beneath him in every direction. Several miles to the west, he saw the sea, glinting in the moonlight. Somewhere over there was the beach with the ship graveyard that he had briefly reached earlier.

Without the obstructive glow of city lights, the night sky glimmered brilliantly, illuminating the empty landscape in dim blue light. A cool breeze blew.

The platform stood high above the plain, at the peak of Hades's mountain, and taking pride of place on it was an elaborate temple-like structure.

Jack took it in.

Whereas the elevator, the catwalk, and the metal stairs were all distinctly modern additions, the temple was unbelievably ancient.

With its sharp pointed corners and strong stance, it looked darkly powerful, as if it had been built in honor of some cruel shadowy power. Every surface was a glistening polished black.

It was two stories tall, with a square base level and a smaller upper level that was accessed by a broad ceremonial stairway. A colonnade of columns supported the upper level.

A wide balcony with no rail ringed the whole space. It was also made of polished black stone. From edge to edge, the whole thing was perhaps thirty yards across.

Jack scanned the details of the ancient temple.

It featured many columns and arches, but as he looked at them more closely, he realized that the whole intricate structure had been cut, amazingly, from a single slab of black stone, the black rock of the mountain's peak.

The rock-cutting skill that had created this place was extraordinary. It was simply exquisite in its precision, way too advanced for primitive man.

The lower level of the temple bore many elaborate carvings on its black stone walls: images of pyramids and suns, stars and planets, fantastical cities and magnificent trees, and several raised images that Jack had seen before.

One depicted the Great Pyramid being struck by a beam of light from the sun.

The Tartarus Rotation.

Another depicted five warriors standing behind four seated kings.

The Five Greatest Warriors and the Four Legendary Kings.

Jack shook his head. It was like reading the story of his life for the last twenty years, as if it had all been foretold.

The last feature of the space that caught his attention were five podiums arrayed around the ceremonial staircase, which he guessed were for—

"Monsieur Vacheron!" Hades said. "Would you please set the first five Golden Spheres in their rightful places."

Vacheron bowed solemnly.

Behind him, five minotaurs held the five Golden Spheres that had been obtained by the champions in the previous challenges. They stepped forward with ritual precision and placed the spheres on the podiums.

No sooner were the glowing spheres set in place than they came alive with an even more intense otherworldly light.

Jack felt a deep rumbling beneath his feet.

He looked around for the cause of it and then he saw it: something rising up out of the upper temple.

"Jesus Christ . . ." Scarecrow gasped from beside him.

Lancing skyward from the upper temple, emerging from deep within the mountain itself, was a towering obelisk-like object.

Rumbling loudly, it rose and rose and rose, until at last it stopped, having added two hundred feet to the height of the already superhigh mountain.

It looked to Jack like a giant black stone obelisk, but instead of having four flat sides, it was cylindrical, its pointed tip conical.

Standing atop Hades's mountain, it looked to Jack like an ancient version of the lightning rod that stood on top of the Empire State Building. The huge black obelisk must have been at least eight feet thick at its base. It literally stabbed the sky.

Hades beamed with pride as the great ancient antenna set itself in place.

Vacheron stepped forward.

"The First Ceremony is complete! The sacred obelisk has risen. Only now can we commence the second phase of the Games. After that, we shall place the final four Golden Spheres on the upper altar and, having proved our worth as a species, the winning king shall receive the Mysteries of the Ancients!"

The assembled royals cheered.

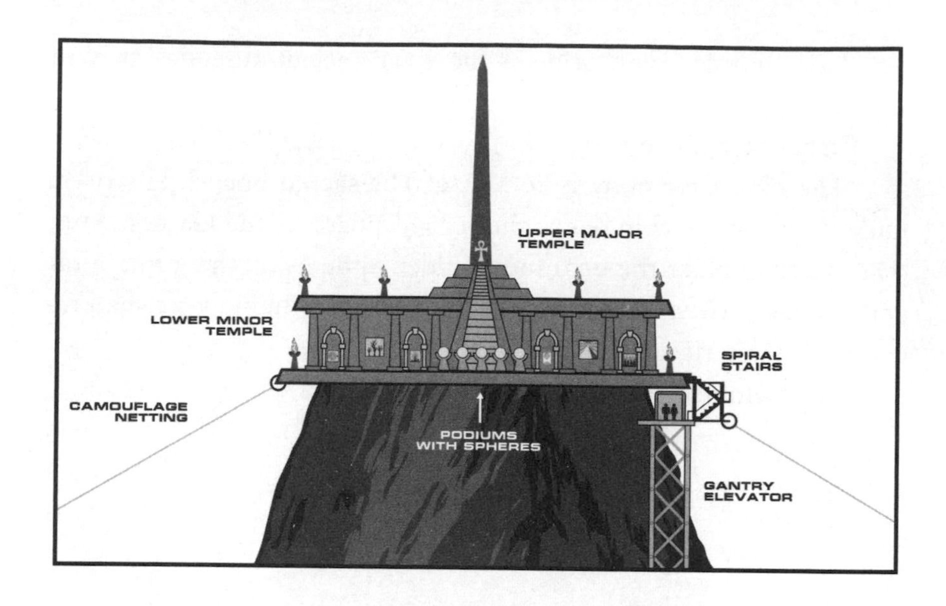

THE SUMMIT TEMPLES (AFTER FIRST CEREMONY)

Vacheron held up his hand for silence.

"My lords and ladies. It is traditional at this juncture in the Great Games for our host, the illustrious Lord Hades, having consulted with his fellow kings, to bestow gifts on certain subjects. This could be an elevation in rank or a grant of land or title. It is entirely his prerogative. My Lord? Do you have any such announcements to make at this auspicious time?"

Hades stepped forward. "I do."

Jack looked around himself and noticed that the assembled royals all stiffened slightly and leaned in closer to hear. Some of them perspired visibly or swallowed in tense anticipation.

This, Jack realized, was the one thing nobles around the world cherished more than anything: advancement. Promotion up the pecking order.

Hades said, "After consultation with my peer, the esteemed King of Sea, it has been decided that his long-serving Master of Coin,

Mr. John Marren of San Francisco, will be elevated to the rank of Duke. He shall be henceforth known as Duke of the Western Shore."

Polite clapping followed as a broadly smiling fifty-something gentleman in a suit—presumably Mr. Marren—gratefully shook hands with the Sea King.

"Likewise, the King of the Sky promotes his good friend, Mr. Geoffrey Yang of Shanghai, to the position of Lord of the Great Mountain."

That announcement was met with impressed oohs and aahs.

Hades went on, "After consulting with my fellow king, his most esteemed majesty, the King of Land, we have determined that a love match will bring our kingdoms closer together. As such, my most noble Master of the Games, Monsieur Vacheron, shall have the hand of the Land King's sister, the beautiful Princess Iolanthe, in marriage."

Jack saw three responses to this announcement.

The crowd cheered happily.

Vacheron positively glowed with joy.

And then there was Iolanthe's response. It only flashed across her face for a split second, but Jack saw it: a look of profound revulsion, which she quickly replaced with a tight smile.

"My Lord"—Vacheron bowed low—"you honor me. I cannot thank you enough."

Hades nodded, but then held up his hand. He wasn't done.

"We have also been graced at these Games with the presence of another most beautiful young lady. A very important young lady whose lineage is perhaps the most pure of them all."

Jack felt his heart sink.

Hades indicated Lily, standing beside Iolanthe. "Of course, I refer to the Ancient Oracle of Siwa, whom I have come to know as Lily. As many of you are aware, my son and heir, Dionysius, has not yet taken a wife. But every king needs a queen—as I know more than most, since the passing of my beloved queen five years ago—last night Dion asked me: 'What better place for the Oracle of Siwa than on the queen's throne of the Underworld?' I have thus determined that at the conclusion of these Games, Dionysius will take young Lily as his bride."

The royal spectators erupted in vigorous applause.

Jack snapped around to look at Lily.

Her eyes met his, wide and horrified.

Beside Lily, Iolanthe gently took her hand.

Hades grinned to his audience. "But such joys must wait. Now we have the second phase of challenges to hold. Let us adjourn to the observatory level for the Sixth Challenge!"

At the same time this was happening, out on the beach to the west of Hades's kingdom, the Typhoon troop truck driven by Sky Monster and containing Mother, Astro, Tomahawk, Alby, and the dogs sped desperately northward.

It was dark now.

The sun had dipped below the horizon and the beach was bathed in inky blackness. Without any kind of city or town nearby, there was not even the faint glow of electric light on the landward horizon. The only light was that of the slowly rising moon.

Sky Monster peered forward as he drove, squinting in the night. He dared not turn on the Typhoon's headlights, lest any of Hades's minions were still following them.

They had been going for about an hour since Jack had destroyed the Alligator chopper, making good progress on the wet sand. About twenty minutes earlier, they had passed a final beached cargo ship and the Typhoon had shot out onto empty open beach.

The placid waters of the Arabian Sea stretched away to their left, flat and languid, while sandy cliffs still bounded the beach on their right.

Mother turned to Alby. "Okay, boy genius. The Huntsman says you've got a brain. So what's the plan? Do we just keep driving till we run out of gas? Or till we run out of beach?"

Alby said, "We keep driving till we find some kind of civilization. If we run out of gas before then, we get out and walk—"

He cut himself off when he heard it.

A deep rhythmic thumping coming from somewhere behind them—

With shocking suddenness, a second Alligator assault helicopter came blasting over the cliffs on the landward side of the beach, searchlights blazing.

The gunship's searchlights quickly found the fleeing Typhoon and the chopper loosed a burst of powerful 30mm gunfire that strafed the beach in front of the truck.

"They've been waiting for us to emerge from the cover of the ships!" Mother shouted above the din. "That thing's got way too much firepower! We're screwed!"

Sky Monster braked and the Typhoon swung into a skid.

The big troop truck stopped on the flat sand of the beach, facing the hovering gunship, bathed in the glare of its spotlights, with nowhere to run and nowhere to hide.

"Damn it . . ." Mother breathed, bowing her head in resignation.

Their escape was over.

SIXTH CHALLENGE

IMMORTAL COMBAT I

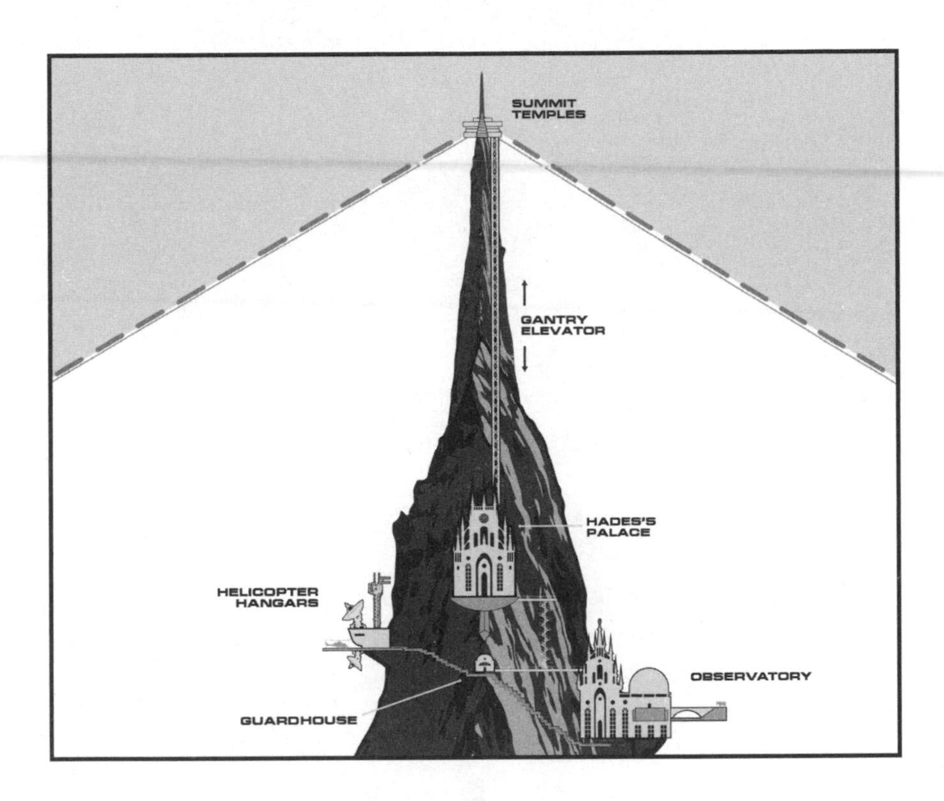

THE HIGH CASTLES OF HADES

If you're going through Hell, keep going.

WINSTON CHURCHILL

Flanked by minotaur guards, Jack and the remaining champions were shoved into the gantry elevator. They were to be taken down to the venue for the next challenge ahead of the royal spectators.

As the elevator whizzed downward, Jack found himself standing beside Scarecrow, Major Gregory Brigham, and Zaitan.

"The final phase begins," Zaitan said to Jack. "No more mazes. No more chases. No more places for you to hide."

Brigham must have seen the confused look on Jack's face. "What he means is it's single combat from here."

"And we are *all* hoping to face off against you, Captain West," Zaitan said nastily.

Jack glanced at Brigham. The British trooper nodded.

"Why?" Jack asked.

"Only one man can win the Games," Brigham said. "But if I don't, I would die a happy man knowing I went down in history as the one who took down the fifth greatest warrior. I will fight all the harder if I know it will get me into a one-on-one battle with you."

"Aye-aye to that," Zaitan said.

Jack swapped a glance with Scarecrow.

The Marine said nothing.

A short time later, Lily rode down in the same gantry elevator with Iolanthe and some of the other royal guests.

While the royals around her chatted and gossiped, she stood stock-still, staring into space, thinking.

She was trying to process everything that had happened. Dion had gotten what he wanted: her hand in marriage. She shuddered at the thought, repulsed at the prospect of spending a lifetime in this place as the wife of a monster.

And then, in the confines of the elevator, she overheard the boorish prince named George whisper to one of his young friends: "Vacheron just informed me that a chase chopper just caught up with those escaping hostages. Fools. To think they could get away."

Lily closed her eyes, biting her lip in frustration.

No matter how she looked at it, she couldn't see a way out. Jack had done so well but she could see he was operating at the edge of exhaustion. If he even survived the final challenges, he would have no energy left to save her from her fate. It wouldn't surprise her, even if he *won* the Games, if Jack met an "accidental" death on Dion's orders. Things couldn't get any worse.

A hand landed gently on her shoulder.

It was Iolanthe's.

"Lily, I know what you think of me. But I also know how you're feeling right now. I want to marry Vacheron as much as you want to marry Dion. To be betrothed to a vile man for my brother's own strategic reasons galls me. Orlando told me it is my fate as a royal woman."

Iolanthe gripped Lily's hand gently but firmly. "Stay strong, Lily. Don't give up yet."

Lily looked back at her with defiant eyes. "I haven't given up. I never give up. I learned that from my dad."

The elevator came to a halt one-third of the way down Hades's mountain.

In the upper reaches of the mountain-palace were several fortresses that hung off the sides of the tapered peak and it was at one of these that the elevator had stopped.

As they walked out of the elevator, Iolanthe said, "These fortresses are known as the High Castles of Hades."

They came in various shapes and sizes—some had multiple watchtowers with pointed roofs, while others had crenellated balconies; others still were squat domed structures. One castle even had an antenna array mounted on top of it.

All were connected by a network of sweeping staircases and narrow paths carved into the mountain.

The lowest of these structures was the one that ringed the waist of the mountain and contained the dining hall and the quarters for Hades's royal guests.

As they walked down some stairs around the outside of the highest castle structure, Iolanthe said, "This is Hades's own palace, his private residence. As one would expect, it is most sumptuously appointed, as befits the ruler of the Underworld."

It was easily the grandest and most complex of all the High Castles. On the outside, it boasted many balconies and towers. Lily could only guess at its magnificence inside.

Descending farther, Lily arrived two hundred feet below Hades's residence and it was here that she saw the oddest-looking of the High Castles.

Jutting out from the eastern flank of the mountain, it featured a very old and very beautiful dome-shaped structure crafted from black stone bricks. It reminded Lily of the Mayan ruins at Chichen Itza.

"We call this the Observatory," Iolanthe said. "It is an ancient astronomical apparatus that keeps track of the Hydra Galaxy."

Fanning out from the dome so that they overhung the thousand-foot drop were three round stages.

They were positioned on three sides of the Observatory—to the south, east, and north—and they rose in a steplike fashion as they swept up and around the ancient dome.

Each stage was different. The lowest one had a hole in its center, like a doughnut. The middle one bore a statue of some kind. The third and highest one had a waterfall running across it and some statues, too. None of the three stages had rails. All three, however, bore small waist-high podiums on which stood a single glowing Golden Sphere.

"What are they?" Lily asked.

"Like the Observatory, they also have a name," Iolanthe said. "They are the combat stages and it is on them that the final four challenges will take place."

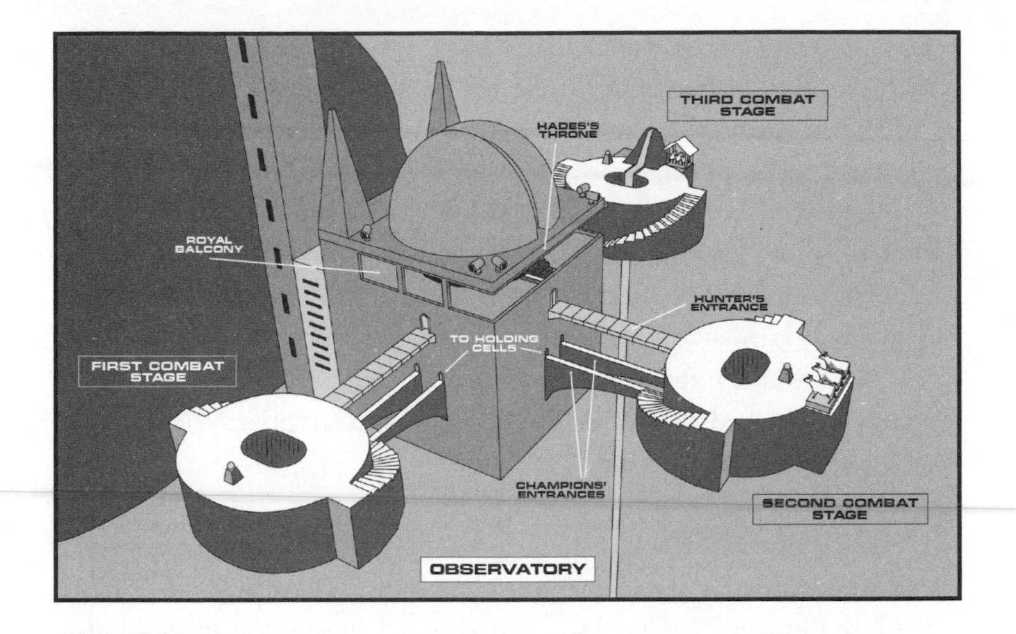

Led by Hades and Vacheron, the royal audience took their places on the upper deck of the Observatory, on a balcony that overlooked the three combat stages. Hades sat in a large elevated throne made of ancient black stone.

It was night now, so the Underworld, beneath its vast canopy of camouflage netting, was dark. Floodlights mounted on the roof of the Observatory illuminated the fighting stages.

Vacheron stepped out onto the first combat stage. He stood beside a podium bearing a single glowing Golden Sphere in a clamp-like mechanism.

"My lords and ladies, it is now that we enter the most celebrated phase of our Games. Here, our champions will either etch their names into the annals of history or they will die.

"We proceed quickly from here. The Sixth, Seventh, and Eighth Challenges are variants of the same trial: mortal combat. Man against man. Hand to hand. No weapons, no aid. To the death.

"The Sixth Challenge will take place on the first combat stage and it will see our champions reduced in number to four. The Seventh will further cull their ranks to two. At the conclusion of each of these two challenges, the Golden Sphere on each combat stage will be placed on Lord Hades's throne."

Hades gestured toward four bowl-shaped recesses carved into the armrests of his mighty black throne.

Vacheron continued, "At the end of the Eighth Challenge, however, only one champion shall remain. After the eighth sphere is brought to Lord Hades, that champion alone will face the Ninth and final Challenge, and the fate of the world will rest on him.

"So esteemed are these first three challenges that the winning champion will also win for his king a special prize: the famed Golden Belt of the Amazons."

Vacheron held aloft a glittering belt.

Made of thick black leather, it was embedded with gold plates and studded with jewels: emeralds, diamonds, rubies.

Lily thought of what Jack had shouted during the Fifth Challenge, that these challenges were the fabled Labors of Hercules.

"The Labors," she breathed. "The Belt of Hippolyta, Queen of the Amazons."

"Correct," Iolanthe said. "In his Ninth Labor, Hercules had to obtain the Belt of the Amazonian Queen. To acquire it, he had to best many men in single combat. That belt is the origin of the championship belts awarded for victory in fighting sports like boxing."

Vacheron continued. "The Sixth Challenge shall take place on the first and lowest combat stage. Two champions will step onto it at a time. Only one will leave." Vacheron grinned evilly. "But there will be a third element to these battles."

The giant figure of Chaos stepped out onto the lowest combat stage. Dressed in his black Kevlar armor and heavy boots, he looked imposing and formidable. He carried in one hand a vicious-looking sword.

Vacheron said, "The two champions will fight while Chaos stalks them. To fight a man to the death is one thing. To do it while another threat lurks is another thing entirely. Only the most worthy champions will proceed beyond this challenge."

Vacheron indicated a computer up on the observation balcony. It had seven screens attached to it.

The screens looked like EKG heart monitors found in hospitals: they each bore a champion's name written above a beeping, pulsing line that represented that man's heartbeat.

"As you know, each of our champions has an explosive chip implanted in his neck. That device also gives us biometric readings, including that champion's pulse and heart rates. Once a champion's pulse has stopped, the surviving champion will be declared the winner and Chaos will immediately cease his interference in the fight.

"Now," Vacheron paused, "it was hoped that at this stage in our proceedings there would be eight champions still alive, which would mean four fights. But, alas, the trials have proven too difficult, so only seven remain.

"This being the case, in his wisdom, Lord Hades has determined that the champion who has won the most challenges so far will be granted a bye through this challenge. This champion is Major Brigham, representing the Kingdom of Land. I am sure he and his sponsor will be delighted to hear this news."

Vacheron gestured to King Orlando up on the balcony. Orlando nodded back approvingly.

Vacheron said, "The other fights have been determined by lot, without manipulation or intrigue. And so, without any further ado, let the challenge begin! Let me go and fetch the first pair of champions."

Jack sat alone inside a cell underneath the Observatory.

It had no windows. The door was solid steel.

He still wore his dirty jeans and T-shirt underneath the white Kevlar armor he had acquired from Fear. With his white chestplate, forearm guards, and greaves, he felt like he was dressed in white police riot gear.

He also felt exhausted.

He had been going nonstop since the beginning of the Fifth

Challenge: fighting, fleeing, driving trucks into helicopters, and then observing the First Ceremony up on the summit—

With a squeal of rusty hinges, his cell door swung open and Vacheron sauntered in, escorted by four minotaur guards who quickly surrounded Jack.

"No time for rest, fifth warrior," Vacheron said. "You're up. Your next challenge is as pure as it is ancient: single combat against another champion. Either you live or you die. I must confess, I am hoping you die soon. I am tiring of your face."

"The Labors of Hercules," Jack said. "Is that what all this is about? Reenacting some ancient myths?"

Vacheron paused, looked Jack up and down.

"Reenacting?" He almost spat the word. "Captain West, as you of all people should know, history is a most inexact science. Just as in the children's game of Telephone a simple statement gets warped in the retelling over the course of a few minutes, so too does a historical event get twisted when it is retold over centuries.

"Take Hercules. The man you know as Hercules was not some half-god of ancient legend. He was the most famous champion of these Games. He is known throughout the ages for the simple reason that he alone won *every single challenge* of the Great Games.

"From defeating the minotaur in the opening cell, to obtaining a sphere in the wall-maze of the Fourth Challenge, to these combat rituals, Hercules won them all. It was a singular and incredible feat and it rightfully attained for him eternal fame.

"But the writers of history are sloppy.

"Over three millennia, they mistakenly took the name of the Lord of the Underworld at that time—a cruel ruler named Eurystheus—and turned him into a petty king who created the Labors that Hercules had to perform. Not knowing the nature of the nine challenges or the metaphorical elements contained in them—bulls, stags, boars, even belts—these historians turned them into 'labors' relating to Hercules.

"The royal families watching these Games know the truth. Now, you know it. Come, it is time to fight."

Vacheron nodded to the guards who shoved Jack down a dark stone passageway lit by flaming torches and lined with other cells.

After about twenty yards, the passage ended at a fork.

The minotaurs shoved Jack down the right-hand fork and shut a steel door behind him.

A whistling breeze buffeted him.

Jack turned and found himself standing on a narrow stone bridge high above the Underworld. He could see the vertical wall-maze of the Fourth Challenge perhaps a thousand feet below him.

A set of stone stairs led away from his bridge, curving up and out of view.

As he walked over to them, Jack heard Vacheron and the minotaur guards go back down the passageway and open another cell. More footsteps. Then the closing of the left-hand door of the fork.

Single combat, Jack thought.

But I don't get to see who I'm fighting until I reach the platform . . .

With a long deep breath, Jack strode up the curving stairs to meet his fate.

Fifteen steps later, the combat stage came into view and Jack stepped up onto it.

A figure appeared from a matching set of stairs on the opposite side and for a fleeting horrifying instant, Jack thought it was Scarecrow, his new ally, his new friend . . .

But it wasn't Scarecrow.

It was Sergeant Victor Vargas, devout Catholic and brutal ex-member of the Brazilian special forces. And Jack's fellow representative of the Kingdom of Land.

At six foot two, Vargas was taller than Jack and heavier, too. He had about thirty pounds on him. With his unblinking black eyes and swarthy unshaven chin, he glared at Jack with the intensity of a psychopath, a psychopath who knows he must kill in order to keep living.

Already waiting on the platform beside a wide hole in its center was the tall black lion-helmeted figure of Chaos. While Jack and Vargas had no weapons, Chaos calmly held a sword pointed downward.

A small podium with a Golden Sphere on it stood at the rear of the stage.

Vacheron resumed his place up on the viewing balcony.

"Our first battle will be between Sergeant Victor Vargas representing the Kingdom of Land and Captain Jack West, also representing the Kingdom of Land!"

He nodded to Hades.

Hades said, "Let the fight begin. To the death."

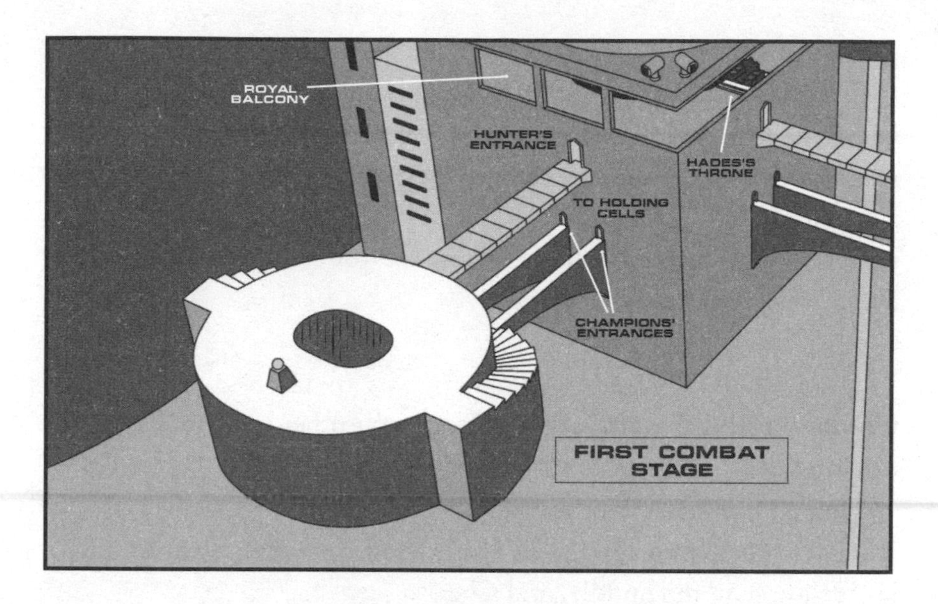

FIGHT 1: JACK VS. VARGAS (VS. CHAOS)

Vargas immediately dropped into a strange low crouch and began to circle Jack like a jungle cat, moving unusually fast for a big man.

Jack recognized his technique instantly. It made sense that a Brazilian soldier like Vargas would utilize it.

It was capoeira, the Brazilian martial art. In a world of familiar Asian martial arts, capoeira was distinctive for one key reason: it was fast.

Its defensive techniques involved quick, evasive movements and its attacks were rapid, hard, and decisive. If the first punch didn't knock you out, the second one would.

Shit, Jack thought.

Lily watched from the royal balcony.

Beside her stood Iolanthe and Cardinal Mendoza.

Mendoza sighed. "This is so unfortunate. Three of our kingdom's representatives make it to this phase of the Games and two of them must fight. What a pity."

Iolanthe didn't take her eyes off the combat stage. "Who will win?"

"Oh, Vargas will win," Mendoza said. "The fifth warrior is brave, of that there is no doubt, but Sergeant Vargas is a capoeira *mestre*, a master of the art. He is a trained hand-to-hand fighter. Besides, look at the fifth warrior. He is spent. His foolish escape attempt wore him out. There is no escape for him this time. If he is lucky, Vargas will make this short."

On the stage, Jack and Vargas circled each other warily, sizing each other up.

In addition to each other, there were three further dangers on the stage that they both tried to keep clear of: the outer edge, the circular well-hole in the middle, and Chaos.

Vargas was mumbling something as he moved, whispering rapidly in Portuguese:

"*. . . ave Maria, cheia de graça, o Senhor é convosco . . .*"

It took Jack a moment to realize what he was saying.

"*. . . hail Mary, full of grace, the Lord is with thee . . .*"

The guy was praying.

Then Vargas pounced.

The move came so fast, Jack almost didn't catch it. It was as if Vargas had lulled him into a rhythm and then exploded out of it.

A high kick came at Jack's head like a bullet and Jack ducked right, and Vargas's boot swished past his cheek, so close that Jack felt the air rush by.

Chaos did nothing.

He just watched from the side of the stage, gripping his sword casually.

Vargas followed up with a barrage of rapid moves—advancing on Jack with a blur of kicks, punches and elbows.

Jack danced backward, avoiding and evading and parrying the blows.

And then one of Vargas's punches connected, slamming into Jack's jaw.

Jack fell, hitting the floor hard, his head overhanging the central well, and as he looked down through the hole at the crater floor far below, time stood still.

The edges of his vision went blurry.

All sound ceased save for a ringing inside his head.

Jack knew this feeling. All boxers and mixed–martial arts fighters knew it: it was the terrifying reaction to being hit hard. You were concussed, stunned, and if you didn't avoid the next hit, you were fucked.

He lifted his head, his mouth dribbling blood.

Vargas came in hard, driving downward with the next blow.

Jack rolled and Vargas missed.

Jack stood and turned—

—to find himself face-to-face with the impassive lion-helmeted face of Chaos.

Chaos punched him in the face.

This time Jack's nose took the hit. Blood sprayed everywhere.

The royal spectators watched eagerly as the small wobbling figure of Jack found himself caught between Chaos and Vargas.

He looked like a trapped animal, glancing back and forth between the two predators.

Lily was furious. "This isn't fair! The lion guy isn't even trying to fight Vargas. They're ganging up on him."

Iolanthe also watched with tight lips. "Jack offended Chaos by killing Fear and taking his armor. And he offended everyone here when he tried to free the hostages. He's being punished before he dies."

Jack staggered backward, blood pouring from his nose, breathing quickly through his mouth, caught between the two deadly men.

He kept an equal distance from Vargas and Chaos.

His mind fought desperately against the haze trying to overcome it. He had about four seconds to figure a way out of this, before he lost consciousness.

Think!

You can't win this fight with muscle. You have to win it with your brains. You have to outsmart these two.

Every man can be beaten.

Okay. What are their strengths? What are their weaknesses?

That's it, Jack realized.

It's the same thing. Their confidence that they are better fighters than me is both their greatest strength and *their greatest weakness.*

I have to let them think they've won . . .

Jack turned his back on Vargas and lunged at Chaos with a weak desperate swing.

Chaos batted away his punch with one hand. The royals on the balcony laughed.

And Vargas made his move.

He grabbed Jack from behind, wrapping one of his thick forearms around Jack's throat.

This was the move Jack had been expecting, precisely because it was the most effective move in hand-to-hand fighting: the choke hold.

By squeezing the carotid artery in the victim's throat, you cut off the blood flow to his brain. Unconsciousness followed, and if you maintained the hold, death came soon after.

Jack scratched at the big hairy forearm squeezing his throat.

Vargas's face was right behind his and he could smell the Brazilian's foul breath as Vargas kept whispering his religious chant:

"*. . . ave Maria, cheia de graça, o Senhor é convosco . . .*"

And as the choke hold began to take effect, Jack began to go limp.

"It's over," Mendoza said. He made the sign of the cross and turned away.

Lily didn't take her eyes off Jack. His body was sagging now, held up by the big Brazilian from behind.

Chaos took a step back, letting it play out.

A tear trickled down Lily's cheek. "No . . ."

Jack sagged fully in Vargas's grip.

And for the briefest of seconds—the tiny half-second when Vargas realized that he had beaten Jack—Vargas momentarily released the pressure and grinned.

That was his weakness: the confidence that he'd won as he'd expected to.

And in that brief half-second, Jack sprang.

It wasn't over. He hadn't been unconscious. He'd sagged deliberately, making Vargas think it was over.

He jerked his head back in a powerful reverse headbutt, slamming his skull up into Vargas's nose, breaking it, partially releasing the Brazilian's grip.

Jack didn't expect Vargas to release him fully. He was too good a fighter for that.

Which was why Jack did something else that no one would have expected.

He reached forward, grabbed Chaos by the chest armor and, with all his remaining strength, pushed off with his legs and threw all three of them into the well-hole in the center of the combat stage.

Every member of the royal audience lunged forward at the sight of the three combatants tumbling into the well-hole and disappearing from view.

Lily clutched the balcony's railing.

She caught her breath when she saw a single figure drop out of the bottom of the well-hole and plummet, screaming, all the way to the bottom of the mountain.

When the man hit the ground there—with a sickening *whump*—one of the beeping heart-rate monitors flatlined and issued a shrill squeal.

Beeeeeeeeeeeeeep!

Everyone spun to see which champion had died, Vargas or West.

The squealing screen had one word written above it: VARGAS.

A moment later, Jack climbed out of the well-hole, crawling slowly and painfully on his hands and knees.

Once he was fully up on the stage, he fell flat onto his face, spent, exhausted.

A moment later, Chaos lifted himself out of the well-hole, too. Jack lay before him on the ground, facedown, totally defenseless. But because Vargas was dead, Chaos was not permitted to touch Jack. Chaos just stood there above the flat figure of Jack, confused.

Then Jack stood, wobbling slightly, his face a bloody mess.

He looked up at the royal crowd, at Hades and Vacheron . . .

. . . and very, very slowly, he flipped them the bird.

* * *

As the three men had toppled into the well-hole, two things happened that Jack had counted on.

First, Vargas had released him.

Released him in the hope of grabbing a handhold. But the walls of the well-hole were sheer and polished. They offered no handholds and Vargas just fell down through the hole, screaming all the way to his death.

And second, also to save himself, Chaos had grabbed the rim of the well-hole.

Jack had banked on that, and so he'd grabbed hold of Chaos as they all tumbled over the edge: which left Chaos hanging from the rim and Jack hanging from Chaos.

When he'd got his breath back, he'd just climbed up Chaos's body and crawled back onto the combat stage.

For a moment, Vacheron was speechless.

He regathered himself. "So be it. Prepare for the second battle!"

FIGHT 2: ZAITAN VS. DEPON (VS. CHAOS)

"Our second battle will be between Zaitan DeSaxe, representing the Kingdom of the Underworld, and Brother Renzin Depon, representing the Sky Kingdom!" Vacheron announced.

Equally formally, Hades once again said, "Let the fight begin. To the death."

The second fight was much quicker than the first.

The Tibetan warrior-monk, Depon, was a skilled hand-to-hand fighter, but after a few exchanges with the equally skilled Zaitan, it was Zaitan who drew first blood.

Chaos lurked at the edges of the fight, only stepping forward when Depon strayed near him—but he hung back when Zaitan came close; he was favoring the son of Hades.

Then Zaitan unleashed two quickfire punches that sent blood flying from Depon's mouth, and the Tibetan, stunned, fell to his knees.

Once he was in that position, it was all over.

Zaitan sprang behind him, wrapped his arms around the warrior-monk's throat and snapped his neck.

Depon's biometric screen on the royal balcony screamed.

On the stage, Depon's body went still and Zaitan kicked it away from him.

The crowd cheered.

Dion clapped especially vigorously.

Two minotaurs scurried onto the combat stage and dragged Depon's corpse away, pulling it by the legs, taking it back to the cells below.

Chaos left the stage as well, his work done.

Now alone on the wide circular platform, Zaitan stood, placed his hands formally behind his back, and bowed reverently to his father and the royal spectators.

Standing in this way, no one saw what he did with his hands behind his back: with a quick flick of his fingers, he slid two razor-sharp skin-colored ceramic blades back underneath the folds in the skin of his knuckles—blades that he had used to slash Depon's face during the pivotal moment of the fight.

All the while, Zaitan smiled up at the cheering, adoring crowd.

FIGHT 3: SCARECROW VS. EDWARDS (VS. CHAOS)

Shane "Scarecrow" Schofield stepped up the curving outer steps of the combat stage and beheld his opponent.

"You . . ." he whispered when he saw him standing on the opposite side of the stage.

"I had a feeling it might come to this," his opponent said with a predatory grin.

It was Jeffrey Edwards of Delta. Another American, he was one of Scarecrow's fellow representatives of the Sea Kingdom, and also the person who, back in Afghanistan a few days earlier, had tricked Scarecrow and his Marines into coming here.

They couldn't have been more different. Scarecrow was lean, clean-shaven; Edwards, as was common among Delta operators, had an unkempt beard and a bulked-up physique.

Scarecrow just glared at him.

Edwards had known all along why he was coming to India. He had trained for the Games. He had prepared. Scarecrow, on the other hand, like Jack West Jr., had been thrown in the deep end and told to sink or swim.

Edwards snorted. "Reckon you're pretty pissed at me, ain'tcha?"

Scarecrow said nothing.

"Tricked ya into comin' here," Edwards said. "A Marine wouldn't like that. Fucking Marines. So damned earnest. Dudley fucking Do-Rights. Had to kill a few Marines in my time, you know:

dumb fucks who saw things they shouldn't have. Now, I gotta kill you."

Edwards clicked his neck, loosening it. He did it casually, like a guy preparing to throw some pitches in the backyard.

Scarecrow's eyes scanned his opponent's body.

Tan combat trousers and T-shirt: no danger there.

Steel-toed boots: significant danger there.

Then he saw Edwards's hands: lots of danger there.

On both hands, Edwards wore a classic piece of Delta kit: sand-colored assault gloves. But these gloves had a more sinister name: knuckle-duster gloves.

This was because they had special domed plates sewn into the knuckles—plates made of steel shot—giving the wearer significantly more punching power. They had the same effect as brass knuckles: a single well-timed punch from them could send a man's nose back into his brain, killing him instantly.

Vacheron called, "Our third battle will be between Major Jeffrey Edwards, representing the Kingdom of the Sea, and Captain Shane Schofield, also representing the Sea Kingdom!"

Hades said, "Let the fight begin. To the death."

Edwards sprang forward, unleashing a flurry of rapid blows, leading with his weighted gloves, driving Scarecrow toward the edge of the stage.

Scarecrow retreated in the face of the onslaught, parrying Edwards's punches while also keeping half an eye out for Chaos.

Then Edwards launched a roundhouse right and Scarecrow ducked and swerved and bobbed up again—

—to see Chaos swinging at him with his sword!

Scarecrow ducked again and the sword swooshed over his head, missing by inches.

He turned back to Edwards as—*whack!*—Edwards's left fist hit him square in the cheek.

The steel shot in the knuckles of Edwards's glove did their thing.

Scarecrow heard his cheekbone crack. Broken.

His eyes began to water, his vision on that side began to darken.

Gotta watch out for Chaos, his mind screamed.

He swung back to check on the lion-headed assassin, just in time to see the big black figure lunge forward, stabbing with his sword . . .

. . . and to Scarecrow's horror, the sword plunged deep into his left shoulder, going right through, so that two full feet of the sword's glistening blade emerged out the other side, protruding from Scarecrow's back!

The royal crowd gasped.

No one came back from such a blow.

Chaos stepped back from Scarecrow, cruelly leaving the sword embedded in his left shoulder.

Edwards moved in for the kill.

Scarecrow staggered, gasping.

He saw the sword lodged deep in his left shoulder and felt the arm below it go limp.

And then Edwards was in his face, raining more punches at him.

Scarecrow pathetically raised his good right arm in defense, trying to ward off the blows.

Edwards spoke as he unleashed his punches.

"I have more training than you!"

Punch.

"More experience than you!"

Punch.

"More knowledge than you!"

Punch.

The last punch knocked Scarecrow's defensive arm away and suddenly Scarecrow was totally exposed.

Edwards made a tight fist with his weighted right glove and coiled himself for the final blow.

Scarecrow held up his good hand and said breathlessly, "But I . . . have more . . ."

Edwards paused, grinning. "What? You have more what?"

"I have more imagination than you."

With those words, Scarecrow dropped suddenly and swept his legs around, taking Edwards's feet out from under him, and Edwards fell to the ground.

Then Scarecrow did the most outrageous thing of all, he leaped up and, gripping the hilt of the sword, dropped his entire body in a backslam . . . right on top of Edwards . . . doing it in such a way that the sword protruding from the back of his left shoulder stabbed Edwards right through the heart.

Blood sprayed everywhere.

Chaos didn't know what to do.

The royal audience watched, aghast.

Silence reigned . . .

. . . except for the long monotone *beep* of Jeffrey Edwards's heart-rate monitor flatlining.

No one said a thing until Prince George guffawed, "Bugger me, that was fucking *intense*!"

Then Scarecrow stood and, still wobbling unsteadily and covered in blood, he yanked the sword out of his body. At the same moment, seemingly of its own accord, the clamp mechanism holding the Golden Sphere in place on the podium beside him snapped open.

At a nod from Vacheron, Scarecrow took the glowing orb from the podium.

To the respectful clapping of the royal crowd, he brought it up to the observation deck and handed it to Hades who placed it reverently into the first bowl-shaped recess on the right-hand armrest of his throne.

SEVENTH CHALLENGE

IMMORTAL COMBAT II

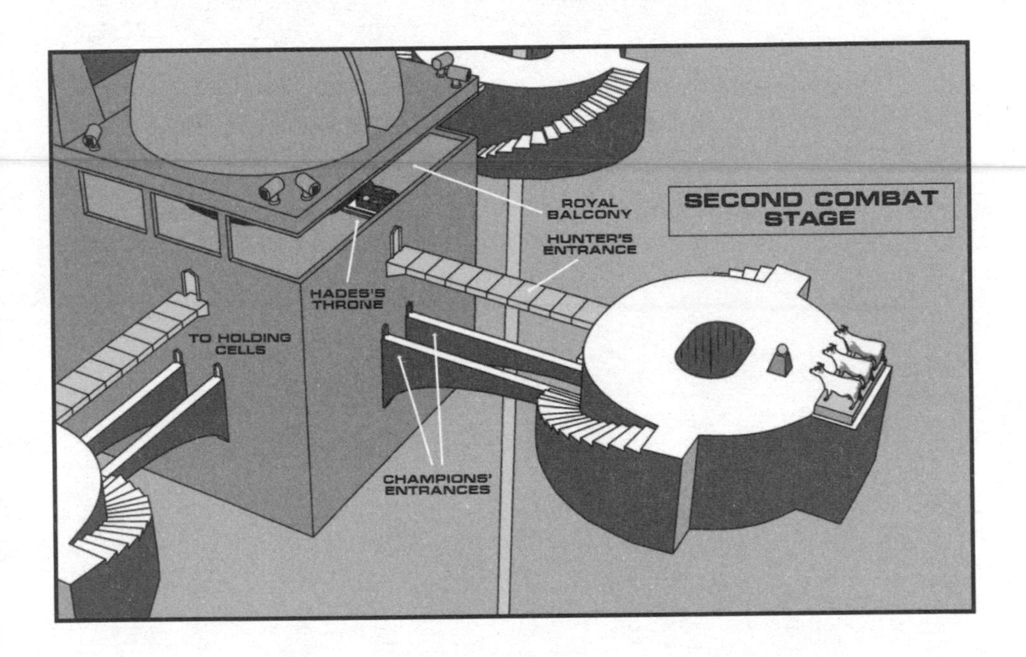

THE SECOND COMBAT STAGE

Only four champions remained now.

Zaitan, the son of Hades.

Major Greg Brigham, the SAS man who had been granted a bye through the Sixth Challenge.

Scarecrow, the Marine with the scars on his eyes.

And Jack.

How they would pair off for the Seventh Challenge, only Vacheron knew, but the royal spectators whispered animatedly, eager for the next round of mortal combat to begin.

In anticipation of this, they moved from the south-facing rail of the Observatory's balcony to its east-facing one overlooking the second of the three combat stages.

Only Hades remained where he sat. His throne moved for him, rotating ninety degrees on an unseen mechanism.

Like the first combat stage, this stage featured a podium with a sphere on it, a hole in its center, and curving entry steps on either side. But it had an extra feature: a raised platform on which stood three large stone statues.

The statues were of three cows, bunched together, cut from a single piece of pale stone. They looked worn and old, faded with extreme age.

"Cattle," Lily said, seeing them. "The Cattle of Geryon. Another of the Labors of Hercules. Hercules wrestled a giant named Geryon so he could steal his cattle."

Iolanthe said, "In truth Geryon was the name of a champion

whom Hercules fought on this very stage three thousand years ago, in the shadow of these statues. Geryon was a towering fellow and a famed wrestler."

Vacheron called, "My lords and ladies! Welcome to the Seventh Challenge! Only four brave champions remain. Bring out the two combatants for the first fight of the Seventh Challenge!"

Jack was once again fetched from his cell by the four minotaur guards.

After the brutal punishment Jack had endured in his first fight, Iolanthe's foppish British physician Dr. Barnard had come by to patch him up. Barnard had used an ice pack to reduce the swelling and the old boxer's trick of Avitene and Vaseline to stem the flow of blood from his cuts.

Thus tidied up, Jack was taken down another forked passageway and pushed through a door which was slammed shut behind him. Another set of curving steps led upward, to another combat stage.

Jack climbed the steps, his head slowly peeking above the flat level of the stage.

He had no clue how the other fights had gone, who had fought against whom and who had won, so he wondered who he would face this time.

As he stepped up onto the stage, his opponent rose up the matching set of stairs on the other side of the stage.

When Jack saw who it was, his face fell.

"Oh, no . . ."

It was Scarecrow.

Jack West Jr. and Shane Schofield faced each other on the ancient fighting platform.

The two men looked like they had been through hell, which wasn't far from the truth.

Despite Dr. Barnard's best efforts, Jack's face was bloody and bruised. His jeans and T-shirt—and the body armor he now wore over them—were dirty and torn.

Scarecrow's left arm hung limply from his shoulder, some tightly bound bandages securing the stab wound there. His combat trousers and Marine T-shirt were similarly dirty and ragged and smeared with blood.

Jack looked deep into Scarecrow's eyes.

Astro and Mother had been right when they'd vouched for Scarecrow. He was the one champion Jack had met during this whole thing whom he trusted and admired.

Scarecrow had saved Jack's life, using his reward to spare Jack when Hades had ordered his head to be blown off.

And now here they stood, facing off against each other in a fight that only one of them could walk away from. A fight to the death.

Jack looked away.

He couldn't see a way out of this.

"Damn . . ." he breathed.

"Captain West," Scarecrow said suddenly. He glanced to the side. Chaos was striding out of the Observatory and would be on the stage in moments.

"This is the only place we can speak freely so listen up and listen good. I need you to kill me now. I don't know enough about these ancient matters, but you do. This is your field. This is *what you do.* If killing me now means saving the world, then that's what you have to do."

Jack was speechless. "No . . ."

Scarecrow looked him square in the eye . . . and then with a flick of his eyes, he drew Jack's attention to something in his left hand.

Jack saw it . . . and frowned.

His eyes snapped up and met Scarecrow's and he nodded.

"You know what you have to do," Scarecrow said.

"I do," Jack said.

"See you on the other side, Captain," Scarecrow said.

At that moment, Chaos stepped out onto the stage armed with his sword, and Vacheron called out: "The first battle of the Seventh Challenge will be between Captain Jack West, representing the Kingdom of Land, and Captain Shane Schofield, representing the Kingdom of the Sea!"

Hades said, "Let the fight begin. To the death."

emerging from the statue of the three cows, something small and red.

"Oh, no," she breathed.

Mephisto crawled stealthily down from the statue, moving like a monkey, silently approaching Jack from above. He gripped the handle of his double-balled flail in his teeth.

Jack never saw him coming—he was too busy holding the writhing and struggling Scarecrow and keeping one eye on Chaos, who was at that moment getting back to his feet.

Chaos stood and took a step toward Jack and Scarecrow.

Then Chaos paused.

It was just for a millisecond, but Jack saw it. Chaos had seen something behind Jack.

Jack dived right . . . taking Scarecrow with him . . . just as the two brass balls of Mephisto's flail came whizzing down from above and clanged together right where Jack's head had been!

The little jester jumped down from the statue and grinned at Jack with his hideous teeth. He began to twirl his flail, increasing its speed, preparing to launch it at Jack when—

Jack dropped Scarecrow and dived toward Chaos, who swung at him with his sword.

This was now a totally crazy fight—Jack vs. Scarecrow vs. Chaos vs. Mephisto—with Jack as the central figure in it all.

Jack somersaulted left, ducking Chaos's blow, just as Mephisto threw his flail and it whipped past Jack, brass balls blurring with speed, and struck Chaos hard in the chest.

Chaos roared in pain and dropped, winded, as Mephisto opened his mouth in shock. He'd hit the wrong man.

He rounded on Jack, only to be side-kicked square in the ribs from the other direction . . . by Scarecrow, lying on the ground! The well-timed kick sent the jester flying into the well-hole in the center

FIGHT 1: JACK VS. SCARECROW (VS. CHAOS)

Scarecrow launched himself at Jack, driving into his belly with his good shoulder.

It was to be expected. The Marine was in a bad way—his left arm was all but useless—and the only way he was going to win this fight was with a quick victory.

He picked up Jack and thrust him back against the podium that supported the three cow statues.

Jack gasped at the impact. Even in his injured state, Scarecrow was strong.

And then Jack saw a flash of silver and out of instinct he ducked as Chaos's sword slashed over his head and hit one cow statue, kicking up sparks.

Jack pushed Scarecrow away from him and side-kicked Chaos in the chest, making him double over.

Scarecrow swung at Jack with his good right arm, but this time Jack evaded the blow and as Scarecrow overextended, Jack stepped in behind him and got the Marine in a choke hold.

The royal audience murmured.

Lily watched tensely.

Then she saw movement above and behind Jack, something

of the combat stage and with a wild squeal, the little red man sailed into the hole and disappeared from view.

"Take that, little fucker," Scarecrow grunted.

Now free of interference from Hades's henchmen, Jack dived back toward Scarecrow. The Marine was getting painfully back to his feet and had just gotten to his knees when Jack pounced on him, once again wrapping his muscly right forearm around Scarecrow's throat in a perfect choke hold.

"I'm sorry," Jack whispered into Scarecrow's ear. "I'm so sorry."

Scarecrow kicked and struggled desperately, but then gradually Jack felt the Marine's body begin to sag and go limp.

Scarecrow's eyes closed.

Jack maintained the choke hold.

Scarecrow lost consciousness. His head flopped forward.

Jack maintained the choke hold.

Scarecrow's breathing stopped.

Jack maintained the choke hold.

And then, as the assembled royals watched in rapt silence, the shrill piercing *beeeeep* of Scarecrow's heart-rate monitor flatlining rang out in the silence.

Jack West Jr. had killed Shane Schofield.

Lily stood stock-still as she watched Jack release Scarecrow's limp body and kick it away from him.

She saw the pained look on his face. Killing any man was not easy, but killing this Marine had clearly hurt him deeply.

On the combat stage, two minotaurs appeared and they dragged Scarecrow's body past Jack and off the stage.

Jack stood and watched Scarecrow go.

Jesus Christ, what have I done? he thought.

A few feet away from him, Chaos rose groggily to one knee, then to his feet.

Jack peered down into the well-hole to see what had become of Mephisto—

What he saw shocked him.

Six feet below the rim of the well-hole, hanging off the side of the slick, polished wall of the hole, was the little red jester.

He grinned mischievously up at Jack.

Mephisto gripped his little mountain-climbing device, the one he had used during the Fourth Challenge on the wall-maze, the pneumatic device that drove a handle deep into the stone, allowing him to hang from an otherwise sheer wall.

Chaos lowered Mephisto's flail into the hole and used it to haul up the jester.

Mephisto sneered at Jack as he stepped back onto the stage. "Tick-tock, tick-tock, I'll be coming back to stop your clock."

Jack just bowed his head.

This was all becoming too much.

Killing Vargas was one thing, but killing Scarecrow was something else. He'd been a decent man, a guy who had wanted the same thing as Jack: for good to prevail.

His mere presence alongside Jack in these hellish trials had given Jack hope, sustenance. He had not been entirely alone in the Games, surrounded by scumbag royals and zealous champions.

But now Scarecrow was gone—killed by Jack himself—and Jack had to survive the final two challenges alone.

Gotta stay strong, he told himself. *This isn't over*.

Exhausted physically, depleted mentally, spent emotionally, and on the ragged edge of his sanity, Jack West trudged off the combat stage escorted by the four minotaur guards and returned to his cell.

FIGHT 2: ZAITAN VS. BRIGHAM (VS. CHAOS VS. MEPHISTO)

The second battle of the Seventh Challenge was no less dramatic than the first.

It saw Hades's second son, Zaitan, pitted against the ginger-bearded SAS major, Gregory Brigham, the man who had so convincingly won two of the early challenges.

"And so we fight," Zaitan said calmly to Brigham as they stood facing each other. "For a chance to win the Great Games and also for the opportunity to kill the fifth warrior."

"I'll enjoy doing both," Brigham snorted.

"Do your worst," Zaitan said.

The fight began with Zaitan and Brigham engaging in a lightning-fast contest of martial arts, but then at the precise moment that the SAS man seemed to be winning, Chaos entered the fray, lunging at Brigham.

In the face of Chaos's attack, Brigham backed up against the big statue of the cows . . .

. . . where Mephisto emerged from his hiding place, just as he had done with Jack, and unleashed his flail.

Brigham heard the rush of air created by the flail too late and swerved his head. The move saved him from death but not terrible injury. One of the brass balls of the flail slammed into his right shoulder and the foul crack of breaking bone echoed out from the combat stage.

Zaitan saw his advantage and took it.

He rushed in on Brigham and unloaded five savage blows with his fists. The blows drew blood—more blood than such hits would normally draw, thanks to the two ceramic blades hidden in the skin of his knuckles.

Brigham was almost out on his feet, bloodied and hideous, when Zaitan unleashed a withering headkick that dropped Brigham, putting him flat on his back.

But he wasn't dead.

Brigham lay on the combat stage, pathetic and immobile, gurgling blood, his right shoulder bent at an odd angle, his left arm outstretched.

Chaos stepped back. Mephisto clambered back up onto the statue of the cows, abandoning his flail.

The royal spectators—grinning with delight—watched in awe as Zaitan, now sauntering casually around Brigham, picked up the flail and tested its weight.

And then Zaitan swung the flail and *slammed* its two brass balls down on Brigham's left hand and wrist.

Brigham's hand exploded in a burst of blood. Brigham screamed, spitting blood. When Zaitan lifted the flail, all that remained beneath it were Brigham's hideously crushed fingers and wristbone.

Zaitan whispered to Brigham. "It will be hard for you to vanquish the fifth warrior, Major, without your hands."

Smash. He flattened Brigham's right hand.

"Or your knees . . ."

Smash. *Smash*.

Two rapid blows from the flail crushed both of Brigham's knees. Brigham howled and began gasping for air. His legs now lay at horrific angles.

Zaitan bowed for the royal crowd and smiled a cruel sadistic smile.

He had completely destroyed Gregory Brigham. The British

SAS major lay behind him, bloodied and broken, a wreck of a human being.

Zaitan then bent over the blood-covered face of Brigham and leaned close so that only Brigham could hear him.

"You are not worthy, Major," he said, "and because you are unworthy, I will now go and claim everything you ever desired when you came here: these Games, the head of the fifth warrior, and your life."

With those words, Zaitan casually kicked Brigham's body into the well-hole.

Brigham fell into darkness, all the way to the base of the mountain, until his heart-rate monitor on the balcony suddenly started issuing a long eerie *beeeeep.*

The royal crowd erupted in applause and Zaitan, still smiling, bowed for them again.

The Seventh Challenge was over.

Once again, the clamps holding the sphere released of their own accord. Zaitan retrieved it and it was set in place on Hades's armrest.

Now, after sixteen champions had started the Great Games, only two remained to proceed to the Eighth Challenge: Zaitan, the son of Hades himself, and Jack West Jr.

EIGHTH CHALLENGE

IMMORTAL COMBAT III

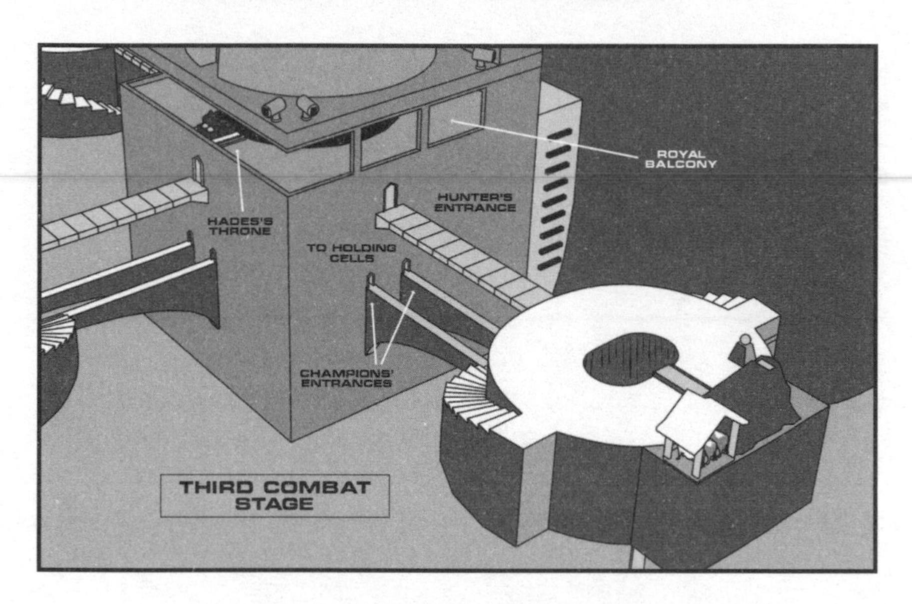

THE THIRD COMBAT STAGE

Hercules's Second Labour was to slay the Hydra, a multi-headed serpent that lived in a swamp near Lake Lerna. But whenever Hercules cut off one of the creature's heads, two more sprang from the stump. Hercules ended up killing the beast in this manner: after he cut off each head, his cousin, Iolaus, cauterised the wound, preventing another head from emerging.

THE GREEK MYTHS,
BY GREG BATMAN
(BODINE BOOKS, NEW YORK, 2005)

EIGHTH CHALLENGE

Jack sat in his cell as Dr. Barnard once again tended to his wounds.

Barnard pressed a cotton pad firmly against Jack's nose, trying to staunch the flow of blood from it.

"We must have you looking your best for your fight against Zaitan," Barnard said.

"Is that who my opponent is?"

"Oh, dear," the doctor said. "I probably shouldn't have said that. Well, never mind. It is only the two of you left now and you would have discovered it soon anyway."

The doctor snapped shut his medical suitcase.

"I was instructed to inform you that you can have an hour to rest before the next challenge, if you want it. Zaitan—I mean, your opponent—has said he is ready to fight now."

"We fight now," Jack said quickly. "I don't want to wait either."

"Very well," the doctor said, standing to go. "Good luck, my dear boy. You've surprised many of us by getting this far and I've got my money on you."

With a quick smile, Barnard left and Jack was once again alone in his cell.

A few minutes later, the minotaur guards came for him.

Jack was marched out onto the third and final combat stage.

Whereas the second stage had been a more advanced version of the first one, the third was an advanced version of the second.

It had a podium with a sphere on it and a central well-hole, just like the first stage.

And it had a large statue of cows like those on the second stage. Jack kept a wary eye on them, watchful for Mephisto. These cow statues, however, had an extra feature: they had a roof over them that looked like a little hut.

What made this stage entirely different, however, was the high water feature near its rear edge: it was a thirty-foot-tall replica of Hades's mountain-palace and from its peak flowed a waterfall that cascaded down several levels before flowing with considerable power down a straight gutter cut into the stage.

The gutter ended at the well-hole in the middle, so that the water gushing down its length poured into the hole before falling a thousand feet to the floor of the crater below.

Jack saw the danger instantly. To fall—or be tossed—into that flowing gutter was to be swept into the well-hole to your death.

His eyes moved from the cattle in their roofed hut to the flowing water. "The Augean Stables," he said to himself. "Which Hercules cleaned by diverting a river through them."

Zaitan was already waiting on the stage.

He glared at Jack with deadly eyes, clenching and unclenching his fists.

Chaos stood off to one side, waiting patiently, holding his sword at the ready.

To Jack's surprise, there was another of Hades's warriors on the stage: the Hydra, dressed in his gray armor and gripping his deadly blade-tipped whip.

"You've got to be kidding me," Jack said.

It was another escalation in the fighting environment, another hazard to avoid while Zaitan, his primary opponent, tried to kill him.

Vacheron's voice cut through the night.

"Zaitan, son of Hades, representative of the Kingdom of the Underworld! Captain West, of the Kingdom of Land! After two days and two nights of valiant effort, only you remain. Alas, only one of you will proceed to the final challenge and have the chance to etch his name in history alongside Osiris, Gilgamesh, and Hercules. The other will die forgotten, for history doesn't care for those who run second. Luck to you both."

He turned to Hades.

The Lord of the Underworld stared down from his throne at both champions.

"Let the fight begin," he said softly. "To the death."

JACK VS. ZAITAN (VS. CHAOS VS. HYDRA)

Zaitan didn't move.

He just stared at Jack, a cocky grin creeping across his face.

Jack frowned.

What's he up to? he thought.

Then Jack's eyes found Zaitan's knuckles and he glimpsed the sharpened ceramic shards sticking out from them. A few of the shards dripped with blood.

Jack looked up at Zaitan. "I thought I'd be facing Brigham. You beat him?"

"Yes."

"With those?" He nodded at Zaitan's sharpened knuckles.

"They are the same claws that will finish you. You should know something, fifth warrior. My brother, Dion, and I are very close. We have planned for this day for a long time. Our father, Hades, is far too noble for our tastes—he actually believes in ruling without fear or favor.

"We do not. We like fear. As soon as these challenges are over, we have arranged for our beloved father to have an unfortunate fall in his private rooms. He will die and Dion will ascend the throne and receive the Mysteries during the final ceremony. We will rule the world as brothers-in-arms. We will share everything: power, wealth . . . and his bride. Know this, fifth warrior: after you are dead, my brother and I will have our way with your daughter every miserable night of her life."

Jack's jaw clenched. His eyes became focused.

"Time to fight, asshole."

"You didn't hear me, warrior," Zaitan said. "I didn't say I would fight you. I said I would *finish* you. These two will fight you."

Zaitan nodded to Chaos and the Hydra and they advanced on Jack.

They didn't even make a pretense of fairness. They were now fighting for their lord's son.

It was one against three.

Jack watched the two armored figures approaching him. In his mind, he visualized the fight that would happen, saw the attacks, saw the defensive moves, saw the outcome.

There was no way he could win this.

He looked from Chaos to the Hydra. Apart from their helmets, the two assassins wore identical Kevlar armor, just painted different colors: Chaos in black, the Hydra in gray. As they advanced on Jack, they both gripped their weapons. The Hydra's deadly metal-tipped whip dangled from its wooden handgrip.

And then Jack saw something.

The Hydra's armor was *not* identical to Chaos's.

It was different at the neck.

While Chaos had a low Kevlar collar protecting the back of his neck, the Hydra did not. Between his shoulder plates and his helmet, the Hydra's neck was bare.

Only the classically educated champion will prevail in the Games. Jack recalled Hades's words.

He now knew those words were a reference to the Labors of Hercules. If you knew how Hercules had performed his Labors—if you possessed that classical knowledge—that helped you win the challenges.

And suddenly Jack remembered how Hercules had defeated the Hydra of his day: the Lernaean Hydra.

Jack now visualized a different fight against these three enemies, and suddenly he saw that if he did a few things right—and did them fast—he could win this.

The two helmeted assassins were almost on him.

Jack called suddenly to Zaitan. "You really want to do it this way?"

Zaitan shrugged. "This is where it ends, fifth warrior."

"You got that right," Jack said.

Then he did something very odd: he smacked his own nose, dislodging Dr. Barnard's temporary staunch, causing his nose to gush with blood again. Blood dripped onto Jack's right hand in large quantities.

What happened next happened very, very fast.

Jack sprang.

Sprang forward with lightning speed . . . at Chaos.

Chaos swung his sword, just as Jack stretched out his hand and flicked out with his fingers, sending a spray of blood *onto the visor of Chaos's helmet.*

It was the one disadvantage of a helmet: having drops of an opaque liquid on its visor meant that the wearer was blinded.

As Chaos tried to wipe the blood clear, Jack wrenched his sword from his hand, elbowed him backward and, leaping forward, swung the sword at the Hydra at the same time as the Hydra lashed at Jack with his whip.

They crossed in midair.

Jack's sword flashed horizontally while the Hydra's whip whistled by his ears, and after they passed each other, they both stopped.

Then, slowly, very slowly, the Hydra's head slid off his still-standing body.

The royal crowd gasped.

Zaitan's eyes went wide.

Jack had sliced the Hydra's head clean off.

Just like Hercules had done.

Thousands of years of myth had transformed the Hydra from a man with a many-pronged whip into a beast with many heads, but the basic method of killing it remained the same: *cut off its head.*

That was why the Hydra's armor had been different from Chaos's. It allowed for such a death. But only the classically trained champion would spot it.

The headless Hydra collapsed to the stage, but not before Jack took something from it.

For his next move was even faster.

What he'd taken from the Hydra was its whip, its deadly flail with the metal tips.

Jack cracked the whip . . . right at the shocked Zaitan.

Zaitan raised his left arm in defense and the whip's vicious metal blades lodged deep into the flesh of his arm.

Zaitan shouted in pain.

But Jack was still moving. He dived left, over to where Chaos stood—still rubbing his blood-smeared visor—and clipped the whip's handle to Chaos's belt.

Then he kicked the unsuspecting Chaos down into the well-hole.

Chaos dropped into the hole . . .

. . . yanking on the whip . . .

. . . which, painfully anchored to the skin of Zaitan's left arm, dragged Zaitan into the hole after him!

Both men disappeared into the hole and fell a thousand feet.

Zaitan screamed, his shrill wail echoing as it diminished, until there came a distant thump and the scream cut off.

Which left Jack standing unsteadily on the stage, alone and victorious.

He glared up at Hades and the royal crowd.

The royal spectators stared back at him in silent, wide-eyed shock.

Some of them glanced worriedly over at Hades, but the King of the Underworld just bowed his head momentarily at the death of his second son.

Only one person in the whole crowd dared to smile: Lily.

★ ★ ★

Up on the royal stage, the shell-shocked Vacheron retrieved the golden belt that was the prize for the winner of the combat phase of the Games.

Of course he didn't present it to Jack. He handed it to Orlando, the King of Land, Jack's sponsor.

Orlando accepted the belt with a satisfied nod.

Standing near them, Lily saw Dion. The young prince was staring in shock at the combat stage, at Jack, and at the spot where his beloved younger brother had last been seen alive.

Then Dion blinked and looked over at Lily with pure hatred in his eyes.

Down on the combat stage, Jack gasped for air, his chest heaving.

He'd done it. He was the last remaining champion.

As he caught his breath, Vacheron appeared on the stage in front of him. The stunned Master of the Games nodded at the glowing sphere on the podium. Jack fetched it and handed it to Vacheron, who carried it up to Hades.

No sooner was the sphere set in place on Hades's armrest than, in the eerie silence, Jack heard something.

Footsteps.

Heavy, purposeful footsteps.

Coming from the bridge that connected this combat stage to the Observatory.

Another fighter appeared on it and Jack's heart fell.

Of course, he thought. *That was the final Labor . . .*

The figure stepped up onto the stage, gripping two weapons, protected by impenetrable armor and wearing a most fearsome helmet.

It was Hades's personal bodyguard, the biggest of them all, the warrior with the dog-shaped helmet. The one everyone said was the best of all of Hades's warrior-servants.

It was Cerberus.

THE FINAL CHALLENGE

THE HOUND OF HELL

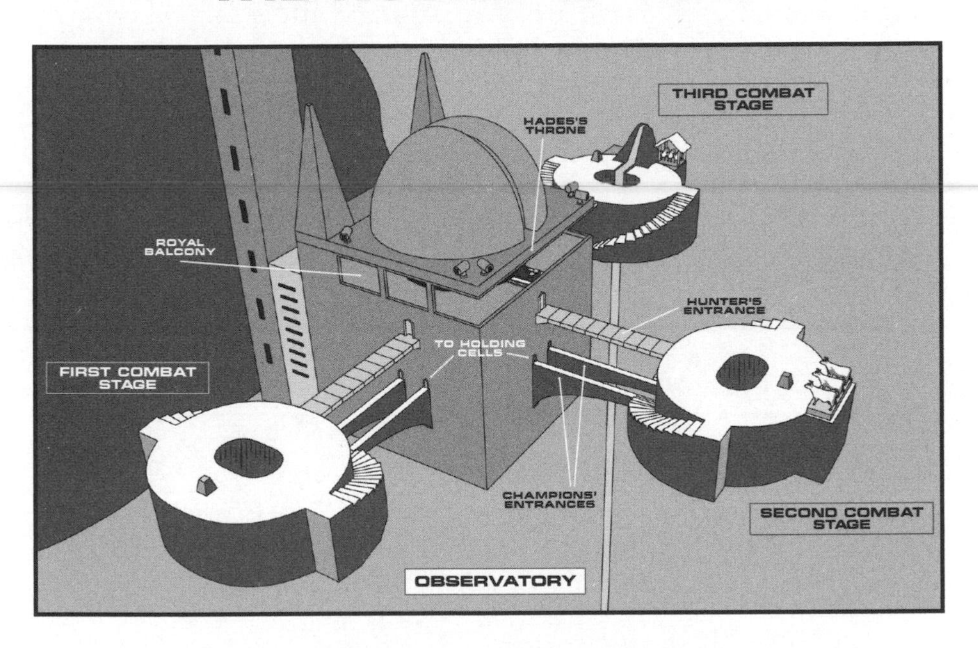

Hercules's final Labour was the most difficult. He had to descend into the Underworld and capture Cerberus, Hades's gigantic three-headed dog. The key element to note here is that, unlike his other Labours involving terrible beasts, this task was to *capture* Cerberus, not kill him. Hercules had to carry the giant hound out of Hell *alive*. His solution was as ingenious as it was surprising.

THE GREEK MYTHS,
BY GREG BATMAN
(BODINE BOOKS, NEW YORK, 2005)

JACK VS. CERBERUS

Jack couldn't believe it.

He was weary, bloody, and wounded . . . and now he had to fight a man, a professional warrior who hadn't expended an ounce of energy in the past two days.

Looking at the giant figure of Cerberus, he saw something embedded in the chest region of the man's body armor: the final Golden Sphere.

Vacheron grinned. "The final challenge of the Great Games is the most famous! The last remaining champion must overcome Hades's most loyal and celebrated guardsman, the Hound of Hell, Cerberus. He must bring him—and his sphere—from the combat stage and present them both to Hades himself."

Jack sagged.

He couldn't see a way to win this.

There were no weaknesses to Cerberus's armor that he could discern.

And the guy under all that armor was huge, at least six foot seven, with tree trunk–like legs and strong muscular arms.

And the big warrior's weapons favored his enormous reach: he gripped a mace in one hand and a curving sword in the other.

Worst of all, however, was the fact that he was fresh. Jack had faced two days of deadly nonstop challenges yet this guy looked like he'd just got out of bed.

Okay, Jack thought. *Can you remember how Hercules got out of this one?*

On the royal balcony, Lily was thinking the same thing: How had Hercules overcome Cerberus in the famous final Labor?

And it hit her.

"Hercules didn't have to *kill* Cerberus," she said aloud. "He only had to bring him out of Hell. Come on, Dad, *think*."

The same thought occurred to Jack at the exact same time.

"The final Labor was to bring Cerberus out of Hell," he said softly to himself. "Not to kill the dog. But how did Hercules do that? No, that can't work . . . Oh, hell, Jack, what have you got to lose? It's worth a try."

With the massive figure of Cerberus advancing quickly toward him, Jack suddenly *turned away* from his opponent and faced the royal balcony.

"Hades!" he called. "I ask for your permission! Will you permit me to bring your dog up to you?"

On the balcony, the younger members of the royal crowd looked at each other and guffawed. What was this?

Alone among them, Lily smiled.

Beside her, Iolanthe whispered, "Oh, Jack, well done. *Well done*."

It was then that Lily noticed that the older members of the royal crowd had begun to do something.

They had started nodding.

Hades's eyes were locked on Jack's.

"You," he said in his deep baritone, "are a worthy champion of the Great Games. Like Hercules before you, you realized that this final challenge is not one of physical strength, but one of humility:

the humility of a hero to seek permission, even after he has won so many battles with strength and violence. The humility of a man who could rightfully think that he owes nothing to anyone."

Hades extended his hand. "You are a noble man indeed, fifth warrior. Having respectfully asked my permission, you may bring my dog to me and he will offer no resistance."

On the stage, Cerberus dropped his weapons instantly and walked over to Jack, essentially giving himself to him.

Doors were flung open, and the way was made clear for Jack to leave the stage, walk across a bridge and through some tunnels and stairways, until he arrived at the royal balcony and stood before Hades's throne with the huge figure of Cerberus by his side.

Jack removed the final Golden Sphere from Cerberus's chest armor and handed it to Hades. Hades then placed it in the final bowl-shaped slot on his armrest.

"My royal brethren," he said, "a champion has proven us all worthy! The final four spheres are now ready to be placed in the major temple atop my mountain. Let us repair to the summit and perform the final ceremony."

He turned to face Jack. "Congratulations, Captain West. You just won the Great Games of the Hydra."

A SECRET HISTORY V

THE SECOND CEREMONY

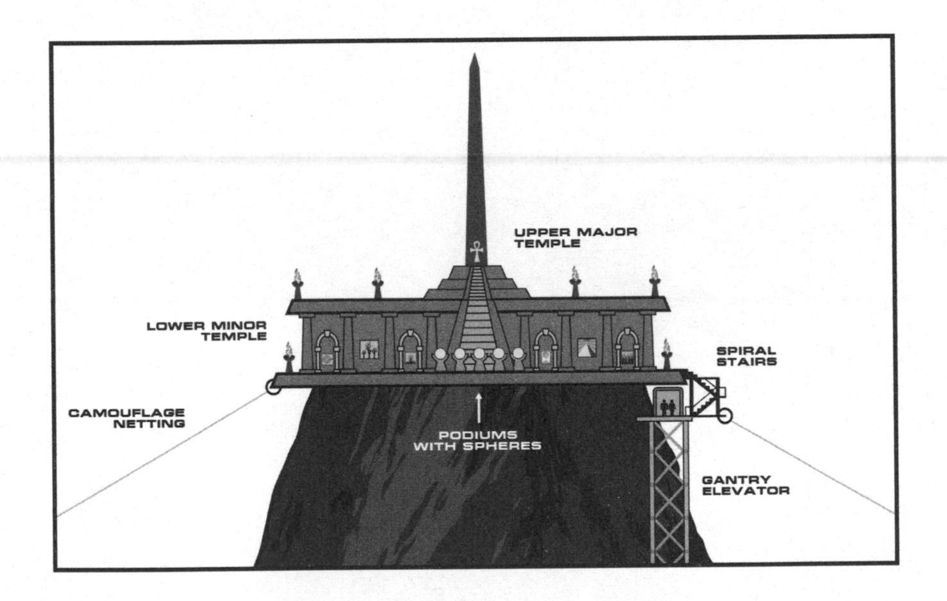

Upon completing his Twelve Labours, Hercules was initiated into the Mysteries of Eleusia and so ascended to Olympus and became a god.

THE GREEK MYTHS,
BY GREG BATMAN
(BODINE BOOKS, NEW YORK, 2005)

THE CEREMONY IN THE MAJOR TEMPLE

Things moved quickly from there.

The royal crowd left the Observatory and ascended in groups in the gantry elevator to the summit of the mountain.

On the ride up, Jack stood with Lily, Iolanthe, and his very proud sponsor-king, Orlando.

All the way up, Orlando was swamped by other royals. They pumped his hand and showered him with congratulations for winning the Games.

"Good show, Orlando!"

"Splendid stuff, Your Majesty."

It was as if Orlando himself had survived the rising water trap, the wall-maze, the wild car race, and several encounters of single combat.

Someone said, "Stroke of genius, Orlando, picking the fifth warrior to represent you. It looked unorthodox at first, I must say, but what a fine choice of champion he turned out to be. You're a smart, smart man."

Jack sensed Iolanthe stiffen, grating at the compliment to her brother and not her. After all, she had been the one to suggest kidnapping Jack to fight for their kingdom.

Jack surreptitiously checked his watch. It had been forty-five minutes. There was still a chance.

His elevator arrived at the wondrous double-leveled structure at the peak of the mountain.

It was fully night now.

The sky was clear and the stars were out. The dead-flat plain of the Indian desert stretched away in every direction, lit by starlight. To the west, way off in the distance, the waters of the Arabian Sea shimmered.

The camouflage netting encasing Hades's kingdom stretched down from the mountaintop like an enormous tent.

Only the two temples protruded above it.

As Jack strode out of the elevator beside Orlando, Hades's heir, Dion rushed up to them.

Dion seized Orlando's hand and shook it vigorously. "Your Majesty, my friend, I'm so pleased for you, *so* pleased. Congratulations!"

"Thank you, Dion," Orlando said.

Dion then turned to Jack and clutched his hand.

"And my sincere congratulations to you, too, champion."

But as Orlando and the others moved on, Dion maintained his grip on Jack's hand and pulled him close.

"You killed my brother, you *fuck*. Once this final ceremony is over and our guests have departed, I will have you brought to my favorite dungeon where I will gut you and strangle you with your own intestines in front of your pretty daughter. Then I shall marry her and, I promise you, make her life a living nightmare."

Dion dropped Jack's hand like a rock star dropping a microphone and strode off.

Jack was left standing there, staring after the prince. After all he'd been through, all he'd overcome, all he'd survived, it still wasn't over.

Hades led the crowd of royals to the higher of the two temples, the major temple.

Four minotaur servants walked behind him, reverently carrying the final four Golden Spheres. They glowed ominously.

The colossal round obelisk soared into the sky from the center of the upper temple.

Cut into its base was a man-sized recess carved in the shape of the ancient Egyptian symbol *ankh*.

With its T-shaped body and round "head," ankh was sometimes called the Coptic cross. Now, as he saw this ankh-shaped recess up close, Jack saw how similar it was to the Christian crucifix. If a man stood inside this recess and stretched his arms out, he would look just like Jesus Christ on the cross.

Suddenly, something occurred to Jack.

He turned to Iolanthe. "The first ceremony caused this antenna to emerge from within the mountain. What happens this time? Your brother said something before about some mysteries being revealed to the winning king."

Iolanthe said, "As the winning king, my brother, Orlando, will stand inside that recess in the obelisk while Hades sets the four Golden Spheres in place around him. Once the spheres are set in place, the antenna will send its signal out to the Hydra Galaxy and the galaxy will alter its course. The Earth will be saved."

"And Orlando? What happens to him inside the recess?"

"That recess is the most holy place in this entire kingdom," Iolanthe said. "Arguably, it's the most important place on Earth right now. This ceremony is the third in a series of five trials the Earth must overcome in order to save the universe.

"Reerecting the Capstone of the Great Pyramid was the first, rebuilding the Machine was the second. This ceremony is more important than those, because it involves the acquisition of *knowledge* required to survive the remaining two trials.

"For the man who stands inside that recess at the moment the antenna sends out its signal will be imbued with the Mysteries, vital sacred knowledge that is required to guide the Earth through the final two ancient trials.

"Because his champion—you—won the Games, that man will be my brother. This will make Orlando all-powerful, the king of kings, the governor of the world for the duration of the trials.

"The last king of kings was the one who sponsored Hercules himself sometime around 1250 B.C. That, of course, was Zeus, who became known to history as the 'king of the gods.'

"But Zeus only repelled the Hydra Galaxy during one of its preliminary passes. He did not live through an Omega Event. When he died, the knowledge of the Mysteries died with him, unneeded and unused. *This* king of kings, however, will govern at a unique time in history. This is why every king so desperately wanted his champion to win these Games."

Jack glanced from the ankh-shaped recess to Orlando standing beside Hades.

Then he asked his big question: "Hades was ready to let the Earth and the universe be destroyed if the spheres were not found and set in place. But what if the spheres *are* set in place and *nobody* is standing inside that recess during the ceremony? What happens then?"

Iolanthe gave Jack a look. "Nobody? I don't think anyone's ever contemplated that."

"What would happen?"

Iolanthe thought about that for a moment. "I suppose, in that case, the Hydra Galaxy would be diverted but no one would receive the Mysteries, and surviving the final two trials would be significantly harder. That vital ancient knowledge would have to be refound, much like you refound the Seven Ancient Wonders and the Six Sacred Stones."

Jack stared at the ankh-shaped recess in the base of the massive antenna, thinking about what it entailed, the power it gave.

Iolanthe said, "Such a question is academic, Jack. There is nothing that can stop my odious brother now. You have won the Games for him and now he shall rule the world."

And so the ceremony—an extremely ancient ceremony—began.

Like a priest of old, Hades stepped forward slowly and reverently and, one by one, he placed the Golden Spheres into receptacles cut into the antenna around the ankh-shaped recess.

One sphere went above the "head."

Two were placed at the ends of the recess's spread-eagled "arms."

And one went below the "feet."

When all four spheres were in place, their glowing intensified and the entire area around Jack was illuminated by their otherworldly light.

And then the great black obelisk came alive.

It began to thrum ominously with some kind of inner power.

Jack gazed up at it.

Thrummmmmm . . .

The noise came from deep within the mountain and it seemed to literally *rise up* through the body of the mighty antenna, gathering in intensity as it did so.

Hades called above the din: "The Age of Trials is upon us and with the revelation of the Mysteries to our chosen governor, we shall overcome those trials. Would the successful king please step forward and take his place inside the sacred tabernacle!"

Beaming with pride, Orlando strode forward. He stopped in front of the ankh-shaped recess and smiled at the royal crowd, gave them a wave, and then—

—an explosion rang out and the mountain shook and Orlando wobbled where he stood. Indeed, all the royals on the major temple were almost thrown off their feet.

Someone at the edge of the stage pointed downward, through the camouflage netting covering the crater: "Look! The minotaurs!"

Jack peered down that way and saw something that totally shocked him.

He saw *the entire population of minotaurs*—a swarming mass of figures, four thousand strong—come charging out of the gates of the minotaur kingdom, rushing toward the Grand Staircase at the base of the mountain-palace.

They looked like an army of ants pouring out of their subterranean city.

Jack squinted.

There was something at the head of the column of charging minotaurs.

A vehicle.

A black Typhoon truck.

And then, with a roar, a helicopter came shooting in low over the mountaintop temple, its rotors thumping, its side-guns blazing, strafing the flanks of the mountain.

The chopper's bullets sheared through the cables anchoring the camouflage netting to the peak of the mountain and the netting dropped away, billowing like a parachute, exposing the entire spectacular crater around the mountain.

The chopper was an Alligator gunship, just like the one Jack had destroyed earlier, and as it thundered by, zooming close to the summit, Jack glimpsed three figures inside its cockpit.

At the controls was Sky Monster.

Sitting in the gunner's seat beside him, squeezed together in the one seat, were two people Jack had never expected to see here.

Stretch and Pooh Bear.

And at the sight of his friends, Jack's heart leaped.

Of course, Jack didn't know what had happened out on the beach before.

As the second Alligator gunship had caught up with the fleeing Typhoon truck containing Alby and the others, it had swept into a deadly hover in front of it, forcing the truck to stop.

A voice over a loudspeaker had commanded, "Get out of the vehicle with your hands raised!"

Totally outgunned, Alby, Mother, Sky Monster, E-147, and Tomahawk had done as instructed and stepped out of the truck.

The heavily armed chopper had been about to open fire on them with its side cannons when without warning a rocket-propelled grenade slammed into it from the other direction, *from behind* . . .

. . . fired by one of three figures racing down the beach from the north in an open-topped jeep: Stretch, Pooh Bear, and Mae Merriweather.

Following their discovery in Karachi, they had arrived by seaplane at the vast beach in northwestern India an hour earlier. Having acquired a jeep in the nearest town, they had begun to sweep down the beach from the north, hoping to find some kind of entry to the Underworld.

What they found was the chopper about to murder their friends.

Rocked by the impact of the RPG, the chopper had dropped to the sand, landing heavily on its belly, and its pilot and gunner were quickly apprehended and bound.

"Are we glad to see you," Sky Monster said, clasping hands with Pooh Bear and Stretch.

Some quick introductions were made to Scarecrow's Marines—including a brief explanation of who and what E-147 was; and the dogs were delighted to see people they knew. Alby briefed Pooh, Stretch, and Mae on what had happened over the previous two days. He also told them how Jack had sacrificed himself to get them away, and how Lily and the Marine named Scarecrow were still in the Underworld. Whether they—or Jack—were still alive or not, he didn't know.

Pooh Bear squinted down the beach. "They're still being held captive back there, you say? Is there any way we can bust them out?"

"Not with a handful of people," Mother said. "We'd need an army to storm Hades's mountain."

"That's right," Alby said, stepping forward. "And I think I know where we can find one."

They'd moved fast from there.

Sky Monster had repaired the Alligator gunship as best he could and somehow got it in the air again with Stretch and Pooh Bear—the freshest soldiers among the group—on board.

Mother took the wheel of the Typhoon assault truck and, with Alby, E-147, Mae, Astro, and Tomahawk with her, she sped back down the beach, heading for the supply dock they had emerged from earlier.

Their target: the minotaur city and the Minotaur King.

Arriving in the minotaur city of Dis, they had been surrounded by half-men, but then the king saw Alby and recognized him as Jack's friend.

Mayhem reigned on the mountaintop temple.

People screamed and ran for cover.

The giant stone antenna kept thrumming, louder and louder, its deep hum gathering in intensity. The thrumming had been so loud before it had prevented anyone from hearing the incoming chopper. Now it was even louder.

Hades spun, not flinching at the gunfire and helicopter noise. He was just trying to figure out what was going on.

Beside him, Orlando looked from the banking chopper to the ankh-shaped recess in the obelisk in front of him. That recess, primed by the Golden Spheres and ready to bestow the Mysteries on the king who stood inside it, was his destiny.

Heedless of the noise and chaos around him, he lunged toward the recess—

—just as someone came flying at him from the side and crash-tackled him to the ground.

"No!" Orlando screamed as he and Jack went tumbling to the stone floor in front of the ankh-shaped hollow.

He clawed and scratched at Jack.

"You fool!" Orlando screamed. "I must be in the chamber when the antenna emits its signal!"

Jack punched him hard in the face, breaking his nose, sending blood gushing over his mouth.

Alby relayed to the king what Dion had told him in the dungeon earlier: about his and Zaitan's plan to kill Hades immediately after the Games and rob the minotaurs of the freedom Hades had promised them.

The Minotaur King had been infuriated by that and the army of minotaurs was assembled and was soon rushing en masse behind the Typhoon toward the mountain-palace.

"I don't think you should rule the world, asshole," he said grimly.

"But everyone will die!"

"I'd rather the whole world died as free people than lived as your slaves."

"What makes you think you, an ordinary man, can speak *for the entire world*?" Orlando spat as he clumsily drew a Glock pistol from inside his coat.

But Jack was on him in an instant and he swiped the pistol from Orlando's hand. Jack looked at the King of Land and saw the sneer in his eyes, the breathtaking sense of entitlement.

"Better me than you," he said simply and he punched Orlando in the face with the pistol, knocking him out, and tossed him like a rag doll away from the recess.

Right then, as its thrumming reached fever pitch, the black stone antenna lit up like a lightning rod and with a colossal *boom*, fired a magnificent white-hot bolt of energy deep into the star-filled sky.

The boom was deafening.

The shockwave of the sound threw everyone on the temple to the ground. A couple of the royals who had raced to the minor temple and stood near the gantry elevator there were hurled off the edge of the mountaintop and sailed to their deaths.

Jack didn't need to see it to know that this was the signal that would divert the incoming Hydra Galaxy. A moment of eerie silence followed as everyone slowly got to their feet.

The only noise was the thumping of the helicopter's rotors as it banked around the mountaintop temple. Its cannons blazed with muzzle flashes as it opened fire on something farther down the mountain.

The royal spectators looked either confused or horrified.

Jack's eyes scanned their faces before suddenly his gaze landed on Vacheron.

The Master of the Games was glaring right at Jack. He smiled nastily as he raised his hand, to reveal . . .

. . . the remote control in it.

He pressed the button on the remote and Jack's blood froze.

Nothing happened.

Jack's head didn't explode.

Vacheron frowned, hit the button on his remote repeatedly.

Still nothing.

And then Jack saw the Alligator assault helicopter sweep around beneath him, and he saw what it had been shooting at moments before:

The antenna array on top of the second-highest castle on the mountain.

"Sky Monster, you've been talking to Alby," Jack said aloud.

The array was now torn to shreds, ripped apart by the chopper's gunfire—which meant the radio link between Vacheron's remote to the explosive in Jack's neck was no longer operating.

Vacheron saw this and with a final furious glare at Jack, discarded the useless remote and bolted for the gantry elevator, following the other royals.

Jack hurried over to Lily and took her by the hand, "Come on, we gotta get out of here—"

He cut himself off when he saw Hades. The Lord of the Underworld was staring blank-eyed and open-mouthed at the empty recess.

"The Mysteries have not been revealed," he said in disbelief. "The sacred knowledge has *not* been received . . ."

He locked eyes with Jack. "Do you know what you've done? Now the knowledge will have to be refound. Before the Omega Event. Before the end of the universe itself. Now, to overcome the two trials ahead, someone will have to *find* the three secret cities and somehow open their vaults. That is the only option remaining for us to obtain the required sacred knowledge and avert the Omega Event. Do you understand?"

Jack nodded firmly. "The world can still survive, it just won't be doing it under some all-powerful king. *We* find that sacred knowledge. You and me."

Hades frowned, genuinely confused. "You and me? You want my help?"

"Yes," Jack said.

Hades blinked uncomprehendingly. "You would accept me after all I put you through?"

"You did your job. You held your Games without fear or favor," Jack said. "Of the four kings, you're the only one who's not in this for himself. You're not a bad man, you're not evil like Dion. He *is* bad; he *is* evil. Zaitan, too. They were planning to kill you right now.

"But you're smart. You're stubborn and unyielding, sure, but you're honorable. If I'm going to try and save the universe, I'll need your knowledge. Come with me. There's nothing for you here now, only a son who wants you dead. Help me."

The look on Hades's face was one of profound confusion now. He was a man who was seeing everything he had ever stood for—ancient rituals, ironclad traditions, divine royal rule—come crashing down around him.

"Our way would have saved the world . . ." he said desperately.

"But it was *the wrong way*," Jack said. "It's better to lose everything the right way than win the wrong way."

Hades stared deep into Jack's eyes . . .

. . . and then he thrust out his hand.

The two men shook.

"We do it your way then," Hades said solemnly.

Jack nodded. “Thank you.”

“Jack,” Iolanthe said. “The minotaurs are swarming up the mountain. When they get here, I don’t think they’re going to differentiate between good guys and bad guys. We have to go. We have to get down to the high castle with the helipad. The hangars are there with a few choppers in them.”

Jack spun. Lily stood with Iolanthe, alongside Iolanthe’s royal doctor, Dr. Barnard.

Once again, Jack checked his watch. “Okay. But we have to make one stop first.”

“What? Where?” Iolanthe asked.

“It’s something I have to do,” Jack said as he snatched Barnard’s medical suitcase and took off at a run. “Follow me.”

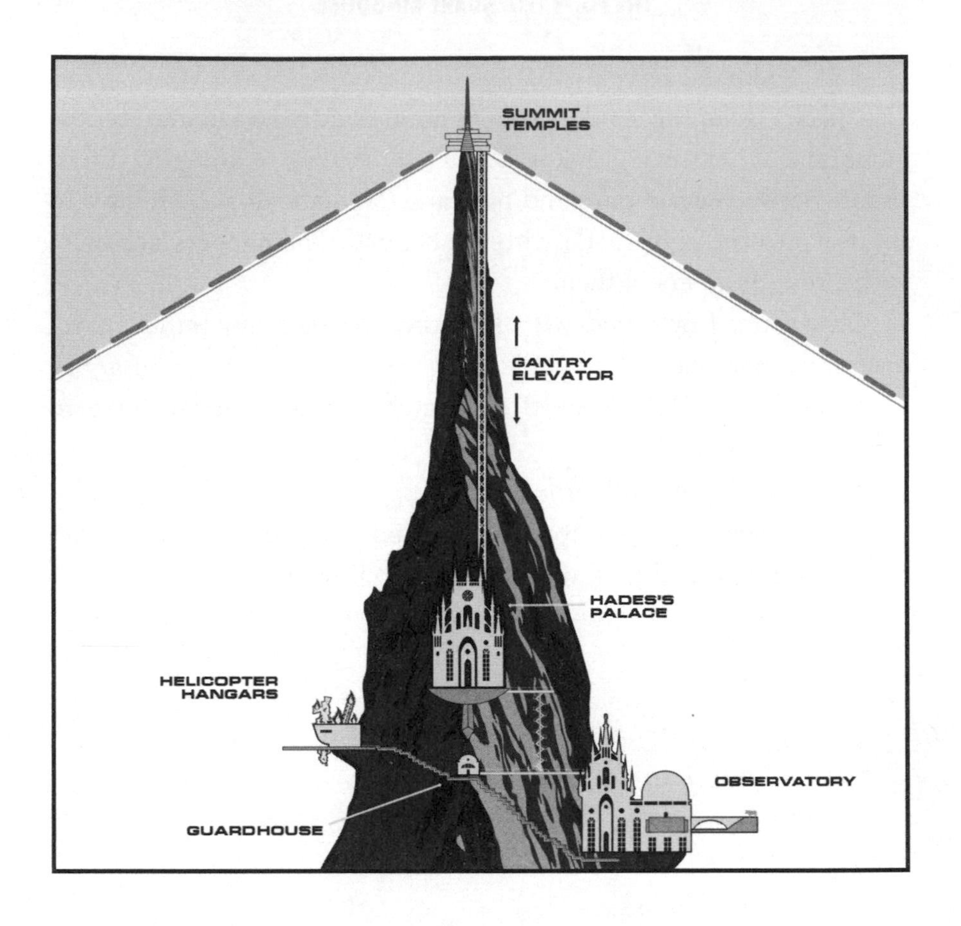

There was movement all over the mountain-palace.

At its base, the teeming mass of minotaurs was rising up the lower slopes. They had reached the battlement level that ringed the waist of the mountain and now swarmed through the guest quarters there.

The rising horde just surged upward, scaling stone staircases or using elevators. They charged through the Observatory and up a curving stone staircase that led to the second-highest of Hades's high castles: the one that contained the Underworld's helipad and chopper hangars.

As the minotaurs rushed upward, the various royal guests fled downward toward the high castle with the helipad.

A leading group of royals emerged from the gantry elevator at

Hades's own palace. As the elevator rose back up to the summit, this first group raced for a sweeping staircase that led down to the helipad castle.

The group was led by three of the four kings: the groggy Orlando; Garrett Caldwell, the American Sea King; and Kenzo Depon, the Sky King.

They arrived at the high castle with the helipad—the wide flat deck sprang out from the fortress that itself sprang out from the mountain.

Inside one of the castle's hangars were several beautiful twelve-seat Sikorsky S-76 luxury helicopters.

The Sea King hit a button on the wall and an underfloor mechanism began to pull one of the wheeled choppers out of the hangar and onto the helipad . . .

. . . just as the first minotaurs arrived, running at speed and roaring with fury.

Truth be told, the minotaurs were searching for Hades's treacherous sons, Dion and Zaitan, but in their panic—the classic panic of the well-to-do fleeing the angry masses—the personal bodyguards of the three kings did something very foolish.

They opened fire on the advancing minotaurs.

The first rank of minotaurs fell, shot dead.

This only served to infuriate the ones behind them who plunged headlong into the group of royals and hacked them to pieces.

As Orlando dived behind a chopper to avoid the melee, the King of the Sea and the King of the Sky, plus their retinues of bodyguards and courtiers, all perished in a hail of blows from the swarm of half-men.

With those royals butchered, the frenzied mob of minotaurs charged up the stairs, desperate to find and stop the princes who wanted to murder their ancient lord.

Up on the mountain's summit, the gantry elevator returned and a second group of panicked royals piled into it.

The elevator's doors closed and it began its descent.

Up on the top level, Jack turned to Hades. "Is there another way down?"

"There are some old stone stairs on the other side," Hades said. "They were built in a time before elevators. They're very steep but they switch back and forth all the way down the mountain."

"Show us," Jack said.

Hades led them to the rear of the mountaintop. Sure enough, a set of stairs led down from there.

Old was an understatement. Steep was, too.

The rock-cut stairs descended at a frightening angle, and they were worn with age. The black stone from which they'd been cut actually shone, polished from thousands of years of use.

Jack led the way, bounding down the steep stairway.

No sooner had he started down the path than the gantry elevator on the other side of the mountaintop creaked loudly.

Then it began to shake.

The minotaurs had arrived at its base and, enraged by the gunshots down on the helipad and acting as a mob, they were wrenching the gantry elevator's frame away from the brackets holding it against the mountain's flank while the elevator car containing the second group of royals was still coming down it!

With a pained metallic groan, the gantry came loose and, like a tree falling in a forest, the frame fell away from the side of the mountain, taking the elevator with it!

Screams and shouts issued from the elevator as the whole combination of elevator and gantry frame toppled off the mountain and tumbled to the crater hundreds of feet below.

Jack and his group hurried down the vertiginous rear stairway.

They passed Hades's personal castle.

"Keep going!" Jack called.

When they passed the castle containing the helicopter hangars, Iolanthe shouted, "Where are we going?"

"The Observatory," Jack said as the dome-shaped fortress came into view, with its ancient telescope chamber and its three combat stages.

He led his group to the cells beneath the combat stages.

Minotaur guards ran the other way, abandoning their posts, fleeing.

Jack came to the cell he was looking for and flung open its door.

He was hoping against hope that the body hadn't been discarded yet . . .

. . . it hadn't.

Jack checked his watch. It had been fifty-five minutes. That could be too long.

"Jesus," he breathed, "I hope I'm not too late."

"Too late for what?" Lily said as she entered the cell behind him and saw the body lying on the floor.

It was the body of Shane Schofield.

The Scarecrow.

Jack slid to his knees beside Scarecrow's body, drawing the defibrillator paddles from Dr. Barnard's medical case as he did so.

Barnard said what everyone was thinking.

"The man's dead, Captain. His heart stopped beating an hour ago. There is no way you can resuscitate him now."

Jack ignored him.

He was thinking of one thing.

The thing that Scarecrow had shown him moments before they had fought, something in his hand.

A syringe with a label on it that read HYPOX-G4–62.

Scarecrow had been silently telling Jack that he'd taken the hyperoxygenated blood additive. As Jack had realized, in addition to giving soldiers extra stamina in battle, Hypox could keep a man's blood oxygenated for some time *after* his heart had stopped beating, so theoretically he could be resuscitated later.

Scarecrow had let Jack kill him in the hope that he would return later and revive him. "See you on the other side" had been his exact words.

Jack fired up the defibrillator paddles.

Whack.

Scarecrow's body jolted.

Jack zapped him again.

Scarecrow jolted again.

Whack!

And suddenly Scarecrow lurched . . . and gagged . . . and coughed as he sucked air into his lungs.

"Scarecrow!" Jack slapped his face. "Can you hear me?"

Another cough, then, "I hear you."

Scarecrow looked up, his eyes slowly focusing on Jack crouched over him.

Jack smiled.

"How long was I dead?" Scarecrow asked.

"Fifty-six minutes," Jack said.

"Glad you didn't wait any longer. Another few minutes and I'd be a vegetable. Thanks for coming back for me."

"It was the least I could do," Jack said. "How did you know it would work?"

Scarecrow said, "I once fought against a renegade US Air Force General named Caesar Russell at a place called Area 7. He used Hypox to stay alive for a while after he was executed for treason. I figured it was worth a try . . . as long as you came back."

Jack lifted Scarecrow to his feet. As he did so, Scarecrow saw the odd group of people gathered in the cell behind Jack: Lily, Iolanthe, Dr. Barnard, and . . . Hades.

"*Look out!*" Scarecrow yelled, shoving Jack away from him, snatching the Glock pistol wedged in Jack's belt and firing it over Jack's shoulder.

Jack heard the sonic sizzle of the bullet whizzing past his ear and he spun in horror at the idea that Scarecrow had just shot Hades . . .

. . . only to see another person standing in the doorway *behind* Hades, gripping a pistol of his own aimed right at Jack.

Vacheron.

The Master of the Games just stood there, frozen in the firing position, a wet crimson patch expanding on his chest. Vacheron heaved for breath, as if willing himself to pull the trigger of his gun.

Blam-blam-blam! Scarecrow unloaded three more rounds into him and Vacheron was hurled out of the doorway by the barrage.

"Never liked that asshole," Scarecrow said, handing the gun back to Jack. "What did I miss?"

Jack said, "I won the Games and saved the world . . . at least for now. My people came back in a chopper just in time and now the minotaurs are on a rampage and overwhelming the mountain."

"Is that all?" Scarecrow nodded at Hades. "What about him? What's he doing here?"

"He's with me now," Jack said. "Come on, the shit's hit the fan and while it's spraying everywhere, we're gonna get out of this place."

Jack slung Scarecrow's arm over his shoulder and together they raced out of the cell.

It was a desperate run up to the helipad fortress.

By now all the members of the minotaur army were climbing the mountain any way they could: up elevators, through internal stairs, and up the steep outer stairs that Jack's group was using.

After a few minutes of running, Jack and his little group came to a junction in the steep stairways: a junction marked by the ruins of a guardhouse.

Three paths met at the ruins: Jack's upward-leading stairway, the steep steps that he had come *down* earlier, and a flat path that led across to the helipad fortress.

The ancient guardhouse was actually strategically placed on a crag on the south face of the mountain. The crag jutted out slightly from the mount, high above a sheer drop, allowing its guards to see east and west, up and down.

It was also seriously old.

Its roof was long gone, so now all that was left of the structure was a stone floor with a low marble fence and a storehouse carved into the mountain. The missing roof's pillars and the knee-high marble fenceposts were either broken or weathered with age.

A huge marble statue of three mighty horses, rearing on their hind legs above three fallen men, stood in the center of the circular ruins.

With Scarecrow still draped over his shoulder, Jack saw the flat path leading westward to the helipad fortress.

"That way! We're almost there—" he said just as a figure emerged from the darkened storehouse embedded in the mountain's wall with a pistol in his hand, aimed directly at Jack's head.

It was Dion.

And he was furious.

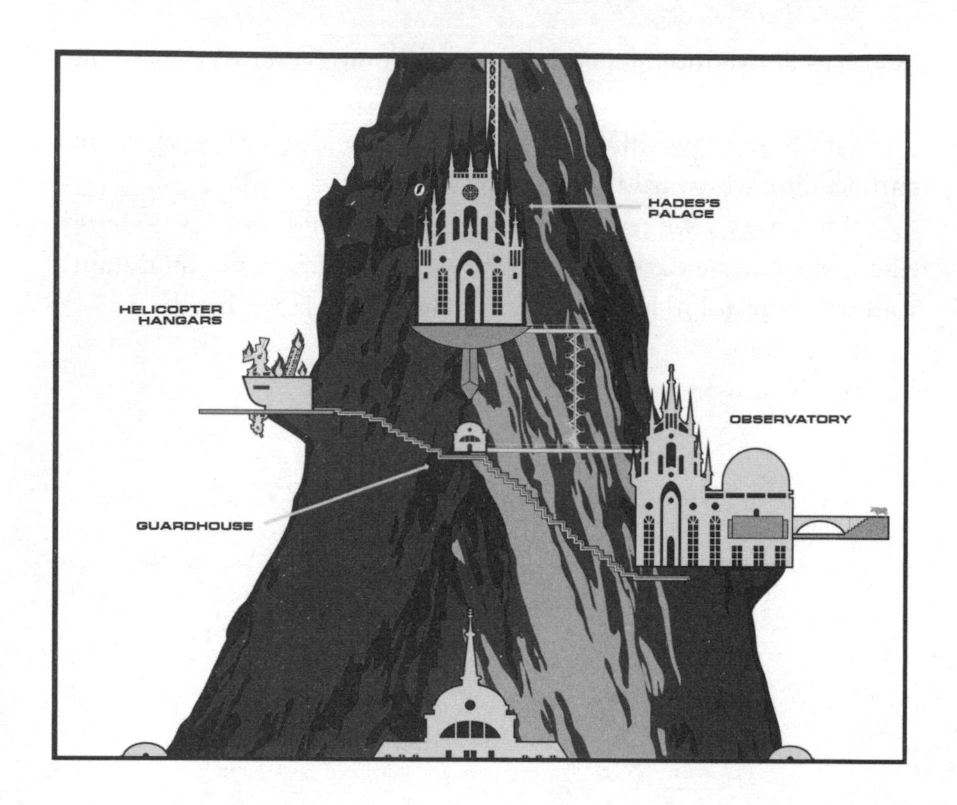

"You!" Dion screamed at Jack. "You ruined everything! The Games! The ceremony! The Mysteries! This kingdom was to be mine! *The world was to be mine!* And now you have condemned us all to die!"

Hades stepped forward. "Dionysius. What were you thinking? Why are you doing this?"

Dion's face screwed up in a rictus of hate and rage. "You grew weak, Father! The Lord of the Underworld should be *feared* throughout the world! The mere thought of him should make men tremble. After I killed you, I planned to rule in a way that would make that happen."

Dion turned his gaze on Lily. "I may not get to marry you and make your life a misery, so I'll do the next best thing and kill your beloved father in front of your eyes. And then I'll kill mine."

He reasserted his aim at Jack.

There was nothing Jack could do. Dion was twelve feet away from him and he himself was weighed down by Scarecrow. He couldn't even make a desperate lunge at the prince.

Dion squeezed the trigger and a single gunshot rang out.

Jack winced, waiting for the bullet to hit him, but nothing did.

Instead, Dion's face blasted outward in a gruesome fountain of blood, shot from behind. He buckled where he stood, his left cheek torn apart, his eyes wide with shock. His gun slipped from his fingers and he fell to his knees and then flat onto his face.

As he dropped, he revealed a group of figures behind him, standing on the flat path leading to the helipad.

It was a cohort of about twelve minotaurs. At their head was the Minotaur King, and beside him, armed with rifles, were Mother, Astro, and E-147. And beside them was a young man gripping a smoking pistol in the firing position.

Alby.

Alby hurried over to the fallen body of Dion and kicked his gun away.

"Alby!" Lily leaped into his arms and kissed him all over his face.

Alby held her tight. "You okay? You're not hurt?"

"I'm good," Lily said.

Alby looked over at Jack. "We came up in an elevator with some of the minotaurs. We went straight to the helipad, looking for you. But then Stretch saw you from the chopper a minute ago and radioed to tell us you were here. Sorry it took us so long."

Jack shook his head. "Don't ever apologize to me again, kid. You're a dead-set fucking legend."

Hades stepped over to the Minotaur King and took his hand.

"Minotus, my friend. As you know, after the Games were done, I was going to give you this kingdom, for I would not need it anymore. I give it to you now. Do with it as you wish. Stay here, and I will ensure that no people come to this place—as far as the world knows, this is all my land. Or venture out into the world, if you desire. I have always appreciated your loyalty to me, but now you are free of any obligation. You may stay, you may go. It is up to you."

Minotus nodded to Alby. "This young man told us that your sons, Dionysius and Zaitan, were planning to kill you, seize your throne and keep us as wretched slaves. We had to act."

"I'm glad you did," Hades said. "Take this kingdom. Make it yours and guard it until it is next needed. But most of all, look after your people and live."

The two men embraced.

As they came apart, Minotus beheld E-147. "Minotaur," he said.

"Yes, my king." E-147 bowed his head reverently.

"Over the course of these Games, you have acquired something that few obtain in their entire lives"—he nodded at Jack—"a true and noble friend. If you desire it, leave this kingdom now and go with this new friend of yours."

E-147 looked from Minotus to Jack.

Jack nodded. "If you want to come with us, you're more than welcome, buddy."

"I will go, Majesty," E-147 said to his king. Minotus clasped E-147's hand and shook it.

Jack said, "Sorry to interrupt, but we kinda have an escape to make. We need to grab a chopper and get out of here."

Now escorted by the Minotaur King and with Scarecrow assisted by Mother and Astro, Jack led the group away from the ruins of the ancient guardhouse and up the path to the helipad fortress.

They rounded a final bend and saw the helipad in front of them.

"Good God . . ." Jack gasped.

He got there in time to see two royal helicopters—both expensive Sikorskys, their rotors blurring, seconds from takeoff—get overwhelmed by a mass of minotaurs that had got there by some other route.

The minotaurs tossed a steel cable into the tail rotor of the first helicopter, causing the rotor to shriek and clank and . . . stop.

Then, working as a mob, they pushed the disabled chopper, *with its cargo of screaming royal passengers inside it*, off the edge of the helipad and the nine-million-dollar helicopter plummeted to the ground hundreds of feet below.

The second Sikorsky's doors were open, so the horde of minotaurs yanked its royal passengers and pilots from it and hacked them to death with their swords. Blood sprayed. The royals screamed. Then the minotaurs began to shove this chopper—its rotor blades still spinning—toward the edge of the helipad.

With the helipad overrun and helicopters dropping off the edge, it looked like the Fall of Saigon.

The Minotaur King stepped in front of Jack.

"I shall get you a helicopter," he said.

Minotus strode across the helipad and commanded the minotaurs pushing the second Sikorsky toward the edge to desist.

They had just managed to shove the chopper's front wheels off the edge when he called for them to stop. They obeyed his command instantly and the chopper remained tilted forward, its nose dangling over the edge of the high helipad.

Minotus waved Jack's group over. "Get in!"

Jack jumped into the pilot's seat. The others piled in the back.

Scarecrow sat next to Jack. "Can you fly a helicopter?"

"Sky Monster's given me a few lessons."

"Here. Shove over," Scarecrow said. "I was in the Air Wing of the Marine Corps before I became a line animal. I didn't survive all those challenges to crash in a chopper flown by a rookie."

Jack scooted over and let Scarecrow take the controls.

Scarecrow powered the Sikorsky up and the big chopper rose off the elevated helipad.

It hovered for a moment in front of the massive black mountain, looking like an insect in front of the towering peak.

"Let's get out of here," Jack said. "Punch it."

Scarecrow hit the thrusters and the chopper peeled away from the helipad fortress. It made a quick stop at the base of the mountain to pick up Mae, Tomahawk, and the dogs, before it leaped skyward and powered away into the night.

Sky Monster's Alligator gunship immediately swept into position beside it and, flying in tandem, the two helicopters swept away from the overrun mountain-palace.

Within thirty seconds, they had risen high into the star-filled sky.

Far beneath them lay the flat desert plain with the wide circular crater cut into it. The tapering mountain-palace of Hades that rose up from the crater's core looked tiny from up here, like a model.

Fires raged in various places on the mountain. The great black stone obelisk that spiked upward from the temple on the mountain's summit looked small, insignificant.

Lit by starlight, the desert stretched away, relentlessly flat and bare, with not a structure or settlement in sight. On the distant western horizon were the waters of the Arabian Sea.

"Go east," Hades said to Scarecrow. "Inland. We will eventually come to one of my mines. There's an airstrip there with all the royal planes. Captain West's plane is parked there, too."

The Sikorsky flew low over the nighttime desert.

The group sat in silence in the luxurious rear cabin of the helicopter.

Lily sat curled in Alby's arms. E-147 sat beside them.

Iolanthe stared out the window, contemplating an unknown future.

Hades did the same.

In the cockpit, Scarecrow flew, gazing ahead at the landscape sweeping by below the chopper's nose. Jack sat at his side, saying nothing because there was really nothing to say.

After about thirty minutes, an open-cut mine came into view, a vast hole in the desert floor.

An airstrip lay beside it.

Three private jets sat parked beside the runway: Gulfstreams and Bombardiers. The crème de la crème of private aircraft.

A short distance from them sat Jack's plane: the black-painted Concorde look-alike that he had christened the *Sky Warrior*.

"Commencing our descent," Scarecrow said as he brought the chopper in toward the airstrip.

As he did so, Jack stepped into the rear cabin and sat down beside Hades.

"So. The Mysteries weren't revealed to us. Which means now we have to find them. How long have we got?"

"We have time," Hades said. "Not a lot, but we have time. The

Mysteries—the knowledge that is required to stop the Omega Event—are kept in vaults in the three secret cities: Thule, Atlas, and Ra. We must now find those cities—and the Trismagi who guard them—and unlock those vaults before the universe ends."

They arrived at the airstrip.

Apart from two late-night security guards, it was silent, empty.

Already agitated by the arrival of one helicopter carrying a load of disheveled and angry rich people, the two security guards seemed positively shocked to see their boss, Mr. Anthony DeSaxe, emerge from this chopper and stride over to them.

"Who else has come through here in the last hour?" Hades demanded.

The senior guard said, "Mr. Compton-Jones, sir, and three of his people, including the Catholic cardinal."

Hades turned to Jack. "Orlando and Cardinal Mendoza. They'll also go after the three cities."

Jack shook his head. "Forget that for now. That's a race that we'll have to run another day. Right now, I just want to go home."

Jack West stood facing Shane Schofield on the empty airstrip.

Behind Scarecrow, the other three Marines—Mother, Astro, and Tomahawk—were prepping one of the royal jets for departure.

"I'm really sorry I had to kill you," Jack said.

"It had to be done," Scarecrow said.

He clasped Jack's hand. "It's been an honor to meet you, Jack West Jr. Looks like you've got your work cut out for you from here. If you ever need a hand, give me a call."

"I will. And thanks. Thanks for being the only other honorable guy in those Games."

"My pleasure," Scarecrow said.

"Yo, Scarecrow!" Mother called from the plane. "Enough with the bromance, already! We gotta hit the road. Later, Huntsman."

Scarecrow gave Jack a final nod. "Good luck."

"You, too," Jack said.

And with those words, the two heroes parted, heading for their respective planes.

As Jack arrived at the *Sky Warrior*, he found his diminutive mother, Mae, waiting for him at the airstairs. Stretch and Pooh Bear stood with her.

"Hi, Mom," Jack said. "Didn't get a proper chance to say hello. Hey, fellas."

"How are you, Jack?" Mae said warmly. "Got yourself into quite the pickle these last few days, didn't you?"

"You could say that. I can't tell you how glad I was to see you guys. I don't know how you tracked us down, but I'm thrilled you did. Thanks."

Pooh Bear smiled. "Anytime."

"You'd do the same for us," Stretch said. "Hey, you *did* do it once for us."

"I guess I did," Jack said, but then he remembered something. "Oh, God, Horus. She was at Pine Gap—"

"It's okay," Pooh Bear said. "We got her. She was a little beat up on account of getting shot and all. We dropped her off at a vet in Broome before we left for Karachi. Explained the gunshot wound as a hunting accident. She's fine. We can collect her on the way back."

"Then let's get out of here." Jack ascended the airstairs.

"Honestly," Mae said, following him. "I'm always saying I want to see more of you and Lily, that you should call me more often. I can't believe it took something like this to get us together."

"Don't speak too soon, Mom. Given your areas of expertise, I think we're going to be seeing a lot more of each other over the coming months and years," Jack said as he stepped inside the plane.

AIRSPACE OVER THE INDIAN OCEAN
FOUR HOURS LATER

The *Sky Warrior* soared over the Indian Ocean, shooting through the nighttime sky.

In his private cabin in the rear of the plane, Jack slept. A quick operation by Stretch with some local anaesthetic had seen the extraction of both the ancient yellow quartz gemstone seared into the back of his neck and the modern small explosive charge that had been implanted underneath it.

Once it was out, Jack peered closely at the yellow gemstone. It looked sleek, old, and oddly powerful. He kept it for later examination.

After that, Stretch stitched him up and, exhausted beyond belief, Jack fell into a deep sleep.

Mae, Lily, Alby, E-147, and the dogs were all in the next cabin, in various bunks, also fast asleep. Pooh Bear, Stretch, Hades, and Iolanthe dozed in some chairs in the main cabin.

Only Sky Monster was awake, flying his beloved plane by the light of the instrument panel.

Jack dreamed.

Of the Underworld and of its deadly challenges. Of its helmeted warriors: Fear, Chaos, the Hydra, and Cerberus. Of men drowning and dying, of combat stages and of an army of minotaurs going on a rampage.

And in that strange way dreams operate, he found himself dreaming of Mephisto. In his dream, he began to wonder: where did Mephisto go in all that chaos?

His brain tried to recall where he had last seen the murderous jester. Was it on the second combat stage? He wasn't sure.

The thought of Mephisto brought the image of the jester's face right in front of his eyes. He saw the vicious little fiend grinning, showing his sharpened teeth and holding up a wicked knife and saying in his twee voice, "You wouldn't forget me, would you? I told you *I* wouldn't forget you."

Jack's eyes flashed open.

Mephisto was crouched over him, his evil red face pressed close to Jack's own, holding a knife right in front of Jack's nose!

Jack hadn't dreamed that voice or those words. Mephisto had said it for real.

His mind raced.

Mephisto must have got out of the Underworld on the first chopper and stowed away on the *Sky Warrior* before they got to it.

The jester slashed at Jack's face with his knife, but Jack caught his wrist and hurled him off him.

Jack snatched up the Desert Eagle pistol he kept beside his bed, chambered a round—

—but Mephisto leaped at him again, hissing through his bared teeth, and pushed Jack's gun hand back against the small window behind him.

Jack struggled as Mephisto knelt astride him. The little jester used his right foot to pin Jack's gun hand to the window while he raised his deadly knife again.

Jack was screwed.

After all the challenges, all the fights and chases, he was going to have his throat cut by this little rat bastard.

"Bye-bye!" Mephisto squealed as he raised his knife for the final blow.

"That's right," Jack said . . .

. . . as he pulled the trigger of his pinned gun.

The gun went off, the blast deafening in the enclosed space, firing *right through* the window behind Jack's head.

The effect was instantaneous.

Cabin pressure was lost and a gale of rushing air went whooshing out the window. Anything not tied down flew out through it: loose paper, blankets, clothing.

In the sudden maelstrom, Jack shifted his weight and yanked Mephisto over him, shoving the jester's head *through* the blasted-open window!

The evil little man shrieked as his body jammed momentarily in the small aperture before—*whoosh*—he was sucked out completely, his body scraping horribly against the jagged edges of the broken window on the way through, never to be seen again.

Gasping for breath, Jack staggered out of the room to find Lily, Alby, Mae, Iolanthe, and Hades rushing up to him, woken by the gunshot and the ensuing wail of alarms.

Sky Monster's voice came over the intercom: "Jack! What's going on? We just lost cabin pressure in your room."

Jack keyed a switch. "I've closed it off, Monster. Restore pressure to the rest of the plane."

"What happened?"

"We had a stowaway," Jack said. "The jester. Never mind. He won't be coming back."

JACK'S FARM
SOMEWHERE IN AUSTRALIA

Nine hours later, the *Sky Warrior* touched down on another isolated airstrip in another isolated desert: the runway at Jack's farm in the vast Australian outback.

The sleek black plane taxied to a halt beside a small shack on the runway.

Waiting beside the shack was Zoe, Jack's wife. She herself had only just arrived back from the Mariana Trench a few hours ago.

When she saw Jack emerge from the plane—cradling Horus in his arms and preceded by the two bounding dogs, and followed by Lily and Alby—she smiled broadly and said, "Wait'll you hear what I saw—"

Her eyes darted from the wounded Horus to Jack's shaved head and the cuts and bruises on his face and her smile vanished.

Then she saw Mae, Iolanthe, Hades, and E-147 step out of the *Sky Warrior*.

She gave Jack a look. "Jesus, Mary, and Joseph! I go away for a week and look at you. What happened? You look like you've been to Hell and back."

"That's a very interesting choice of words, honey," Jack said. "Let's go inside and sit down. I've got a lot to tell you, too."

EPILOGUE

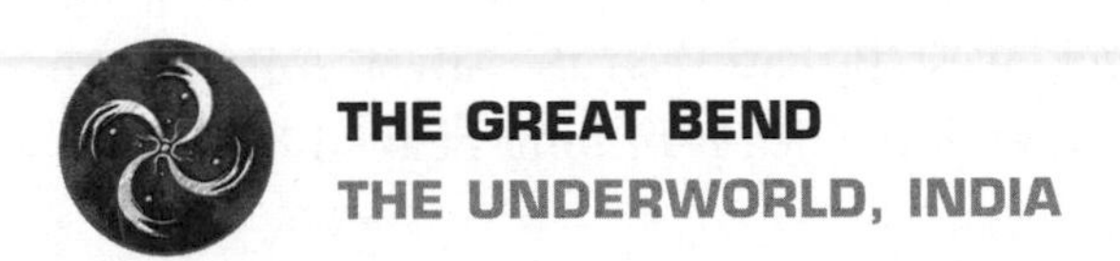

THE GREAT BEND
THE UNDERWORLD, INDIA

In one of the innermost corners of the Underworld, at the farthest point of the enormous racetrack that had played host to the wild car race of the Fifth Challenge, all was still.

The floodlights that had illuminated the gargantuan cavern during the challenge had been turned off. The only light came from some dim battery-powered work lights spaced along the railless roadway.

The enormous pyramid that sat inside its box-shaped shelf stood somberly in the semidarkness.

The wrecked vehicles and dead bodies of the champions who had come to grief near the pyramid during the challenge still lay where they had fallen, to be collected by a crew of minotaurs at some later time.

A smashed Typhoon truck lay on its side at the base of the pyramid.

The dead body of the black Navy SEAL champion, DeShawn Monroe, lay on the ground in front of it.

A crossbow bolt protruded from Monroe's forehead an inch above his lifeless eyes. They remained wide open, staring at nothing.

Near Monroe lay the corpse of his SEAL companion who had also died from a crossbow shot.

Their bodies lay near the summit of the massive upside-down building that hung suspended off the edge of the abyss that formed the core of the Great Bend.

The building loomed in the dim light, as it had done for thousands of years.

Deep shadows cut across the hundreds of rectangular recesses hewn into its flanks in regular rows, veiling the many silver coffins in them in deeper darkness.

Of all the champions who had blasted through here during the Fifth Challenge, only Jack West Jr. had seen the silver coffins with their eerie carvings of men with the heads of long-beaked birds.

All was silent.

All was still.

Nothing stirred.

And then, very slowly, from within, one of the silver coffins began to open . . .

THE END

ACKNOWLEDGMENTS

When I write a novel, I spend countless hours by myself . . . in a room . . . typing. I immerse myself in history, myth, the plot, future plots, booby traps, mazes, twists, escapes, characters, and things like where Jack got his fireman's helmet (if you want to know, check out the short story "Jack West Jr and the Hero's Helmet," which is available for free online). This is why, with a book like *The Four Legendary Kingdoms*, I need a second and even a third set of eyes to look over the manuscript, to make sure I haven't overexplained or underexplained things or just forgotten an entire character. (Yes, it is true that Wendy the cute seal died in the first manuscript of *Ice Station*; I forgot about her, so in that draft she was left behind in the cavern to be blown up by the nuclear missile. Whoops. Fixed it in the rewrite.)

In other words, it doesn't happen without help.

I'd like to send out a big thank-you to my publisher at Pan Macmillan, Cate Paterson, who is still the first to receive my stuff and who still offers wise and constructive feedback.

To my editor, Alex Lloyd, who helped in the background on *The Tournament* and *The Great Zoo of China* but who stepped up into the big leagues for this one and assumed the title "Editor." Editing one of my novels is not your usual editing job: it requires corralling drawings, diagrams, endpapers, and enduring all of my patented

"Matthew Reilly Last-Minute Additions and Comments About the Cover." Thanks, Alex!

Tracey Cheetham once again handled my publicity with her trademark aplomb and grace, and Zoë Caley helped me navigate social media.

The cover art and the internal images were done by the wonderfully talented Gavin Tyrrell, a superb Australian graphic designer and artist (he also does movie stuff, which is how I met him). Gavin did the awesome cover art for *The Great Zoo of China* and the Roger Ascham short story *Roger Ascham and the King's Lost Girl*, but I think he outdid himself with the cover art for this. For the internals, he worked from my pretty woeful original sketches, which thankfully you the reader never get to see!

As always, family and friends gave great support, from my girlfriend, Kate, to my brother, Stephen, and my parents, Ray and Denise Reilly. And of course, my little furry writing buddy, Dido.

To anyone who knows a writer, never underestimate the power of your encouragement.

AN INTERVIEW WITH MATTHEW REILLY

SPOILER WARNING!

The following interview contains SPOILERS from *The Four Legendary Kingdoms*. Readers who have not yet read the novel are advised to avoid reading this interview, as it does give away major plot moments in the book.

Okay, Matthew, you just put the two biggest heroes from your Jack West Jr. and Scarecrow series in the same novel! Take us through it all. What inspired you to do this, how did you plan it, and what were you trying to accomplish by doing it?

Very often over the years I've been asked by fans, "Can you *please* put Jack and Scarecrow together in a book?" What many of those very kind people may not have realized was that this had been on my mind, too. I just needed the right story.

To me, the Jack West Jr. books are quite different to the Scarecrow novels. Largely this is because of Lily. It was Lily who softened and humanized all the gung-ho military characters, from Gunman and Zoe to Pooh Bear and Jack himself. Those stories also usually take place over a long period of time. In contrast, the Scarecrow novels (at least, to me) are a bit harder-edged. They usually take place over a short time period and the characters are very, very intense—from what Scarecrow has endured with Gant to the rampaging presence of Mother.

When I conceived the story of the Great Games of the Hydra, however, in which each king would choose a few champions to represent him, I realized that I had the chance to bring Scarecrow into Jack's world.

One thing was very important: *The Four Legendary Kingdoms* is a Jack West Jr. book. The characters of Scarecrow and Mother (and to a lesser extent, Astro) would just make a special appearance in it. From the outset, I said to myself, "This book is part of the series that began with *Seven Ancient Wonders* and continued with *The Six Sacred Stones* and *The Five Greatest Warriors*. First and foremost, it has to appeal to the fans of those books. It must be about Jack and his larger journey through a world filled with ancient places and myths, giant galactic-scale danger, and, of course, booby traps." I was simply going to add some cool characters to it.

And so I thought about how I would do this.

I didn't want to just toss Scarecrow in there. He had to be threaded into the story slowly. Early on, we read about a Marine with reflective glasses. Then we glimpse him and his large female companion in the Third Challenge. By this stage, I figured keen readers of my novels would know exactly to whom I was referring (mind you, I was also aware that in this age of social media, word that Scarecrow was in *4LK* would get out pretty fast).

To explain his entrance into Jack's world, I used the common link between the two series of books: the character of Astro, who appeared with Scarecrow in *Hell Island* and with Jack in *6SS* and *5GW*. I decided that the best way to bring Scarecrow into Jack's world was to have poor Astro inadvertently suggest his name to someone looking for a champion.

Then the fun began.

It was tremendous fun for me to write the scene where they meet for the first time. What would these two heroes say to each other? What would Scarecrow make of these ancient challenges and shadowy kings? I figured Scarecrow would be very wary. I also liked the idea that Mother would have met Jack at some point in her career . . . and would naturally greet him in her usual way!

And then came the biggest scene . . .

You made them fight to the death. What inspired that?

When I see a crossover movie like *The Avengers,* a cool story that brings together heroes from different series, I'm always wondering what the storyteller will do to make it interesting.

When I decided to put Jack and Scarecrow in the same book, I asked myself, "What would I, as a reader, want to see?"

The answer was simple: I'd want to see them fight! I'd want to see who'd win a fight between Jack West Jr. and Shane "Scarecrow" Schofield. More than that, what if that fight was a fight to the death in front of an audience where one of them *had* to actually die.

I love the moment in *4LK* when Jack steps up onto the combat stage and sees that Scarecrow is his opponent. That was one of the first scenes I conceived for this novel.

As a story,* The Four Legendary Kingdoms *is very large in scale, even by your standards. Why is this so?

Mainly because, in addition to seeing Jack and Scarecrow fight, I also wanted to see them *team up*. Now, over the course of seven novels and one novella, Jack and Scarecrow have separately done some pretty big things. I wanted to see what they could achieve as a team. This was the reason for making the Great Games so big and huge, with so many villains like Hades, Chaos, Fear, the Hydra, and Mephisto, not to mention Dion, Zaitan, Brigham, and the other champions. If you're gonna have two major heroes team up, then you have to have a supersized story for them to do battle in.

What was the genesis of the idea of four kingdoms ruling the world from the shadows?

I love conspiracy theories, I really do. And when I look at the world, I often wonder if there is something else going on in the background.

The notion of four powerful rulers controlling world affairs from the background is something that I've pondered for a long time (as quite a few fans have noted, I first mentioned "four kings seated on thrones in front of five warriors" back in *The Six Sacred Stones*, which I wrote way back in 2006).

Maybe it comes from the profound dissatisfaction I feel when I look at politicians these days. I rarely get political and I won't do so here; it's just that I find politicians and political parties don't seem to care about representing people anymore: they're just in it for themselves and the pursuit of temporary power. My notion of the four legendary kingdoms is perhaps my way of saying "If you think our politicians are shallow and venal, you're right. They're not actually in charge anyway. The four kingdoms simply allow them to *think* they are in charge."

When I announced the title of this book earlier this year, I watched the responses of fans on Facebook and online, watched them speculate on what the legendary kingdoms might be. None anticipated four "shadow kingdoms," so I was kinda pleased about that. I pride myself on coming up with new stuff that keeps my readers guessing!

Tell us about the idea for the Great Games. Where did that come from?

It's no secret that I enjoy themes of competition in my novels. *Contest* had it. So did *Hover Car Racer*. *The Tournament*, even though it was ultimately about a gifted young girl and her wonderful teacher, also had the chess matches going on in the background.

Competition is fun to watch or read about because it is intrinsically dramatic: two characters want the same thing—to win—and that is the essence of good drama. (This is why legal and hospital shows are so popular on television: in a courtroom, you have two sides who both want to win the case; similarly, in an emergency room, you have a team of doctors trying to save ill or wounded patients; in essence, they want to defeat death.)

With the Great Games I wanted to come up with the coolest, most insane challenges imaginable and hurl my unknowing hero, Jack, into them. It was imperative to me that Jack enter the Games entirely unprepared, not knowing a thing about what is going on. This is why the book starts so quickly, with Jack waking up in the dark, with his head shaved, having been kidnapped . . . and then a minotaur attacks him with a knife. He is on the back foot from the get-go. (I also loved dressing him in a Homer Simpson T-shirt and depriving him of shoes.) This becomes important when the tide turns, and Jack starts surviving against the odds: the people who kidnapped him disrespected him when they did that; and so when Jack dines with Hades in his T-shirt and bare feet, he gets his revenge by disrespecting them.

If *The Four Legendary Kingdoms* is similar to any of my previous books, the closest is probably *Contest*. But *Contest*—written when I was nineteen and much less experienced in the ways of the world—does not have the breadth of backstory or cultural relevance that *4LK* has. *Contest* was a good old-fashioned fight to the death. It is a lean, mean, thrill-a-minute machine. That's what it was designed to be. *4LK*, on the other hand, is ultimately about ruling and being ruled.

And this leads me to one of the major themes of the book: Should a small group of privileged people place themselves above everyone else? In our present-day world, where we see a small subset of the population owning so much wealth, are we creating a world of the elite and the rest? The haves and the have-nots? If the haves own *too much*, will the have-nots eventually riot?

(That Anthony "Tony" DeSaxe is a superwealthy mining and shipping magnate whose wealth goes back generations is very deliberate. There are clusters of superwealthy individuals in the world today—from the more reclusive Rothschilds to the well-known modern billionaires like Bill Gates, Warren Buffett, and Mark Zuckerberg. I wanted to suggest that the ones with real power might be the ones you never hear about, the ones who are very quiet about their wealth and influence.)

And connecting the Games to the Labors of Hercules? What inspired that?

I've always enjoyed reading about ancient myths and stories, from Hercules and Achilles to tales of Atlantis and fire-breathing dragons (hello, *Great Zoo of China*). And I love the idea that mythological characters like Hercules, Hades, or Zeus were once real people, but that their stories have been distorted over time. The Greek philosopher Euhemerus mentioned in the story was a real guy.

Having said that, over the years, I've particularly enjoyed reading about the Twelve Labors of Hercules, especially the part where Hercules defeats the Nemean Lion, which was famous for its impenetrable hide. (Hercules defeated it, skinned it using its own claws, and then used the Lion's pelt as his own impenetrable armor.) I wanted to reinterpret the Twelve Labors in a modern and interesting way.

And so I reimagined the Labors as something different: that Hercules was actually a guy overcoming a series of challenges—the challenges of the Great Games. Further to that, he became globally famous because he was the only winner of the Games *to win every single challenge*.

I particularly enjoyed reimagining Eurystheus, the cowardly king who sent Hercules on each of his daunting tasks. I made Eurystheus the Lord of the Underworld of that era. This would explain how a cowardly king could boss around a warrior as great as Hercules.

Tell us about the minotaurs.

Just as I've enjoyed reading about Hercules over the years, I've always been fascinated by the legend of the Minotaur. A man with the head of a bull, lurking inside a labyrinth on Crete, has always just, well, intrigued me.

As with Hercules, I decided to create a real explanation for this legend. My idea was that, firstly, a minotaur was actually someone in a bull-shaped *helmet*. This isn't exactly earth-shattering. But the second element would be quite different: my minotaurs would be *Neanderthal* men in masks.

I like the notion that Neanderthals—a variety of hominid that preceded *Homo sapiens*—walk among us today. It's entirely possible. I also like the idea that Neanderthals aren't stupid brutes; they can be as bright as any modern human, if they are allowed to be. And I *love* the idea that a small group of them has been living in a secret kingdom in a remote corner of India and has never made contact with modern man; such a group would be *pure* Neanderthals. And I just wanted to have an army on hand that could go on a rampage!

You included a mention of four kings way back in* The Six Sacred Stones. *Are there any other story elements in* The Four Legendary Kingdoms *that we should look out for in future novels?

Of course! First, I think it's pretty clear that the next book will be about Jack's search for the three secret cities (hmmm, could be a good title there . . .).

Truth be told, one of the reasons it took so long for me to produce a fourth book in the Jack West Jr. series (*The Five Greatest Warriors* came out in 2009) was that I wanted to plan ahead and set up the last three books in the series. So, yes, there are a lot of things mentioned in *The Four Legendary Kingdoms* that will come back in future books: the three secret cities, the Omega Event, the Trismagi, even some unusual trees . . .

This book is designed to set the scene for three massive books to come. That's the challenge I set myself and it's why it took so long to conceive and write it.

Are there any other interesting things in the book that you'd like to share?

Over the years, I've been asked by charities to put up a character's name for auction at fund-raising dinners. A few characters in *The Four Legendary Kingdoms* acquired their names in this way.

Tony and Colleen DeSaxe were the winning bidders at a lovely charity golf day put on by Vivienne Freeman, so of course, I made Tony the Lord of the Underworld. Who wouldn't want that? (I figured.) **George Khalil** was the underbidder at the same event, so while Tony became Hades, George became a drunken young prince.

Conor Beard's parents, **Allyn and Julie Beard**, successfully bid at Smokey Dawson's wonderful Charity Challenge Ball, as did **Mark and Michelle Finn**, who, in an original twist, asked me to include their two *dogs*' names in a novel. This is how **Ash** and **Roxy** got their names (I had been thinking of giving Jack a poodle for a while, so that worked nicely!). And **Greg Batman**'s name appears in this book after his brother, **Gary Batman**, bid on his behalf. I did my best, but in a world of superhero movies, it's hard for an author to name a character Batman (even if you do pronounce it Bat-*mun*)!

And a *very* special mention must go to **Tim Bowles**, a trooper from the Australian Army. Tim has waited for a long time to see his name in one of my novels and I really must publicly thank him for his incredible patience.

At a charity dinner in 2011 in aid of the Welfare Trust (which supports the families of soldiers killed in the line of duty) Tim bid for a character name. He asked me especially if he could be in a Scarecrow novel and fight alongside Scarecrow. Two things conspired against Tim: first, I had just released *Scarecrow and the Army of Thieves*, so I wasn't planning a new Scarecrow novel for some time; and second, he made his bid when I was going through a bit of a tough time, so I wasn't even thinking of writing a book at all. And so he waited patiently. I released *The Tournament*, but it wasn't right to put him in that. Then I wrote *The Great Zoo of China*, which didn't feature Scarecrow. I asked Tim if he would mind being in a Jack West novel, and he said sure. I didn't tell him that he would get his wish and fight alongside Scarecrow but in a Jack West book!

As the book was about to go to print, I did tell him, so Tim was one of only a few people outside a very tight inner circle who knew Scarecrow would be appearing in this Jack West book. I even gave him what I think is one of my cooler call signs: *Tomahawk*. He has only a brief role in this book, but rest assured, when Scarecrow returns, Tomahawk will be with him. Thanks for your patience, Tim.

In early 2015, you moved to Los Angeles. How is it going there? Any movies on the horizon?

It's been great, thanks, and just what I needed. I wanted to find a new place to live and explore, and to immerse myself in a world of storytellers, which is exactly what LA is.

I've met some fantastic people already, from brilliant producers and directors to successful screenwriters. I'm constantly doing meetings about film or television adaptations of my novels (*The Great Zoo of China* has been optioned by Sony, I myself wrote the screenplay for *The Tournament*, and I have met with a top screenwriter about turning the Jack West books into a TV series). If a few pieces fall into place, we could be all systems go, but you've got to be in it to win it.

Any final words?

As always, I just want to show people a good time. This was a really fun novel to write. For a long time, fans have asked me if I could put Jack and Scarecrow in the same novel and it was a challenge I threw myself into. I hope I have delivered the goods in an unexpected and original way that has left those fans and all my other readers feeling satisfied.

It is my job to entertain. So, as I always say, in the end, I just hope you enjoyed the book.

Matthew Reilly
Los Angeles
July 2016